From the bestselling author of the
award-winning novel Pig Trouble on
Sullivan's Island . . .

. . . comes a captivating new tale that explores the deep ties of friendship, family, and community—and the hidden cracks that can fracture even our strongest connections.

The Sullivan's Island Supper Club

Sunsplashed Southern Stories

BY SUSAN M. BOYER

Carolina Tales Series

Big Trouble on Sullivan's Island

Beginnings - The Sullivan's Island Supper Club (Prequel)

The Sullivan's Island Supper Club

Trouble's Turn to Lose (April 8, 2025)

Hard Candy Christmas (October 28, 2025)

The Liz Talbot Series

Lowcountry Boil (A Liz Talbot Mystery # 1)

Lowcountry Bombshell (A Liz Talbot Mystery # 2)

Lowcountry Boneyard (A Liz Talbot Mystery # 3)

Postcards From Stella Maris (Five Liz Talbot Short Stories)

Lowcountry Bordello (A Liz Talbot Mystery # 4)

Lowcountry Book Club (A Liz Talbot Mystery # 5)

Lowcountry Bonfire (A Liz Talbot Mystery # 6)

Lowcountry Bookshop (A Liz Talbot Mystery # 7)

Lowcountry Boomerang (A Liz Talbot Mystery # 8)

Lowcountry Boondoggle (A Liz Talbot Mystery # 9)

Lowcountry Boughs of Holly (A Liz Talbot Mystery # 10)

Lowcountry Getaway (A Liz Talbot Mystery # 11)

The Sullivan's Island Supper Club

A CAROLINA TALE

SUSAN M. BOYER

STELLA MARIS BOOKS
LLC

The Sullivan's Island Supper Club

A Carolina Tale

First Edition | September 2024

Stella Maris Books, LLC

5052 Old Buncombe Road, Suite A-273

Greenville SC 29617

https://stellamarisbooksllc.com

This is a work of fiction. All of the characters, places, organizations, and events portrayed in this novel are either products of the author's imagination or are used fictitiously.

Cover Artwork © 2023 by Marina Kaya, Qamber Designs, used by exclusive license

Cover design by Elizabeth Mackey

Author photograph by Mic Smith

ISBN 978-1-959023-28-9 (E-book)
ISBN 978-1-959023-29-6 (Trade Paperback)
ISBN 978-1-959023-31-9 (Hardcover)
ISBN 978-1-959023-32-6 (Large Print Paperback)
ISBN 978-1-959023-33-3 (Audio Download)

Printed in the United States of America

 Created with Vellum

For my mother, Claudette. I miss her terribly, yet I feel her close to me every day.

The Sullivan's Island Supper Club

MEMBER	HUSBAND/ESCORT
Sarabeth Boone (March 2021)	Tucker Boone
Hadley Cooper (June 2021)	Cash Reynolds
Norah Fitzgerald (June 2022)	Knox Fitzgerald
Libba Graham (May 2017)	Jake Graham
Camille Houston (May 2017)	Fish Aiken / Tennyson Sumter
Birdie Markley (May 2017)	Vernon Markley
Quinn Poinsett (May 2017)	Redmond Poinsett
Tallulah Wentworth (May 2017)	Tennyson Sumter / Fish Aiken

Chapter One

Present Day—Saturday, October 29, 2022, 7:10 a.m.
Morning after the Fall Meet and Greet
Sullivan's Island, South Carolina
Boone Home, I'On Avenue
Sarabeth Mercer Jackson Boone

The morning after we hosted the *Titanic* of all neighborhood parties, Tucker and I were dead to the world, blissfully oblivious —at least for a few sweet hours—as to how spectacularly my plans to sow the seeds of unity in our small, fractured town had failed. I had tried my best to build bridges, I did... and every one of them had blown up in my face. Could there possibly be any bigger party fail than having to call the police, who hauled off several of your neighbors in handcuffs? My fall meet and greet was an unmitigated disaster of epic proportions is what I'm telling you.

Tucker and I slammed into wide-awake the next morning when the doorbell went off, ringing urgently in rapid-fire succession like maybe the house was on fire and somebody was trying to save us all. A woman was hollering and the dogs were barking and we bolted straight up out of the bed. It's a miracle we didn't both have massive heart attacks at that very moment. We are, after all, in the grandparent demographic and at an elevated risk.

We grabbed our robes and threw them on and went flying down the stairs. And of course the girls and Deacon and the dogs all came too. Tucker threw open the door and we huddled in behind him, the girls kneeling down to grab ahold of the dogs. Clutching the top of my robe together to be sure I was decent, I peered over his shoulder at Josephine Huger, who's our neighbor behind us, and her English bulldog, Petunia—who was flat losing her mind—there on the porch.

"Call 9-1-1," Josephine gasped, a hand to her chest. "There's a body out here in your front yard."

Well, at first I confess I thought, *Poor Josephine is just confused. Those are our Halloween decorations.* We had one of those spooky graveyards under the big live oak in our front yard?

Tucker stepped out to the edge of the porch and leaned over the rail for a better look.

Then he dashed down the steps for a closer perspective on things. The rest of us stepped onto the porch and clustered in the spot he'd vacated.

Tucker looked up at me.

The expression on my husband's face was just... He was thunderstruck. "Call 9-1-1."

"Girls, get inside and get dressed," I said as I dashed for my phone, which was on the table beside our bed. I called 911 and told them we had a body in our front yard and to please send someone right away but I had no further information and needed to get my clothes on, thank you very much.

I must've been in shock, because it wasn't until I was on my way back outside that it hit me Tucker hadn't said *who* was dead in our front yard. At that point, I just assumed it was a random stranger. Probably some poor soul who overserved themselves at a party and through some series of misadventures passed out in our front yard and died of alcohol poisoning or some such thing.

Tragic and horrifying but connected to us only by the accident of location. It never entered my mind it was one of our friends.

I've given a lot of thought as to how, exactly, we came to that moment. Looking back on everything that's happened, if someone asked me when the whole thing started, initially I would've said it was with the May supper club. For me, of course, everything began the morning Tallulah Wentworth rang my door-bell—three days after we'd moved in, in March of last year—and asked for a drink of water. She *said* she wasn't feeling well. Then she invited me to supper club. Actually, I guess if I really thought about it, the entire series of events was set in motion years ago, back when the supper club first started. I'm not saying any of this was Tallulah's fault. Perish the thought.

But none of this would have happened if it weren't for supper club. There was just no getting around it.

Chapter Two

Rewind to Wednesday, April 5, 2017, 5:00 p.m.
On the beach near Station 22
Sullivan's Island, South Carolina
Tallulah Wentworth

"Eugenia thinks I should get a dog." Tallulah's tone painted the idea absurd. "We've never been the sort of people to have a dog. Why do you suppose that is?"

We traveled too much for dogs. Wouldn't've been fair to them. And I distinctly remember deciding against any pet that might require us to venture out in this sort of miserable weather. Seriously, Tally, the fog is so thick I can barely see three feet in front of me. Even with my golf umbrella, you're soaked to the bone. Let's go indoors and dry off by the fire, shall we?

"Nice try." Tallulah raised an eyebrow at her husband. "You'll not talk me out of this, Henry Charles Wentworth. Not on your life."

That would be a sorry bet now, wouldn't it?

The pain grabbed Tallulah by the throat. "I should've taken better care of you," she whispered. It was all she could manage. "Should've paid more attention to what you were doing. Washing down Bufferin with bourbon every night. Of course you had a bleeding ulcer. And everyone knows hospitals are just crawling with pneumonia. It was an entirely preventable tragedy."

It was, yes. But it was hardly your fault, now was it? Last I checked, I was perfectly capable of reading warning labels myself. And for the record, you harped on my NSAID habit plenty. There's nothing to be done about it now. You, on the other hand, can best avoid pneumonia by coming inside with me.

"Oh, I'm coming with you all right. That's precisely what I'm going to do." She'd waited long enough.

Tally, the ocean is full of hungry creatures. You've always said so. You never, ever swim in water when you can't see the bottom. You haven't been in this part of the Atlantic past your ankles since you were seven years old. You're going to mess around here and get shark bit, that's what's about to happen. Tally, please. Don't do this.

Tallulah stopped walking and studied the churning sea and sky. The weather was morose and fitful and suited her mood. It was unseasonably cold, a rare April day on Sullivan's Island, with nature orchestrating the full symphony of elements. The thermometer had struggled to reach the midsixties with the wind and rain making it feel much colder. The wind whipped through the air, carrying with it the scent of salt and seaweed. A gust plowed into Tallulah and urged her along the beach. She struggled to control the umbrella. Her toes dug into the cold, wet sand as raindrops pattered all around, striking different notes on the water, the umbrella, and the sand. Fog blanketed the shoreline, cloaking everything in a soft, mysterious haze, blurring the lines between sea and sky. Waves crashed against the shore with a rhythmic intensity, their roar muffled by the thick mist. A pair of intrepid seagulls, separated from their colony, glided gracefully by, their calls echoing eerily in the distance. Despite the inclement weather, there was a wild beauty in the desolation of the beach. The rest of the world had faded away, isolating Tallulah in a bubble where time seemed suspended.

"Did you know seagulls mate for life?" Tallulah asked her dead husband.

Mm-hmm. Most birds do, I think. Has to do with needing both of them to care for the offspring.

"How much different things would be if we'd only been able to have children."

I suppose if we'd seen this far down the road, we might've decided to adopt after all. But we had a good run, didn't we, Tally? We swam with sea lions in the Galapagos, went on safari in the Serengeti, and followed the footsteps of the ancient Incas in Machu Picchu—we traveled to every continent. How many people can say that?

"It was a magical ride," said Tallulah. "No one could ask for more. But it's over now. I've stayed too long at the fair, I'm afraid. There's nothing for me here with you gone. You and I... We were wrapped up in our own world. Oh sure, we had friends. But you know... our happiest adventures were just the two of us."

I suppose we did tend to isolate ourselves a bit.

"I'm just so alone, Henry."

I know, my darling, and I'm terribly sorry.

"Have you seen my brother Grayson?"

Yes, I have, as a matter of fact. And now that you mention it, he's asked me to tell you to abandon this fool notion immediately. And your parents. Your father has spoken quite sternly on the issue. Your mother is beside herself. I speak for us all when I say please, for the love of Heaven, go back inside the house. You've no idea how short life on Earth actually is in the scheme of things. We'll all be together again soon enough.

"I don't think my parents were ever the same after we lost Grayson. None of us were. He was the golden boy. Good at everything he tried. And so handsome. Some men who are that good-looking are insufferable. But not Grayson. He had the kindest heart... so proud to serve his country. I was twelve when they sent him home from Vietnam in a flag-draped coffin. I've lost everyone I've loved, Henry."

You're having a dark day, Tally. It's this weather. Tomorrow the sun will be out, and you'll feel so much better. Also—and please don't be angry with me, darling—but I think perhaps you should ease up on the gin. I'm not suggesting complete abstinence, nothing so rash as that. Perhaps a short break would be the thing. I know—how about a week or two at a spa? I understand the one in Marrakech is quite nice. They don't starve you there like they do at so many others. That might be just the ticket.

"I'm grieving, Henry. I don't need to dry out."

I tell you what, why don't we see how you feel in the morning? Maybe look at some of the spas online when you're feeling a bit more clearheaded.

"Thank you, but no. Nothing will be different in the morning. I've given it a year. You've been gone a year, Henry. And the pain still takes my breath away. I can't do this without you. I'm sorry, I just can't."

Nonsense, Tallulah. You can do anything you put your mind to. You're the strongest person I know. There are people here who need you—think of the poor souls at the homeless shelter... the women at the group home... What about your friends? Have you considered how this will devastate poor Eugenia? She's just finished yet another round of chemotherapy. You know Everette is useless when it comes to taking care of anyone other than himself.

"Eugenia will be just fine. She has her children, and Birdie, of course. And Fish. Do you know Fish sat with her during every bit of her chemotherapy? He's taken her to every radiation appointment, every scan, every biopsy..."

Yes, Fish Aiken is a prince, of course. And he needs you as well. The man is practically homeless. How many nights has he stayed in one of our guest rooms? What's he going to do, for Heaven's sake, if you go through with this?

"Oh please. Fish has more friends than anyone I know. If that's the best you've got for an argument, it's time to get on with things."

Tally, wait—

"There's no point."

This has gone far enough. I must insist you come indoors. The water is churning like a washing machine today. And there's not a soul out in this nasty weather to help.

"That's rather the point, Henry."

You know, I've heard drowning is a horrible way to go. And that's the best-case scenario that could possibly come from getting in this water really—drowning, that is. The sharks will likely get you first. Darling, please—your clothes are getting soaked with seawater. What is that you're wearing, by the way?

"It's called a caftan. It has oversized pockets."

Pockets? What on earth—?

"I've stuffed them full of the river rocks the landscaper used in the bed around the outdoor shower. I'll see you shortly."

Tally, for the love of—

"Yoo-hoo, Tallulah!" Eugenia's voice trilled out through the fog.

"Hey, Tallulah, wait up!" Fish called.

Oh, thank Heavens. The cavalry has arrived.

"Couple of meddling so-and-sos," muttered Tallulah.

Eugenia and Fish hurried up the beach. Tallulah's oldest friends looked like they'd hopped off a frozen-seafood box with their bright yellow rain slickers. It was a shame they'd have to witness this, but maybe it was for the best after all. No one would have to wonder what happened now, would they? Tallulah plowed into the waves.

A large swell broke and slammed into her, pushing her back towards the shore, as if the ocean were trying to spit her out. She steadied herself, hunched down, and leaned into the surf.

"Go away," she hollered. "Leave me alone."

"I don't think so." Eugenia waded into the water. When she was close enough, she grabbed ahold of Tallulah's arm. "Come celebrate with us." Her voice was downright joyous.

"Have you lost your mind?" Tallulah threw a scathing glare over her shoulder.

Fish sloshed around behind them and attached himself to Tallulah's right arm. "Eugenia's finished her chemotherapy. She got to ring the bell today. We're going to open a bottle of champagne."

The news hit Tallulah like a body blow. How had she forgotten today was the day?

"Well, why haven't you already done that?" she demanded. Oh! She squeezed her eyes shut against the fresh tears. Happier news she could scarcely conjure. A better person would've been focused on her very sick friend. Tallulah sorely wished she were a better person. As it was, she was apparently succumbing to her soul-sucking grief. "What the devil are the two of you doing out here in this awful weather?"

"Why, looking for you, of course," said Eugenia.

"That doesn't make a lick of sense," said Tallulah.

"Given that we found you," said Eugenia, "I'd say it makes perfect sense. And thank goodness we did. You might've drowned yourself."

"Given that you weigh all of ninety pounds soaking wet anymore, I'd like to know how you think you're going to stop me."

"Now you listen to me," said Eugenia. "I've spent three years fighting to save my life. The very least you can do is come inside and celebrate with me. You can throw yours away tomorrow if you're still of a mind. But it's awfully selfish of you, I must say."

"Selfish?" Tallulah crowed at her.

"You heard me. Yes. Selfish."

"How do you figure?"

"It's self-indulgent. You miss Henry. I get it. You were married to him for thirty-six years. Of course you miss him."

"There's nothing left here for me."

"Life is a precious gift, not a wilted bouquet of hydrangeas," said Eugenia. "You should be ashamed of yourself. I know people fighting with their last ounce of strength for one more month, one more week, one more day. You have your health, and you have things yet to do in this life," said Eugenia.

Eugenia and Fish tugged Tallulah back towards the shore.

"Says who?" asked Tallulah. "Get your hands off me." She leaned into the surf.

"Says God," growled Eugenia as she tightened her grip and pulled back hard. "Or he would've hauled your sorry hind end home already."

"I'm so weary of this life."

"Snap out of it."

Eugenia nodded at Fish, and with one last big yank, they all toppled over and landed in the sand, a tangled mess of arms and legs and Tallulah's caftan. The foamy edges of the spent waves lapped at their feet.

Fish howled with laughter.

"Ooooooh!" Tallulah wailed indignantly.

"You need to get your mind on something else," said Eugenia. "Someone else."

"Well now, therein lies the problem, Eugenia," said Tallulah. "I'm all out of someone elses."

"That's ridiculous," said Eugenia. "This world is overrun with people who need a friend, a hand, a meal, or a hug. If you'd just get busy helping someone else, you wouldn't have time for this foolishness."

"Who do you think I am? Mother Teresa of Calcutta?" asked Tallulah.

"Come now," said Eugenia. "I know you far better than that. I just think you'd be happier if you focused more on other people and less on creative ways to kill yourself."

"I'll have you know, every penny of my money is going to charity. Everyone will be far better off with me gone," said Tallulah.

"Everything is not about money," said Eugenia.

"Name me one person, anywhere on this entire planet, who needs *me* more than they need my money."

"I do, Tallulah." Eugenia's voice was soft, barely loud enough to be heard over the roiling sea.

"Aww, come on now..." Tallulah screwed up her face in aggravation. "You have more friends than you can count."

"But I only have one of you," said Eugenia. "And it's not just me. Fish needs you too."

"It's true," said Fish. "I depend upon you."

"You're both full of manure," said Tallulah. "And you've ruined everything."

"Well, thank Heavens. That was our plan," said Eugenia. "I'm sorry we were late. Chemotherapy took me longer today."

"What do you mean late?" asked Tallulah. "It's not like I was expecting you. Far from it. I've never been less happy to see either one of you."

"We knew today would be hard for you," said Fish.

"Henry's been gone a year," said Eugenia. "I wanted to spend the day with you. I'm so sorry I wasn't able to reschedule my treatment."

Tallulah closed her eyes, sucked in a long, deep breath. "Oh, Eugenia. I'm so deeply sorry. A fine friend I am. With everything you have on you, you don't need to be worrying about me. I'm thrilled, truly, that you've finally finished treatment. You've beaten that horrid disease—you're a miracle. And you deserve a huge celebration. A better friend would've planned one. It's just"... tears slid down her face... "Henry was my whole world, you know?"

Eugenia's eyes glistened. She pursed her lips together and nodded. "I do."

"Everything I've done that was worth doing, since I was twenty-two years old, I did it with Henry. His memory is everywhere I turn. I can't escape it. Living is just too painful."

"We've got to get you busy doing *new* things," said Eugenia. "That's the trick—things you never did with Henry."

Tallulah scoffed. "I'm far too old for new tricks."

"Nonsense... What's something you've always wanted to do but never got around to?"

"Don't you understand? Henry and I chased every dream we ever had. I've had a full life—"

"Give me a break. There are oodles of things you haven't done."

"Is that a fact?"

"Yes... yes it is."

"Name one."

"Well... you've never been skydiving as far as I know... How about running with the bulls? Did you and Henry ever do that?"

"No, but this is a much less painful way to kill myself."

"We'll think of something," said Eugenia.

"You've got no business whatsoever out here in the wind and the rain," said Tallulah. "You should be in bed. Just look at you. Eugenia, you're white as a sheet."

"I'm not going indoors without you."

"You are a royal pain in my derriere."

"Come on, Tallulah," said Fish. "Let's get you girls inside and into some dry clothes. I'll make us something to eat. How about a steak?"

"A steak?" Tallulah scoffed. "Eugenia won't let us have anything but leaves and twigs and grass anymore."

"Nonsense," said Eugenia. "I'll happily have a celebratory steak with you. You may as well come inside. This isn't happening. Not today."

"Fine," said Tallulah. "I want a big fat filet mignon. No—a rib eye."

"There's our girl," said Fish. "I'll make you one with a crab cake on top and some béarnaise... all of it atop a buttery piece of grilled French bread. How would that be?"

Tallulah lifted her chin and sniffed. "If you insist on interfering, I suppose it will do... with some mashed potatoes. And I want a big slice of cheesecake—Carnegie Deli, there's really nothing that compares. I have one in the freezer."

"If all that saturated fat doesn't kill you, it will be a miracle," said Eugenia.

"If it doesn't, I'll finish my business when I have more privacy."

"That may be a while," said Eugenia. "I'm going to need someone to take care of me while I recuperate from my treatment. I'd love to convalesce here at the beach. What do you say?"

"Where the bloody Hell is Everette?" asked Tallulah.

"Cabo San Lucas," said Eugenia. "Fishing for striped marlin with some of his cronies. He said something about going to Bermuda for wahoo next. Who knows when he'll be home?"

Probably just as well. If there were any justice at all in the world, God would've taken that sorry excuse for a man Everette Ladson instead of her Henry.

"It's really not safe for me at the Tradd Street house by myself," said Eugenia. "All those stairs…"

Fish crawled to his feet and offered Eugenia a hand. When she had her balance, they each reached for one of Tallulah's arms and tugged.

Tallulah didn't budge.

Eugenia's eyes grew large and round. "How many of those cheesecakes have you been through?"

"Oh, put a sock in it, Eugenia," said Tallulah. "I've got rocks in my dress."

"Of course you do." Eugenia regarded the Heavens. "Why don't you leave those here, Tallulah?"

"I'm going to put them back where they go in the yard. Here, just let me get my feet under me." She pulled her arms free.

Fish walked behind her, hooked an arm under each of hers, and hoisted her up. "Now, that's got it."

Tallulah steadied herself. "Thank you, Fish." He'd always been such a gentleman.

"My pleasure."

Eugenia put her arms around her friend. "Everything's going

to be fine. You'll see. We'll find you a new project or two by the time you've finished nursing me back to health."

"I may put us both out of my misery before this is over with," said Tallulah.

"Tallulah, I've got it!" Eugenia grinned from ear to ear.

"Got what?"

"I've just remembered something you enjoy doing, but rarely did, because Henry was not a fan."

"No."

"What do you mean, no?"

"I was quite clear," said Tallulah.

"Tallulah, you love to entertain. You should throw a dinner party— No, I know... You could start a supper club. I've always wanted to belong to one of those. This is going to be such fun!"

"It's not happening," said Tallulah.

"You have no choice whatsoever in the matter," said Eugenia. "This is how I want to mark finishing chemotherapy. A good friend would plan a huge celebration. You said so yourself. Well, I don't want a *huge* celebration. I'd like an enduring one."

Five Months before the Fall Meet and Greet

Chapter Three

Saturday, May 28, 2022, 7:45 a.m.
Boone Home, I'On Avenue Sullivan's Island
Sarabeth Mercer Jackson Boone

Above all the other pretty beaches in our home state of South Carolina, this spot on the map called to both Tucker and me. Recently I've been wondering if that wasn't a siren's call we heard, one that's lured us onto the rocks.

As children, both our families vacationed here, though our paths never crossed. This half-wild salty piece of land held memories that were precious to us both, sweet memories that bandaged over some of the rougher scrapes and bruises of typical middle-class American childhoods. Later we brought our own blended family here as often as we could. Sullivan's Island was our sanctuary.

Tucker and I have dreamed since before we were married about living on Sullivan's Island. Actually, we both dreamed about it long before we even met. It was one of the first things we learned about each other that we had in common—both of us had always fantasized about living here.

I grew up in Florence—South Carolina, not Italy—and Tucker's from Abbeville. We met in school at Clemson, if you happen to wonder. Of course, we weren't involved back then. Our story didn't start until later, after we'd both married other people and had children. People in my family seem to go through a stupid phase between the ages of eighteen and twenty-something. It passes quicker with the girls. I can't speak to why Tucker chose the wrong person the first time.

We worked hard, scrimping and saving, forgoing fancy vacations and new cars. Still, property here is outrageous, and by the time we were able to make our dream a reality, neither of us were young anymore. I worried that maybe that was a young person's dream. It would be different if we were wealthy. We're not, not at all.

Tucker works for a consulting company out of Columbia. He makes good money, but he works really hard and travels a lot. I'm an author and not one you would've heard of, so my income is... sporadic. I worry about the toll all that travel takes on Tucker. I mean, he's fifty-eight years old. He should be thinking about retirement in a few years, right? Had we made that impossible? Was it my fault? Should I have persuaded him that we should stay in Summerville? We raised our kids there—three of his and one of mine. There are no ours. We figured we'd be doing good to get four children raised. But Summerville is a lovely town.

Those were the thoughts running through my mind as unthinkable things rained down on my head from a broken pipe.

This was literally happening, but also, it was a metaphor for the past fourteen months. A year ago in March, Tucker and I moved into the only house on Sullivan's Island we could possibly afford. The real estate agent called it a fixer-upper, but really, that might've been a euphemism—a kindness not to hurt its feelings. We had a long list of things we wanted to do to fix the house up, make it ours, and a very small budget that would allow us to do a few of those things at first and, hopefully, the rest over time.

That was our plan. We *did* have a plan to address things like the roof, energy-efficient windows, refinishing floors, paint, insulation, and outdated appliances. And we managed to do *some* of those things in the fifteen minutes before things started breaking, one thing right after another.

First it was the air-conditioning, not a huge deal in March, but it had to be fixed before summer arrived. Next the hot water heater went out, followed by the refrigerator. As soon as it got cool, the larger, main floor furnace gave up the ghost, and the repairman found a bad coil in the one upstairs while he was here. The lights in the family room flickered ominously when you ran the washing machine.

In other news, our youngest son—technically he's my son, but his biological father has been minimally involved, and Deacon calls Tucker Dad—called night before last. There were complications with him getting his paycheck—I could've told him there would be, but I've learned to save my breath. He and a bunch of his friends decided to go in together and get rich growing hemp, but that's a whole nother story for a different day.

The salient point for our family that particular day was that Deacon was not getting paid, so he couldn't make rent, which meant he and the girls would need to move back in with us. I had no idea how I would tell Tucker this. This was supposed to be our empty-nest house. We'd never had an empty nest. Our nest has been filled to overflowing from the I dos.

We started over, the two of us, twenty-nine years and eight months ago with nothing but four children and a mountain of debt from a lengthy custody battle. We loved our children, but they were full-grown people now. The youngest—Deacon—was *thirty-four years old.* We had been looking forward to having this new-to-us, sixty-five-year-old house to ourselves, like the honeymoon period we never had, you know? Does that make me a bad person?

And now an upstairs pipe had burst.

My favorite spot in our breakfast room—it faced a big window that overlooked the side yard—was right underneath the pipe in question.

This house we'd dreamed about for so long was literally spewing poop at me.

My husband was on a plane, returning from a business trip to Boston.

The plumber's phone went to voicemail.

I might have been in a fugue state.

Then the doorbell rang—the first of three times it rang that morning. That's one thing that worked, the doorbell. That day, every time it rang, it heralded someone who would change my life, which seems to be a pattern with me—people ringing the doorbell unexpectedly and changing my life.

I grabbed a handful of paper towels from the kitchen counter and dashed for the door, praying the plumber had gotten my desperate message and come rushing right over. There wasn't a peephole in the door. When I swung it open, Frances Tennant, the small, white-haired lady on my front porch, holding a cake carrier, might've had trouble processing my appearance. Her lips parted, like she wanted to say something but maybe couldn't think just what.

"Hey, Frances, how are you?" I offered her my sunniest smile as I dabbed at the sewage on my head. Frances lived a couple of blocks over, on Atlantic. We'd first met when she brought me a pound cake the day we moved in. Frances loved to bake, and she often brought us treats.

"I've brought you a lemon-blueberry pound cake. It's my latest experiment." She spoke with a delightful British accent and wore a genuine smile. Her pixie haircut gave her an impish look.

"Oh! How sweet of you! Thank you so much. Please forgive my appearance and me not inviting you in this morning, but we've just had a pipe break, and I'm having trouble getting ahold of the plumber."

"Oh dear," she said. "You might try Ronnie Aldean. His company's called Pipe Wizard. He's reasonable and reliable."

"Thank you so much. I will surely give him a call."

"Tell him I sent you and that he should get to you right away.

Ronnie was one of my students." She smiled mischievously. Frances was a retired English teacher.

"Well, here you go then." She tried to hand me the cake carrier.

"I'm afraid to touch anything," I said. "Would you mind setting it down? If you could just put it on the little table right here?" I opened the door wider. "I apologize for not inviting you in. Things are still a hot mess from several other projects we've had going on, and now the pipe situation." My face warmed with a flush. I really did need to work on my tendency to over-apologize.

"I quite understand," she said. "No worries a'tall." She stepped inside and set the cake carrier on the table. "Listen, I don't know what's going on with your plumbing, but if you need anything at all—an extra bathroom or whatever, please don't hesitate to call."

"That's so sweet—thank you. I'm sure we'll be fine. The bathroom with the leak is upstairs, but our primary bathroom is on the main level. Hopefully this will be a quick fix." I sent up a silent prayer that Ronnie Aldean could fix the upstairs bath before Deacon and the girls moved in at the end of the month.

"Yes, hopefully. Well, let me know what you think of the cake."

We said our goodbyes, and I closed the door. Frances Tennant was just precious. I was smiling in spite of the fact I was still covered in filth. Now here is the CliffsNotes version of how Frances changed my life. She was somewhat of a local activist. The first time I returned her cake plate and she invited me in, Frances told me all about the local conservation groups she was part of— and, well, also some of the local online groups. I was so eager to get involved in all the local goings-on. I just didn't understand at the time how controversial some of the goings-on were.

The online groups for neighbors came in handy when there was a power outage, or the bridge got backed up, or someone's dog went missing. That's why I joined initially. It's an easy way to reach many of your neighbors quickly to get word out when you need to. It never occurred to me how that technology could be used against me.

I called Ronnie Aldean, and thankfully he said he'd be here as soon as he finished the job he was working on, about forty-five minutes. There was nothing I could do about the pipe except put a bucket under it, which I'd already done, so I decided to get myself cleaned up.

Thirty minutes later, I'd scrubbed myself raw and changed my clothes and was making myself a glass of iced tea when the doorbell rang for the second time that morning. I glanced at my watch. If it was Ronnie Aldean, he was ahead of schedule. My natural optimism rebounded a notch. I had a spring in my step as I approached the door.

Then I heard dogs barking on the other side. What in this world? Before I could get the door open more than a crack, in rushed two medium-sized shaggy dogs with brightly colored print bandannas around their necks, one pink, one blue.

"Gigi!" My granddaughters followed the dogs in. Deacon stood on the porch with an ominous-looking terrarium I couldn't see inside of because of the way he was holding it.

I opened my arms wide and hugged Lennox (age fifteen) and Calliope (who'd be fourteen in two weeks) close. "How are my girls?"

"We're good," they chimed. They looked happy to be here. They usually were. Their dad wasn't a bad person, but I think it's fair to say it took a special kind of man to be both parents to teenage daughters. Deacon did his best. The other thing that was fair to say is that I'd spoiled him rotten, despite Tucker's best efforts to rein him in. We'd decided early on that whenever we disagreed on anything to do with the kids, he had the final say with Gemma, Gillian, and TJ—Tucker junior—and I had the final say with Deacon. You could just look at where each of those kids were right now in life, and it would tell you everything you needed to know about how well that worked out. I was just too tenderhearted. No, that's not right either. The truth of the matter is that I was a pushover with a tendency towards being gullible in certain situations.

"Who's this you have with you?" I gave Deacon a look over the girls' heads I'm confident he could easily decipher. We hadn't discussed pets, and I was certain he was counting on my inability to say no to my granddaughters.

"Aren't they adorable?" cooed Calliope. "I named mine Daisy, and Lennox's is Hutch. We rescued them." The dogs dashed off through the house, sniffing everything and occasionally barking.

And now I'm rescuing all of you. I sighed and squeezed the girls tighter before I released them. "And who does your father have?"

"That's Elvis." Lennox avoided my gaze.

"Elvis?" I asked.

"He's a blue iguana," said Calliope. "Gigi, he is so pretty."

"Deacon Ford Dawson, what could you possibly be thinking?" I asked, like any reasonable person in my situation would.

"Well, Mom, I didn't set out to adopt an iguana. He belongs to my friend Amber. Her boyfriend got abusive. She was in a tight spot, so I let her sleep on the sofa for a few days. She left yesterday morning, but Elvis did not leave the building. To be honest, I don't know what to do with him."

"But why—?" My eyes darted to the driveway. His truck, which was backed up to the bottom of the steps, was overflowing with furniture and boxes. "Are y'all here to stay?" I stepped through the door and craned my neck to get a better look at the truck. "I didn't think y'all were coming until the end of the month." I stepped back inside, opened the door wider, and motioned him into the house. I needed to get him and that iguana off my porch while I figured out what was going on.

Deacon carried Elvis inside. "My landlord already has new renters lined up. He said he'd get me my deposit back if I went ahead and moved out. I didn't think it would be a problem."

"*That's* not a problem," I lied, my eyes transfixed on the blue iguana. There were several problems.

"Isn't he beautiful?" asked Calliope.

I might've taken a step or two backwards. "Well, he's a pretty color." It was a shade of blue you don't often see on living creatures, at least not in this country. He looked like a miniature dinosaur, and he was giving me a hostile look. "Deacon, you're going to have to locate this lizard's rightful owner."

"Mother, I plan to," he said in this patronizing tone he uses with me sometimes that works my last nerve. And let me tell you, my nerves were already frayed to the point of snapping that morning.

I should tell Deacon no, he needs to wait until the end of the month, like we agreed. He could just figure things out with his landlord. Maybe he wouldn't get his deposit back after all. Given the level of chaos in my house, maybe this once my needs would take precedence.

But the truck was already loaded and backed up to my steps.

Did he still even have a key to the apartment?

Poor Tucker. What an unmitigated disaster all of this was to come home to. Could I just meet him at the airport? Maybe board a plane to the Caribbean and get jobs bartending or something? Because I was likely going to need another source of income. How in the name of sweet reason was I going to meet my deadline with the house falling apart and the kids moving in?

"You okay, Gigi?" Calliope asked. She smiled her positively angelic smile and sidled over to give me a hug.

I must've still been staring at the lizard.

"I'm fine, sugar," I said brightly. I squeezed her tight and did the only thing I possibly could. "Well, let's get y'all settled upstairs."

The stairs were just at the edge of the entryway. I started up and they followed, the girls chattering happily.

"Can we go to the beach later?" asked Lennox.

"Sure," I said.

"It's so cool we're living at the beach," said Calliope. "I'm going to learn to windsurf."

"I didn't expect y'all till the end of the month," I said. "I haven't had a chance to move my office." Selfishly, I guess I resented having to move out of the largest of the guest rooms—the one I'd painted Sherwin Williams Waterscape, a color that just made me feel happy. I'd spent the better part of a month decorating and organizing my creative space so that I could be productive. Giving it up hurt, I'll admit that. But family sacrificed for family.

We all stopped at the doorway to my office. "Deacon, if you'll help me, we'll move my desk and so forth into the bonus room. That way the girls can each have their own room." That was important at their ages. I'd be fine in the bonus room. Tucker and I could watch TV downstairs. We'd just need to rearrange the sectional sofa and chairs that were in the bonus room and make room for my office furniture.

Deacon set the terrarium down on my desk. "I've still got that king-sized bed y'all gave me, so I guess I'll be in here."

Lennox chose the room overlooking the backyard, and Calliope didn't object. She was the easiest going one of us all.

"Listen, a pipe broke in the bathroom," I said. "It's an awful mess, but the plumber will be here shortly, I hope. In the meantime, if you need to use the bathroom, there's a powder room downstairs."

The doorbell rang for the third time that morning. Please, God, let that be Ronnie Aldean. Or the Publishers Clearinghouse. If I won that, I could pay Deacon's rent for him.

The dogs bolted for the front door, barking like we were under attack.

Tucker loved animals. He did not love them inside the house. The yard wasn't fenced, and in terms of home improvements, that just wasn't a priority right now. What on earth were we going to do? I was reasonably certain he wouldn't divorce me at this stage of the game, but you shouldn't take that sort of thing for granted.

I dashed down the steps and to the front door. "Get back now," I said to the dogs. "Daisy, Hutch... shoo. Girls, call the dogs please."

The girls obliged, and the dogs went racing back up the stairs.

Ronnie Aldean, the much anticipated plumber, was not your plumber from central casting. Neatly dressed, fit, and tanned, he looked more like a marine than a plumber. He was very apologetic for being later than he'd estimated. He offered a sincere explanation, and I'm certain it was a good one, but to be honest, by that time, my nerves were so shot I wasn't paying good attention. It didn't matter. He was there. I was saved. All would be right—with the plumbing at least—before Tucker got home. That's what I was thinking anyway.

I showed Ronnie to the breakfast room and gestured to the pipe that had failed so dramatically with the bucket underneath, not that he could've missed the problem. Our house has an open floor plan, with the main living area—family room, dining room, breakfast area and kitchen—all one big room, really, separated only by small sections of wall with oversized pass-thru doorways.

Needing to sit, just for a minute and gather my wits, I took a seat in the family room. I figure it was a good idea to be easily accessible while Ronnie was working, you know, in case questions came up. I considered, for a moment, if it was too early for a gin and tonic. Yes... yes, it was. My granddaughters needed better than a day-drinking Gigi.

Deacon, the girls, and the dogs came noisily down the stairs. "We're going to start moving things in if that's okay," said Deacon.

"Of course." There was nothing else to be done. I'd just as well make the best of it. My son and granddaughters needed me. Having them with us again would have its share of joys.

"We went ahead and moved your stuff to the bonus room," said Deacon.

I swallowed hard. I knew well my son's strengths and gifts. Organization was not among them. Especially given the amount of time that had elapsed, he'd no doubt thrown all my things in a huge pile. I could not give him what for, though I had a desperate, burning need to do exactly that, in front of my granddaughters and a plumber. "Be careful carrying things up those stairs."

"We will," called the girls as the three of them tromped out the front door.

"Y'all just moving in, ma'am?" Ronnie's voice was deep and melodic but had a pleasant country twang.

"Well, some of us are—my son and my granddaughters."

"Ma'am, it's hard to believe you've got teenage grand-children."

That was a bit familiar. Was he flirting with me? Surely not. Well, he did call me ma'am, but in the South, women of all ages were called ma'am. It was a sign of respect and deference, not an indication of age. Well, not always anyway. Like a lot of Southern things, the translation varied. I laughed at myself. "I could not agree with you more. And yet Deacon insists I do."

"You must've been a child bride."

I gave him a sideways look. He did sound a little flirty. But he was at least twenty years younger than me, and I seriously doubted he was into grandmothers. "That's very kind of you." I had married Deacon's dad when I was very young and very fool-ish. That much was true. The other true thing was that Deacon had made me a grandmother at a ridiculously early age due, in part, to his genetic predisposition towards sowing his seed widely.

"Ma'am, I'm going to check things out upstairs," said Ronnie.

"I'll just be right here. Let me know if you need anything."

Someone banged on the front door.

I hopped up and darted over to open it, but just as I reached for the doorknob, the door opened. I backed out of the way, and Deacon and one of his pot-smoking buddies carried a mattress upstairs.

"You remember Corey, Mom?" said Deacon as he backed up the stairs.

Breathe in, breathe out. "Yes, of course. How are you, Corey?"

"Hey, Mrs. B. I'm good."

I caught a whiff of Corey as he slowly maneuvered his end of the mattress up the stairs. I could've gotten high just standing next to him. If I hadn't been in desperate need of the plumber upstairs and therefore required to stay and talk to him about whatever repairs he recommended—and pay him, of course—I would've taken my granddaughters and gone out for a while, just until Deacon and Corey had the big pieces inside and Corey had, with any luck at all, left.

It's not that I opposed pot in general. I'm pretty much a live and let live person. And to be honest, if it were legal, I'd likely be making some brownies with an extra ingredient on occasion. But I didn't want my impressionable granddaughters exposed to that lifestyle.

Who was I kidding? There was no telling what all they'd been exposed to. Deacon was a free spirit. That was the most charitable way I could put it.

Ronnie Aldean came down and checked the primary bathroom and the powder room, then the kitchen and the laundry room. Finally he crawled under the house. Our house wasn't raised as high as many of the others on Sullivan's Island, the ones with garages underneath, but we did have a decent-sized crawl space. Ronnie seemed to be making a thorough inspection of anything plumbing related. I was impressed.

After he'd been here a little more than an hour, he rang the doorbell again. I was feeling optimistic as I went to the door. He seemed to be very meticulous. I would definitely be keeping Ronnie Aldean's number for the random clog or leak. Hopefully, he would have everything wrapped up and be on his way before Tucker got home. We had supper club at five that evening. I still needed to decide what to wear. I smiled widely as I opened the door.

Ronnie Aldean stood on the porch, dusting himself off.

When he looked up, he wore a pained expression. "This is just heartbreaking, ma'am."

Something with icy talons grabbed a handful of my internal organs and squeezed. What now? I dreaded the answer to that question more than I could adequately express. "I think I'd better sit down. Please come inside." I moved to the closest chair in the family room and slid into it. "Please have a seat."

He followed me inside, tugging at his collar, his wince deepening. "Nah, I'm okay. I've got my work clothes on. Now this pipe in the kitchen, that's not a problem itself. It's old pipes, is what it is, ma'am, and I guess maybe they've been cleaned with chemicals and what have you over the years. That won't take long at all to fix, and then you'll just have your cleanup, fixing the drywall, repainting, and whatnot."

"And the heartbreaking part?"

"Well, I thought I should check out the drain pipe in the other bathrooms to make sure you didn't have the same situation going on somewhere else. Unfortunately, you do in the primary, but that's not the worst part. I brought some pictures I took with my phone."

He squatted by my chair. "You see this area right here? This is underneath the house, right below your primary bath. It's hard to see in this picture, but this area is covered in mold."

"Mold?" News stories about houses that had to be burned to the ground because of mold flashed before my eyes. Didn't our insurance exclude mold? Mold!

"Yes, ma'am, I'm afraid so. You've got a leak under the shower. Looks like it's been leaking for a long time, and mold is just covered over everything down there."

"Do we need a hazmat team to clean it out?" I might've been stammering by that point.

"The floor... ma'am, the wood underneath there is all rotted. It can't be cleaned. It's going to have to be tore completely out. That water got into your sub-floor, the joists... I'd say the whole bathroom is going to have to be ripped out down to the studs and redone."

"But the mold—"

"When they rip everything out that has mold on it, it won't matter anymore as long as it hasn't spread. Doesn't look like it has. You might want to get an environmental company to take a look just to be sure."

It took me a minute to get the question out. "Is this... the tearing out and so forth... does it have to be done right away? I mean, from the inside everything looks just fine. I just had a shower this morning—"

"Ma'am, it's a wonder you or your husband hatn't fallen through that floor. It's not safe to use at all. It's rotted."

"But—"

"You're going to need a contractor. This is way beyond what I can fix. Do you know anyone to call?"

I leaned over, elbows on my knees, and held my head in my hands. "I don't. Can you recommend someone?"

"There's a guy I go to church with, name's Luke Baldwin. He might have time to take a look. He's another one of Miss Josephine's former students, so she'll vouch for him too."

I nodded. "Could you give me his number please?"

"Sure, I'll send you his contact information. I sure am sorry about this."

"Thank you, Mr. Aldean."

"Ma'am, Mr. Aldean is my daddy. Call me Ronnie. I'm gonna get your pipe fixed for you in here so you'll at least be able to use the upstairs bathroom. The powder room looks fine—you can use that too. Of course you can't shower in there. I would fix the drain in the primary bath, but that's all got to be tore out, so it ain't any point."

"Thank you, Mr.—Ronnie."

How much would it cost to fix this? Ripping out and completely redoing the biggest bathroom in the house... that had to be expensive. The best we could hope for was it would take all the remaining money we'd set aside for other repairs.

What had we done? This house was a money pit. How much more money could we sink into it before we weren't just risking our dreams of what our next act looked like but our security when we were old and at our most vulnerable? Especially if I missed my deadline and couldn't settle into a regular publishing schedule because I lived in utter chaos? Were we going to be one of those desperately sad old couples living in a broken-down trailer park with newspapers on the windows, eating cat food, or some government-run old-folks home? Did they even have such a thing anymore?

How had the home inspector missed rotted floors? I understood how the Johnsons might've not known there was a problem. We certainly hadn't noticed anything wrong in the bathroom. But wasn't this sort of thing why you had home inspections done?

I needed to make a run to the liquor store before Tucker got home. We were both going to need a stiff drink tonight. I needed to get something to make for dinner, maybe pick up some chicken at Publix. That would be an easy—

Oh my Lord... we had supper club tonight.

Chapter Four

Tallulah did a last-minute scan for anything out of place. Dinner that evening would be served on the lower deck. It was one of several dining areas incorporated in the outdoor living space and the one she used most often for supper club. It was a lovely spot, down a half flight of steps, situated beneath the branches of a sprawling live oak. For the occasion, she'd replaced the all-weather dining set with a large, heavy wooden dining table. It fit her motif of "alfresco dinner in the Italian countryside" rather well, she thought. The table was surrounded by whitewashed ladder-back chairs with cream-and-tan striped cushions. Strings of white lights were strung from the live oak branches, giving everything a magical glow.

She'd gotten the idea for the table scape off Pinterest. Chunky candles in low wooden holders, votives, pots of herbs, and small vases of hydrangeas were scattered across a simple flax-colored linen runner. The table was set for fourteen with alternating cream and sage dinnerware. Who would have guessed that Tallulah would ever take so much pleasure in setting a table? She loved entertaining, and she loved making everything beautiful for her friends. Somewhere tonight, Eugenia Ladson was quite pleased with herself.

Oh, Eugenia, you should be here for this.

Life could be so bloody unfair.

Tallulah tried to shake her melancholy mood. The others would be here soon. She needed to find her joie de vivre and get changed.

Change. That was the problem. Too much had changed. Six years later she still missed Henry, of course she did. She always would. But aside from missing *him*—her heart, her better half—she was lonely.

Yes, she had broadened her circle and had a group of dear friends who felt like family. Eugenia had cobbled together the members of the supper club, choosing a mix of a few lifelong friends and people she felt could use a friend. And Tallulah adored them all.

But when they all went home at the end of the evening, she was very much alone. Rattling around that big house by herself was probably a mistake, but she couldn't bring herself to sell the only home she and Henry had ever shared.

And she missed Eugenia.

Eugenia had quite literally saved her life. She'd stood by Tallulah, pretending to need her, until she was out of the woods. Friends like Eugenia were one in a million. And she deserved so much better than what life had handed her. Losing her, when Tallulah was just finding her stride again, had been devastating. If it hadn't been for her friends, for people to bear that loss with, she might well have sunk back into the dark place she was in when Eugenia and Fish dragged her out of the ocean kicking and screaming. Fish. Bless his bohemian heart. He was a true friend as well—her best friend since Eugenia had passed away.

Tallulah brushed a speck off the table runner. It didn't seem possible Eugenia had been gone for a year. Tallulah's phone buzzed with a notification. She retrieved it from the table and glanced at the screen.

Oh good grief. More drama. She needed to change her settings so she didn't get so many social media and app updates. The good people of Sullivan's Island were losing their minds, and Tallulah needed a break. What would Henry think of all this hullaballoo about the maritime forest? He'd passed away before things had gotten so completely out of hand.

How *had* that happened?

Sullivan's Island had a somewhat rare situation. Most sea islands fought erosion constantly. They brought in sand periodically to renourish the beaches because they're forever washing away. Sullivan's Island had that problem on the northeastern end, but the rest of the island was actually growing rather than shrinking, because sediment that would otherwise be washed on down to Folly Beach or other points south was accreting to Sullivan's Island. It was the opposite of erosion, and it had been going on since the jetties went in, in the late 1800s, to fix the problems with Charleston Harbor.

The jetties are, simply put, two three-mile-long underwater stone walls, laid out rather like a funnel with the small end towards the ocean. One of them juts out from Sullivan's Island, the other from Morris Island. They created one deep channel that comes directly into the harbor. It took seventeen years and more than a million tons of stone. And, Tallulah supposed, it did what they designed it to do quite nicely.

Trouble was, the resulting changes in the way sediment behaved nearly wiped out Morris Island and damaged Folly Beach. And Sullivan's Island received the windfall, if you will. Before the jetties were built, Sullivan's Island had erosion problems and several temporary fixes. But once the harbor jetties went in, well, everything changed. Sullivan's Island had been accreting land for well over a hundred years. But the difficulties started after Hugo.

Over time, as sediment builds, you get new dunes on the beach. Then come grasses, flowers, and shrubs. Along the way, you might get another row of dunes or two. Eventually trees begin to grow and a forest is born. Today Sullivan's Island is home to a maritime forest of nearly two hundred acres that *technically* reaches almost to Breach Inlet. Tallulah scoffed at the notion. It's nothing but sea oats, flowers, and a shrub or two on the northeast end. But on the opposite end of the island, it's a thriving stand of a hundred and twenty-five or more different kinds of plants and trees—including wax myrtles, cedars, pines, magnolias, young live oaks, and on and on.

To some, the maritime forest was an incredible gift—a stunningly beautiful Eden that served as a buffer between the island and hurricane storm surges and rising sea levels. It was a sanctuary for nesting sea turtles, all manner of birds, rabbits, and other wildlife, butterflies, and bees.

To others, the maritime forest was a vermin, snake, and coyote habitat that blocked million-dollar views and ocean breezes.

The newly accreted land belongs to the town, not to the individuals who bought the lots closest to the ocean. Back in 1991, in the aftermath of Hugo, the town realized the growing natural area could give rise to problems. They sold the accreted land for ten dollars to the Lowcountry Open Land Trust, a nonprofit corporation created to preserve natural areas. The land trust in turn deeded the property back to the town but with deed restrictions. Essentially, the land must be left in its natural state, but the town has the authority to take measures to control the vegetation as deemed necessary for the common good. Regrettably, Tallulah thought, therein lay the problem. Opinions as to the "common good" varied widely.

There was controversy and compromise for years but with the town passing increasing restrictions on what could be cut on town-owned lands. With less cutting, nature took its course and the forest flourished.

The most controversial topic in their little town was neither politics nor religion.

It was trees.

Some of the neighbors filed a lawsuit. The ocean views they paid top dollar for when they bought their property had disappeared. Rats invaded their living rooms. They worried about the fire hazard in the underbrush. There were rulings and appeals and so forth for more than a decade. Then an abomination of a settlement, followed by an election that threw everything back in flux. And the whole time, bitterness grew between neighbors. Dueling newspaper editorials were published. Groups were formed. Everything was continuously debated across multiple platforms.

What would her parents say? Their home—the house Tallulah had grown up in—had been all but destroyed in Hurricane Hugo in 1989. She had to believe they'd be in favor of preserving the barrier that now buffered much of the island. But it would devastate them to know how neighbors were turning against neighbors, all the ugliness, especially online. Temperatures were definitely rising.

It all just made Tallulah deeply sad. And tired. Sometimes she didn't even recognize her hometown. So many things had changed in the years—decades now—since Hurricane Hugo. In many ways the island was a different place altogether. But nothing had changed more than the way so many people had developed an utter contempt for compromise. Both sides of the argument seemed absolutely convinced they held the moral high ground, and any sort of compromise spelled catastrophic disaster. It was all too depressing for words.

When Tallulah was a child, Sullivan's Island was a close-knit town of everyday people, for the most part—people who rarely locked their doors at night, neighbors who looked out for each other and kept a watchful eye on all the island children. She'd had a charmed childhood in many ways—up until they lost Grayson anyway.

Tallulah and her motley crew of friends had mapped every

inch of the island on their bikes. They'd crabbed on the back side of the island, hidden from each other in deserted forts, and spent endless summer days on the beach, riding the waves, splashing around the tidal pool, and eating sand-flecked pimento cheese or fresh tomato sandwiches for lunch. It was an idyllic way of life.

Hurricane Hugo changed everything, at least to Tallulah's mind, destroying more than just the homes of many of her friends and neighbors. Of course, she was thirty-two years old at the time. She and Henry lived in the same house then as she did now. They'd fared better than many and better than they'd expected when they returned days later, given that the entire island had disappeared under the sea for nearly an hour. Afterwards... it was like living through the aftermath of an atomic bomb. Hugo left them with a bridge sideways up, boats on land, houses in the middle of the street, fish in houses, no utilities, and snakes everywhere.

Some of the same families were still here, of course. But many had left after Hugo, unable to face rebuilding and risking losing it all again. There were so many new people in town, most perfectly lovely people who wanted to be a part of the community—like Sarabeth and Tucker Boone, and Libba and Jake Graham. But it hurt Tallulah's heart that Wall Street bankers and celebrities were buying up homes at sky-high prices, then letting them sit empty most of the time. The fabric of their community frayed in several spots.

Tallulah drew a long, slow breath and squared her shoulders. It was time to get ready. Her friends would be there soon. She hoped none of them wanted to talk about the latest legal wrangling in the dispute over the maritime forest at the dinner table—again. For Tallulah's part, she was well pleased that the mayor had won reelection last May and with him a town council that had a decidedly conservationist mindset.

It was the first step, though they had a long way to go. For the moment at least, the town was still legally bound to a forest-thinning agreement, though that was being challenged in court.

Tallulah was a conservationist. She wanted to see the maritime forest preserved. But that wasn't what she worried most about anymore. What kept her up at night was the growing tensions tearing at the town she loved. They lived in an idyllic, magical seaside village. What was wrong with people that they couldn't just be grateful for that?

Chapter Five

Saturday, May 28, 2022, 5:00 p.m.
Monthly Meeting of the Sullivan's Island Supper Club—
Happy Hour
Home of Tallulah Wentworth
Sarabeth Mercer Jackson Boone

I think Tallulah sees supper club as her mission in life. Some people might see that as a trivial thing, but I'm here to tell you, it changed my life. Not because of the food, which is always delicious, or Tallulah's beautiful home. Those things, of course, are quite trivial.

But the women I call friends because Tallulah Wentworth rang my doorbell that day... those women are precious to me. For most of my life, I didn't really have close girlfriends, well... not since high school anyway. Oh, there were girls I ran with in my misspent youth, but calling them friends would be a stretch. Anyway, that's a whole nother story and not one I care to tell.

You know, I always envied women who traveled with a posse of true friends who knew the absolute worst thing about each other and loved each other anyway. The kind of friends who would always have your back no matter what. I know what that feels like now, though the cast of characters who make up my tribe are not who I would've imagined.

My imaginary friends were all my same age, and they were all the same kind of pretty. Not as me—I don't mean I think *I'm* pretty. But in my fantasy, my friends looked like maybe we were all in the same sorority back in college. I was never actually in a sorority. And while I went to college—several of them, in fact—I never did graduate. Bobby Earl Dawson happened to me when I was nineteen, followed soon thereafter by Deacon, but that's a whole nother story too.

Anyway, back to the May supper club this year. I suppose that's the best place to start. That particular Saturday evening we were enjoying cocktails on the pool deck at Tallulah's, the way we always did if the weather was nice. The weather was perfect, the warm air like silk on your skin. There was a soft breeze blowing, and even though Tallulah's home isn't ocean front—it's second row—we could smell the salt in the air, and if you listened closely, you could hear the mesmerizing roll of the surf.

They say if you live near the beach you don't appreciate it. I've always heard that anyway, but it's certainly not true in my case. I was grateful every day I lived on this sandy slice of paradise. And I was trying hard to stay in the moment, because who knew how many more evenings like that we would have? At what point would Tucker and I be forced to cut our losses, sell the house for whatever we could get, and move someplace more affordable? It was bad enough to think about leaving this beautiful place. But that wouldn't be the worst part. It would gut me to leave my friends.

Tallulah's outdoor living space was something out of a fancy magazine, with several different sections—like outdoor rooms—on three different levels. The centerpiece was the pool. It was a large, free-form affair with small firepits and planters artfully arranged here and there and a built-in hot tub off the side closest to the house. There'd been nights supper club had ended with a soak or a dip. We all knew to bring suits just in case. Around the edge of the pool, groups of loungers were arranged with bar-top tables and stools scattered in. It was a space designed for entertaining large groups, and Tallulah seized every opportunity to do just that.

To the right of the pool was the tiki bar, which was huge and also housed an outdoor kitchen. Tallulah'd brought in someone to bartend—she often did that. Fish would've been happy to do it, but Tallulah said because he's always someone's escort, he doesn't need to be behind the bar.

About Fish... Fish is a nickname, of course, short for Fisher, which is one of a long list of names his mamma gave him. Tallulah and Fish grew up together more or less, and they've known Birdie and Vernon Markley since childhood. All of them are Charleston area natives, though Tallulah is the only one who's lived on Sullivan's Island her entire life. The four of them are all around the same age—in their midsixties. Fish comes from very old Charleston money, but he blew it all years ago. He's an easygoing soul who looks like an aging hippie, with wavy grey hair on the longish side and a tendency towards wearing Hawaiian shirts.

That evening, Fish was Camille's date. Tallulah brought a retired realtor named Tennyson Sumter—she's never brought the same date twice except for Fish, who was technically one of us anyway. Camille and Tallulah passed him back and forth like a favorite sweater they'd shared so long they'd forgotten whose it was to begin with. Anyway, none of us knew very much about Tennyson, but we weren't expecting to see him again.

The rest of the usual crowd was there: Tucker and me, Quinn and Redmond Poinsett, Libba and Jake Graham, Birdie and Vernon Markley, and Hadley Cooper and Cash Reynolds. I know, that's a lot of names, but I promise you'll get to know everyone in no time.

"Does everyone have a drink?" Tallulah stood near the edge of the pool and waited for everyone to quiet. The fountains were silent that evening, and she'd floated candles and flowers in the pool, which added to the festive ambiance. "We're celebrating a couple of things this evening. Y'all may or may not recall, but this evening is actually the fifth anniversary of the Sullivan's Island Supper Club."

A wave of delighted oohs and aahs passed through the group, then Tallulah continued. "I'd like to offer a toast in honor of our dear friend, Eugenia Ladson, without whose nagging and bullying this supper club would never've come to be. In her darkest hour, when she was recovering from chemotherapy herself and didn't even know yet if it would be effective, Eugenia set out to save me from myself. She made me her project, the way Eugenia did. I know some of the rest of you know what I'm talking about. She was special, our Eugenia, and I count myself quite fortunate to have been her lifelong friend. To tell y'all the plain, unvarnished truth, Eugenia handpicked each of you, well, the ladies I mean, of course. She saw something in each of us... somehow knew we needed each other. So here's to Eugenia, the best of us... Until we meet again, may God hold you in the palm of his hand."

Everyone echoed, "To Eugenia," and we all toasted her with her favorite cocktail, prickly pear margaritas, which I have to admit I'd developed a fondness for myself. I was all misty-eyed, thinking about Eugenia. I think most of us were.

"Also in honor of our anniversary," continued Tallulah, "we're having the same menu we had the night of the very first supper club in May of 2017—and also the first time Sarabeth and Tucker joined us a little more than a year ago. I called it La Vida Dolce back then, which means, of course, the sweet life. That first night—well, it was Eugenia and Fish and one of Fish's old friends they'd conned into escorting me, though I wasn't fit company for man nor beast at the time. I declare, I don't even recall his name." She searched the group for Fish.

"Probably for the best," said Fish. "He turned out not to be supper club material."

"Indeed." Tallulah laughed. "Quinn and Redmond were here and Libba and Jake. Camille and one of her doctors." Tallulah met each person's eyes and gave them a little nod as she went around the group.

"He wasn't *my* doctor," said Camille. "Well, not at the time anyway."

"...and of course Birdie and Vernon," continued Tallulah. "There were twelve of us that first night, and since then we've added Sarabeth and Tucker and later Hadley, who brought us Cash, and we're all hoping she lets us keep him."

Cash spoke up. "I'm hoping for that as well, Tallulah." He had his arm around Hadley, and he was smiling, looking at her the way a man does when he's found what he was looking for and he knows it.

Cash Reynolds was, at that time, a South Carolina Law Enforcement (SLED) agent, which gave him lots of interesting dinner conversation to contribute, well, when he could, of course. He and Hadley—Hadley Cooper—are just so cute together. She's a private investigator and a really good one, though you'd never in a million years guess to look at her what she does for a living. She looks like she should be a kindergarten teacher. She's tall and thin with long brown hair and big, soft brown eyes, and she's one of the kindest people you'll ever meet.

Hadley blushed bright red and grinned as the rest of us chuckled, and Jake Graham, who was standing beside Cash, turned his head and said something private to Cash. I suspected Libba and Jake and Hadley and Cash enjoyed each other's company outside of the bigger group. They were all of a similar age—early to midforties—and seemed to get along so well.

"Oh dear, did I say something I shouldn't have?" Tallulah feigned remorse. "Enough of me chattering on. Everyone enjoy your *aperitivo*—which is the Italian version of happy hour and appetizers, as best I understand it anyway. A butler will be passing arancini with basil pesto, broccoli-and-garlic-ricotta toasts with hot honey, and bruschetta. There are vegan versions of everything for those of that persuasion. *Buon appetito.*"

Tucker leaned over to speak directly in my ear. "You feeling better?"

I flashed my husband a smile that might not've made it all the way to my eyes. I was the luckiest woman I knew. I'd hit the husband jackpot. He was handsome but didn't seem aware of that fact. But more importantly, I'd never for a second doubted that he loved me. He was patient and kind and had a soothing way about him. Tucker was my security blanket.

I leaned into him. "It's stress, is all." I was trying hard not to think about how our house was falling down as more people moved into it and our savings were rapidly disappearing. "I'm fine, really. Let's just enjoy the evening."

He squeezed my elbow. "Listen, we'll get through this. We're going to be fine."

"I know." I nodded, looking at nothing in particular across the pool deck. I was still reeling from the final bit of news we'd gotten that afternoon.

Luke Baldwin, the contractor Ronnie Aldean had told me about—and actually ended up calling for me because I think he might've been afraid I was losing my grip on sanity, which was valid—had come straight over to talk to Ronnie about our disastrous plumbing leaks and damages. Luke concurred with everything Ronnie recommended, and then, as if Luke'd said, *Hold my beer*, he one-upped Ronnie with an even bigger catastrophe to do with the foundation.

"We'll get another estimate," said Tucker. "The foundation repairs may not be as major as Luke thinks. We need someone with a lot more experience with this kind of thing to take a look."

"Okay," I told him in a voice that let him know in no uncertain terms that I didn't want to discuss it anymore. The truth was, fear gripped my insides in a cold, steel vise. Tucker and I had sunk everything into that house. We didn't have the means that most everyone else in our group had. We were one more piece of bad luck away from losing everything. I shook that idea out of my head, took a deep breath, and rejoined the moment. I sorely needed this distraction.

Tallulah never does anything halfway, and I love that about her. A butler appeared in front of me with the broccoli toasts and offered me a napkin. I took my appetizer and drifted towards the gas fire pit, which occupied the left-hand side of the deck and was surrounded by Adirondack chairs. Tucker wandered over to talk to Redmond Poinsett and Vernon Markley, and Quinn and Libba took Adirondack chairs on either side of me. We sipped and chatted and munched on appetizers with the butler materializing every time we had an empty hand.

Quinn is the youngest of our group, and she shares my birth month—February. She turned thirty-six this year. You wouldn't think we'd have that much in common, but I know what life looks like from where she's standing, and somehow we clicked. Quinn's long brown hair is lighter than Hadley's and has caramel highlights. She wears it wavy most of the time, and it suits her. The most remarkable thing about Quinn is her megawatt smile.

"Quinn, I meant to tell you before and it slipped my mind," I said. "I finally met your mom and dad. They volunteered to help with the Arbor Day festivities last month. They are just the sweetest couple. And hard workers."

Quinn gave me the oddest look, like maybe she was waiting for me to say something more. Then she said, "I'm happy to hear they were on good behavior. You can't always count on that."

"Well, I thoroughly enjoyed them. It's not often you see couples their age who are still so demonstrably in love with each other." I really had only the vaguest idea what age the O'Leary's were. With some people it was really hard to tell. Maybe around Tallulah's age? Though they acted younger and were both quite... vigorous.

"Oh, they are demonstrative, to be sure." Quinn's hazel eyes got bigger. "They're Irish, so when they're in love with each other, they're deeper in love than anyone ever has been in the history of time immemorial. And when they hate each other... well... you'd better steer well clear of them. Bystanders have been known to be hit with flying debris."

"They're precious," said Libba. "They're Irish, seriously? Like, they were born in Ireland?"

Now, Libba is a petite blonde with a chin-length bob. For reasons I can't quite understand, she thinks she's fat, but she's not. She's healthy-looking, for goodness' sake—not to mention gorgeous. I think it's hard for a lot of women to be happy with their appearance. But then, I was reading *Seventeen* magazine when I was twelve and *Cosmopolitan* by the time I was twenty, so I understand a thing or two about unrealistic expectations.

Anyway, poor Libba had been going through a really hard time ever since I'd known her. She'd had a horrible case of endometriosis and had to have a hysterectomy not long after I met her. That is something else I understand a thing or two about. I have walked that road. And I know it's taboo nowadays to suggest a temperamental woman might be dealing with hormone issues. But let me tell you, that is a real thing when they yank your ovaries out. It takes a while for the chemistry in your body to get readjusted, and in the meantime, well... mood swings doesn't really cover it. I'll tell you one thing: Jake has been very supportive.

"They're first-generation Irish American," Quinn said. "Their lives are quite dramatic. Just ask them."

"They have the most charming accents," I said. "Everything about them is charming. I do hope they'll be getting more involved." I sent up a silent prayer I'd still be living here next year on Arbor Day.

Arbor Day was fun on Sullivan's Island. I'd never lived in a place where they made quite as much fuss about it or at least that I'd noticed. But anything to do with the environment was a popular cause in our town, as in many coastal communities, I supposed. It was important to me right from the start to give back to the community. Tucker and I hoped to make this our forever home. It was important to be a part of things.

Quinn took an appetizer from the butler. "What is in these little balls?" she asked us after we each had one and the butler had moved on to the next huddle. She didn't wait for the answer but bit right in. That's Quinn for you.

"That's arancini," said Libba. "Fried risotto with cheese and pesto."

"They're delicious," said Quinn. "So Arbor Day was a success?"

"I'd say so," I told her. "We gave away so many saplings. I hope they all get planted. And we had several presentations, a band, a scavenger hunt—it was a fun day."

"I need to get involved in some of your conservation groups," said Libba. "Unfortunately, it might be after the kids go to college. Right now they're keeping me hopping. I don't know how you manage it all, with all your renovations and trying to write a book. How's that going, by the way?"

By way of answering Libba's question, I gave them the Cliff's Notes version of my day.

"I can't believe you're here," said Quinn. "I'd have had to take to my bed, I'm afraid."

"Oh, I wouldn't miss this for the world," I said.

"So..." Libba made a face like *let me get this straight.* "You gave up your office—your writing sanctuary? You *love* that room."

"Well, the girls are teenagers," I said. "They need their own space. And two of the upstairs bedrooms are really small."

"So the bonus room is your office now?" asked Quinn. "It's actually bigger, right? Maybe it won't be so bad once you get settled. You want us to help paint it that same pretty shade of blue?"

"Thank you so much," I said. "That's actually a great idea. I might take you up on it. But... well, it'll be my office during the day. In the evenings the kids will use it as a den. They don't watch the same stuff on TV that we do. You know how it is."

Now here's the interesting thing about that. Libba had three teenagers: Mia, Maeve, and Mills. They were fifteen, fourteen, and thirteen, bless her heart. Quinn, whose husband, Redmond, was a bit older, had twin sixteen-year-old stepchildren she'd raised since they were three, Sutton and Shepherd, and a little boy, Oliver, who was hers and Redmond's. Oliver was much younger—I'm thinking he was seven at the time. My grandchildren would soon be going to school with Libba and Quinn's children is what I'm saying. And because my granddaughters' mother wasn't around much, I would no doubt be filling in all kinds of gaps. It would keep me young. That's what I was telling myself.

I just had to figure out how to still finish the book I was working on, write the next one, and repeat, while helping to raise my granddaughters.

"So, it's not actually your dedicated office then?" asked Libba.

"Not exclusively."

"How are you going to finish your book?" asked Libba. "And write the next one? I've heard you say a hundred times how important having your own space was."

"I'm just going to have to suck it up and do it," I said. "This won't be forever."

"How long is it for?" asked Libba.

"We haven't really discussed that."

Libba and Quinn exchanged a look.

"Look, y'all, I know this is a train wreck, and no, it's certainly not what I had planned. But the alternative is homeless grandchildren, which, I'm sure you'll agree would be a bad thing."

They both made soothing noises and rushed to say of course they understood.

"Thank y'all. I really do appreciate the support."

"Just let us know how we can help, okay?" Libba said. "Once school starts, we can figure out a car pool."

"That would be absolutely amazing," I said.

"You just finish your book." Quinn smiled. "I'm looking forward to it."

"Hey, has anyone heard anything on the appeal of the settlement agreement?" asked Libba.

She was referring to the agreement reached between the town council and some of our neighbors who'd sued the town in a lawsuit that dragged out through an entire decade. Very few people were happy with that settlement, which cleared the way for the maritime forest to be thinned out and cut back.

"No," I said. "The attorney filed for a judicial review in February, but it'll take months I bet, maybe longer."

"Well, I hope they get it thrown out," said Quinn. "It's just crazy the way the settlement was written. They got what they wanted—a compromise to allow cutting—and then tried to fix it where it could never be reconsidered. Who's ever heard of one town council tying the hands of all the future town councils to come?"

"At least we have a town council now that supports preserving the maritime forest," I said. "Surely they'll get that settlement tossed out."

"I hope so," said Libba. "Have they caught whoever cut all those trees?"

"No." Quinn's eyes traveled the perimeter of the deck. "But I worry about—"

"Vernon would never cut the trees." I lowered my voice and looked to be sure Vernon was still on the opposite side of the pool. I thought about that after I said it. The truth was, Vernon was a certified character, with a reputation for being a bit of a loose cannon. There was really no telling what he might do. "Besides, that was near Station 26. And how does that even happen in broad daylight and without anyone noticing? Seems like that kind of thing would require a chainsaw. Now, if you hear someone has been surreptitiously chopping down trees around Station 24..." I thought about it for a second, then shook my head. "No. I just can't see Vernon doing that."

"I don't know." Libba tilted her head and raised her eyebrows. "He's always agitated about what he calls the 'jungle' between their house and the ocean. And he does have those goats..."

Birdie appeared from nowhere. "Shush now, you'll get him

started and we won't be able to talk about anything else tonight except his jungle. And no, he did not cut down those trees. I would kill him deader than Elvis, and he knows that."

Birdie always tickled me. She was so down to earth. Somewhere along the way, she'd picked up a little country twang in her sweet Charleston drawl. Birdie had a delicate look to her, like fine china. She wore her long, wavy hair—it was mostly grey with light brown streaks—pulled over her shoulder and tied with a blue ribbon.

Libba turned a delicate shade of pink. "Birdie, I'm so sorry—"

Birdie waved the apology away. "He's the one who's made himself a suspect. I should never have allowed him to keep those danged goats. But they're cute little boogers—and smaller than a lot of dogs. I'd bet money most people who see them from a distance assume they're dogs. To be honest, it's the underbrush they eat that's the biggest problem for us. All kinds of stuff lives in that." She shivered and shook her head.

"But how do they—?" I started to ask.

"Everyone, it's six o'clock," called Tallulah. "Let's gather at the table, shall we? The *primo* course is about to be served."

I had so many questions about those goats, but apparently they wouldn't be answered that evening.

I scanned the group for Tucker, my eyes catching his across the deck. He met me halfway to the steps down to the lower deck and slipped an arm around my waist. I leaned into a hug. He was my rock. He'd told me we'd be okay. I trusted him.

I took a deep, cleansing breath and smiled up at my husband.

Chapter Six

Saturday, May 28, 2022, 6:00 p.m.
Monthly Meeting of the Sullivan's Island Supper Club—Primo
Home of Tallulah Wentworth
Tallulah Wentworth

As was her custom, Tallulah had put place cards out so no one would have to wonder where they should sit. It always stressed Tallulah when hostesses failed to do that. She moved to her chair at the far end of the table, waited until everyone had found their places, and took her seat. Once they were all seated, Hank, who'd tended bar, came around to offer everyone wine. Fish had helped Tallulah choose a nice pinot grigio and a red blend, either of which worked well with the menu, she thought. She wasn't one to get caught up too much in wine pairings. Everyone should drink what they liked.

Tallulah quelled the urge to say what everyone knew, but she somehow still wanted on the record. While Tallulah had been often accused—perhaps with some merit—of being a bit over the top, she did *not* have this much staff in every month. Typically it was just Hank to bartend. But this was a special occasion. Sometimes they all pitched in getting dinner on the table like normal people. They *were* normal people, well, some of them were anyway. Sometimes they had a buffet. Once they'd even had a picnic on the beach. But that night under the stars none of them had to hop up for a single thing. And that was simply sublime.

Once they were all seated and everyone had made their wine choice and been served, Tallulah asked Fish to say grace. He might've had a little more to say to the Lord that night than he typically did, but they had so much to be grateful for after all. Fish always did a nice job with the blessing.

"Thank you, darlin'." Tallulah patted him on the hand, and his blue eyes twinkled as he smiled at her. Fish really did have nice eyes. They were kind. Kindness was a quality often undervalued in men. Her Henry was the kindest man she'd ever known.

Technically, Fish was Camille's date that evening, but Tallulah wasn't one to allow technicalities to interfere with her preferences. She'd thought it would be better to have him next to her so they could confer if necessary. Fish had been in on supper club from the very beginning after all—had been instrumental in the forming of the group. He often served as Tallulah's sounding board, troubleshooter, and runner when needed. Libba was seated beside Fish, with Jake right beside her. With the exception of Fish and Camille and Tennyson and Tallulah, Tallulah had seated the other couples together that evening.

A server delivered the first course, deftly setting pasta bowls on top of dinner plates.

When they'd all been served, Tallulah said her piece. "I have to apologize for the primo course not being more imaginative. Five years ago, when I planned this menu for the first time, I was deep into my comfort-food stage. Fettuccini Alfredo is my absolute favorite pasta dish. I hope y'all will enjoy this recipe. Hadley, darlin', yours is, of course, the vegan version."

"That's so sweet of you—thank you," said Hadley. "You always go to too much trouble on my account."

"Nonsense," Tallulah told her, sounding to her own ear a bit like Eugenia, who'd had a particular fondness for the word.

As she picked up her fork, Tallulah cast a glance down to the other end of the table, to Tennyson—her date for the evening. Her late husband, Henry, was the love of her life, and she had no intentions of trying to fill that void. But a lady needed an escort on occasion, and Camille insisted they share Fish. Never having the same date twice kept things simple. So did sitting them at the far end of the table where they were less likely to get ideas, though she had to admit, Tennyson was a handsome devil. He reminded her a bit of Richard Gere.

Tallulah might be lonely, but she could never bring herself to allow anyone else to occupy Henry's place in her life. It would feel like cheating. Henry would always be her husband even if they occupied different worlds for the time being.

Not everyone felt as though remarrying was disloyal to their original spouse, and that was perfectly fine. Camille wanted to remarry. That was her choice, of course. Poor Camille had buried her husband relatively young—in her midfifties, in Texas—and had moved to Sullivan's Island for a fresh start. But that had been nearly fifteen years ago.

It was nice that Camille was enjoying Tennyson's company even if he was *technically* Tallulah's date. Tennyson didn't seem too unhappy with his seating arrangement. At that moment, Camille was enthralled by something he was saying. Was there anything a man liked better than an adoring audience?

Camille laughed. She didn't seem to mind the seating chart either. Humph... he could've at least acted like he was disappointed to sit so far away from Tallulah.

"Oh look!" Libba pointed at something above Hadley's head. "Is that a comet?"

Tallulah slid back her chair and turned to see. "Where?" All she could see was the deepening blue of the evening sky.

"I see it," said Sarabeth. "I bet it was a comet."

"I must've missed it," said Birdie.

"It just streaked right across the sky over the ocean," said Libba.

Apparently everyone else missed it. They settled back in to finish their first course. A moment later, Libba excused herself. Was she feeling all right? She looked a bit peaked, at least Tallulah thought so. Libba'd had a rough patch a while back, health wise, but Tallulah thought she'd turned the corner on all that. Jake and Libba were such a handsome young couple, and their children were positively precious. Three stair-step teenagers with Libba's light blond hair. They'd be heartbreakers, every one of them. And Libba did such a good job with them. She was very thorough, very focused. If every child had a mother like Libba Graham, the world would be a far better place. Of course, Quinn was an excellent mother as well.

The fettuccine was delicious, naturally. Tallulah had given the caterer her own recipe, which she'd worked on over the years until she had it exactly like she liked it. She'd say this much: when the busboy came to clear the dishes, every bowl was perfectly clean.

"Did you enjoy the fettuccine?" she asked Fish.

"It was so good I can feel my arteries hardening."

"Well, we can all eat some kale tomorrow to make up for it." Sometimes these health nuts got on Tallulah's nerves. Oh, that wasn't fair. Fish didn't have extreme opinions about anything. He was the easiest going person she knew. The fact was that Tallulah keenly missed the biggest health nut—Eugenia.

Libba returned to the table, and Tallulah thought she looked like she was feeling better. She smiled as she slid into her seat. "Tallulah, that fettuccine was amazing," said Libba. "Honestly, the best I've ever had."

"Well, thank you, sugar," said Tallulah. "I'm so happy you enjoyed it."

An odd expression flashed across Jake's face—he looked angry, Tallulah thought. Then he turned to say something to Vernon. Maybe she'd imagined it.

Tallulah watched Libba from the corner of her eye. Libba and Jake exchanged a few private words. A hurt look spread across Libba's face. She looked at Jake like maybe he'd been the one to hurt her, which surprised Tallulah, because it had always been her impression that Jake doted on Libba. Tallulah made herself a mental note to check in with Libba next week, make sure she was okay. It was probably nothing. Everyone quarreled. She and Henry had certainly had their share of disagreements.

"The sauce was delicious, but the pasta itself was excellent too," said Hadley.

"The chef made it fresh," said Tallulah. "I think you can really taste a difference, but I don't go to the trouble usually."

As they waited for the second course, it struck Tallulah, now on high alert, that Libba and Jake were awfully quiet, which was unusual for them. Tallulah tried a couple of times to engage Libba in conversation but didn't get very far. Her smiles fell flat, Tallulah thought. What *was* going on there?

Tennyson's voice carried the length of the table. He spoke in melodic, velvety tones that soothed something in Tallulah. "My third or fourth—to tell you the truth, I lose count—great-grand-father was a revolutionary war hero." He sounded every bit the Southern gentleman he was.

Tallulah caught just snippets of whatever he was telling that end of the table. They all seemed entertained. Thank goodness Tennyson Sumter had joined her Sunday school class a few months back. She'd been fresh out of dates for supper club, having run through all of her friends long ago, then friends of friends and everybody's cousins. Camille was no doubt pleased that Tallulah had met him in church. She was always carrying on about how it was better to meet men at church than with some app, which were all, according to Camille, full of psychopaths. Perhaps Tennyson would join the regular rotation, like Fish. Everyone seemed to enjoy his company.

For the next little bit, the group chatted with whoever was beside them or across the table. Tallulah reckoned there were three or four different conversations going on when Vernon said, rather loudly, "You've got foundation problems now?" He was across the table diagonally from Sarabeth, who wore a queasy look.

Every other conversation stopped. Vernon had everyone's attention. "On top of everything else you've been through, now it's the plumbing and the foundation too? I've never seen anything like it. It's a shame there's not someone to sue. I mean, you could sue the Johnson widow, but—"

"Vernon!" Birdie chided.

Tallulah closed her eyes and sighed. She dearly loved Vernon and Birdie. They were among her oldest and closest friends. But Vernon Markley could test one's patience. He must've picked up on a piece of someone else's conversation intended for an individual, not the table.

"Calm down, Birdie, I wasn't suggesting they do that. I was just saying when there's that much wrong with a house, you've only had just over a year, there ought to be someone you could sue. I'm just being empathetic here."

Tucker gave a little shrug. "Sadly, I don't think—"

"Surely you had a home inspection," Vernon said. "I'd start with the inspector. Sue him."

"Unfortunately, most home inspectors—ours included—have contracts that limit their liability," Tucker said.

"What's the point in having one then?" Vernon asked. "Who're you going to get to fix the foundation?"

"We're not sure yet," said Tucker. "We've just been made aware of the issue today."

"What's the problem, exactly?" asked Fish.

Tucker hesitated, and Sarabeth looked away. It was obvious she didn't want to discuss this, and Tallulah didn't blame her. Dinnertime conversation shouldn't be stressful. It should be pleasant. Tallulah gave Fish a look, and he lifted his chin in a half nod of understanding. After all these years, they understood each other quite well.

"Let's—" Fish started to change the subject, but Tucker spoke at the same time.

"It seems our house is not actually sitting on its foundation. Possibly it's been that way quite a while. Might've been hurricane related—who knows? Fixing it, apparently, is going to involve jacking the house up a section at a time and adding a support beam."

"Sounds expensive," said Vernon.

"I think that's a fair assessment," said Tucker. "But we'll get a few more estimates."

Tallulah reckoned Sarabeth's expression—part smile, part wince—suggested she'd still be grateful for a change in topic, but she leaned into Tucker, who for his part seemed untroubled. That was the thing about Tucker Boone. You rarely saw him rattled. He often defused awkward situations before they could morph into something bigger. For all their troubles, Tallulah had a strong sense that Sarabeth and Tucker's marriage was solid, which was a blessing. Shaky marriages did not weather crisis well.

The rest of the men asked a hundred questions and commiserated with Tucker. The Boone home was the topic of conversation until the next course had been served. Sarabeth looked more and more unhappy, bless her heart. When were those two going to catch a break?

Tallulah looked around the table at her friends, one by one. They were an interesting group, representing four different decades. In the beginning she'd been concerned about what they'd find in common with some of the younger couples. But Eugenia had been right, as usual. Age doesn't define you. Every phase of life is just a snapshot—a moment in time. Each of us might be in different moments right now, but we're all the same inside where it counts.

Tallulah felt the same inside as she did when she was Quinn's age, which seemed like the day before yesterday. Time was moving far too fast. They were all on a continuum—sometimes it felt more like a merry-go-round—each of them looking at life from a slightly different perspective, with that perspective constantly changing. Even though they were all at different places in their lives, they shared a connection to this place and to each other that was quite remarkable.

This group was such a blessing. And Tallulah loved the menu planning and the decorating and varying her seating arrangements for keeping conversation lively—but hopefully not too lively. She wished she'd started hosting supper club as a younger woman. But then she and Henry had been busy with other things, and Henry was not a particularly social animal. He might've tolerated this type of evening occasionally for her sake. But he would never have fully embraced it.

Could Henry see her now?

What would he make of the broken life she'd rebuilt without him?

Chapter Seven

Saturday, May 28, 2022, 6:20 p.m.
Monthly Meeting of the Sullivan's Island Supper Club—Secondo
Home of Tallulah Wentworth
Libba Graham

When everyone had been served the next course, Tallulah grabbed the opportunity to change the subject. Libba watched a smile of relief spread across Sarabeth's face.

"The *secondo* course," said Tallulah, "is oven-roasted branzino with figs, apricots, Mediterranean spices, and a citrus saffron butter sauce, accompanied by parmesan risotto and a *contorno* of roasted vegetables. *Buon appetito.*"

Birdie smirked at Tallulah. "You like saying that, don't you?"

Tallulah laughed because they all knew it was true. "I do. *Buon appetito,* Birdie."

"Enjoy your dinner, Tallulah," said Birdie with an affectionate little eye roll.

It used to be Eugenia who picked at Tallulah. They picked at each other like old friends will. And Birdie had known Tallulah just as long as Eugenia had. More and more, Birdie seemed to be slipping into that role. They both had Eugenia-sized holes in their lives—we all did.

There was a slight lull in conversation as everyone tasted the fish. Libba didn't want to give the men an opportunity to hop back on Sarabeth and Tucker's problems with the house. It had been really sweet of Sarabeth to pretend to see the imaginary comet. She was likely curious what that was all about. Libba would have to think of something to tell her besides the truth: Libba couldn't possibly eat fettuccine Alfredo. It had a million calories and ten million grams of fat, and Libba had done nothing but put on weight since her hysterectomy a year ago.

Her hormones were completely out of whack. Hopefully the new prescription Dr. Harris had given her yesterday would help. Libba was desperate to get some of this weight off.

But she didn't want to put a damper on the evening by talking about calories and diets, and she couldn't let Tallulah think she didn't care for the pasta, so she staged a distraction, snatched the nest of fettuccini out of her bowl, carried the fistful of saturated fat to the bathroom, and flushed it down the toilet at her first opportunity.

Of course Jake had seen her. She just prayed no one else had. Why did he feel compelled to raise the subject while they were still at the table? Could he not wait until they were home to call her out like a child? He knew full well what she was going through.

She needed to change the subject. Also, she wanted to send a message to Jake Graham. She was unfazed by his callous disregard for her feelings. Libba picked up her fork and glanced around the table. "Has anyone met the new couple who moved into the Henderson house?" She was proud of how composed, upbeat, and engaged she sounded. It was nothing like how she felt, which alternated unpredictably between tired, wired, and angry, mostly due to the hormone swings.

"Over on Conquest Drive? Overlooking the cove?" asked Redmond. "Big grey house with a dock?" Redmond was such a gentleman. *He* seemed interested in what she had to say.

"Yeah—yes." Libba corrected herself, nodding. One of her self-improvement goals was to speak better, a little less like a hill-billy. She'd noticed Jake sounded less like their Tennessee roots these days. What was up with that?

"I haven't met them," said Redmond. "But my understanding is that he is a retired investment banker."

"Retired?" Birdie's forehead creased. "I thought they were younger. Mid to late forties is what I heard at the hair salon."

"They are both," said Fish. "Younger and retired. He is anyway. I haven't met his wife."

"You've met him?" asked Tallulah. "What's his name? That's a lovely home. Quite large. I wonder if they have children."

Libba glanced at Tallulah. The house on Conquest was about the same size as the one Tallulah lived in by herself. Libba wasn't judging her—not at all. It was just curious how people often examined others far more closely than themselves.

"Knox Fitzgerald," said Fish. "It's just him and his wife. No kids."

"When did you meet him?" asked Tallulah.

"He was having lunch at Dunleavy's on Thursday," said Fish. "I happened to take the barstool next to him to grab a mahi-mahi sandwich. We chatted briefly."

"Where are they from?" Libba hoped her expression concealed the fact that she did not give a single fig—or cluck. She'd trained herself to think the words fig and cluck so she wouldn't accidentally say the other word out loud. She was not raising potty-mouthed children, and children repeated what they heard at home.

"New York," said Fish.

"Well, if he's an investment banker who retired in his forties and bought real estate here, perhaps he's someone we should get to know," said Vernon. "Maybe he's got the magic touch."

Fish winced. "I'm not sure we'd have a lot in common with him."

"What makes you say that?" asked Tallulah.

Fish gave a little shrug like maybe he'd opened his mouth and said something he wished he could take back. Then he took another bite of his branzino. "This fish really is delicious. I love the figs and apricots with it."

"Was the man a jackass?" asked Vernon.

"Vernon," Birdie said sternly.

Libba downed half her water. She knew the temperature outside was a pleasant seventy degrees that evening, but she was hot as fire. She'd love to take an ice cube from her glass and put it on the back of her neck, cool herself down.

"What, Birdie?" Vernon looked indignant. "It's a legitimate question."

"Did you not like him?" Tallulah asked Fish.

"I barely spoke with him for ten minutes," said Fish. "I hardly know the guy."

"But it's fair to say you know him as well as you'd like?" asked Redmond.

"Yes." Fish widened his eyes briefly in an emphatic little expression and took a sip of wine like he was hoping that'd be the end of it.

Tallulah said, "Hamilton Alexander Hughes Fisher Ravenel Aiken, I've rarely known you to meet anyone who you didn't want to get to know better. Now I'm really curious. What didn't you like about this man?"

Fish made a face like he'd tasted something sour, sighed, and then nodded. "Fine. He's apparently made fast friends with Richard Kinard and that bunch. He was spouting off at lunch about property rights and so forth. Protecting the views and the breezes. Y'all know the talking points."

So Knox Fitzgerald was a cutter or had aligned himself with them. Libba probably should give a fig about that. Normally she would. But truthfully, tonight she gave zero figs. Her life was coming apart at the seams, and she felt like someone had doused her in Tennessee whiskey and struck a match. Someone else would have to save the trees.

Diagonally across the table from Libba, Quinn set down her fork. "But his house is on the other side of the island. Why is he worried about ocean views?"

"It seems he's standing on principal," said Fish. "Perhaps he's bored since retirement."

"So he's a pot stirrer," said Cash, who was directly across the table from Fish.

"Precisely." Fish's eyes grew with meaning and he nodded at Cash.

"Just what we need." Jake's words dripped with sarcasm.

Libba looked at her husband. Except for calling her down, he'd been so quiet all evening she was happy he was participating in the conversation at all. But he was clearly in a sour mood, had been since before they left the house. Why can men not simply answer a simple question? "Do you like this dress?" didn't seem like a trick question.

And when, exactly, had she started even needing to ask the question? What happened to the man who used to tell her every day how beautiful she was? And it's not that Libba ever thought she was beautiful, but she loved that Jake thought that—or used to anyway. He didn't see her that way anymore. She could see it in his eyes.

What else was she seeing in his eyes? Or who?

That new associate artist he'd hired was nothing but trouble. Roxie Harlow. Had she made that name up? And how many women did you see in woodworking anyway? Jake had started making furniture and carved pieces when he was in junior high school. By the time he opened Graham Custom Woodwork in Mount Pleasant, he'd worked for two other shops in Nashville. Libba knew everyone he'd ever worked with, and this was the first time there'd been a woman in the mix, unless you counted wives who did bookkeeping. Maybe Libba should volunteer to do Jake's bookkeeping. She could keep a closer eye on Miss Roxie.

Directly across the table, Hadley flashed Libba a curious look.

The conversation continued around her, but she'd zoned out. What had she missed?

"Is everyone's fish all right?" asked Tallulah.

Everyone raved about the fish, even Hadley, who rarely ate fish. For the next few moments, they all enjoyed their dinner with occasional comments about the flavor combination, the risotto, and exactly what kind of fish branzino actually was—Mediterranean Sea bass, not to be confused with its Chilean cousin.

The Fitzgeralds didn't come up again until dessert was served.

Libba would later regret not having paid better attention when the Fitzgeralds were being discussed.

Chapter Eight

Saturday, May 28, 2022, 7:00 p.m.
Monthly Meeting of the Sullivan's Island Supper Club—Dessert
Home of Tallulah Wentworth
Quinn Poinsett

Quinn savored a bite of the Pistachio Stracciatella Gelato, which might've been the best thing she'd ever eaten. For a few moments, it got her mind off her parents. Then she looked across the table at Sarabeth, and the conversation they'd had earlier flashed like lightning through her brain. Quinn shifted restlessly in her seat.

Redmond, seated to her left, glanced at her and she smiled. Nothing to see here. Everything's fine. Quinn clutched her napkin.

Her parents had been getting out a lot more lately, which, on the one hand, she knew was good for them, especially if they were doing age-appropriate things, like volunteering instead of thrill seeking. But on the other hand, it worried Quinn. It was risky. Arbor Day—anything remotely connected to the issues with trees —had the potential to draw attention.

Just look at what had happened to Sarabeth. She'd only lived on Sullivan's Island a little over a year. But she'd gotten involved in the controversy and she'd been attacked online several times. Drama created more drama, which got people to talking. Sarabeth's name was out there. She'd become high-profile. Her parents could not afford to be high-profile.

"You know, I was thinking..." Birdie snapped Quinn back to the moment. Birdie twirled her gelato, spooning the air like maybe it was helping her pull the idea from her brain. "I bet if Eugenia were here, she'd've already invited that Fitzgerald man's wife to supper club. What's her name? Does anyone know?"

Fish frowned, shook his head. "Birdie, I don't—"

"You know, you're probably right," said Tallulah. "I can just hear her now. It's not a bad idea. Perhaps they just need different friends."

"I think it's a terrific idea," said Vernon.

"Of course you do," said Birdie. "You would have to agree not to discuss your jungle issues with Mr. Fitzgerald. That's the last thing he needs."

Vernon attempted an innocent look. "I just wanted to see what he's investing in."

Redmond casually rested a hand on Quinn's leg. The knots in her stomach relaxed a bit. As always, his touch was reassuring. How had she been so lucky? Redmond was everything a husband should be—calm, good-humored, and so patient, with her, with the kids—with everyone really. He had a steady hand at the tiller. He was her rock.

The secret she kept from him ate at her insides like acid.

Sarabeth said, "Maybe we could help them settle in. Maybe make sure they fully understand what's at stake before they get too involved with folks who are only concerned with their own gratification."

"Hold on now." Vernon sat up straight. "Not everyone who would like to see the underbrush cleared out is a selfish SOB."

"Well, of course not, Vernon." Spots of color appeared on Sarabeth's cheeks. "I didn't suggest any such of a thing. From what Fish said, this Fitzgerald person is carrying on about views. The underbrush is another issue entirely."

"For Heaven's sake, Vernon, you know that's not what she meant," said Birdie.

Vernon settled back in his chair. "Just don't go lumping all of us together. Some of us just want the varmint habitat controlled so we don't have rats running shamelessly through our living rooms and coyotes attacking our pets."

"And that is certainly a valid concern," Sarabeth said.

"That's all I'm saying." Vernon nodded, and Sarabeth nodded back at him. They were calling a truce, thank goodness. That line of conversation could quickly get out of hand, even among friends.

Quinn glanced at Tallulah, who might've been telegraphing something to Sarabeth along the lines of *We don't discuss that at dinner or any other time, so hush up.*

"About the Fitzgeralds...," said Camille. "We don't know anything about these people. Maybe Cash could do a background check before we invite them to dinner. Just to be on the safe side."

Cash and Hadley laughed like they thought she was joking, but Quinn was pretty sure she was not. Camille was a big fan of vetting folks, though she usually suggested Hadley do it. They all rather liked having a private investigator as a friend. It came in handy.

"For goodness' sake, Camille," said Tallulah, who knew full well Camille's tendency towards fretting about the monsters under the bed. "They're our neighbors. They're hardly going to rob us at gunpoint."

"You never know," said Camille. "I'm sure Bonnie and Clyde were someone's neighbors."

Scattered laugher rolled through the group, mostly the guys. The women just smiled and shook their heads. Except for Libba, who stared at her water glass. Was she feeling all right?

"Perhaps I'll take them a basket of muffins or a pound cake," said Tallulah. "Meet the wife, nose around... If she seems nice, I'll invite them for June."

"You'd better take someone with you," said Camille. "Just in case..."

"I'll go along," said Birdie. "Camille, no one did a background check on you when you moved here from Texas, just so you know."

"You should have," quipped Camille. "I might've been a sociopath."

"You mean you're not?" Tallulah smothered a laugh.

Camille raised her eyebrows in an expression that might've meant *If I am, I'm coming for you first.*

Tennyson placed a hand on Camille's arm and patted her. He leaned in and said something that made her smile at him and bat her eyes like he was George Clooney or maybe Richard Gere. He actually looked a bit like Richard Gere, now that Quinn thought about it. He and Camille had been acting flirty all evening. Quinn was happy to see that. Camille seemed lonely to her.

Birdie said, "Tallulah, I'll bake a cream cheese pound cake tomorrow after church. I've got some fresh strawberries I can slice and take along. You want to go over there late tomorrow afternoon?"

"That sounds good to me," said Tallulah.

"I'd like my objection to this entire plan noted," said Fish.

Tallulah waved a dismissive hand at him. "You are nearly as much a worrywart as Camille."

"I've met the man, Tallulah," said Fish. "And I'm telling you, this is not a good idea. But you will do as you please, as is your custom." He smiled to gentle what he was saying. But Quinn could tell he was not happy.

Chapter Nine

Sunday, May 29, 2022, 5:30 p.m.
Fitzgerald Home—Conquest Ave
Tallulah Wentworth

Tallulah and Birdie crossed the grass carefully, watching where they stepped. Birdie carried the pound cake, which was nestled inside her mother's vintage aluminum cake carrier, the pink one with yellow daises. Tallulah ferried Birdie's cut glass bowl with the sliced strawberries.

"I don't understand why they don't have a walkway," said Tallulah. "And the steps are hidden by the overgrown bushes."

"Well, they just moved in, Tallulah," said Birdie. "They probably haven't had a chance to get to the landscaping."

"This house has been here for twenty years. Someone could've put in a walkway. And there's no excuse for those bushes."

"Why are you so cranky this afternoon?" asked Birdie.

"Am I?" Tallulah raised her chin and squinted, looking left, then right as if searching for the answer, though she was keenly aware of her foul mood and knew precisely what caused it. Tallulah was nothing if not self-aware.

"Yes, you are."

"Hmm... I'm not sure why, actually," she lied. She'd been out of sorts since the moment last night when Fish had failed to embrace her plan for inviting the Fitzgeralds to supper club. It annoyed her. She was accustomed to Fish playing the tambourine for any tune she called. Perhaps she was spoiled to that. "Nice screened porch. I like a screened porch on the front of a house."

They climbed the steps, opened the screen door, and proceeded to the center set of French doors flanked by potted pink hydrangeas. Tallulah pressed the doorbell.

After a few moments, Birdie leaned over and peered through the glass.

"It's not as if the view is any better that way," said Tallulah. The whole front of the house was lined with sets of French doors. They could see half the first floor from where they stood.

"Gorgeous house," said Birdie. "Do you reckon they're not home?"

"It's hard to say," said Tallulah. "They may just not care for strangers. Or perhaps they're enjoying one another's company in the owner's suite with a bottle of champagne. For all we know, he has her tied to the bed at this very moment." She pressed the doorbell again.

"*Tallulah.*" Birdie stared at her, mouth agape. "I cannot believe you just said that. What is wrong with you today?" She pressed the bell button herself for good measure.

"It's anybody's guess. A vitamin deficiency? I saw on Facebook where not enough B12 will make you psychotic."

Movement from inside the house caught their attention. A tall man with unruly brown hair crossed the family room towards the door.

"Nice," said Tallulah devilishly. "How old do you suppose he is?"

"Not nearly old enough. And married." Birdie looked towards the Heavens. "Like you're even looking for a man of any age."

"I'm just window shopping, Birdie. No harm in looking."

Though she did feel a pang of shame, truth be told. It wasn't her habit to admire strange men, or any other man aside from Henry actually.

The subject of their discussion opened the door. "Hello. What can I do for you ladies?" He spoke with a subtle British accent, one that sounded vaguely secondhand.

"Good afternoon," said Tallulah. "Are you by chance the man of the house?"

"Indeed I am," he said. "Knox Fitzgerald at your service."

"How nice. I'm Birdie Markley, and this is my friend, Tallulah Wentworth. We just wanted to welcome you to the island."

"Thank you so much. I appreciate that." He did not step back, open the door wide, and invite them in.

Tallulah was flummoxed. Could the man not see they'd brought cake? Did he have no manners at all? "Is Mrs. Fitzgerald at home by chance?"

"I'm afraid she's out at the moment, but I will be sure to tell her you stopped by." His smile was a meager thing.

Tallulah sized him up, her gaze traveling from his leather camel-colored sneakers to his odd little goatee and then to his cold eyes, which mocked them. Clearly this cretin had no interest in getting to know his neighbors on even the most superficial level. He was probably one of the Wall Street part-timer crowd.

Birdie extended the cake to him. "We've brought you a little welcoming gift. It's my grandmother's cream cheese pound cake with fresh strawberries. We didn't bring cream. I prefer it without to be honest with you."

Tallulah glanced at Birdie, willing her to cease trying to be nice to this obvious cad.

"I'm terribly sorry you've gone to the trouble," said Knox. "Unfortunately, we won't be able to accept it."

"Oh no," said Birdie. "Are you gluten-free? I should've known —so many people are these days."

"No, it's not the gluten. It's the sugar, you see. Mrs. Fitzgerald has quite the sweet tooth, and we can't have her piling on the pounds, now can we?"

Tallulah and Birdie blinked at him. Could they possibly have heard him correctly? A gentleman would never say such a thing about his wife to anyone but even more assuredly not to strangers.

Tallulah laughed without humor. "You're quite the comedian, aren't you?" Surely this was his poor idea of a joke.

"Oh, I'm quite serious."

Birdie squinted at him. "Is she diabetic?"

"No, not at all. Just has absolutely no self-control whatsoever."

Tallulah and Birdie nodded and put on sympathetic expressions because they'd been raised to be polite no matter what. Clearly this imbecile had no such training. What sort of husband appointed himself sheriff of the pantry?

"Well, I'm certain someone else can use it." Birdie smiled brightly and pulled the cake back towards her chest. "Perhaps your wife would like the fresh strawberries. They're really nice, and I didn't put sugar or anything on them."

"Food of any sort is a bad idea, sadly. She really does struggle." He said that as if she had a life-threatening disease. Clearly this obnoxious jerk was toying with them for some unknown reason.

"So she doesn't eat at all then?" asked Tallulah, her words frosty but coated in sugar and dipped in sprinkles. "How very *in-te-resting*."

"I guess you all wouldn't be interested in joining us for supper club in that case." Birdie tilted her head and gave him a sympathetic look. "What a shame."

Tallulah, having come around to Fish's way of thinking on the subject, cut Birdie a quelling look.

Birdie looked sideways at her friend and wrinkled her nose in confusion.

"I'm sorry? What exactly is supper club?" inquired Mr. Fitzgerald.

"I'm sure you wouldn't be interested." Tallulah should've

listened to Fish. They should never have come here. She should've trusted his judgment.

"To the contrary," said Knox. "I'm already intrigued."

"It's a celebration of food and friendship," said Tallulah. "So... as food is problematic in your household—"

"I said it was a problem for my wife," said Knox. "I have no such limitations. Having food in the house that isn't on Norah's plan isn't a good idea. It could be a stumbling block for her. But one meal, that wouldn't be a problem at all. It would give us a chance to meet some of our neighbors, wouldn't it? Is everyone in the group around the same age?" He looked from Tallulah to Birdie and back as if to inquire after their age. He tacked on a fake smile in a flimsy attempt at civility.

What on earth was he playing at?

"Wait." Alarm spread over his face. "Would we need to host?" The word seemed to taste sour. "Is it the sort of thing where you take turns having everyone 'round to yours?"

"Yes, of course." Tallulah smiled widely. "You'd need to decorate appropriately for the theme of the month. Last month we did Australian Adventure, and the hostess had live kangaroos. It was such a treat. As for the food, you'd serve an eight course sit-down meal for thirty, plus ever how many children were coming. That does tend to fluctuate, but plan for at least twelve. Shall I sign you up? Perhaps you'd like to host in June. I think we have an opening in the calendar."

He sucked in air through a pained expression. "On second thought, it's probably not actually a good idea to tempt poor Norah. All that food in the house." He shook his head. "It just wouldn't be fair to her to have to cook for everyone and not be able to eat, would it?"

"You're such a thoughtful husband." Tallulah's lips turned up, but her eyes assured him of her insincerity. "Well, it was *niiice* meeting you." She stretched out the word nice the way every Southern woman did when something was decidedly *not* nice. "Bye now."

Tallulah turned to go and Birdie followed.

When they'd reached the car, climbed inside, and locked the doors, they both stared at the house the way you might if you suspected a house was haunted.

Birdie said, "What an insufferable ass."

"Indeed," said Tallulah. "I will never question Fish Aiken's judgement again. But don't dare tell him I said that."

Chapter Ten

Wednesday, June 1, 2022, 5:00 a.m.
Graham Home
Libba Graham

The day started out like any other Wednesday during the school year, with Libba in their third-floor home gym at five a.m. She spent thirty minutes on the Peloton, thirty minutes on the elliptical, and then did fifteen minutes of free weight arm work. Later in the day, if she had time, she'd spend thirty minutes on the rowing machine. If she didn't work out every... single... day... of her life, the scale started creeping up again. She still hadn't figured out how to get the numbers moving in the other direction. Since her hysterectomy, her body waged war with her on several fronts.

The hot flashes, mood swings, and the weight she couldn't lose were bad enough, but they weren't the worst part of it. The complete and utter loss of all inclination to have sex with her husband of twenty-two years at the age of forty-five—which, let's face it, was still young by today's standards—that was killing her. These should be her prime years—everyone said so. She didn't *feel* any older than she felt the day she married Jake. Except for the no interest in sex thing.

Up until very recently, Jake had been so patient with her, so loving, so understanding, so upbeat and certain she'd be her normal self in no time. But lately his optimism seemed to be fraying at the edges. Lately she'd begun to think the unthinkable. One minute she was convinced he was cheating. And the next she castigated herself for being ridiculous, certain it must be the hormones making her crazy. Even good men—very patient, loving men—reached their limit, didn't they? To say that she wasn't the woman he married would be a massive understatement. Libba knew she couldn't go on like this much longer.

She sent up yet another prayer that the new prescription would do the trick. She'd been staring absently out the window, striding frenetically on the elliptical machine, when suddenly the view, the one of Inlet Creek, and beyond that, the Intracoastal Waterway, smacked her upside the head. She was so fortunate in so many ways. Thank God the surgeon had gotten all the endometriosis and the biopsies had been negative for cancer. Thank God for her children's health and Jake's... for this beautiful place they lived.

In sane moments, Libba appreciated exactly how lucky she was. She had been raised in a trailer park near Nashville. It was better than some—tidy and well maintained—but a trailer park nevertheless. Her daddy never did realize his dream of being a country music star. He paid the bills working as an HVAC repairman and hung out at the Blue Bird Café every chance he got. Her mamma was a waitress who sold Mary Kay on the side. Neither of her brothers had gone to college. One was an electrician who'd done pretty well for himself. The other worked with her daddy, paid child support to three different women, and smoked way too much pot.

Libba had worked hard for her scholarship to University of Tennessee. There was no way her parents could ever have afforded college even if they'd been inclined to send her. But her daddy had subscribed to the notion that women didn't need to go to college. It wasn't good, he'd told her, for women to have more education than their husbands. And in *his* plan for her life, Libba would've married one of the guys she'd dated in high school—all of whom had tradesmen-type jobs, not that there was a single thing wrong with that—and lived within a five-mile radius of her parents. She would've had three or four children and occupied her place in the life her parents built. It wasn't a bad life. They were all happy, more or less. But it wasn't the life Libba envisioned for herself.

She'd met Jake the summer after she'd graduated with a degree in advertising, and they'd married the following year, waiting eight years until they were well established before having the first of three children, then two more one right after the other. Jake was from Nashville too, but he'd attended College of Charleston for their program in historic preservation. He had dual degrees, one in studio arts, specializing in wood sculpture. Her parents had laughed when she'd told them what he'd studied in college. They were convinced he'd wasted his parents' money and would be the most educated carpenter they knew.

Wildly talented, Jake had made a name for himself in sculpture and custom furniture. He'd fallen in love with the Lowcountry—Sullivan's Island in particular—while in school. After vacationing here a few times, they'd decided to make the move while the kids were still in elementary school, before uprooting them would've been more traumatic.

Because she had the luxury of choice, Libba decided to focus on getting them all established in their new lives—to not look for a job at first but prioritize their family. She'd told herself this was just a short break, that she'd go back to work soon enough. But she'd gotten so incredibly busy and the time had flown by. They'd been here six years and Libba hadn't worked since they'd moved. Was she even employable in advertising anymore? Certainly not at the level she'd been in Nashville. Things changed so fast in the advertising industry. It would no doubt be like starting over. She didn't regret putting her family first—never. But when she was honest with herself, she had to admit she missed the challenge of developing a knockout campaign. And she actually missed going to the office every day... dressing up in a cute outfit, stopping for coffee, and having lunch with coworkers.

The school year was almost over, and Libba had mixed emotions about summer's imminent arrival. On the one hand, they wouldn't have to worry about homework, class assignments, and projects for a while. But summer for her children didn't mean the same thing as summer had meant for her as a kid. The lazy, honeysuckle-scented, seemingly endless summer days that tasted like homegrown tomato sandwiches on white bread, honey-sweet cantaloupe, and homemade peach ice cream, when you spent the long, hot afternoons on a quilt spread under a shade tree with a book after chasing the other kids through the woods to the local swimming hole when your chores were through... days before children had cell phones and tablets... those happy, carefree days would no doubt leave her kids bored and maybe even scared. It was difficult to conjure an image of her children in the landscape of her childhood.

Mia, Maeve, and Mills had a series of activities planned for summer. They'd all spend two weeks at camp on the North Carolina coast—Camp Seafarer for the girls and Camp Sea Gull for Mills. Then they each had a week at church camp. Mia had cheer camp, Maeve volleyball camp, and Mills baseball camp. Each of them had summer practice for their respective sports and a summer reading list. She and Jake were taking them to Yellowstone for a family vacation the only week in the summer one of the kids didn't have a conflict. Libba was exhausted just thinking about summer, though to be fair, the weeks the kids were at camp, she and Jake would have some needed quality alone time, and she'd get a break from the running—running one child to a friend's house, another to practice, and the other to the movies or the trampoline park. If she had lived a couple of blocks from the Atlantic Ocean as a child, she would've spent every single summer day on the beach from after breakfast until her mamma made her come in for dinner.

When the kids were younger, she'd taken them to the beach

every day all summer long. They still spent time at the beach, of course, but now it was usually with their friends. Libba was still allowed to be *on* the beach, just not too close to the clusters of teenagers. After all, they could need something, a snack, a cold drink, more sunscreen, or a wet, chilled facecloth. Having her close by was handy sometimes. But they didn't need her to help build sand castles or look for seashells or help them fly a kite or watch them ride the waves in on their boogie boards. Oh, she still watched them, of course she did. Like a hawk. But there was no more "Watch this, Mommy!" Those days were gone forever.

By six thirty, Libba had showered, dressed, verified the kids were up and on schedule, and stopped by the laundry room to throw in a load of towels. If she didn't stay vigilant, the laundry multiplied, morphing into a mountain. She took the load of darks from the dryer and popped back into the primary suite. Jake was in the shower—she could hear the water raining down on tile. Libba set the laundry basket on the bed and made quick work of folding Jake's underwear, socks, T-shirts, and pajama pants. She carried a stack into their closet and set it on the drawer island.

As she separated the underwear from the stack and reached for the top drawer, she noticed Jake's cell phone on top of the island, next to the clean laundry. He must've laid it there when he was getting clean clothes before showering. The phone lit with a notification, a text from Roxie.

Oooh! The nerve of that girl, texting Jake before seven in the morning. Before Libba could read it, it disappeared.

She glanced over her shoulder. Jake was still in the shower.

She picked up his cell phone and swiped to unlock it. The Face ID screen popped up, followed by a prompt to enter a password when her face wasn't recognized.

She sucked air. When had Jake turned on the password for his cell phone? He'd never wanted to bother with it before. She'd nagged him about it, told him it was a security risk, for years. But he'd insisted the phone was never out of his sight when he was away from home. What had changed? What was he hiding?

Reeling, she put the cell phone down, put the rest of the laundry away, and went downstairs to the kitchen. She couldn't afford to get behind. On Wednesdays she made waffles with fresh berries and maple syrup for Jake and the kids. She had a green smoothie every morning.

Moving fast, she preheated the warming drawer, started the coffee, and whipped up the waffle batter. Jake was having sex with that child, Roxie. He had to be. There was no other reasonable explanation. Libba had put him off for months—nearly a year with very few exceptions, and every time they'd tried, things had ended with her in tears. Her body simply didn't function the way it used to. She'd tried the gels and all that, but that stuff only fixed part of the problem. It couldn't make her weak-kneed with desire the way she used to be. Jake had clearly gotten tired of waiting and sought his entertainment elsewhere. What, what, *what* was she going to do? She swiped at the tears that welled up and slipped down her cheeks.

When the last waffle was in the iron, Libba spun around to grab her smoothie ingredients. She had the steps down to a science. Greens first: romaine, spinach, and frozen kale, then the ginger, hemp hearts, chia and flax seeds, fruit on top—frozen mango, pineapple, and banana. Lastly she poured in the coconut water.

The waffle iron beeper went off.

She flipped the blender on high as she turned towards the waffle iron.

Something wet smacked her on the back of the head. Confused, Libba glanced over her shoulder.

Green smoothie was splattered all over everything—the cabinets, the backsplash, the counter—everything.

Libba screamed and lunged for the blender. *Cluck, cluck, cluck!*

She'd been so distracted she didn't put the lid on. *Stupid.* She smothered a litany of curse words. She did not need this mess this morning. She switched off the blender.

"Yuuuuk," said Mills as he strolled into the kitchen. "That's disgusting." He held her green smoothies in contempt under normal circumstances.

"Mom, the waffle is burning." Mia took her place at the table in the breakfast nook, her eyes glued to her phone.

Cluck-a-mighty! Libba whirled back to the waffle iron and raised the lid. She pulled out the waffle, which was admittedly darker than any of her crew would want. And she had no time to mix more batter.

"I'll get our plates on the table." Maeve, her sweet middle child, took in the situation from the doorway and rushed into the fray to help.

Jake was right behind her. "Here, I'll get the plates. Maeve, will you pour the juice, sweetheart?" He assessed the situation and smothered a grin. "Appliances acting up this morning?"

Libba grabbed a paper towel and wiped the smoothie off her face. Her husband seemed so normal. The same easygoing guy who'd always handled life's little disasters with such grace and efficiency—the guy who'd always loved her. How? How could he stand calmly in the kitchen with their children when he was clearly betraying her in the worst possible way?

"I'm running late anyway," said Jake. "I'll pick something up on the way into the office. Don't worry about the waffle."

She didn't say a word—she couldn't. She was afraid of what might come out of her mouth if she dared open it. She nodded, then went to cleaning up the mess.

"You okay?" Concern creased Jake's face—faux concern, obviously.

Here is what flashed through Libba's brain: loose screws.

On the way home Saturday night after supper club, Jake tried to make a joke, said maybe the new prescription would tighten up her *loose screws*. This in response to the fettuccini incident at dinner and his subsequent jackassery. At the time, she'd been tired and worried and she just let it go. But this morning it flashed on and off in her brain in smoothie-green neon.

She ground her teeth, tried with all her might to just keep her mouth shut. She positively vibrated. Something shifted inside her, rose up.

The words exploded out of her like hot lava and fireworks. "My clucking screws are not clucking loose. The brother cluckers are clucking *missing*. They've been clucking surgically removed, do you clucking understand? And please... for the love of all that is holy, stop clucking asking me if I am clucking okay when the kitchen looks like someone clucking projectile vomited all over it and I have not even had my clucking coffee."

She drew a long slow breath and felt the crazy burning in her eyes. Then she dashed for the powder room.

Chapter Eleven

Wednesday, June 1, 2022, 12:10 p.m.
Burton's Grill, Mount Pleasant
Libba Graham

Libba hadn't thought this all the way through. She'd rented a nondescript white Camry, put her hair under a baseball cap, donned her biggest sunglasses, and followed Jake from his studio on Hungry Neck Boulevard to Burton's Grill, a restaurant less than a mile away. But now what? She'd parked and watched him walk across the parking lot and through the front door by himself. It wasn't unheard of for Jake to have lunch by himself. At least he'd left Roxie back at the studio.

Then again, maybe he was being careful, avoiding the appearance of... what? That didn't even make sense to Libba. There was nothing wrong with coworkers riding to lunch together or having lunch together to begin with. But Libba wanted to see how he was with her. Was he professional, explaining the business to her over lunch? Or did he flirt with her? Worst of all, did she make him laugh? Libba hadn't seen Jake laugh in a while.

Libba couldn't dare go inside the restaurant. That was way too risky. She knew Jake at a hundred paces from the way he moved. Surely he couldn't fail to notice her if she went inside. Burton's was in the parking lot of Mount Pleasant Towne Centre, an outdoor mall. Should she just go inside and say she'd been on her way to Barnes & Noble or Ulta or Palmetto Moon and had seen him pull in and decided to see if he needed company for lunch? Maybe they could talk. Maybe she had things all wrong. He'd explain everything and they'd laugh about it. Yes, going inside and talking to her husband was absolutely the best plan.

No... no, she couldn't possibly do that, because she couldn't bear to see it in his eyes if he wasn't happy to see her. Worse yet if he said "Yeah sure, let's have lunch together, what a happy coincidence," but she could read the pity in his eyes. No. She needed to stay the course. She needed a closer look. She was going to have to go inside, or this was just a waste of time.

Libba scanned the parking lot for any sign of Roxie, then climbed out of the car. She crossed the parking lot, went inside, and waited at the hostess stand. A quick glance told her Jake wasn't in the bar. Her eyes darted around the restaurant, at least what she could see. Where was he?

The hostess smiled. "One for lunch?"

"Yes, please," said Libba. Where should she ask to be seated? She needed to see but not be seen.

She followed the hostess to a seat at a small table near the middle of the banquette that formed the wall between the dining room and the bar. At least half a dozen tables, some for two, some for four or six, lined the wall, and most of the tables were full. She'd blend into the background here.

"Thank you," she said as she slid into the padded bench side.

A waitress appeared, handed her a menu, and went off to get her an unsweetened iced tea. Libba held her menu high enough to partially hide behind it but low enough to get a look around the dining room. There. Jake sat alone in a booth across the room and to her right. A glass of iced tea sat in front of him.

White-hot lightning seared Libba's chest.

Two menus lay on the table.

He was expecting someone.

The tears came fast and hot. Oh dear goodness. She could not make a scene. He wouldn't fail to recognize her if she caught his attention. She raised the menu and swiped at her eyes. Enough of this. She should cry later. She had to be strong now. It had to be that tramp Roxie. Had to be.

Why had she encouraged Jake to hire an associate? Because business was so good he was having to turn clients down or tell them they'd have to wait months for their table or bookcase or whatever. But why did it have to be Roxie? Why not a scruffy, overweight, middle-aged man in overalls?

The waitress set down her glass of iced tea. "Are you ready to order?"

"Yes, please." She had to order something, and better to get it out of the way so the waitress didn't need to keep coming back to talk to her. "I'd like a roasted vegetable bowl."

"Any protein with that?"

"No, thanks." She wasn't going to eat anything anyway.

The waitress reached for her menu.

"Oh... if you don't mind, I'll hang on to this. I'm still looking. I might decide to add an app or a dessert."

"Sure thing. Let me know if you decide on anything."

Great. Now she'd be back. But Libba felt much better with the menu between her and Jake. Holding the menu in her left hand, she picked up her tea glass in her right and took a long sip. She nearly spewed it when Jake stood as an exotically gorgeous woman approached his booth. This was definitely not Roxie.

This was so much worse than Roxie.

Libba struggled not to cough. The woman was tall and athletic with luminous, medium-toned black skin. She wore a casually elegant tropical print shirt dress and sandals. The woman exuded class and confidence. Was this a client?

Libba grabbed ahold of the idea like a life preserver. Surely that was the most logical explanation. Of course. Jake typically held new client meetings in the studio so he could show examples of his work, but perhaps she'd requested they meet for lunch. Maybe this wasn't an initial meeting, but for some reason Jake had to talk to her. Maybe…

They'd settled into the booth. The woman was talking. She leaned in slightly, as if she was speaking confidentially. Libba studied her husband. He was watching the woman, listening intently, occasionally nodding. Their waiter appeared and left with their menus. When he stepped away, the woman resumed talking. Jake was mostly listening, contributing short answers periodically. This did not look like a client meeting to Libba. What exactly was going on here?

Jake leaned in towards the woman and spoke. He wore an earnest look, as if he was trying to convince her of something. This wasn't a first date or anything like that. No, this was a serious conversation. How well did Jake know this woman?

Who was this woman?

This was above Libba's pay grade.

Hadley.

Libba needed Hadley. It was handy, at times, having a good friend who was also a very good private investigator. If Libba stayed here much longer, she risked being discovered. Hadley could easily find out who this woman was—learn everything about her. And find out what Jake's relationship with her was.

Why on earth had Libba not called Hadley to begin with?

Libba pulled two twenties from her purse, left them on the table, and making as few sudden movements as she could, stood and slipped out of the booth. One foot towards the door, it hit her that Hadley would need something to go on to track this woman down. She slipped her phone out of her purse.

Jake was still very focused on the woman across the table from him.

Libba drew a deep breath and made a show of pretending to check something on her phone while she snapped a picture of her husband and her worst nightmare.

Seeming to sense she was being observed, the woman turned her head and looked straight at Libba.

Libba darted for the entrance, praying no one would call out her name before she reached it. When she cleared the door, she ran to her car, climbed in, slammed the door, and locked it. Heart racing, she waited. But no one chased her down to see what on earth she was up to.

How did Hadley do this every day? It tore Libba's nerves to pieces. She called Hadley on the way back home.

Chapter Twelve

Wednesday, June 1, 2022, 1:30 p.m.
On the Beach near Hadley Cooper's Home,
Marshall Boulevard, Sullivan's Island
Libba Graham

Libba made her way across the soft sand towards the pair of canvas-and-wood beach chairs under the striped umbrella. Only a few wisps of white cloud disturbed the brilliant Carolina blue sky. The tide was on its way out, the foam-crested waves rolling and dashing themselves against the hard-packed sand, slipping forward, sliding back. Sunlight danced across the water, scattering a blanket of diamonds across the deep turquoise surface.

Libba could feel her blood pressure drop as she slid into her chair. "This view never gets old, does it?"

"I was just thinking the exact same thing," said Hadley.

"You didn't need to go to this much trouble, putting out the chairs and umbrella and all," said Libba. "I can't stay long. I've got to pick up the kids at school."

"All the more reason why you need a few minutes of peace. Slow down. Have a few lungfuls of salt air."

They sat for a few minutes, watching the pelicans dive for

lunch and the sea gulls sail by in formation. Libba focused on the rhythm of the surf, breathing in and out.

Finally, Hadley said, "You sounded really upset on the phone."

"I am." Libba wondered briefly if she was overreacting. No, she didn't think so. "I need to hire you."

Hadley's head spun towards Libba. "What on earth for?"

"I think Jake is having an affair."

Hadley's chin drew back. Disbelief washed over her face. "Libba... that's... no. Just no. There's no way. I've come across a great many adulterous men in my time. I have a highly developed nose for tomcats. Jake? No."

"He finally password protected his phone, after I've nagged him about it for years. What else would he be hiding from me? Then, I saw him having lunch with a strange woman. A drop-dead gorgeous woman. I don't think she's a client. I need to know who she is and what's going on."

"I highly recommend you talk to your husband," said Hadley. "I know Jake. There is a simple, non-adulterous explanation. There has to be."

Miserable, Libba shook her head. "I don't think so." Tears slid down her cheeks.

"Oh, sweetie..." Hadley leaned over and put her arms around her friend. "I know you're not feeling yourself..."

"Oh please. That's the understatement of the year," said Libba. "And the worst part is, I can't even blame Jake. I haven't been myself, or anyone I remotely know, for a year now. And it breaks my heart. Since the first time I laid eyes on Jake, I've never given another man a second look. He's it for me. We've always been... like... We're that couple who would meet each other in a hotel bar and pretend to be strangers and spend the night in the hotel doing the wild thing, you know?"

"I know."

"I have a whole chest full of lingerie, and I'm not talking your mamma's nightgowns here."

"I know."

"We have a toy box—"

Hadley pulled away and held up both hands, nodding furiously. "I get the idea. I do."

Libba nodded with her through her tears. "But lately... I just... I'll be in the shower, and Jake'll come in there with this wild-eyed wolfish expression on his face, staring at my boobs and making these twisty, pinchy gestures with his hands like he's about to grab them, and I just want to stab him in the neck."

"Oh—"

"He knows, intellectually, that I've lost all sex drive. But there's a part of him that sees that as a challenge—like he thinks he can cure me. And we do still try... every once in a while..." Libba sniffed.

"Oh, sweetie..."

"And I know this is hormonal. I love my husband—you know I do. And it was supposed to be getting better. But it's not. And look at me... I'm super chunky. I've never been chunky in my life. You know Jake does not want a chunky wife. I mean, look at him."

"You are not chunky," said Hadley. "You're gorgeous. And Jake loves you for more than just the way you look anyway."

"Listen... it's not like I believe that my only worth as a human being is as a sex object, and I have to be appealing to my man or I have no raison d'être. But on top of everything else my body is throwing at me, you can understand how feeling fat would be bad for my self-esteem, right?"

"Of course. I know you're struggling, and I know it's the hormones. Once you get that all straightened out, everything will look much differently. Maybe you should see another doctor?"

Libba shook her head. "I love my doctor. But there's only so much they can do. I'm damaged goods."

"You are no such thing."

"But this... what I saw this afternoon... *this* is *not* my hormones nor my imagination," said Libba. "At least I'm pretty sure it's not. If he's not cheating, well, you'll find that out quickly enough, and then we'll have a good laugh at my ridiculous suspicions."

"Libba, please don't ask me to surveil Jake. He's my friend."

"But I'm more your friend," said Libba.

"Yes, of course you are," said Hadley. "But... this is just wrong. First because I know he can't possibly be cheating. He clearly adores you. But secondly because it's just not a good idea for investigators to investigate their friends."

"Don't think of it as investigating Jake," said Libba. "Think of it as proving to me that I'm wrong because I'm clearly crazy."

Hadley closed her eyes and sighed deeply.

"Please, Hadley? Do this for me. I don't want to get a stranger involved in this. What if you're right and I'm nutty as a fruitcake? I don't want some random stranger dissecting our lives... following Jake around when he's got the kids. It feels wrong. You know us. It'll be so much easier for you to spot something suspicious. And of course you can come snoop around the house anytime you want. I don't want an old guy in a trench coat who smokes cigars rambling around my house."

Hadley sighed deeper and hung her head in defeat. "For the record, you are nuttier than any fruitcake ever baked. But I love you. I will do this under extreme protest, only because I'm convinced you're wrong, and the quicker I prove that, the quicker we can get you the professional help you so clearly need."

"Some things you shouldn't joke about," said Libba. "It's just too close to reality."

"Oh gosh, I'm an idiot. I'm so sorry." Hadley rubbed her eyebrow. "How are you otherwise? Is that new prescription not—"

"Still absolutely no interest in any kind of sex whatsoever," said Libba. "It's like I'm a eunuchess. No wonder my husband is having an affair."

"It probably just takes a while to get into your system, you know? And your husband is so not having an affair. Just you wait and see."

"How much do you charge? Don't we need a contract?" Libba recalled Eugenia signing a contract with Hadley to follow her husband. Icy fingers crawled up Libba's spine. She sure hoped things worked out better for her than they had for Eugenia. Of course it wasn't Hadley's fault what happened. And she *was* the one who figured things out.

Hadley shook her head. "No. Absolutely not. I will not take your money, and we are not signing a contract."

"You had a contract with Eugenia."

"I had just met Eugenia. She became a client and a friend at the same time. She wasn't my friend to begin with. You are. I will do a quick verification of marital fidelity on the friends-and-family plan. It would take more time to fill out the paperwork than it will for me to prove you're wrong."

"No really. I wouldn't have asked if I'd known you wouldn't take my money. This is how you make your living. I can't have you out on a stakeout for me for free. That's like someone asking Jake to make them a live-edge table as a favor."

"It's nothing like that," said Hadley. "Jake invests a lot of time in making a table. This will not take long. Let's call this a bet, how's that? You bet me that your husband is a philanderer, and I will take that bet and prove I'm right. Now... tell me about this woman you saw having lunch with him."

Libba replayed the scene in the restaurant.

"Were there any displays of affection?" asked Hadley.

"No, but there was something about the conversation that didn't feel professional."

"Did you happen to get a photo of her?"

Libba widened her eyes and smiled, proud of herself. "I did." She pulled out her phone, swiped up, and pulled up the picture.

"Good work," said Hadley. "Text it to me, would you?"

"Sure."

"Be figuring out where you're going to take me to lunch when I win this bet," said Hadley. "Someplace nice."

Libba made a squeamish face. "I don't have any idea what to feed you. Do vegans eat anyplace nice?"

"I'm not a vegan—"

"Yes, I know. You eat a whole-foods, plant-based diet. I'll take you anywhere you want to go. Just don't make me figure that out. Trust me, if you're right, I'll happily buy you a bowl of hummus and lettuce from wherever you like."

Hadley rolled her eyes. "I'm going to broaden your horizons. You have to eat too, wherever we go."

"Haven't I suffered enough?"

Hadley gave Libba a stern look.

"Okay, okay. Fine."

Chapter Thirteen

Saturday, June 11, 2022, 6:00 p.m.
High Thyme—Middle Street, Sullivan's Island
Tallulah Wentworth

Fish held Tallulah's chair.

This was unexpected. Had he always done that? He was a gentleman, always, of course. But she couldn't recall him holding her chair before—well, not in a very long time anyway. She and Fish went back a long way, most of their lives. They'd never attended the same schools. Supporters of the public education system, her parents had sent her to the East Cooper public schools while Hamilton Alexander Hughes Fisher Ravenel Aiken, an only child and heir to a considerable fortune, attended the best private schools in the area. But their families traveled in the same social circles, and Tallulah and Fish had attended birthday parties together before they were old enough to remember the occasions. They'd simply always been part of the fabric of each other's lives.

"Thank you." She offered him a smile and settled into her seat. They hadn't had to wait long for a table on the porch, which was their preference as it was quieter outside.

Fish took his seat across the table from her. He wore a freshly pressed pale blue button-down collared shirt and khakis. These days, for Fish, this was dressed up. A memory surfaced, of seventeen-year-old Fish in white-tie with long tails, clean-shaven, his hair cut short. Goodness, that was a long time ago.

"You look handsome this evening." There was a twinkle in his bright blue eyes, she thought. What was he up to?

"Thank you, my lady. And you are gorgeous as always."

"You are too kind, sir." It was so pleasant sharing a meal with an old friend, comfortable. There was nothing to stress about at all. Over the past year, she and Fish had occasionally had dinner together, sometimes at home and once in a rare while, like tonight, in a restaurant. Why, all of a sudden, was she looking around, wondering if anyone they knew was having dinner here tonight or driving by to see them on the porch together? Would the casual observer think they were on a date?

This was *not* a date. They were two old friends enjoying a meal together, nothing more, nothing less. She was not being disloyal to Henry. Everyone needed companionship.

The hostess handed them menus, and the waiter took their cocktail order. For the next few minutes they chatted about their favorites and made their decisions. When the waiter returned with their Spicy Margys—a margarita made with jalapeño tequila—they were ready to order.

"We'd like the seared scallops to start," said Fish. "The lady will have the arugula salad, and I'd like the romaine please. Then the lady would like the spinach and mushroom risotto, and I'll have the grilled pork chop."

"Very good, sir."

"And please bring us each a glass of the Piper Sonoma Blanc de Blancs with the scallops, the Domaine Cherrier Sancerre with the salads, and a bottle of the Châteauneuf-du-Pape with our entrées."

The waiter nodded and hurried off.

"I'm surprised you didn't want the steak." Fish grinned at her. "You're not adopting Eugenia and Hadley's diet are you?"

"Perish the thought," said Tallulah. "I simply adore risotto, and I was in the mood for it. I'm past the age where I'll be depriving myself of the things I love on the hope of a few more days on this earth. God will take me when he's ready, either way." Fat lot of good all that deprivation had done Eugenia.

"Hear, hear." Fish stared at his cocktail for a moment. "I'd like to propose a toast."

Tallulah smiled and lifted her glass.

"To old friends," said Fish. "They're irreplaceable. As they say, one can never make new old friends."

"To old friends. Cheers." They touched glasses and sipped their drinks. Fish seemed to study her, searching for the answer to an unasked question. Whatever it was, he'd make his way around to it sooner or later. Oh, what the heck, she'd encourage him a bit. "You seem introspective this evening."

"I suppose I am," said Fish. "It'll be a year tomorrow since we lost Eugenia. And I don't mean to get us off on a sad track. I don't think for a moment Eugenia would want us to spend our time crying over her premature exit. And truly, I know on a cellular level that she's in a far better place, probably watching us on some big-screen TV in Heaven."

"Wouldn't surprise me one bit." Tallulah's eyes misted. Was Henry watching too? Would *he* think it looked like a date?

"It's interesting the turns your life takes that you'd never anticipate. I think for a long time I perhaps took my friends for granted."

"Oh, I wouldn't say that," said Tallulah.

Fish nodded. "It's true. I was off seeing the world, chasing the next adventure, spending time with women of no importance. I should've been here, tending the garden the good Lord blessed me with."

"I think everything we experience helps to fashion us into who we're meant to be. You shouldn't have any regrets." Tallulah sipped her margarita.

"I don't regret the travel," said Fish. "As education goes, travel is the best investment, I think. And I have a few good stories to tell. But I do regret the extravagance. All the money I wasted could've been put to better use. Do you have regrets?" After Fish's parents had been killed in a plane crash, he was mad with grief, then fell into an existential crisis of sorts that sent him on a mission to live life to the fullest. Nearly thirty years later, he'd spent everything his parents left him and was living simply in an Airstream trailer on a beach in Mexico when a friend tracked him down to let him know about Eugenia's cancer diagnosis. He'd bummed a plane ticket home and taken care of her when Everette wouldn't.

Tallulah laughed without humor. "A million of them."

"Perhaps you should take your own advice."

"Touché." She raised her glass to him.

This was so much nicer than having dinner alone at home. She ate by herself far more often than not. Tallulah felt the urge to draw things out, delaying as long as possible the moment she'd go home to an empty house. They passed a few minutes in comfortable silence, the way old friends do, then the waiter delivered the champagne and the seared scallops.

"These look amazing," said Tallulah. "And I adore champagne with scallops. To be honest, I have a particular fondness for champagne in general."

"So I recall." A hint of a smile played at the corners of Fish's mouth.

A warm, happy feeling fluttered up into Tallulah's chest and she smiled, then covered her smile with her hand. She blushed. She hadn't thought about that in ages. She'd had too much champagne at a party the spring they'd graduated from high school—him from Porter-Gaud and her from Wando. Fish had walked her home along the beach.

Though she'd been more than a little tipsy, the memory was painted vividly in her mind, with bold strokes and saturated colors, like an impressionist painting. The sky was a deep black velvet, scattered with a million diamonds. They'd strolled along the hard-packed sand, him pointing out constellations and pulling her away from the incoming tide when the waves pushed too close. When she remembered that night, she could hear the soundtrack of the surf, smell the salt, the confederate jasmine, and his aftershave.

They'd sat on the back porch at her parents' house and talked until the sky lightened just before sunup. So much was in front of them then. They were both leaving that fall for college, her to Duke and him to Harvard. Everyone knew his parents had high expectations of him. She was still trying to figure out what to do with herself. But that night... she would always cherish the memory of that night. They'd never crossed the line between friendship and something more. She couldn't say why. It was a time when gentlemen still made the moves, at least in the circles Tallulah traveled. But there'd been a moment when she'd been tempted and willing. She would've sworn the sparks were mutual. She hadn't thought about that night in a very long time.

"A gentleman never reminds a lady of her indiscretions." Tallulah raised her chin, a tease in her tone. She delivered a bite of scallop to her mouth.

"My apologies," said Fish. "It's a very pleasant memory."

"Indeed."

They were quiet, both reminiscing as they finished their appetizers. It was such a happy time, ripe with possibilities. Life was still in front of them. Tallulah had been strong and vibrant and... well, all right—desirable. She'd felt none of those things in a very long time, not since Henry had passed away.

Somewhere over the salads, when Tallulah was well into her second glass of wine, she said, "You clean up nice, Mr. Aiken. I was recalling earlier how handsome you were at seventeen in white-tie attire."

It was his turn to blush. "I'm afraid I was a poor excuse for an escort to the St. Cecilia Ball."

"Why on earth would you say such a thing?" asked Tallulah, mystified. "You were the catch. Every girl who debuted that year envied me, several have never forgiven me. And you were the best dancer there. It was magical."

"And now you're too kind. I seem to recall stepping on your toes a time or two after you were kind enough to allow me to escort you."

"I saved you from—how many girls asked you to escort them? As I recall, you were catnip to every mother in town. Handsome, from a well-respected family—with money, of course—and great expectations. My, yes."

"Technically, only one other young lady inquired. After I told her I'd committed to you, word got out. You were a good friend. And look what disasters you might've saved another girl from. My great expectations as you put it turned out to be so much dust in the wind. You were a true friend. Always have been."

"Well, I had a lovely time. And there was so much less pressure than if I'd been escorted by someone I was hoping to marry, for goodness' sake. There was some rumor going around about the percentage of girls who married their debut escort. It's different now, I'm certain. Women have so many more choices. But in the early seventies, most of my friends were more interested in a husband than a college education. Oh they went to college, of course, but it was for that Mrs. degree."

"That's not what you were looking for from college as I recall."

"No, indeed. I had big dreams. I wanted to be a trailblazing journalist, follow in the footsteps of Barbara Walters, push the boundaries for women even further, and see the world."

"And then you met Henry."

"He's not one of my regrets." Tallulah drained her wineglass. "But... I was young and in love. I couldn't imagine leaving Henry and traveling by myself. He couldn't imagine such a thing either. You have to remember, Henry was eleven years older than me. Times were different, but even still. I could never have sacrificed our time together for a career, even if jet-setting career women had been more commonplace at the time. I'm not unhappy with my choice."

"You and Henry had a happy life together. And you did get to see the world."

"Yes, but I left a lot undone." Had she and Henry spent too much time traveling and not enough time building a life? Would a firmer foundation have left her in a better place when she lost him? She was beginning to think so.

"The ride's not over yet," said Fish.

"No, it isn't," said Tallulah. "I don't feel old, do you?" She was surprised that she meant that. She didn't feel old, not really. She felt lonely. She'd built her life around Henry and lost him. Then Eugenia was helping her rebuild, and she'd lost her too. And she was discouraged, at times, by some of the ways her world was changing. But old? No. Perhaps she needed to give all of this more thought when she wasn't feeling a bit tipsy.

"What's that Willie Nelson song? 'Don't let the Old Man In'—that's it. I've adopted it as my theme song. Age is nothing but a number."

"I thought that was Toby Keith."

"Ah, they both sang it. Anyway, it's a good philosophy."

A member of the waitstaff cleared their salad plates, and their waiter brought the bottle of Châteauneuf-du-Pape. As Fish went through the ritual of tasting the wine, Tallulah's mind wandered to the hundreds of times she'd watched Henry do the same thing. She still missed him just as much as the day she'd lost him. She didn't suspect that would ever change. After all, they'd been married for thirty-six years. But with the help of her friends, she'd made it to a place where she could still find the joy in life, well, some days she could anyway. Some days she talked a good game.

The waiter brought their entrées, inquired after their needs, and slipped discreetly away.

Fish speared a roasted brussels sprout and delivered it to his mouth. "Ummm." He closed his eyes, a blissful expression on his face. "Here, try one of these." He forked another and fed it to Tallulah.

"Those are tasty." She smiled, suddenly shy. It had been a long time since a man fed her from his plate. "I love them too. I wish they served them as a side dish. I just wasn't in the mood for the pork chop."

"Have you ever asked for them as a side with another dish?"

"No, I don't suppose I have," said Tallulah. "I've never been one of those who considers the menu a list of mix-and-match suggestions. I imagine the chef has put hours of testing into everything he or she serves. I figure she's already hit upon the best combination."

"Perhaps that's a matter of taste. Who's to say what's best? You really should color outside the lines more, Tallulah. I've always liked your name."

"Thank you. I like yours too, though it's quite long." She smiled and took a bite of her risotto.

"It is, isn't it? I can't imagine why my parents thought a baby needed so many names."

"You know exactly why," said Tallulah. "Every name you have is a family name."

"I bet if they'd known how I was going to turn out, they'd've been less eager to identify my lineage." Fish sipped his wine.

Tallulah lifted her glass, tilted it, and twirled the stem, admiring the rich hue of the wine with the light shining through it. "There's nothing wrong with the way you turned out. You're one of the finest men I know."

Fish blushed and grinned like a teenager. "That's very kind of you. Tell me, of all the places you've traveled, what's your favorite?"

"I couldn't possibly choose one," she said. "Every place we traveled, Henry and I, is a beautiful memory. What about you?"

"You know, there was something special about every place. But I guess I must've liked the Baja Peninsula the best because I stayed there. Well, I was out of money, so there's that. But it's a beautiful place."

"Henry and I went to Cabo San Lucas once. It's quite lovely, parts of it anyway. I'm not sure Mexico is safe anymore, is it? The news reports of tourists and businessmen being kidnapped are terrifying."

"I think Cabo is generally safe. There are parts of Mexico I'd hesitate to travel to these days. Have you been to Capri?"

They lingered over their dinner and the wine, telling stories of their favorite trips. When they were both quiet for a few moments, Tallulah asked, "Do you miss it? Do you think you'll ever go back to Mexico?"

He raised his eyebrows, an expression of what might've been regret slipping across his face. Then he shook his head. "Nah. I'm home. I'm happy here. I'd still like to travel some, maybe go back to Mexico for a visit. There are a few other places I'd like to spend some more time. But I don't see me ever living anywhere else. Sullivan's Island is pretty special."

"I've never wanted to live anyplace else," said Tallulah. "Are you happy in Eugenia's house? Well, your house now, of course." Eugenia had left her beachfront house on Sullivan's Island to Fish, along with plenty of money to maintain the property.

"It took some getting used to," said Fish. "I mean, I miss her, and everything in the house screams Eugenia. At first I couldn't bring myself to move from the pool house to the main house. I just sort of went there to visit occasionally."

"But you've done that now? Moved?"

He nodded. "A few months ago. I guess I didn't think to mention it. We're always either on the beach near Eugenia's or at your house."

"Do you think we should have supper club there sometimes?" asked Tallulah. "It does have a lovely view."

"Sure. I think Eugenia would like that, if you're sure you don't mind. You've always seemed pretty sure about having it at your place."

"Well, it's my project. I might possibly be a bit of a control freak. If anyone else were to host, well, I wouldn't get to be in control, would I?"

Fish gave her a wry grin and nodded. "But you're reasonably certain I won't wrestle you over the menu."

"Exactly. I think it would be fun. Let's do it in June, shall we?"

"Fine with me. Just let me know what you want me to do."

Fish had always been there if Tallulah needed him for anything when she was planning supper club. But this was different—like they were partners now. She was surprised at how much she enjoyed the feeling. The little smile on her face seemed to stay there.

Later, after Fish had walked her home along the beach, kissed her on the cheek, and bid her good night, Tallulah washed her face and sat at her dressing table doing her nightly skin routine: antioxidant recovery serum, wrinkle serum, eye cream, neck cream, and facial mousse with retinol and peptides—and lip cream. Holding back the years took a lot of work. Age might just be a number, but wrinkles made it harder to ignore that number. She wouldn't let the old woman in if she could help it.

This evening had been fun. She and Fish didn't often have dinner in a restaurant just the two of them. In fact, she couldn't recall the last time they'd done that. When Eugenia was alive, the three of them had dinner together at least once a week, sometimes going out and sometimes eating at Eugenia's house, but never at Tallulah's. She and Fish had always deferred to Eugenia, who always wanted them at her place. She'd be happy to know they were having supper club at her house. She probably planted the idea somehow. Tallulah didn't doubt for a minute that Eugenia continued to prod them into doing her will from the viewing room in the sky.

Fish was easy to talk to. They shared so much history. She didn't have to explain things to him. Henry had grown up in Charleston too, but because of the age difference—he was eleven years her senior—they didn't know all the same people or share the same experiences. She was going to ask Fish to be her supper club date for June. Tallulah and Camille had been sharing him since Eugenia passed away, but maybe she just needed to tell Camille she wanted Fish as her permanent supper club date, especially if they were going to have it at his house sometimes. Yes... that was a better plan. She was tired of the endless rotation of dates. She had very little in common with any of them, and she always had the best time when Fish was her escort.

Camille would understand. She'd really seemed to like Tennyson Sumter anyway. Who knew? Maybe she'd ask him back again. Maybe he would become a regular part of their group. Tallulah would let Camille figure that out. As she turned out the light, Tallulah wondered what Fish would think of the new arrangement.

Chapter Fourteen

Wednesday, June 15, 2022, 2:45 p.m.
Beardcat's Sweet Shop
Sullivan's Island, South Carolina
Quinn Poinsett

When Quinn was growing up, her parents had taken her to get ice cream on summer afternoons. They'd driven over to Mount Pleasant, to Ye Ole Fashioned Ice Cream and Sandwich Café on Highway 17. There were closer places to get ice cream, but her father loved the banana splits at Ye Ole Fashioned. It was a pleasant memory in a somewhat tumultuous childhood. So Quinn was pleasantly surprised when her mamma called and suggested she meet them at Beardcat's Sweet Shop for gelato. Quinn needed a distraction.

She watched as her dad pulled the silver Mercedes into the parking lot. Beardcat's was on the ground floor of a building that housed the Obstinate Daughter upstairs. The sweet shop and the restaurant shared the patio space. Quinn waved at them from the little bench that circled around the live oak tree that shaded the patio.

111

Myrna and Finn walked across the parking lot hand in hand, smiling at each other. Quinn sent up a silent prayer of gratitude. They were having a good day. She took a deep breath and tried to exhale the stress that stayed coiled inside her. She stood and met them at the corner of the patio.

"Hey, Mamma, hey, Daddy." She leaned in to hug them both.

"Where are the kids?" her mamma asked.

"They're with Redmond's parents," Quinn said. Had her mother expected the kids to be with her? She hadn't mentioned it. Myrna and Finn weren't what you would call involved grandparents, not consistently anyway.

Her mamma raised an eyebrow. "And Elaine's?"

Quinn winced. "Yes. They're all playing golf this afternoon." Redmond's parents—Banks and Lydia Poinsett—were good friends with Redmond's first wife, Elaine's, parents, the Radcliffes. Tragically, Elaine died giving birth to the twins, Shepherd and Sutton.

Elaine's parents had always made a point to be a part of the twins' lives, and Quinn understood and supported that. They were the twins' grandparents. But if Quinn's own parents were somewhat sporadic in their interest, the Radcliffe's were the polar opposite. There was probably a diagnosis code associated with their level of involvement. They could be overbearing at times, attempting to substitute their judgment on a long list of things for Quinn's and even Redmond's.

Their antics also made things a little weird for Oliver, who Quinn worried felt like a fifth wheel. They always insisted on including him, which was sweet, but... Quinn wondered if maybe Oliver wouldn't sometimes prefer to be left to his own devices. For example, he had no interest in golf, which they were all playing today. Oliver would be eight in July. The twins were sixteen. Of course they had different interests. The twins—like the Radcliffes and the elder Poinsetts—were athletic and outdoorsy. Oliver was more bookish than his brother and sister, a little quiet. He was a lot like Quinn.

The Radcliffes hadn't warmed to Quinn quickly. She'd married Redmond when the twins were three, so she's the only mother they remembered. But Elaine's parents, understandably, wanted to make sure the twins knew who their *real* mother was. And they seemed not to mind comparing Quinn to Elaine unfavorably. The relationship with the Radcliffes could be challenging at times, with Redmond's parents often in the middle.

All of which made Quinn eager for gelato that June afternoon.

Quinn's mamma, Myrna, shook her head. "Well, Finn, let's get our girl some ice cream."

"All right then, ladies..." He held the door for them, leaning down to whisper something in Myrna's ear as she walked through that made her giggle.

Quinn surveyed the display case. She loved too many of the flavors to pick a favorite. Strawberry today or honey almond? Or maybe milk chocolate... no... Today she'd have the olive oil and sea salt. It was unexpected but delicious.

She glanced up to see if her parents had made a decision.

Oh *no*. They'd commenced with the public canoodling, each with an arm around the other, their foreheads nearly touching, staring into each other's eyes. It was like no one else was around. Neither she nor the ice-cream scooper nor the people in line behind them existed.

Quinn gave the woman behind the counter a look that carried an apology and a shrug. "I'd like a small olive oil with sea salt please. Mamma? Daddy? Do y'all know what you want?"

"A milk chocolate and a strawberry," said Myrna without taking her eyes off Finn. "We're traditionalists."

Quinn held her eyes very still, willing them not to roll. Nothing, not one single thing about her parents was or ever had been traditional. These public displays of affection were an embarrassment Quinn had lived with her entire life. Beyond the mortification, they terrified Quinn because they called attention to her parents, which confused Quinn because they'd ingrained in her how critical it was to remain under the radar. She had a recurring nightmare where the monster pursuing them broke into their house in the middle of the night and killed them all in their beds.

When the woman behind the counter handed Quinn her gelato, she glanced over her shoulder at her father and said, "He's paying."

She took her gelato outside and sat in the shade under the oak tree in the same spot she'd occupied earlier. She'd just enjoy her gelato and head home to get a start on dinner. Quinn took a bite and relished the contrast of the creamy sweetness with the bit of savory.

Moments later, Myrna and Finn came outside and sat at one of the little tables. "What are you doing over there?" asked Myrna. "Come sit with us."

How was she supposed to know where they wanted to sit? Quinn sighed and stood to go join them. Several other couples were scattered around the patio along with one group of four. The only person she recognized was Josephine Huger, who was there with her English bulldog, Petunia. Hopefully her parents would be able to keep their hands off of each other long enough to eat their gelato.

Quinn was one step away when trouble started.

They'd been talking quietly, hands on their gelato, when Finn raised his voice and said, "At least I clean up after myself."

Oh no. Quinn recognized the starting bell. This was a familiar argument and going nowhere good. She quickly took a seat at their table. "Do you guys have plans for dinner? I've been craving potato pancakes—"

"Are you suggesting I'm a slob?" Myrna glared at Finn, her voice louder than his had been.

Quinn could feel the eyes on them. The loud voices upset Petunia, and she started howling. Quinn's anxiety rose and gnawed at her stomach. They could not afford a public scene.

"Guys, really. Please. Don't do this here." Bile rose in Quinn's throat. Their behavior wasn't *just* mortifying—though it *was* mortifying. It was reckless.

They ignored her, eyes locked on each other, leaning into the argument.

"No, darling, of course not," Finn shouted. "I'm stating the fact. You are a slob of the first order. If they gave awards for slovenly achievement, you'd take home first place."

"I am begging y'all—" Quinn's voice quivered.

Myrna stood up, threw her arms wide and her head back and shouted something to the sky.

"Mamma." Quinn's voice was an urgent, angry whisper. She tugged on Myrna's arm. *"Stop this."*

Myrna kept shouting. No one else would likely have a clue what she was saying, but Quinn recognized it as an Irish curse. Myrna called down all manner of torment on Finn. Then she dumped her gelato on his head.

"What is the matter with you?" Quinn wheezed. She was on the verge of a panic attack.

Finn jumped up and scooped his gelato out of the cup with his hand—

"Daddy! No!"

—and smeared it all over Myrna's face—gleefully.

Quinn drew back in horror.

Not to be outdone, Myrna snatched the upside-down cup from his head and got herself a fistful of what looked like strawberry.

Finn backed away, and Myrna threw it at him and screamed, "Find someplace else to sleep tonight." The ball of strawberry hit him square on the nose.

He yelled back at her, "A nest of rattlesnakes would be more hospitable."

Myrna turned around and ran for the parking lot, and Finn chased after her. Quinn covered her face with her hands. When she looked again, they were wrestling each other, both of them trying to get into the driver's seat of her daddy's silver Mercedes.

Myrna fell to the ground.

Quinn tried to stand, to help her mamma, but found herself paralyzed with a cocktail of fear and humiliation.

Finn climbed inside the car and slammed the door and locked Myrna out. He almost ran over her while backing out of the parking space.

But Myrna wasn't ready to concede the match. Screaming like a banshee, she scrambled to her feet, climbed up on the hood of the car, and grabbed ahold of it up near the windshield, hanging on for dear life.

Quinn sat there in shock, watching as Finn drove out of that parking lot as if Myrna wasn't even there. She could've been killed.

Quinn wrapped her arms around herself and rocked back and forth. All of this happened, of course, right across the street from town hall, the police department, and fire and rescue. It was a miracle her parents weren't arrested, and it would be an even bigger miracle if her mamma made it home alive. It was only a mile to their house, but a mile would be a long way to hold on to the hood of a moving car.

Her parents had always been volatile. This sort of wild swing from crawling all over each other to trying to kill each other wasn't rare by any means. But they'd never behaved like that in public. They'd always known the risks. It's like they were trying to blow up all their lives.

Quinn wanted badly to leave, but she was shaking and felt sick to her stomach. The bathroom was upstairs inside the restaurant, but she didn't trust herself to climb the steps. She had no doubt everyone was gawking at her. She stared at the patio and took deep breaths. When she felt steady enough to try, she threw her melted gelato in the trash and walked quickly to her car.

When she was safely inside and the door was closed and locked, she dissolved into tears. She'd spent her whole life trying to live by the rules they told her they all had to follow. The conse-quences of not following the rules had been plainly spelled out to her. She'd lived her life in fear of unspeakable violence, and now her parents were courting disaster.

She had to talk to Redmond.

She couldn't talk to Redmond, not about this.

Quinn knew she had to figure something out. She was near her breaking point.

Chapter Fifteen

Thursday, June 16, 2022, 7:15 a.m.
Sullivan's Island Nature Trail
Sarabeth Mercer Jackson Boone

I have never been the outdoorsy type, and by that I mean you wouldn't see me camping in a tent or hiking anywhere that requires clunky boots, especially not with a backpack. And you definitely won't find me anywhere modern, clean indoor plumbing isn't readily available. Except, of course, our house, where that was a challenge lately.

Honestly, I don't want to be anywhere bugs are a problem either. Mosquitos love me, and I purely hate putting chemicals on my skin. Of course I adore sitting in a swing or a rocking chair on the porch, especially if a book is involved. I usually burn a citronella candle and keep one of those tennis racket bug zappers handy on the porch. I do enjoy riding my bike—I've been all over this island many times now, well, the paved streets anyway. And I love spending time on the beach, either walking or sitting in a beach chair under a canopy. I burn so easily. I enjoy nature at a safe distance with all the necessary precautions is what I'm telling you. I'm no Henrietta Thoreau.

So it was an interesting situation I found myself in. My friend, Frances Tennant—she was one of the first people I met after we moved here a little more than a year ago—is what I guess you'd call a naturalist, or an environmentalist. She drives an electric car —please, nobody get my husband started on how bad electric car batteries are for the planet—and she eats plant based, like Hadley and Eugenia, and only runs her air-conditioning when it's scorching hot outside and the alternative is a heatstroke.

There's a long list of equally admirable things she does, trust me. Frances has lived on this island forever, and she's very active in all the environmental groups. She makes really good points about everything, and she's such a sweetheart it bothered me how mean some people were to her, especially online where the cowards could hide behind their computer screens. It's easy to bully elderly ladies online. It's a disgrace.

In any case, to be perfectly honest—this is somewhat embarrassing—while I have been a vocal advocate for our maritime forest since shortly after we moved here, I'd never actually *seen* very much of it up close, and we live right next to it.

Okay, now, yes, of course I've seen the trees and shrubs and all from the beach. I walk on the beach nearly every day. And *technically*, I understand from the Sullivan's Island for All folks that the maritime forest extends all the way up nearly to Breach Inlet, though up on that end it's just dune grasses and flowers, not anything resembling a forest. There's a lot I still don't understand, because I also understand there's an erosion problem near Breach Inlet, and even I can see the houses between Station 30 and Station 32 are sitting in a pretty precarious position.

But if you're walking down the beach, you can definitely see shrubs growing in the sand starting around Station 28 1/2, and by the time you get to Station 26, you can sympathize with Vernon Markley when he's ranting about the jungle even if you agree with protecting the forest. So I suppose there's a point somewhere, where sand stops accreting and starts eroding, but I'm not exactly sure where that is. Anyway, everything that accretes is protected, and if something grows on it, that's protected too, and it's technically part of the maritime forest. The island is shaped like a J with the top pointing east-northeast and the biggest chunk of the maritime forest at the elbow—the southwest end. This was the part I had failed to enjoy up to that point.

Okay, I decided that if I was going to be involved in advocacy, I needed to learn a little bit more about what I was advocating for. I'd read a bunch of stuff online—mostly articles from the *Post and Courier*, but I needed to actually get a look at this maritime forest I'd heard so much about, which sounds strange, I know, since Tucker and I have always been so crazy about Sullivan's Island. You'd think we might've investigated this whole issue a little bit before we went so far out on a limb buying this house. But frankly, we love this island for the beach and the small town vibe and the little strip of restaurants and shops along Middle Street. We were oblivious to the situation with the trees until Frances brought me up to speed.

Now the other thing going on with me was that with all the crazy in our house—the kids, the dogs, the demolition of the primary bath, which had Tucker and me showering outside because the alternative was sharing a super-small bathroom with the kids—I was finding it hard to write. I won't use that word that starts with *b* and rhymes with rock. I don't believe in that word. But suffice it to say my story wasn't gushing out of me onto the page. I've heard that spending time in a forest relaxes you. They call it forest bathing, and it's supposed to cure everything from depression to high blood pressure to dialing down your fight-or-flight response, which was an issue for me, because I was still occasionally daydreaming about running away with Tucker to a Caribbean island.

So that morning in mid-June, I, the girl who likes to enjoy nature from a bit of a distance, decided to go for a walk along the Sullivan's Island Nature Trail, which goes, of course, through the aforementioned maritime forest. I was going to try my hand at forest bathing. If I had told Tucker what I was planning, I have no doubt that he would've talked sense into me, maybe suggested I wait until he could come with me. But I didn't mention it to him. I didn't think it was a big deal really. Frances raves all the time about how fabulous this nature trail is.

I walked down to where Atlantic Avenue dead-ends into Station 16 where the nature trail access point is. Now, I wasn't completely ignorant. I did put on some bug repellent made from essential oils, and I wore a pair of lightweight pants and a white long-sleeved shirt—one of those Columbia knock-offs—and a hat that looks like Tucker's Tilley hat, you know, those broad brim hats that are shaped kinda like an Indiana Jones hat, but they're made of nylon? I wore sneakers with socks to protect my feet, and of course I slathered on the sunscreen. I want you to know I passed several groups of people with small children in shorts and flip-flops, but they were headed to the beach, not the nature trail.

I have to say right off that the signs gave me pause. Of course I'd heard all about the coyote issue at that point, but I'd never seen one myself. I really didn't want to run into a pack of coyotes nor any other wildlife, for that matter. So far my fight-or-flight response was exacerbated, not soothed. But I recollected that someone had said coyotes were nocturnal creatures. Surely they wouldn't bother me in broad daylight. I mean, if they were a problem on the nature trail, we'd be seeing an all-out effort to deal with them, right? People would be talking about it online. We let our children walk on this nature trail, so it must be safe.

Gathering my wits about me, I took a deep breath and walked right past the warning signs, made a right turn off the beach access path, and set out on the trail. Among other things, the sign here warned me to respect the local wildlife. I had plenty of respect for it and frankly no desire to interact with any of it, so what kind of fool was I?

I hadn't gone fifty feet before I felt the tickle of a spiderweb on my face. I swiped at my face with my hands and spat—well, I blew air out to get rid of any potential strands on my lips. I don't really know how to spit. It's just not something I ever needed to learn. I was certain a brown recluse had gone down my shirt. I spent the next minute or so sorta shaking my clothes out as best I could. Then I continued down the trail.

It really is beautiful—so wild and green and lush. The path was a thick blanket of leaves with occasional big mucky spots where you could see tire tracks. Someone had been driving something through here. Along both sides of the path there was a mix of plants that formed a thick ground cover. Who knew what lurked in there? I shivered at the thought.

But the birds were nice. The forest was thick, so it was quiet along the path except for the warblers or sapsuckers or whatever they happened to be and all the other critters I tried not to think too much about carrying on. Oh my goodness, there were so many feathered friends singing along the trail, and I don't know the first thing about birds, but there must be a big variety because their chirps and hoots and whistles were all different. Listening to them was very relaxing at first.

For a little while, I just meandered along the path and enjoyed the avian sounds and the butterflies and just being in all the green. I did feel like it was soothing me, maybe even lowering my blood pressure a bit, which, frankly, I was taking two different prescriptions for. I was really enjoying myself.

I was thinking about Tucker, to be honest. I worried about him a lot, about his stress level. He was in the midst of those years when you hear about men having heart attacks or strokes or being diagnosed with something, and you weren't all that surprised because past a certain age, it happened to lots of people.

We were doing the only thing we could possibly do under the circumstances—letting the kids move back in. But what was the cost to my husband? Having Deacon back in the house with his very different and implacable ideas about things—for example, smoking marijuana—and two teenagers who were absolutely precious but still teenagers nevertheless, well, it was stressful. How much of this could Tucker take before the stress caused some health emergency? I had to find a way to help Deacon get on his feet for Tucker's sake. If I could just finish this book, it would help matters.

Maybe Deacon's daddy should fiddle with all this for a while —that's what Tallulah suggested. The thought was laughable. Bobby Earl Dawson—first, what exactly had I been thinking? I was nineteen and stupid and clearly not thinking at all. My first marriage had lasted barely more than three years and wouldn't have lasted that long if it hadn't been for Deacon coming along. Bobby Earl was a good-timing Southern good ole boy built in the mold of my daddy. Bobby Earl was everything I knew I didn't want, and yet somehow I'd succumbed to his brand of charm long enough to derail my education. I transferred home from Clemson and went to Francis Marion until Deacon was born. Later, I'd taken more classes at College of Charleston. I had an impressive number of college credits, from three different schools, but not enough in any one program to get myself a degree. Well, I didn't really need one, did I? The best way to study writing novels was to read them, and I certainly did my share of reading. But if I had that degree, would it have been easier to get a more lucrative publishing contract? Platform meant a lot, I knew that was true. Who was I kidding? I was a woman of a certain age with few credentials.

Tucker and I needed some time alone. Nurturing a relationship with your husband was difficult with three other people in the house. Both our sunny dispositions were wilting. We were starting to snap at each other, which wasn't like either of us. I honestly couldn't remember how we managed when all four of our kids were teenagers. But everyone deals with that, everyone who has kids anyway. At a certain point you think—

Something moved in the path in front of me. I froze and leaned forward a bit to see and screamed.

Oh. My. Stars. A snake. It was thick as a pool noodle and maybe six feet long. It was the biggest black snake I'd ever seen.

Sweet baby Moses in a basket—another one jumped out of a tree and landed on the path.

And another one!

I screamed again and backed up.

But what if there were snakes in the trees behind me too?

I spun around and stared down the path.

Who knew snakes climbed trees? Why in Heaven's name had *that* not been on a sign?

I whipped back around and studied the path in front of me. Three long black snakes writhed and slithered off into the brush. I shuddered.

Which way was shorter? The way forwards, or back the way I came?

I was about to hyperventilate. My heart was racing. My blood pressure had to be through the roof. I gulped for air. Oh sweet Lord was I having a stroke? Save me, Jesus—and this was a sincere prayer. I do not take our Lord's name in vain.

I knew for certain there were snakes ahead of me, but there could just as easily be snakes behind me too. Well, I couldn't just stay out here until it got dark and the coyotes got me. I took a few steps backwards, tripped over a clump of grass, and got tangled up in myself and landed in the scrub on the side of the trail, hollering the whole way down.

I put my hands down to push myself up and must've put my hands on sand spurs.

"Ouch!" I had to get up. There were probably snakes and who knew what all else in this scrub.

I was hollering and making all kinds of unintelligible racket, trying to pull myself up—I'm certain none too gracefully—when I heard someone on the trail.

The woman ran towards me. "Are you all right?" She was tall and slender, and she spoke with a natural authority. She was dressed for exercise and appeared to do it regularly.

"I think so," I called. "Oh, thank goodness!"

She reached my side and took in the sand spurs I was pulling from my hands. "Those are wicked nasty. Here, let's get you out of there."

She reached under my arms and lifted me back up to the trail and steadied me.

"My goodness you're strong. Thank you so much."

"My pleasure. You okay?"

"Yes, just very clumsy apparently. I was startled by a snake jumping out of a tree up ahead."

"That's disturbing." She drew back her chin and studied the trail.

I brushed off my clothes. "My thoughts exactly. I don't want anything to do with snakes of any kind. Do you walk here often?" I asked.

"Yeah, well, I have every morning since we got here anyway. I've never seen a snake jumping out of a tree."

"I've never heard of such a thing. Is it longer that way"—I pointed down the path—"or back that way?"

"I think we're right in the middle," she said.

"Oh joy." I winced.

"Come on, we'll make a lot of noise. If the snakes hear us coming, they'll stay in hiding."

"All right," I said. "But if a snake lands on me, I will faint dead away. Just call my husband. He's on speed dial."

We made our way quickly back to the main beach access trail, which is wider, sandy, and well traveled. I breathed a sigh of relief when my shoes touched sand.

"Where on earth are my manners? I'm Sarabeth Boone, by the way."

She reached out a hand. "Norah Fitzgerald."

"I can't thank you enough for helping me up and escorting me out of there. I should've had better sense. Are you visiting, or do you live here?"

"I just moved into the Henderson house on Conquest a few weeks ago."

Well, my, my. "It's so nice to meet you." I took her hand. Had Tallulah and Birdie already invited them to supper club? "Are y'all from Boston?" She sounded like she was from Boston.

"Originally, thereabouts," she said. "Yeah, but we lived in New York before we moved here. My husband is from Brooklyn."

"Welcome to Sullivan's Island. Have your ears been burning?"

"I'm sorry?" She squinted, tilted her head, and gave me a little smile.

"A group of my friends has supper club once a month. When we heard you'd moved in, we wanted to invite you. In fact, I think perhaps you met some friends of mine a couple of Sunday afternoons ago? Tallulah Wentworth and Birdie Markley?"

"No, but I generally spend Sunday afternoons on the beach. Did they stop by? I must've missed them."

"Oh, that's a shame," I said, "but since we've run into each other, I'll extend the invitation myself. We meet once a month, the last Saturday of the month, at Tallulah Wentworth's house over on Atlantic near Station 22. We'd love to have y'all join us."

"Sounds fun, thanks. I'll speak to my husband. How can I reach you to confirm?"

We swapped phone numbers, and I went home to take a shower and a Valium. I had seen all the nature trail that I ever would. Women like me had absolutely no business on a trail with tree-climbing snakes. And unless there was a guaranteed snake-free forest somewhere, I think it was safe to say foresting was not going to be the answer to either my blood pressure or my word-count problems.

Chapter Sixteen

Friday, June 17, 2022, 5:00 p.m.
Beach Cabana near Fish's House
Sarabeth Mercer Jackson Boone

I love meeting everyone for happy hour at five at the cabana. It gives me something to look forward to on days when my life spins out of control and crash lands way beyond the splintered guardrails of sanity. Also, breathing in the sunshine, digging my toes into the sand, and listening to the waves roll in is cheaper than therapy, which I cannot afford. When Eugenia was alive, we did this five days a week, but over the past year, everyone has gotten so busy that it's hit-and-miss. A handful of us are here every day, but it's a different mix.

Because Tucker had been out of town on business—was he traveling more lately, or was it my imagination?—and I've had to meet with engineers, foundation repairmen, and contractors, in addition to navigating the end of the school year for two teenagers, I had missed two full weeks of happy hour, which explains why I was behind. That particular Friday, everyone showed up.

I was two sips into my prickly pear margarita and had

recounted in harrowing detail my close encounter with nature the day before when Birdie filled me in on the incident at the Fitzgeralds' the Sunday before last.

"Well, what did y'all do with the pound cake?" I asked.

"We took it back to Birdie's house, sliced it, each had a big piece to calm our nerves, and froze the rest," said Tallulah. "It was quite good. Too good to waste on that horrid man."

"Why didn't anyone tell me?" I gulped my drink. I should never have taken it upon myself to issue an invitation to someone else's house. Mamma would be so ashamed at my disgraceful breach of etiquette.

"I suppose no one envisioned the woman would rescue you from tree-climbing snakes," said Tallulah.

"She seemed really nice," I said.

"I'm going to go out on a limb here and suggest that anyone who came along that trail at that particular moment would've seemed like an angel sent from Heaven," said Quinn.

"I suppose you're right about that. I was terrified." You would never, ever catch me on that or any other path labeled as a nature trail again in this lifetime.

"Well, there's nothing to be done about it now," said Birdie. "We can hardly uninvite them."

"Why on earth not?" Fish gave Faulkner, the Bichon Frisée Eugenia had left in his charge, a treat. "It's all in how things are handled. Why not just say that you were mistaken about the particulars and we'll be in touch? Be vague. That's always best."

"It's not like you to be ungracious." Tallulah gave Fish a look that suggested she might like to pinch him and not in a good way.

"Tallulah, you have met the man," Fish said. "You know what an insufferable ass he is. None of us want to put up with that during dinner. Aggravation is horrible for the digestion."

"It does make you wonder," said Libba. "If she's so nice, why would she stay married to him? Why would she have married him to begin with? Maybe he wasn't born a jerk, but he has some sort of chemical imbalance."

"You won't hear me passing judgement on anybody's marital decisions," I said. "I am positively mortified every time Bobby Earl Dawson crosses my mind, which is about every time I lay eyes on my son, who has way too much of his daddy in him. This is God's way of punishing me for my misspent youth."

Libba gave me a sly look. "Spill your guts, girl. I want to hear all about your misspent youth."

I took a long, slow breath and shook my head. "You really don't. It's not pretty at all. You know, I often suspect it was biological. I mean, every single person in my family has lost their minds between the ages of eighteen and twenty-six. Thank Heavens for Tucker Boone. That man saved my life, just ask my mamma. She prayed for him for years."

"Now I'm intrigued," said Birdie.

"Please don't be," I said. "There's not much in my pre-Tucker past I'm proud of. It's... tawdry. I don't want to talk about it."

"Sarabeth," admonished Tallulah, "every single one of us— every human walking this earth—has regrets. How fortunate indeed one is if she can look back on her life and not see something that causes her pain. Stop flogging yourself for things you did when you were a child. Now, tell us more about Norah Fitzgerald. I'm intrigued by her."

Thankful for a change in subject, I told them everything I could recall, which wasn't much. "Like I said, she seemed really nice to me."

Camille said, "Why don't we plan for something casual? We're having the June supper club at Fish's house, right? That'll give us an excuse to switch things up, make it simpler. Then, if things start going sideways, Tallulah, you can give us a signal, and one by one, we'll say we're making an early night of it or feign a headache or something."

"I like that idea," said Tallulah. "How about American Cookout for our theme? There would only be happy hour nibbles and then dinner—not a long, drawn-out multicourse affair."

"I could smoke a brisket," offered Fish.

Faulkner barked his approval. He understood certain words, like brisket.

"That sounds divine," said Camille, who was, after all, from Texas. "My grandmother had a killer brisket recipe she bequeathed to me. It was a deep family secret, handed down for generations. My brother was livid she left it to me and not him. It's one of the reasons I had to leave the state of Texas. I could help you with the brisket."

She might've batted her eyes at Fish when she said that, which caught my attention. I hadn't noticed Camille flirting with Fish before. He'd always been everyone's platonic friend, but there'd never been the suggestion of romance.

Tallulah caught the eye batting too, and I don't think she cared for it one bit. "That won't be necessary, Camille. Fish is a prize-winning outdoor chef. His brisket is legendary."

"I've had his brisket before, Tallulah." Camille's tone was snippy, which was very unusual. What on earth was going on here?

"Well then," said Tallulah, "you know he doesn't need help in that department. As for everything else, Fish and I have it all under control."

"Listen," I said, "why don't you let us all bring something, just for a change of pace? It'll be so much less work for you and Fish. I could bring my mamma's potato salad if you like?"

I could tell Tallulah's mind was whirring, no doubt struggling with relinquishing control of the menu. Finally she said, "Thank you, Sarabeth. That's a lovely offer. I'm certain your mamma's potato salad is divine. What does everyone else think?"

"I could make cowboy caviar." You could tell by Camille's tone she was still miffed.

"My family really likes my pasta salad," said Quinn. "I could bring that."

"How about if I bring some apps?" asked Libba. "I could do a veggie/hummus tray, and Jake could smoke some wings."

"I'll bring some baked beans and a dessert," said Birdie.

"Maybe we could make homemade ice cream. What are we going to do about what you told that jerk? You told him they'd need to host, remember? And there were thirty of us plus children."

Tallulah waved the question away. "I can't be bothered with what that cretin thinks. Sarabeth, when she calls to confirm, just give her the details, and we'll let it go at that. I'm certainly not ever going back to that man's house."

"Do you suppose he abuses her?" wondered Birdie. "I mean, maybe this is a situation where offering her a network of friends helps her get herself out of a bad situation. Eugenia would expect us to help a neighbor in need."

I winced and shook my head. "I really don't see her as being abused. She seemed very self-reliant to me."

"You never know," said Libba. "That happens to women you'd never guess. It can happen to anyone."

Up until then, Hadley hadn't said a word, and I hadn't noticed until she spoke up. "I may have a bit more information about Norah." She exchanged a look with Libba, who nodded.

"Well, do tell," said Tallulah.

"Norah Fitzgerald is a US marshal," said Hadley.

Everyone got confused looks on their faces.

"Really?" I asked. "Well, she did seem very self-confident."

"Maybe she's not really married to the jerk," said Birdie. "Maybe he's in her custody and this is some sort of case she's working."

"No, that's her husband," said Hadley. "Today is their twenty-fifth wedding anniversary."

Everyone gasped a little and made incredulous noises.

"How did you come by this information?" asked Tallulah.

Hadley made an apologetic face. "I'm afraid I can't divulge that. Client confidentiality."

"Someone hired you to investigate these people?" asked Birdie.

"No," said Hadley. "This was incidental information."

"Hadley, darlin', that is a very unsatisfying answer," said

133

Tallulah. "Is there anything else you *can* tell us about the woman or her husband? For example, does he have a criminal record?"

"He does not," said Hadley. "Other than that, I don't think I know much that y'all don't already know anyway. He was a Wall Street banker, managed a hedge fund. He did very well for himself and retired at fifty, about a year ago."

"Hmmm. Is she younger than him?" I asked.

"No, they're both fifty-one," said Hadley.

"She looks younger," I said. "I would've guessed early forties."

"Can I just say how happy I am to have you as a part of our coterie?" Tallulah grinned from ear to ear. "It's quite handy that someone hired you to do... whatever it was... and you were able to look into these folks. It gives me an idea."

Hadley's eyes grew. "Really? Sounds dangerous."

"Well, you recall Tennyson Sumter, the gentleman who escorted me to dinner last month?" asked Tallulah.

"Yes," said Hadley. "Interesting name."

"Yes, well... his parents apparently had a fondness for Victorian poetry. In any case, I wondered if you might do a background report on him. I don't know him well at all. I believe he's from Walterboro."

"Are you planning to see more of him?" Hadley regarded Tallulah over the top of her sunglasses.

"That depends," said Tallulah. "I was thinking Camille seemed quite taken with him, and you all know how nervous she is about serial killers, conmen, and all such as that."

"What makes you think I was taken with him?" asked Camille. "He was your date."

"He was," said Tallulah, "but I did notice you seemed to enjoy his company."

"I was simply being friendly to the person seated next to me," said Camille, "though I did wonder why I wasn't seated next to *my* date like everyone else."

"I needed Fish by me for logistical purposes," said Tallulah.

"Since we're keeping things so simple this month, you shouldn't have that sort of limitation," said Camille.

"I was thinking Fish would be my escort this time." Tallulah looked at Fish.

"Camille has already made arrangements." Fish might've blushed a bit.

"You didn't mention it to me." Tallulah's voice sounded hurt. She looked at Camille like she'd smashed her grandmother's favorite china.

"I didn't realize I needed permission," said Camille. "And since I didn't get to enjoy his company last month…"

"It's fine," said Tallulah in that tone that left absolutely no doubt at all that things were anything but fine.

I declare, it was almost like the two of them were fighting over him. And Tallulah didn't say another word to Fish that afternoon.

Chapter Seventeen

Friday, June 17, 2022, 5:45 p.m.
Beach Cabana near Fish's House
Quinn Poinsett

Quinn might've been having some sort of breakdown. Everyone was chattering around her, but her fingers tingled and she felt like she couldn't breathe.

What was a US marshal doing on Sullivan's Island? Why was she here?

Thank goodness no one seemed to have heard about the awful scene her parents made at the ice-cream shop. Had the US marshal heard about it? What on earth was Quinn going to do? She was going to have to figure something out. Her parents were headed straight for a divorce, and then Quinn's whole world would come crumbling down around her head.

Redmond was growing more and more distant. Or was it her? Was she putting walls between them? Of course she was. She'd been lying to him since the day they met, and they'd been married thirteen years. Of course they were growing apart. Secrets were toxic, the assassins of intimacy. She'd torpedoed her marriage before she'd even said her vows, and Oliver would pay the price.

Did Hadley know why the woman was here?

Hadley.

Maybe Hadley could help her.

———

At six o'clock, everyone headed home for dinner. Quinn had parked at Eugenia's—Fish's house—but she followed Hadley up the beach towards her house.

"Hadley?" she called.

"Yeah." Hadley stopped in the sand and turned and smiled at her. Hadley had such a warm, friendly smile. And she really was a kindhearted person.

"You got a few minutes?" Quinn asked.

"Yeah, of course. You want to come sit by the pool?"

"Sure. That sounds good." Quinn was second-guessing everything now. Hadley could only help her if she told Hadley what the problem was. But she couldn't do that, could she? This was a bad idea. But Quinn didn't have a good option. She followed Hadley up the beach, through the gate, and navigated to the pool deck.

Hadley's house was much more modern than anyone else's in their group. It was only a little more than a year old, and it was all concrete and glass. Hadley walked to a drink cooler and pulled out a couple of bottles of water. She handed one to Quinn and settled into an outdoor sofa.

Quinn took the chair next to her and leaned in. "Are things you tell a private investigator... is it like with an attorney? It stays confidential?"

"It depends," said Hadley. "There are some exceptions, but generally, as a matter of ethics, a PI will not divulge what you tell them unless you ask them to. But aside from all that, I'm your friend. Of course I'm not going to blab what you tell me."

"I need to hire you in a professional capacity."

Hadley looked like maybe she'd swallowed something too big. "There's an awful lot of that going around."

"I'm sorry?"

"Nothing— Never mind. Listen, why don't you tell me what's up. If I can help I will, but you're not going to hire me."

"No, I insist—"

"It's my new friends-and-family program," said Hadley. "I can't take your money. But I will help you if I can."

Quinn's stomach roiled. "I need to run to the powder room."

"Sure. You know where it is—"

Quinn hopped up and ran to the pool deck powder room. Could she do this? Could she break the confidence she'd held so long? Betray her family? How could she?

She splashed water on her face. Her parents were on the verge of betraying them all. She had to do something. Hadley was a professional. She wouldn't divulge her secrets. She would never endanger Quinn's family.

Quinn steadied herself. She took a few cleansing breaths, then went back outside and slipped back into her chair.

"Talk to me, Quinn," said Hadley.

Quinn took a long drink of water, then nodded. "I'm ready."

Hadley leaned in.

"I've never told a soul this," said Quinn. "I can't. I'm breaking all the rules talking to you."

"Whose rules?" asked Hadley.

"The witness-protection rules."

"You're in wit-sec?" Hadley's voice registered shock.

"My parents are," said Quinn. "Well, we all are. When I was a child, they were art dealers, working together for years before I was born. Their jobs involved a lot of travel, and it was difficult for them to continue in that career after I came along. I was a surprise, I think. I mean, they never said that, but it's a safe assumption.

"Things fell apart after I was born. We left Alabama when I was six and moved again and again for the next five years. We were in New York... There was some big mafia type who hired Mamma and Daddy to appraise a painting—a Monet, supposedly. Who knows if he owned it legitimately or if it was stolen? Anyway, while they were at his house, they witnessed a murder. They barely escaped with their lives. And of course they went straight to the authorities. They testified against him, and we were relocated here when I was eleven. We were so lucky in so many ways.

"We built a life here. And after we'd moved so much, well, all I wanted was a place to call home. I was sick of the constant moving. Thank goodness my parents had saved enough they were able to retire at a very young age. We've just always been told to lead as quiet a life as possible, keep our heads down. And that's the problem.

"I don't know if you've caught wind of it, but lately my parents have been having issues. They've always had a volatile relationship. They're very passionate people. But now I'm afraid they're headed for divorce. And I'm wondering if this US marshal has been sent here to evaluate our situation. If they feel protectees have been compromised, they move them."

Hadley's forehead creased. "But, Quinn, you're an adult now. You're married... Even if they were relocated, for any reason, either separately or together, you would have the choice to stay here. You and Redmond have a life here... the kids. I mean, I get that you're upset about the situation with your parents, but as an adult, your situation is much different than when you were a child."

"But if I stayed here, I'd put myself in danger, and by association, Redmond and the kids. And if I left... I can't imagine Redmond sitting still for me taking Oliver. And of course his paternal rights to the twins outweigh my own."

"When you say you've never told a soul..."

"Redmond has no idea."

Hadley seemed to be taking that in, processing it.

"I didn't tell him in the beginning because my parents convinced me that would put us all in danger, him included. Let's just say I find their arguments less convincing than I once did. But

I can't tell him now because I've been lying to him for thirteen years, and when he finds that out, he might well leave me, and I couldn't blame him. It's just such a mess. Such an awful, awful mess."

"I can see that," said Hadley.

"So you'll find out why she's here?"

"I can try. But the simplest thing might be for you to just talk to her. Ask her if she's here about your parents and see if she has any advice."

The notion took Quinn by surprise. Could she actually do that?

No, she couldn't. Her parents would absolutely kill her. What if Norah weren't here to evaluate their situation but Quinn triggered some sort of review? Aside from that, they'd drilled into her the need for absolute secrecy and loyalty. She shook her head. "Nothing involving my parents is ever simple. Please would you see what you can find out?"

"Okay." Hadley patted her arm. "Sure. But Quinn?"

"Yeah?"

"How would you feel about telling Libba what you told me?"

Quinn squinted at her. "Why would I do that? I've never told anyone. Telling you was huge for me. I feel like I've betrayed my family. I probably won't sleep for a week."

Hadley winced. "I know. It's just..." Her eyes widened and she bit her lip. "I can't tell you why, but I think you should trust Libba with your secret. She's our friend. She'd never betray you. And it will make things so much simpler for all of us."

Four Months before the Fall Meet and Greet

Chapter Eighteen

Saturday, June 25, 2022, 5:00 p.m.
Monthly Meeting of the Sullivan's Island Supper Club—
Happy Hour
Home of Fish Aiken
Libba Graham

Happy hour that evening was on the sand-toned travertine pool deck, which was situated at ground level in the L-shape created by the back of the white, raised two-story, beach house and the complementary-styled pool house. Around the left side of the wide patio, rope hammocks were strung between light-twined trees and poles anchored in the sand. Beyond the row of hammocks, expertly lit planting beds held a riot of trees, plants, and shrubs. Libba recognized crepe myrtles, oleander, Hibiscus, dwarf sabal palms, sea oats, and beach sunflowers, but there were still a few she couldn't name.

Fish had put out the tiki torches, lending a festive ambiance, and while the outdoor living space at Fish's house was much less grand in scale than at Tallulah's, it was plenty big enough to comfortably accommodate the sixteen of them. Best of all, Fish's pool deck opened to an unobstructed ocean view. The white picket fence surrounding the backyard was well below eye-level. Beyond the fence, the low, dense row of scraggly greenery in the soft sand wasn't yet tall enough to impede the view. The soothing cadence of the surf offered the perfect soundtrack for the evening.

Libba smiled as she arranged the pretty paper napkins with the brightly colored sea creatures on the table near the pool house where she'd set up the appetizers. She put the cast-iron starfish on top of the napkins so the breeze wouldn't scatter them everywhere and stepped back to admire her handiwork. The pool house featured a two-sided, indoor/outdoor bar beneath the pool house porch overhang. Everyone huddled around and helped themselves to one of a few wines or beers Fish had selected for the occasion. In a twist none of them could've predicted, Tallulah had stuck to the plan and kept things simple. That was probably easier to do at Eugenia's house—Fish's house. Libba might never get used to thinking of it as Fish's house. But here, there were no memories of supper clubs past, no expectations. Libba quite liked the less-formal vibe this month. She felt more relaxed than she had in a while, lighthearted even.

Libba inhaled deeply and savored the mingled scents of sweet confederate jasmine and salt. She put a few vegetables and some hummus on a clear plastic appetizer plate, picked up her glass of prosecco, and made her way to the ocean side of the pool deck where Quinn stood staring out at the waves. Libba set her glass on a nearby bar-top table. "Isn't this fabulous?"

Quinn turned towards her and smiled, but the smile didn't reach her eyes. "Simply glorious. It's so much more laid-back. Don't tell Tallulah I said this, but I wouldn't mind if we came here every month."

"Yeah, me too. The vibe is much more relaxed here. Every-thing all right? You seem somewhat less effervescent than usual."

Quinn sipped her drink. "I'm fine. Just..." She shrugged and made a circular gesture with her hand. "You know."

They'd had lunch at Libba's house on Tuesday. Quinn had spilled everything about her parents and asking Hadley to find out what Norah Fitzgerald was working on. And, in turn, Libba had confessed to suspecting Jake of having an affair with Norah. Quinn's problems gave Libba new perspective. She couldn't imagine living with that awful secret—and the fear that mobsters might find your family and kill everyone at any point. How did anyone live with that hanging over them? So much of Quinn's reticence to open up was explained.

"It's pretty funny we both asked Hadley to investigate the same woman, and right over there she is," said Libba.

They both turned and nonchalantly scanned the pool deck, not stopping too long at the spot near the bar where the Fitzgeralds chatted with Vernon and Birdie. Everyone else had scattered across the patio in clusters. Hadley was making her way in their direction. "Yeah, I guess I can see the humor in it. Poor Hadley. She can't get any work done because her friends keep needing her services. Did you finally talk to Jake?"

Libba nodded. "I did. Worked up my nerve last night actually. I did *not* tell him I'd hired Hadley to put him under surveillance. But I did tell him I followed him to lunch."

"How did that go over?" Hadley joined them in time to hear what Libba said.

"He was not happy with me," said Libba. "He seemed really hurt that I thought he might be cheating. But how can I be sure he's not just gotten really good at playing the part? I got sidetracked—blindsided by catching him with Norah. But Roxie is the one who was texting him before breakfast. She's the real threat."

"Come on now," said Hadley. "I told you. Jake's no cheater."

"He did sound sincere." Libba wanted so badly to believe him. "Oh—and he told *me* what Norah told *him*."

"Really?" Hadley's eyes got big. "What was that? I've basically gotten nowhere with what she's working on."

"Jake says she's investigating a fugitive who could be in the area living under an assumed name. She was asking Jake about one of his clients. She quizzed him about what all he'd noticed when he went to do the installation—Jake made him a really high-end home library."

"But surely Norah works on more than one case at a time," said Quinn. "That doesn't necessarily mean she's not also checking up on my parents."

"I guess that's true," said Libba.

"The only way you're going to *maybe* get the answer to that question is if you ask her," said Hadley.

"I just can't do that," said Quinn. "I've already betrayed my family talking to y'all."

"Well, then maybe you should talk to Redmond," said Libba. "Take it from me. It will make you feel so much better. Honesty, or something close to it, is the best policy."

Quinn smirked at her. "Says the woman who hired a PI to tail her husband."

"I take your point," quipped Libba with a nod and a smile from underneath raised eyebrows, "but I don't care for your tone. You're attempting to apply logic in a situation where logic is useless. I'm hormonal, remember? Logic doesn't enter into it. Anyway, living with that secret is probably making you sick."

"Agreed," said Hadley. "You should talk to Redmond. He's your husband. I'd bet my mamma's pearls your parents assume you told him years ago."

"Oh no." Quinn shook her head. "They made me take an oath I would never tell him."

"That's... messed up," said Hadley. "Secrets are toxic in relationships."

Sarabeth walked over to join them. "Cheers, everybody." She extended her arm and raised her glass towards the three of them. They all clustered up into a little huddle, clinked glasses, and said cheers.

"So what've I missed?" Sarabeth asked.

"Not much," said Hadley. "We're just trying to figure out if Vernon is trying to get stock tips or enlist Knox's help with his jungle."

"Woo-wee," said Sarabeth. "With Birdie right there, I'd wager neither. I'm guessing he's on good behavior, at the moment anyway."

"For as long as he can stand it," said Libba.

They all laughed.

Sarabeth said, "I just hope Knox is too. If there's unpleasantness, it'll be all my fault."

"That's ridiculous," said Hadley. "You're not responsible for his behavior."

"Don't look now, but Birdie bailed on the conversation and went to talk to Tallulah and Camille. Norah's on her way over here." Quinn stood with her back to the ocean and had a view of the outdoor entertaining area.

Sarabeth took a step back, turned around, and smiled widely at Norah. When she was a few steps away, Sarabeth said, "Poor Hadley doesn't have the coolest job in the group anymore. Norah, come tell us what it's like to be a US marshal. Are you packing heat?"

"Who says being a PI isn't cooler?" Hadley feigned offense.

"I'm betting it's way cooler." Norah laughed. "But I'm actually a deputy US marshal. Important distinction. And yes, actually, I'm always armed."

"Well, that's certainly good to know," said Libba. "If any snakes jump out of the trees, you've got us covered."

Laughter bubbled through the group.

"Is it supposed to be a secret? You being a deputy marshal?" asked Sarabeth. "Are you undercover?"

"No, it's not a secret," said Norah.

"I imagine it's an exciting job," said Libba.

"Some days." Norah gave a little shrug. "But there's an awful lot of paperwork."

Libba scrunched up her face. "What do marshals do exactly?"

"All kinds of things," Norah replied easily. "We protect judges and witnesses, track down the bad guys."

"Fascinating," said Libba. "Are you, like, dedicated to one

case, or do you work several at the same time, like a police detective?" If Quinn wouldn't talk to Norah, maybe Libba could find out something helpful.

"It varies." Norah turned to Hadley. "What sort of cases do you work?"

"Ha," said Hadley. "That varies too, but basically, whatever I'm hired to do. I work a lot of criminal defense cases for a local attorney's office. And whatever else comes through the door." She looked sideways at Quinn, then Libba.

"Now see, I think *that's* fascinating," said Norah.

"So your husband is retired?" asked Sarabeth. "He's awfully young. I cannot imagine having Tucker home all day and me out working. The house would be a wreck."

"That is a problem," said Norah. "I'm trying to encourage him to take up some volunteer work. Anything to get him out of the house."

"Have you thought about retiring?" asked Quinn.

"Ah, no," said Norah. "I love my job. Knox would like for me to retire and entertain him full time. But that is not happening."

"Didn't you tell me your husband is from Brooklyn?" asked Sarabeth. "He has a little bit of a British accent, doesn't he?"

"He does," said Norah. "Knox's parents are British. He was raised in the States but spent a lot of time in the UK growing up. To be honest, I think he cultivates the accent."

"I just love a British accent," said Sarabeth.

"And I was just admiring your Southern drawl." Norah smiled. "All of you have lovely accents, but they're all a bit different, aren't they?"

"Tallulah, Birdie, and Hadley are from here," said Sarabeth. "I'm originally from Florence, South Carolina. That's a couple of hours north. But Libba's from Tennessee, Quinn's originally from Alabama, and Camille is from Texas."

"Well, that explains it," said Norah.

"So who are you assigned to protect?" Libba continued her fishing expedition. "A federal judge? Or someone in wit-sec?"

Norah winced. "I can't really talk about my job much. I mean, it's not a secret who I work for, but that's really about as much as I can say, aside from, you know, the general types of things that we do."

"Oh, I'm sorry," said Libba.

"No need to apologize," said Norah. "I get that type of question a lot. It's kind of a problem because I can't talk about my job. Makes me a bore at parties."

"Oh now, that's crazy," said Sarabeth. "Hadley's the only one of us besides you who *has* a job. We're just trying to live vicariously through y'all."

"Sarabeth, that's not true." Libba gave her a look that said *What the heck?* "Sarabeth is an author."

"Wow," said Norah. "That sounds like an amazing job to me."

Sarabeth sighed. "I suppose I'd forgotten I had a job. I haven't been able to actually do it in a while. There's chaos in my house."

"I'm sorry to hear that," said Norah. "What kinds of books do you write?"

Sarabeth beamed. "Mysteries. They're cozy-ish."

"I'll check them out," said Norah. "I read all the time, and I love cozy mysteries."

"Aww—thank you!" said Sarabeth. "You'll have to let me know what you think."

"I will," said Norah. "Hey, is there a neighborhood book club?"

"Several," said Quinn, "but some of them are a little strict with the rules. We prefer to just talk about what we've read while having a glass of wine or whatever."

Libba flashed Quinn a warning glance.

"That's more my speed too," said Norah. "Do you do that on a regular basis?"

A loud clanging noise rang across the deck. They all looked for the source and found Fish ringing a big black dinner bell atop a post.

Libba and Quinn exchanged a relieved look. They'd been

saved by the bell. If Norah were to be invited to happy hour, which is where book discussions occasionally took place, though not according to any schedule, Tallulah would need to invite her.

"Well, that bell is new," said Sarabeth. "I wonder what Tallulah thinks about it."

"I bet if she didn't like it, he'd have already taken it down," said Libba. "Shall we?"

Where had Jake gotten to? Things seemed a bit more relaxed between them since she'd asked him about Norah. The air was clearer. She still wasn't convinced that Roxie wasn't a threat to their marriage. Part of Libba was convinced that Jake had given in to temptation, because Roxie clearly pursued him, and there was a distance between Libba and Jake that might have given Roxie an opening.

Something was going on. Libba was sure of it. The question was, was it simply that Roxie was flirting with him but he had ignored her? Or did Jake have casual sex with her out of loneliness? Or was he—please God, don't let this be it—in love with Roxie but anchored to Libba because of the kids? Could Libba forgive a casual affair? If it were just sex and not that he was in love with Roxie, could Libba get past it?

Chapter Nineteen

Saturday, June 25, 2022, 6:00 p.m.
Monthly Meeting of the Sullivan's Island Supper Club—Dinner
Home of Fish Aiken
Tallulah Wentworth

Tallulah and Fish stood near the top of the steps leading to the deep back porch. They all gathered around.

Tallulah placed a hand on Fish's arm. "After Fish says grace, y'all help yourselves to the buffet up here on the porch to my left. Now, the dish that looks like pork barbecue is actually jackfruit—which is tastier than you might imagine—for our plant eaters, but there's plenty for anyone who's curious to try it. Hadley made that for us, and I have to say, I was pleasantly surprised. Several of the sides are all plants—the pasta salad, the Texas caviar, and the beans. Now we are, of course, less formal this month, but you will find your names on place cards at the table over here to my right." Her eyes swept over the group and back to Fish. She smiled brightly, then noticed Camille, who was standing behind him and one step up and had put her hand on his shoulder, like she was laying claim to him or something.

Fish smiled back at Tallulah, then bowed his head and returned thanks.

The tumultuous uproar inside Tallulah confused her. She and Fish had dinner again just last week at Poe's Tavern. The week before they'd gone into Charleston and eaten at FIG, which was one of Tallulah's long-standing favorites. It was becoming more common for them to go out together, Tallulah supposed, and she was already looking forward to when they might see each other alone again. To the casual observer, who didn't know they were old friends, it must look like they were dating. What did it look like to Henry?

After they'd all said amen, Tallulah opened her eyes and glared at Camille in what might've been an un-Christian manner. Well, she supposed Fish was Camille's date that night, technically, but my goodness, they were friends—they were all just friends. One shouldn't paw at one's friends at dinner.

She stepped up to the porch and backed out of the way. "Fish, darlin', why don't you and Camille go first and lead everyone down the buffet line? Y'all, both sides of the table have some of everything, so you can go down either one, but start at the far end now, and come down this way."

Fish and Camille did as she'd asked, and Tallulah stood to the side with Tennyson, who'd graciously agreed to escort her that evening. Tallulah had the idea he was lonely and grateful to be invited. Whoever his dinner partner was on any given night, he was pleasant company and a good fit for the group. Hadley never did check on his background, at least as far as Tallulah knew. They'd just sort of dropped the idea when Camille said she wasn't interested in dating him. Of course, his deceased wife was his best reference. Zelda Boykin's family was well known in the area. That really was all the reference they needed.

"Now, Fish's brisket is excellent, y'all," called out Camille, like a carnival barker or what have you. "But if you'd also like to try some genuine Texas brisket, I brought some of that as well. Let me know what you think."

Tallulah blinked several times rapidly. When exactly had Camille snuck her brisket onto the buffet? What was wrong with her? They'd discussed this, and what's more, they didn't need more brisket. Fish had smoked more than enough for all of them and leftovers to boot. It was downright rude—suggesting that Fish didn't know what he was doing. Tallulah felt her blood pressure rising.

She waited until Hadley and Cash were getting biscuits at the end of the table, then moved to the other end of the serving station and picked up a plate. Tennyson followed her, piling Fish's brisket on his plate and then following her example and skipping over Camille's platter—which of course didn't match the other serving dishes—and adding a taste of the barbecued jackfruit and small servings of the potato salad, Texas caviar, pasta salad, baked beans, watermelon salad, and biscuits. They settled into their places at the far end of the large teak dining table, Tallulah at the very end and Tennyson to her left. This time, much to her chagrin at that moment, Tallulah had kept Fish and Camille together with Fish immediately to Tallulah's right and Camille in the chair beside him.

"Camille, my compliments on your mighty fine brisket," said Fish. "It's delicious. You'll have to let me know your secret."

Tallulah gave Camille a look that telegraphed her displeasure, which Camille completely ignored.

"Yours is delicious too," said Camille. "Very tender and moist."

"These are Callie's Hot Little Biscuits, aren't they?" asked Cash, who had piled four of them on his plate.

"They are," said Tallulah. "Two kinds, buttermilk, and cheese and chive."

"Aah—I'm addicted to these things," said Cash.

"Is that a family recipe?" asked Norah.

"Well, yes, actually," said Tallulah. "But not my family. Carrie Morey is a local entrepreneur. She's created a biscuit empire. It's named for her mother, Callie, I understand. You can buy her biscuits from a couple of grab-and-go shops downtown and even in the freezer section in some of the grocery stores. Carrie's on television now too, I understand."

"Well, these are delicious." Norah picked up a biscuit to take another bite. Her plate had generous helpings of everything.

"Norah, darlin', I should've asked in advance if you—or Knox —have any dietary restrictions. I'm well acquainted with everyone else's by now. I apologize for my oversight."

"Oh no, we both eat everything," said Norah.

Well, that was interesting. Tallulah gave Knox Fitzgerald, who sat next to Camille, a sideways glance. His wife was slim, fit, and apparently in possession of a healthy appetite. Did she know what kinds of ridiculous things he told strangers coming to her door? What was he up to anyway?

Knox smiled, what to all appearances was a genuine, open smile, and said, "They are quite good. I particularly like the cheese and chive."

Tallulah raised her eyebrows but resisted the urge to ask him if he was monitoring what his wife ate.

"Small crowd tonight?" Knox raised his eyebrows back at her, no doubt recalling what she'd told him about thirty people plus children.

"No, actually, everyone is here," said Tallulah. "And we're so happy y'all could join us."

"Thank you so much for having us," said Norah. "What a lovely evening. And I was just admiring the table. I'd love to have one similar." She ran her hand along the table.

"It's teak," said Tallulah. "I ordered it online. I can show you where. We needed one long enough for all sixteen of us in a hurry. Thank goodness they were able to ship it quickly. But I tell you what, if you're looking for a table, Jake's are simply gorgeous. We would've much rather have had one of his live-edge tables, but there wasn't enough time. He's backed up till next year sometime aren't you, Jake?"

"Not quite that long." Jake sat on Norah's right side. "I'm

happy to show you some samples. Most of our work are custom jobs."

"I'd like that," said Norah. "Maybe Libba and I can go to lunch one day and she can bring me by." Norah leaned forward and looked past Jake at Libba.

"Sure," said Libba. "Just let me know when."

Tallulah's mind was hopping in two different directions, between Knox, whose behavior so far had been better than feared but whom she still felt the need to keep a close eye on, and Libba, who seemed a bit happier than she had in recent months but still not quite herself.

Underneath it all, Tallulah wondered, more and more, what Henry thought about how she was living her life. She so enjoyed spending time with Fish and wanted to do more of that. But she couldn't help feeling disloyal to her husband of thirty-six years. Then again, everything in her life was different than when Henry was alive. She was doing different things with different people, and really, what else could she do? Maybe she needed to talk to someone, perhaps Reverend Goodall.

"Tennyson, you didn't try my brisket?" Camille's tone was hurt, but it was that fake hurt, not the genuine article. She stared at his plate.

"Well, I—"

"There are two different kinds," said Camille. "Did you miss it? Here, I'll get you some."

"That's not—" Tennyson started to say.

"It's no trouble at all." Camille was up and moving, chattering along the way.

Tallulah exchanged a look with Tennyson, whom she realized she'd been neglecting. There was so much going on this evening. Why on earth did Camille feel the need to further complicate things? And why was she worried about what Tennyson had on his plate? Let the poor man decide for himself what to eat.

Camille returned moments later with the platter and forked a generous serving onto Tennyson's plate. "Does anyone else need more brisket?"

"I'll try a bit," said Knox.

Camille served him a helping, then set the platter on the table, pushing aside one of the hurricane lanterns to make room.

Tallulah ground her teeth. Why was she so on edge about the small stuff this evening? It really was so out of character for her, but Camille was getting on her last nerve. She'd made such a fuss about Fish being her date, and not only was she basically ignoring him, she'd tried to compete with his brisket.

"Quite good." Knox nodded approvingly at Camille. "Did you try some of this, sweetheart?" He turned to Norah.

"I did," said Norah. "I have some of everything on my plate. It's all delicious."

"Can I get you more of anything?" Knox asked sweetly.

"No, but thank you." Warm smiles passed between the two of them. Tallulah felt like telling them enough already. It was almost like they were making a point to show how well they got along and how Norah suffered from absolutely no eating disorders. What had he been playing at the day she and Birdie came to the door? Had he told Norah what he'd said?

"Tennyson, you are from Walterboro, I understand," said Fish.

"Originally, yes," said Tennyson. "I moved to Charleston in 1971 when I married my wife. She passed away about four years ago."

"I'm sorry to hear that," said Fish.

"Thank you," said Tennyson. "We were married forty-seven years. I still miss her every day."

"I lost my husband, George, in 2010," said Camille. "You never really get over it."

Things were falling apart. Tallulah was so off her game she'd ignored both Fish and Tennyson, and now the conversation was reduced to departed spouses. Anything would make for more lively dinner conversation.

Apparently Vernon agreed. From near the far end of the table, in his outside voice, Vernon said, "You know, I think it's a mistake to ban politics at the dinner table. Just look where it's gotten us. Nobody in the country can have a conversation with people they disagree with anymore."

"Vernon, no more alcohol for you tonight," said Birdie.

"I'm serious here. I say we should all be like Ginsberg and Scalia. They—"

"That's enough," said Birdie.

Tallulah drew herself ramrod straight and lifted her chin. "Here is what I know about politics, Vernon: The partisan mind is small and tribal. You can agree with your dear friend about virtually everything, work beside them in the soup kitchen, have dinner with them and their spouse, celebrate their child's birthday, make chicken pot pie for them when they're sick, sit beside them in the pew at church—all of it, and the two of you love one another and get along beautifully, just as long as neither of you labels yourself as conservative or liberal or republican or democrat or what have you. Because it's that one thing, that label—or perhaps it's simply the admission that one of you supports a given candidate or likes a certain news program that really gets under the other's skin—that ONE THING. It wipes everything else out. It assigns you to a team, a tribe. And we're all about the team anymore in this country. We're dug in, all of us, fans. Fanatics. Your team, your tribe outweighs every positive connection you ever had with your friend who backs the other team. And it's a disgrace, and I'm personally convinced that the Russians or the Chinese have instigated all this animosity, but that's where we are. So I do not care to know the first thing about anyone's politics, thank you very much. And I damn sure won't be sharing mine."

For a beat, no one spoke. Vernon's eyes had grown to the size of saucers. Birdie gripped his arm but didn't say another word.

"Well." Sarabeth smiled brightly and glanced around the table. "If anyone needs anything investigated, we have three detectives at the table this evening. Isn't that something?"

Tallulah nodded appreciatively at Sarabeth. "Indeed. Yes... Have they caught whoever is responsible for cutting those trees by Station 26? Perhaps y'all could collaborate on that."

Fish touched her arm at the same moment she realized she'd gone the one place she hadn't wanted to go. Trees were as bad as politics—worse. But Fish's hand on her arm felt so nice. Tallulah couldn't quite catch her breath.

Tension swirled around the table as everyone held their breath to see if Knox would rise to the subject.

Birdie looked at Knox and Norah. "Have y'all been over to Bowman yet to see the UFO Welcome Center?"

Tallulah couldn't read their expressions, as Birdie was at the far end of the table and everyone had turned in her direction.

"I'm sorry, the what?" asked Knox.

"The UFO Welcome Center," said Birdie. "It's about an hour and fifteen minutes up I-26 past Harleyville."

"Is this a real thing?" asked Norah.

"Well, I couldn't tell you how many visitors from other planets have been served there," said Birdie, "but they have a billboard along the interstate. And Steven Colbert had a segment on it... Oh, law, when was that?"

"It's been twenty years ago or more," said Vernon. "You know, Norah, Colbert has a home here. He grew up in Charleston. Several other celebrities live here at least part of the time... Bill Murray, Reese Witherspoon, Darius Rucker, Judge Judy..."

Norah laughed. "Seriously? Judge Judy?"

Vernon nodded emphatically.

Normal, happy table cacophony resumed as Jake explained the UFO Welcome Center to the Fitzgeralds, and everyone else told each other either their UFO Welcome Center tale or their celebrity encounter.

"Crisis averted," murmured Fish. "All is well."

"For the moment." Tallulah might've looked too long into

Fish's smiling blue eyes. Something inside her was fluttering. Maybe a chat with Reverend Goodall was the thing.

Chapter Twenty

Saturday, June 25, 2022, 7:00 p.m.
Monthly Meeting of the Sullivan's Island Supper Club—Dessert
Home of Fish Aiken
Quinn Poinsett

Birdie had outdone herself on dessert. She'd set up an ice-cream bar on the far end of the porch, with homemade peach, as promised, along with butterscotch, bourbon, butter pecan, and vegan blackberry peach. There was a crumbled shortbread topping, along with a variety of nuts, syrups, and candy toppings. Quinn savored a small dish of peach. She loved ice cream, and even though she'd lived most of her life in the South, where homemade ice cream was a summertime tradition, she'd never had it until she'd become friends with Birdie, who had mastered the art form.

Everyone was enjoying their dessert and talking quietly with whoever was right beside them. Quinn's eyes met Libba's directly across the table. Next to her, Jake chatted with Norah on his other side. Quinn couldn't wait to hear what Libba had to say about tonight's seating chart. Tallulah couldn't have known, of course, that Norah had interviewed Jake in her professional capacity or that Libba had suspected Jake of having an affair with Norah, before Libba knew who she was. Libba hadn't shared those tidbits with anyone except Hadley and Quinn.

"Is the peach good?" Redmond murmured.

Quinn turned and smiled at her husband. An unruly lock of brown hair curled across his forehead. She leaned into him ever so slightly and inhaled the heady scent that was uniquely him, a blend of sandalwood, leather, and a spice she couldn't name. "Delicious. You want a bite?"

"No, no. I overserved myself with the butter pecan." Something in the tone of his voice, no matter what he was saying, soothed her. Thirteen years, one month, sixteen days, and one hour. That's how long they'd been married. And she was still just as head over heels in love with him as she had been the day he first came into the Beach Hair Affair to get the twins haircuts and she'd fallen hard and fast. How had she let her parents convince her that lying to him was the only way? The secret ate at her insides like acid.

"It sounded positively decadent." Her eyes met his and held them.

"It is that. I was thinking we might take a walk on the beach later, after we get home."

Quinn tried to read what was in her husband's soft grey eyes. Desire, for sure. But was there something more?

"Would you like that?" he asked when she didn't respond.

"Yeah, of course." The distance between them had grown so gradually it was hard to put her finger on when it started. If she was honest with herself, she supposed it had always been there. She'd never completely let him in. She could feel him reaching out for her, trying to bridge the gap neither of them could deny.

What was she going to do?

Norah could easily be the harbinger of the destruction of Quinn's carefully constructed world. Quinn studied her, two seats down from Libba. Norah seemed really nice. Maybe she should talk to her. Would she be able to tell her if she was there to check up on her parents? And even if she were, did that mean she'd automatically relocate them if they'd called attention to themselves? What if Norah wasn't here about her parents and had no idea who they even were, but Quinn's questions put them under scrutiny? Quinn's stomach clenched, anxiety crawling up her throat. She set down her spoon.

"Had enough?" asked Redmond.

"Too much." Something tightened and twisted in her chest. Was it too much of a coincidence, Norah, a deputy marshal, turning up here just as her parents' bad behavior was escalating?

Birdie placed a hand on Vernon's arm. She'd been speaking quietly with him, likely admonishing him about what all he wasn't supposed to be talking about. She patted his arm twice, then turned to Quinn with a smile. "Did y'all try some of the shortbread topping? It's my grandmother's recipe."

"Yes, it's fabulous with the butter pecan," said Redmond.

"Everything is delicious, Birdie," said Quinn.

"Darlin', are you feelin' all right this evening?" Birdie's brow knit in concern.

Quinn smiled at her brightly. "Yes, of course. I've just over-served myself, I'm afraid. Excuse me, would you?" Quinn rose and headed inside towards the powder room. She needed a few minutes to herself to breathe.

"Well, I know it wasn't something *I* said," she overheard Vernon say.

Chapter Twenty-One
〜〜〜

Saturday, June 25, 2022, 7:00 p.m.
After-Dinner Drinks
Sarabeth Boone

It surprised me, to tell you the truth, that no one left after dessert. It had been an awkward evening, and things have never, ever been awkward at supper club before. It was the Fitzgeralds. Everyone was torn between not discussing the trees at all because the issue was controversial—and who needs controversy at dinner?—and trying to gently influence the Fitzgeralds in the general direction of the preservationist mindset most of us shared. It was a delicate tightrope to walk. And then of course there was that odd business with the pound cake. I still don't know what to make of that. And what was Vernon smoking, trying to bring up politics? It's a sad state of affairs when politics is the best topic anyone can come up with.

After dessert, we all refilled our drinks at the pool house bar and scattered into pairs and groups around the pool deck. I guess it was so tempting because that pool deck is a front-row seat to the ocean. The beach isn't as wide at Fish's house. It's near Station 28 1/2—beside that dome house?—and the dunes don't amount to much. That pool very nearly sits on the beach—it's that close. Tucker and I were out at the far corner by ourselves, just soaking in the evening, which was nice. He'd been gone all week to a client near Los Angeles, and we'd barely had ten minutes alone. Things between us were somewhat strained. We both understood all the problems, and neither of us had a solution different from what we were doing. But we were both still disappointed, if we were honest, and felt guilty because of it. We were adults. Life was full of ups and downs. We had a lot to be grateful for, but... But just then, all of that seemed to be on a back burner, like we'd called a time out and were just enjoying the moment.

It was right about what photographers call magic hour, still an hour and a half till sunset, and the fading sunlight was catching the foam on the waves and the tips of the sea oats just right. It was magical really. I guess that's what made what happened next so shocking.

Tucker excused himself and went to the restroom, so I was standing there by myself, enjoying the sound of the surf and sunlight on the water, waiting for my husband to come back. I was staring at the ocean, and I didn't even hear him walk up.

"Lovely evening." Knox Fitzgerald just sort of appeared, catlike, at my elbow.

"Yes, it is." I smiled.

Everyone else was somewhere else—near the bar, across the pool deck, over by the porch—somewhere. So I was alone with him. And he'd been real pleasant all evening, so I wasn't particularly concerned. But then he leaned in close to me.

"I've heard about another group here in town that gets together monthly," he said.

"Really?" I asked. "Another supper club?"

"Hmmm... well..." He gave me a look that might've meant *not quite*, but then he nodded. "They do have dinner, I'm told, but it's not as structured."

We'd had a pretty unstructured evening for us, I thought. There were paper napkins with the appetizers. Everything had been served buffet-style. I tilted my head and asked, "What do you mean?"

"It's a pot-luck affair. And the main event is the after-dinner entertainment."

"Movies?"

He raised his palm and shrugged. "I suppose some of them may watch films."

"I'm afraid I don't understand you."

"Well," he said, "they all drop their keys into a large bowl when they arrive. Each of the keys has a tag with their home address. After dinner, they all grab a key and go to the address on the label. Then they get better acquainted with whoever else shows up."

I heard myself gasp as realization dawned.

"You're talking about a—"

"Yes, quite. A sex club."

"I don't believe you. No one in this town does such a degenerate thing as that."

"Are you quite sure? I do understand what you're saying though. It does seem a bit risky. I mean, what if you ended up paired with someone who wasn't your type? I like girls, you see, and wouldn't be at all interested in the biblical knowledge of another man."

"I don't believe for a minute that there's any kind of sex club in this town. You are making that up." What a horrible man. How could he go from so pleasant one moment to so... so... debased in the next? What was wrong with him? How was that sweet Norah married to this... this reprobate?

"Am I?" He gave me an amused look. "I wonder if they color code the keys? Maybe you drop in the color you are and pull out the color you like? That would work, wouldn't it?"

"I think you're just trying to get some sort of reaction out of me. You like to toy with people, don't you?"

"Hmm... well, I like to play anyway. The question is, do you?"

"I beg your pardon?"

"Have *you* ever been to the key-exchange party?"

"I most certainly have not."

"Pity. Well, perhaps someone else can steer me in the right direction. Nice chatting with you." He nodded and sauntered off.

I was so shocked I just stood there. Could there possibly be a swingers group in town? Surely not. Was Knox Fitzgerald really looking for such a group, or was he just playing with me for sport?

Poor Norah seemed so normal compared to her husband. I really did like her, and she was closer to my age than anyone in our group. Should I tell her what he'd said? Would she believe me? Would she think I was making things up about him?

"Quinn and Redmond are leaving," Tucker called as he made his way back to our oceanfront spot. "Did you want to say goodbye?"

"I'm coming." I was ready to go home myself.

Actually, that wasn't true. Our bathroom was down to the studs. We could see the ground through the floor joists. The plumber had set off the smoke alarm soldering pipes yesterday eighteen times, and every time he did, the dogs went crazy. It was no wonder I couldn't focus on my book.

I wanted to get on a plane with my husband and fly far, far away.

Tucker read my mind. "Want to check into a hotel in Mount Pleasant for the night?"

"We can't afford that." I smiled up at him, loving him for the thought.

"I have Hilton Honors points."

"How many? How long can we stay?"

We laughed, said our goodbyes hand in hand, and drove straight to the Hampton Inn. I didn't give Knox Fitzgerald or anything else another thought that evening.

Chapter Twenty-Two

Tuesday, June 28, 2022, 5:45 a.m.
On the Beach
Sarabeth Boone

Needless to say, I was not going back on that nature trail. But after missing my exercise for nearly a week due to the need to meet contractors, supervise grandchildren, and drive back and forth to Florence to see about my mamma and daddy, I was committed to getting back in my routine. It was so easy for me to let one day become two, then five, then a whole month would go by without me getting exercise. Aside from all the other health and self-esteem benefits, exercise is, I understand, very good for your brain.

My daddy had been diagnosed a few years back with something the doctors were calling "cognitive decline" but which my sister insisted was Alzheimer's. She might well've been right, but they couldn't do the test to know for sure because it costs more than twenty thousand dollars and the insurance won't pay for it. According to the doctor, the treatment is the same, so it really doesn't make any difference. I had a lingering suspicion we didn't have all the facts.

In any case, if you could see me standing next to my daddy,

you'd understand my self-protective instincts. I look just like him. Mamma has always maintained I act just like him. Genetically speaking, my apple fell *reeaallly* close to his tree, is what I'm saying. So I worry. And I get my exercise, and I try to eat brain-healthy food, and I do my word games.

Also, not for nothing, I needed an hour of peace and quiet to work through a particularly thorny plot problem. Another benefit to an early-morning walk was that I could avoid strangling my son for smoking pot in our house—against Tucker's very explicit wishes—if I didn't see him this morning before he left for work. Tucker was in Vermont that week and therefore blissfully ignorant of everything going on under our roof. It was no doubt saving my marriage that my husband could escape from the crazy.

I power walked down to the closest beach access path to our house, which is at Station 18 1/2, right by the lighthouse. At the end of the wooden walkway, I went left, in the opposite direction from the nature trail. I didn't want to be anywhere close to those tree-climbing snakes. The sky was just beginning to lighten, the horizon painted in shades of pink and orange. When the weather warms up, I like to walk early before it gets hot. The air was fresh and crisp, the breeze carrying the salty tang of the ocean. The tide was on its way out, the gentle lapping of the waves accompanied by the distant calls of sea gulls and the sporadic squawk of a heron. A few scattered shells and an occasional footprint were all that marred the smooth expanse of sand. I had the beach to myself.

I was somewhere between Station 22 and Station 23 when I saw him—or her. I really couldn't say whether it was a man or a woman. Whoever it was, they had on what looked like a white hazmat suit—one of those things that covers you up from head to toe?—and they were walking around up in the dunes, where no one is allowed, carrying one of those little plastic canisters like the ones you put bug spray or weed killer in, with the little wands. And they were broadcasting something all over the bushes growing on protected land that belonged to the town. It had to be some kind of poison—right there near the beach. What on earth was this idiot thinking? They were contaminating the ground-water and no doubt doing a long list of other horrible things I hadn't even learned about yet.

I should've had better sense.

"Hey," I hollered out, like I was calling down an unruly child.

Dang the bad luck. I was wearing my Apple Watch but had left my phone at the house, so I couldn't take pictures. I ran towards them, hollering, "What do you think you're doing?"

Whoever it was took off running towards the Station 22 1/2 beach access path. I darted after them. Well, it was as close to a dart as I get anymore. They were a good ways ahead of me, but I hoped I could catch them. Surely it would be difficult to run in that getup. Apparently whoever was in the hazmat suit was younger and spryer than me.

When they reached the end of the path, they turned right on Atlantic. But by the time I got there, there was no sign of them. He or she must've ducked under someone's house to hide. Surely it must've been someone who lived in one of the beachfront houses right along there. It stood to reason that the only people who would do such a thing were people trying to protect their views.

I was standing there holding my side and catching my breath and stewing about what to do when someone on a bicycle came flying down the street and came to a sudden stop.

"Sarabeth?" a woman asked.

I took a closer look at the woman wearing a bike helmet. "Norah. Hey."

"Good morning. Are you all right?"

"I'm fine," I said. "I just chased someone who was spraying something—probably some sort of plant killer—near the dunes."

"Where did they go?" she asked.

"I don't know. I lost them."

"Are you going to report it to the police?" asked Norah.

"Yes, of course."

"I'll walk with you over there," said Norah.

"Thank you so much. I just can't believe anyone would do such a thing."

We headed down Atlantic Avenue towards Station 21. Norah was quiet on the way to the police station, which was only a couple of blocks over and a couple of blocks down. The town hall and police department sat next to fire and rescue at the intersection of Middle Street and Station 20 1/2. When we arrived at the raised white building with the front porch and metal roof, I was surprised when she asked me if I wanted her to go inside with me.

"That's okay," I said. "I don't imagine this will take long. I doubt there's much they can do, but it seems like the right thing to report it."

"Why don't I wait outside then?" she asked. "You feel like a smoothie? I was on my way home to make one."

Now that was really awkward. I liked Norah. And she was new in town, and I know what that's like. But her husband was just not someone I wanted to run into ever again in this lifetime. I hadn't told anyone about what Knox Fitzgerald said to me Saturday night. It would've ruined the moment with Tucker, and we needed that moment. Then later, well, the right time just hadn't arrived. "Well, I—"

"Knox is playing golf at Wild Dunes this morning."

Could she read my mind? "Oh well, all right then. A smoothie sounds lovely. Thank you so much."

Norah secured her bike to a light post, then followed me up the steps and sat in one of the black wooden front porch rockers. "Real homey for a police station."

"It is, isn't it? Well, it's the town hall too. I'll just be right back."

It turns out that was wishful thinking. Making an official report isn't quite as quick in reality as it was in my head. It was nearly seven when I walked back out on the porch.

"Hey, you want to just pop over to the Co-op for that smoothie?" asked Norah. "They make a pretty good one. I mean,

I'm happy to make them, but it'll take us a while to walk to my house. I live almost at the tip of the island. I'm getting a little hungry. How about you?"

"That sounds good," I said. "I'll get my five miles in tomorrow. It's been a stressful morning."

Diagonally across the street there was a little strip of restaurants and shops: Sullivan's Fish Camp, A Maker's Post, which is a local artisan shop, the Co-op, which is a grab-and-go sandwich, coffee, and breakfast operation, and a Pilates studio. We crossed the street, waited less than five minutes for them to open, then went inside and got our smoothies. I ordered Snow on the Beach, which is what they call strawberry banana, and Norah had something called an Antihero, which had strawberries and dragon fruit. We brought them back outside to one of the tables out front.

"These probably taste better than what you'd have gotten at my house," said Norah. "I put kale in my smoothies."

"I wish I could make myself do that," I said.

"You actually can't taste it if you put enough fruit in. That's the key."

"I'd have to put a lot of fruit in to not taste kale. I don't think I'd be able to drink it all."

"You might be surprised," said Norah. "Listen, I wanted to thank you again for inviting Knox and me to supper club. We really had a good time Saturday night."

"Oh, I'm so happy to hear that. It was our pleasure." My insides clenched. Was she expecting to be invited back? Should I mention Knox and his... curiosity?

"I think maybe Knox got off on the wrong foot with Mr.—ah, Fish. Knox told me he met him at Dunleavy's Pub."

"Yeah, I think he mentioned that." I studied my smoothie.

"Knox has some issues," said Norah.

You are telling me. I tilted my head and gave her a sympathetic look that meant *that's just awful and I'm not going to pry but if you want to talk, I'll listen.*

"I think I mentioned that his parents are British. What I didn't say is that they are his adoptive parents. Knox was in the foster care system for several years."

"Oh no." I know there are many amazing foster parents. But it's the horror stories that stick with you.

"That's actually one of the things we bonded over in the beginning. We're both former foster children. We both have some scars from the experience."

"Norah, I had no idea." Bless her heart. And his too. Bless his perverted heart.

"How would you?" She smiled. "And Knox eventually ended up with a lovely family. But... the thing is, Knox can be a bit clingy to me and a bit insecure. He'd never admit it, but he tends to like it best when I don't have friends aside from him."

"That's just awful." I said it out loud that time. It was awful. And potentially indicated other awful things might be going on in their household.

"I bet you wonder why I'm telling you all this." Norah shook her head. "We're really just getting to know each other. I don't mean to overshare. It's just I want this to be our forever home. I want to put down roots, make friends, join a book club, get involved. That frightens Knox a bit. He worries I won't need him anymore."

"Ohhhh. Bless his heart." It really did soften my heart towards him even as my concerns grew. It was a sticky situation.

"He has many beautiful qualities, and I love him to distraction."

"Of course."

"But sometimes I want to wring his neck."

I nodded. "About that..."

She got this terrified look in her eyes. "What did he do?"

I winced. "Saturday night after dinner he asked me if I knew anything about the local sex club? Where people put their keys in a bowl and take someone else's..."

"Oh no." She set down her smoothie and pressed her eyebrows with her fingers. "I am so sorry. I can't believe—"

"Oh no... you don't have anything to be sorry about. I didn't know he was—"

"There's no excuse for that." She shook her head. "He knew we'd met on the trail and that you'd been the one to invite us to supper club. That was a deliberate effort to sabotage any friendship between the two of us."

"And did you know about the pound cake?" I might as well get it all out.

"Pound cake?" Her forehead creased in confusion.

I explained about what happened with Tallulah and Birdie when they tried to drop off the cake and invite them to supper club.

"I love pound cake," she said. "I cannot believe him. Every bit of that is made up. He just thought if people were nice enough to drop off a cake, maybe I'd be making friends and he wanted to nip that in the bud. He did this same exact thing with the neighbors in our building in New York. They couldn't even look me in the eye. I just really wanted things to be different here."

"It will be," I heard myself saying. Could he possibly be abusing her? Isolating their wives... that's what abusers did. But Norah was a US marshal... she was strong and capable... and yet I knew all kinds of women were abused.

"How can it? He's already managed to destroy every opportunity I might have to make new friends."

"That's not true at all." I reached out and put a hand on her arm. "Listen, maybe he just needs more time to see that friends aren't a threat to him. We need to get him some friends of his own. Who's he playing golf with anyway?"

"He went by himself."

"Now that's just so sad. I've never even heard of a man doing that. Don't they have to go in groups of four? I don't know the first thing about golf. Tucker tried to get me to learn to play, but really, I'm happy driving the cart or, better yet, staying home and reading a book."

"Yeah, that's one of the things Knox hopes I'll do when I retire, which he wishes I'd do right now. I think I'd rather have my thumb pierced."

"He should play with some of the guys. I know Vernon plays golf. Tucker does when he has the time, but he hasn't had much time for anything lately." Tucker had precious little free time. I was reasonably certain he didn't want to spend any of it with Knox Fitzgerald. But someone needed to befriend the man. "I'm honestly not sure about the rest of them. Listen, y'all come back to supper club in July. Let him get to know everyone a little better —maybe connect with Vernon."

"Oh no, we couldn't."

"Why on earth not?" I asked.

"You guys have been so welcoming, so kind. And he's behaved horribly. I am really sorry."

"I insist," I heard myself say. "I'll let you know if it's at Fish's house again or if we're going to be at Tallulah's. Y'all be there or we'll come and get you. I mean that now."

Tallulah was going to kill me, sure as the world. But Norah needed friends. She needed a strong support group, especially if it turned out her husband was abusive, which who knew if he was or he wasn't? He certainly was an odd duck, with some challenging issues. But Heaven knows, he wasn't unique in that regard. All God's children needed friends. Unless he was an abuser. Then he needed a jail cell.

Chapter Twenty-Three

Friday, July 8, 2022, 5:00 p.m.
Beach Cabana near Fish's House
Tallulah Wentworth

There were only four of them that day for happy hour: Tallulah, Birdie, Camille, and Sarabeth. Fish had an appointment in Charleston that afternoon and hadn't made it back in time, so Tallulah played bartender.

"I hope the gin and tonics are okay," said Tallulah. "I decided to keep things simple."

"They're delicious," said Camille. "Cheers."

"Cheers," everyone called out as they raised their tumblers.

For a few moments, they took in the afternoon sunshine glistening on the water and let the sound of waves frolicking on the sand soothe them. Tallulah loved sitting this close to the ocean. It was therapeutic, and the good Lord knew she needed therapy or something like it.

"Looks like we have the varsity squad here today," said Camille.

"I suppose that's one way to put it," said Birdie. "Were you ever a cheerleader, Camille?"

"I was," said Camille. "Rah-rah, rah-rah-rah, team, team, team!"

"Me too," said Birdie. "Of course, that was back before they did all the gymnastics. We did the occasional pyramid, but they were pretty tame. It wasn't an actual sport unto itself when I did it."

"Oh goodness, me either," said Camille. "I could turn a cartwheel, and that was somewhat remarkable back then."

"I twirled the baton," said Sarabeth. "Sometimes we soaked the ends of special batons in dry cleaning fluid overnight, then on Friday nights they'd turn out the lights in the football stadium, and we'd twirl fire at halftime."

"That sounds dangerous," said Tallulah. "I wasn't involved in any of that. I was focused on my studies, though I was editor of the school newspaper."

"I bet you were valedictorian, weren't you, Tallulah?" Sarabeth asked.

"As a matter of fact, I was." Tallulah smiled. "Seems like a lifetime ago.

"I suppose the younger crowd is busy with the kids this evening," Camille said.

"Cash is taking Hadley someplace special," Tallulah said.

"She's not the only one who's being squired around town." Camille looked at Tallulah over the tops of her sunglasses.

"Have you been seeing Tennyson?" Birdie asked.

"We've been out a time or two," Camille said like *it's no big deal*. "As a matter of fact, we saw Tallulah and Fish last night at Peninsula Grill."

Tallulah gave Camille a long, steady look. She'd seen Camille and Tennyson across the room. It didn't look as casual as Camille made it sound. How did she and Fish look? "We're just two old friends having dinner."

"Why is that, Tallulah?" Sarabeth asked gently. "If you don't mind my asking."

Tallulah stared at the Atlantic. "Henry was the great love of my life. I won't dishonor his memory."

"Oh, now wait just a minute," said Camille. "I loved my George to distraction. But I didn't die with him. He's in a better place, and one day hopefully I'll see him again. But it wouldn't dishonor him if I chose to remarry."

"I didn't mean that it would, Camille," said Tallulah. "Everyone has to decide these things for themselves. I think it's fine if you want to remarry."

"Well, thank you." Camille sniffed and raised her chin. "But I wasn't looking for your blessing."

Tallulah rolled her eyes elaborately. "I'm merely saying that just because I choose not to remarry and want to honor Henry, it doesn't mean I'm making any sort of statement about whatever you choose to do."

"Don't you think Henry would want you to be happy?" Sarabeth asked, her voice light and soothing.

"Of course he would." Tallulah kept her eyes on the foam-topped waves. "But I imagine he'd want me to be happy on my own. I'll see him again one day. I know I will. That's the only thought that sustained me in the beginning."

"Of course you will," Birdie said gently. "But, Tallulah, you know you won't be anyone's wife in the next life, not Henry's nor anyone else's. Marriage is for this world. You're still in it. Henry's not."

"Some people choose to remarry." Tallulah shrugged. "Others don't. I'm in the latter group. Why is this an issue for everyone?" She was starting to feel a bit defensive.

"We only want you to be happy," Sarabeth said.

"I *am* happy," Tallulah said. "I'm the very picture of jubilation most of the time, everyone knows that."

"Well, you might be even happier still if you allowed yourself the option of remarrying," Birdie said. "It seems like you've discarded the notion altogether. And I'm just saying, why not be open to the possibility? It doesn't take away from what you had with Henry, not at all. It just acknowledges that that part of your life, however beautiful, is over. Maybe it's time to move forward."

"I don't think people were meant to live alone," Sarabeth said.

Tallulah sighed. "I know this will come as a crushing disappointment, but we won't be putting it to a vote."

"I say we do." Camille grinned. "It's clear to me that you need some sort of intervention."

"Mind your own business, Camille." Tallulah's tone betrayed her increasingly testy mood.

"All right then," said Camille. "So I guess that means you're fine with me dating Fish? I mean, if you're not available, you wouldn't be so selfish as to stand in the way, would you?"

Tallulah stood. "I think I'd like to take a walk on the beach. I need to move around a bit. I'll be back shortly. There are refills in the cooler if anyone needs one."

Tallulah headed down the beach towards the lighthouse. Her emotions were all over the place. What business was it of anyone's if she chose not to remarry? Birdie was right though. Tallulah knew there was no marriage in Heaven. Was she being foolish, choosing to be alone and then feeling lonely most of the time?

One thing she knew for sure. She most certainly was not fine with Camille dating Fish. Not at all.

Chapter Twenty-Four

Wednesday, July 13, 2022, 7:15 a.m.
Bonus Room/Office
Boone Home I'On Avenue Sullivan's Island
Sarabeth Mercer Jackson Boone

I'd just gotten back from my morning walk on the beach, made my smoothie, grabbed my coffee, and settled in at my desk. Early in the morning, before I start work for the day, I look at the news and fiddle with social media while I have my smoothie. That morning I was trying a new one—Norah had given me the recipe, and it's a lot like the one Hadley makes with blueberries. It wasn't bad, maybe an acquired taste. But it did have a lot of brain-healthy things in it, including, yes, kale, so I was giving it a chance.

Now, we used to subscribe to the newspaper. It was delivered to the house. Tucker might see one of the neighbors as he stepped out to get ours, if Tucker happened to be home, and perhaps they'd say good morning or even stop for a chat. Tucker and I would pass the sections back and forth at the breakfast table. It was all quite civilized.

These days, I read the news on my iPad. I have digital subscriptions and apps, and they send me notifications constantly.

It can be annoying, and yes, I know I can turn the notifications off, but then I worry what if there's urgent news? Then again, I have no need to be this up-to-the-minute. It's not like there's anything I can do about any of it.

After I've been sufficiently traumatized by the morning news, I click over to scroll my Instagram feed. If you're an author, you have to be on social media. It's just a job requirement. And honestly, I enjoyed most of it. I just had to be careful to not spend too much time on it. You could lose a couple of hours if you weren't careful. I finished on Instagram, flipped over to Facebook, and started with my groups.

Most of the groups I'm in are book-related, some reader groups and some author groups, a few to do with recipes and cooking. But the first one that came up that morning was the one for Sullivan's Island locals.

Someone—not anyone I know—posted about the incident a couple of weeks ago where I ran across someone spraying what was likely herbicide on part of the town-owned property. The initial post was supportive, for which I was grateful. It just basically said shame on you, whoever you are, for trying to destroy something that doesn't belong to you. Forestation of the accreted land protects us all from storm surge, et cetera. And of course, the accreted land and everything that grows on it *is* owned by the town, and only the town can do anything with it, yada yada—I'm paraphrasing.

Actually, I'm not a hundred percent sure even the town can take plants out anymore. Seems like the last time they were going to, DHEC—the Department of Health and Environmental Control—got involved and permits were going to have to be issued. And then I read the Army Corps of Engineers was monitoring everything. I wouldn't be one bit surprised to hear Congress had gotten involved.

The thing is, for the record, I did sympathize with property owners whose lots keep moving farther from the beach. They had no legal right to remove anything growing between their property line and the ocean. I didn't blame them for being frustrated, especially the ones who had ocean views when they bought the property. And if they were paying taxes on that lot valued as ocean front... well, that just wasn't right, and it should be addressed.

But... I happened to believe the arguments for protecting the island from storm surges and so forth were more compelling arguments, especially in light of what happened during Hugo. That's just me, and I get one vote, just like everyone else who lives here.

And yes, I realized we all had our opinions, and we didn't all agree.

But there was just no excuse whatsoever for all the ugliness online.

Naturally, one of the folks in favor of the cutting responded to the very civil post with a civilly expressed, well-reasoned counterpoint about the underbrush and everything living there and how the rats drew snakes and so on. This was a valid concern that deserved serious solutions.

Well, that was the end of reason right there. The post and the first comment.

The next person allowed as to how I should mind my own business. Probably the person wearing the hazmat suit.

Then someone defended me saying we should all be willing to take a stand to protect the island and everyone who didn't enjoy the natural landscape should move elsewhere. I'm paraphrasing again. What was said wasn't *nearly* that civil.

Back and forth they went. Names were called. Lineage was maligned.

Multiple people suggested other places I would be happier living. My, my... how *considerate* of them to offer their suggestions.

Poor Frances hopped in to defend me, and someone told her she needed to move into assisted living—people her age shouldn't have a voice in what the future here would look like.

What on earth is wrong with people? When had it become

acceptable—even expected by some—that we disregard the humanity of people we disagree with?

That morning, there were four hundred and seventy-eight comments. Most of them should've been removed by a moderator if anyone wanted my opinion. But I understood they've gone through several moderators already, and people went completely crazy when their comments were deleted. Then they all turned against the moderator and started screaming about free speech and their constitutional rights.

I'm sorry, but some of our neighbors clearly didn't understand their right to free speech. That's between them and the government, not them and Facebook or any group moderator on Facebook. Now, the Supreme Court could rule and change things, but at that moment, social media companies were not bound by the first amendment, and neither were private groups on their platforms. And why, exactly, were people looking to cloak themselves in the first amendment so they could be as nasty as they liked anyway? Seriously.

Why couldn't we all just talk to one another face-to-face in a neighborly manner and work things out? Come to a compromise? What affliction caused full-grown people to lose their minds and spew all kinds of vitriol online? How did they justify that? I couldn't even look some of my neighbors in the eye anymore knowing what kinds of thoughts ran through their heads.

If you asked me, it was a sign of society's imminent collapse. I mean, it's one thing to keep up with your children who live on the other side of the country or your high school classmates who have scattered to the far corners of the earth with social media. It's quite another to use a Facebook group as a way to vent your frustrations at your neighbors, saying any mean thing that pops into your head because there's absolutely no filter on some people online. How had it come to this?

It's just like Tallulah was saying at supper club last month. It's just exactly like politics—worse.

I blame the Russians, possibly the Chinese.

Can I just tell you, on top of everything else going on in my life just then, I so did not need this stress? *I better check my blood pressure.*

Now, when I took a deep breath, I had to admonish myself of one salient fact—, okay, two: We lived in a magical seaside town. Most of our neighbors were kind, thoughtful, generous, wonderful people—people who brought pound cakes and invited you to supper club and looked out for one another.

There were a few bad apples whose mammas didn't raise them right who were creating all this drama. Unfortunately, those few miscreants on the lunatic fringe were creating havoc, as was so often the case.

Chapter Twenty-Five

Monday, July 18, 2022, 12:15 p.m.
Mex 1, Sullivan's Island
Libba Graham

Libba and Hadley sat at a high-top table on the deck at Mex 1, munching on chips and the triple dipper.

"I can't say I'm not relieved to not be going to a juice bar or one of those places that serves fake meat," said Libba.

"I don't eat fake meat," said Hadley. "It's less healthy for you than the actual meat in a lot of cases. Too much saturated fat, and it's highly processed. I avoid highly processed foods at all costs."

"Noted," said Libba. "I'm just trying to get full on chips and dip because I'm still not sold on cauliflower tacos."

"Just keep an open mind," said Hadley. "That's all I ask."

Libba made a face and loaded another chip with corn-and-black-bean salsa.

"How are you feeling? Has the new prescription helped any?"

Libba rolled her eyes. "If anything, my mood swings have gotten worse. This morning I had to call the insurance company —car and home. I'd gotten a cancellation notice in the mail, and I knew I had paid them. I just knew it. I had a receipt. Well, I've never had any patience with automated phone systems. I mean, whatever happened to customer service? They take up so much of my time making sure they don't have to spend a minute of theirs. By the time I finally got to talk to a person, my blood pressure was so high I'm lucky I didn't have a stroke. I was fit to be tied.

"Anyway, the woman I was talking to... oh my gosh. I probably drove her to have a nip from the bottle stashed in her desk drawer. I was, shall we say, venting my frustrations on her rather eloquently, if I do say so myself, when I looked down and noticed what I wish had caught my eye sooner. The receipt I had pulled from the file was from *last* year. The whole thing was completely my mistake. And I made an utter fool of myself and probably gave this poor woman a nervous breakdown on top of everything.

"I think she must've known I was on the brink and she felt sorry for me. There at the end she was all, 'I'm just so happy we could straighten this out,' and 'Is there anything else I can do to be of service today?' But I just felt like the world's biggest idiot."

"That kind of thing happens to everybody," said Hadley.

"Hmm... maybe. But then I took a hammer and bashed my computer senseless. Completely destroyed it."

"What did it do?" Hadley's eyes grew round.

"I could not make my keyboard work. All of a sudden, some of the keys worked, but others didn't. I turned it off and back on. But I had to press the button to do that because the keys I usually use didn't work. The third time I turned it on and couldn't do the simplest thing, I got one of Jake's hammers and just beat it to a pile of little plastic bits and glass and squiggles of wire."

"You know, next time call me. I'm not anybody's idea of a computer expert, but I know a thing or two. And maybe in the time it took me to get there you could've, I don't know, recentered or something, and we could've figured it out."

"Thanks, but it was really therapeutic, taking the hammer to it. I'm going to the Apple Store after lunch to get a new one."

Hadley shook her head. "What a waste, Libba."

"I know. I should be ashamed of myself. I could've donated it.

But it's like I'm telling you. I lose my mind several times a day." Libba's eyes filled with tears. "I get so angry. It just wells up inside me, and I can't control it. This is not me. I have never been this way. And a little while later, it's all sunshine and flowers. The distance between the highs and the lows gives me whiplash. And none of this is helping things with Jake."

"I still say you need to see a different doctor," said Hadley. "They all have different areas of expertise. Maybe this one is good at surgery but not so great at balancing your hormones afterwards."

"I guess I don't have anything to lose," said Libba. "Maybe I will. I have to try something."

"So... supper club was weird."

"Yeah... what did you think of the Fitzgeralds?" asked Libba.

"They both seemed really nice," said Hadley. "If Knox is some sort of crusader for the cutters, he left that at home. Do you think they're coming back?"

"Who knows? As far as I know, Sarabeth just invited them for the one time, but then again, they know it's a regular thing, and Tallulah and Birdie did invite them to join. Maybe." Libba shrugged.

"I'd like to find out, nonchalantly, if Quinn's parents are on her radar," said Hadley. "Quinn's really freaked out, and I'm thinking it's probably for nothing. I mean, it just seems to me like US marshals wouldn't pussyfoot around. If she was here to check on Quinn's parents, she'd knock on the door and tell them to straighten up and fly right."

"Have you ever met Quinn's parents?" asked Libba.

"No, have you?"

"I met them Arbor Day with Sarabeth. From what I understand, they've kept to themselves pretty much until fairly recently. I mean, they're not recluses or anything. They just never really socialized much. They're a cute couple—really youthful. What was it Quinn told you they did for a living before they moved here?"

"I promised her confidentiality," said Hadley. "But I know she talked to you about this, and we all discussed it together the other night, so I guess it's okay. She said they were art dealers."

"Interesting," said Libba. "They must've been really good at it to make enough money to retire here—in one of the most expensive places to live in the country—when Quinn was a child. They would still have been pretty young."

Hadley made a face like something bothered her. "Yeah, I guess so."

"Do you think they were... I don't know, maybe mixed up with the guy they testified against? Like maybe their fortune wasn't completely amassed through strictly legal methods?" Libba wasn't judging them. Everyone made mistakes. But if they weren't simply innocent bystanders, did that change anything? Did someone watch them more closely?

"Who knows?" said Hadley. "They may have made some sort of deal for immunity. I think that's pretty common."

A server set their tacos in front of them, refilled their water, and asked if they needed anything else.

"No." Hadley smiled. "These look great, thanks." Her grin widened as she watched Libba give her plate a wary look, then poke at her tacos with her fork.

"Cauliflower... in a taco."

Hadley picked up one of hers and took a bite. "Ummm."

"Okay, fine." Libba picked up one of her tacos and tasted it. She chewed, her expression flipping from skeptical to okay maybe to wow. "Oh my gosh!"

"I know, right?" said Hadley.

"It's actually good," said Libba.

"I told you."

"Yeah, but I didn't believe you."

"You should learn to trust me more."

For a few minutes, they both focused on their lunch. If Libba hadn't been so wrapped up in her own troubles, she might've noticed something was clearly on Hadley's mind.

Chapter Twenty-Six

The O'Leary home occupied a half-acre lot on I'on Avenue between Station 27 and Station 28. It wasn't a fancy place. It had the look of an old-fashioned beach house—white-painted wood, one-story, raised, with wide porches front and back. Quinn had always loved that house, modest though its size may be. It was the first place they'd lived that was a real home to her that she was old enough to remember. Built in 1920, it had weathered its share of storms. But it was solid, well constructed, and had been lovingly updated several times now, most recently by her mother, who had impeccable taste, an artist's eye, and an eclectic style that might've been a blend of coastal and bohemian.

That morning, Quinn was in her favorite spot, the back porch swing. Two sprawling live oak trees shaded the backyard, and the back of the house was still comfortable, though the high that day was supposed to be well into the nineties and the air was thick and heavy with humidity. A ceiling fan swirled the jasmine-scented air.

Her parents occupied the cushioned love seat that sat at a right angle to the swing.

"What has you so upset, Katie Quinn?" her dad, Finn, asked. "As happy as we are to see you, you don't typically drop by on a random Thursday morning. And you're fidgeting like an eight-year-old in need of her Adderall."

"Finn." Her mamma, Myrna, tilted her head and gave him a look.

He issued a long-suffering sigh, widened his eyes, and looked sideways like he was thinking, *women*.

"Talk to us, sweetie." Her mamma reached out and squeezed her hand, then had to let it go because Quinn pushed her feet against the floor to keep the swing swinging.

"I'm just so, so worried about the two of you," said Quinn.

"Us? Why?" They spoke over each other, both looking at her with baffled expressions.

"Because you're becoming the topic of gossip lately. So much gossip. What were you thinking with that spectacle at the ice-cream parlor?"

"Well, now—" her dad started.

"That's between the two of us." Her mamma straightened.

"If only that were true," said Quinn. "Whatever was going on, you shared it with everyone. This is a small town. News travels fast, especially news that entertaining."

"I'm sorry if we embarrassed you," said her mamma, in a tone that let Quinn know she absolutely did not mean it, and what's more, she was offended by the whole conversation.

"Mamma, listen." Quinn stopped the swing. "I'm glad the two of you are getting out and making friends. The Arbor Day thing—at first that worried me, I'll admit, but that was probably fine. But you can't be making spectacles of yourselves. People will talk."

"Let them," scoffed her mamma.

"Really? *Really*? Are you serious? You can't be." Quinn looked at both of them like they'd lost their minds. "All my life, you've impressed upon me how important it was we keep a low profile. Our safety depended upon it, you said. People would always be looking for you, and if they found you, they'd kill us all. *This* is what I've lived with since I was eleven years old." Her voice was getting louder.

"Katie Quinn, calm yourself," said her dad.

"I'm sorry we gave you such a difficult life." Her mamma raised her chin and turned her head.

"Oh no... no." Quinn shook her head. "No. You don't get to act like I'm being ungrateful. I have lived most of my life in fear of our being discovered and killed in our beds. That's a real thing, not some made-up childhood nightmare about monsters under the bed. These monsters are all too real. You made me understand that as a child. And I can't for the life of me understand why all of a sudden, the two of you are acting like I'm overreacting. Like I'm building this into something it's not. Both of you know that's not the case. What are you two *thinking*?"

Her dad sighed. "Ah, Katie Quinn, I guess the truth of it all is that we're tired of lying low. We're been doing it a very long time, and it's not really in our nature at all. Your mother and I are passionate people. Perhaps this is making us a little crazy after all these years."

"Is this some kind of late-in-life crisis?" Quinn asked.

"Hey, what do you mean by that?" Her mamma looked offended.

"Oh my—"

"Age is just a number," said her dad. "And we are dedicated to staying young and not acknowledging the numbers."

"Well, could you possibly do it more quietly?" asked Quinn. "Because if the two of you are outed and you get relocated... I am a thirty-six-year-old woman now. I have a husband and children. If the two of you get sent to Phoenix or Idaho or wherever, guess what? I won't be going with you this time."

"That's not going to happen," said her mamma.

"Mamma, I might never see y'all again." Tears filled Quinn's eyes. "And what about me... and Oliver, your grandson? And Redmond and the twins? The people who are hunting you would likely kill us all for spite."

Her mamma stood and crawled into the swing with her and put her arms around her. "No, no, no. Quinn, sweetie, you are overreacting here. That is not going to happen. We are not going anywhere. No one is going to hurt you and Oliver and Redmond and the twins."

"How can you say that?" The volume on Quinn's voice rose again.

Quinn's dad climbed into the swing with them and wrapped his arms around her. "Let's make a Katie Quinn sandwich. It's all going to be okay, me darlin'."

Quinn eyed her dad. Sometimes he embellished his accent to the point he sounded like the Lucky Charms commercial. "I just wish I could be sure of that."

"You know," said her dad, "I haven't heard from anyone from our past life in so long. And the mob boss—the guy we testified against—he was old back then. Probably dead by now. Probably died in prison years ago."

"Wouldn't someone have told you that?" asked Quinn.

"Eh, maybe, maybe not," said her dad. "Perhaps I'll look into it if it would ease your mind."

"Well, certainly it would ease my mind to know we were out of danger."

Quinn's mom nodded. "Me too. Finn, why don't you make some phone calls. Set all our minds at ease."

"You could probably just ask our new neighbor," said Quinn. "I'm sure she could check for us." Quinn wouldn't dare talk to Norah without their blessing. But what if they gave it? Maybe there was a simple way for all of them to get some peace of mind.

Her dad gave her a confused look. "What do you mean by that?"

"Norah Fitzgerald," said Quinn. "She's a US marshal. She and her husband just bought a house over on Conquest. I thought...

It scared me when I found out she was with the marshal's service. I figured she was here to check up on us. And then the two of you were making public scenes..."

She looked from her mamma to her dad. They'd both gone quiet.

"No, I'm sure that's not the case," said her mom.

"Absolutely not," said her dad. "We have an assigned contact. They don't just send people around to make sure you're behaving."

Quinn felt her brow furrow. "You always told me that's exactly what they do."

"Well, yes," said her mamma. "But it's the people you know. They'd send the marshal who's assigned to us if there was a problem."

"Who is that?" Quinn asked.

"He's an old man," said her dad. "With white hair. Name's John Walters. Probably nearly as old as your ancient parents. Definitely not this Norah. And believe you me. If there was a problem, John would have let us know."

"So you don't think it's odd there's a US marshal living here now?" asked Quinn. "You're saying it has nothing to do with us?"

"Absolutely nothing," they said in unison.

Quinn sighed. "I feel like there's something you're not telling me." But then she'd felt that way her whole life. Her parents were so wrapped up in each other she always felt like she was on the outside.

"Well, there's not." Her mamma hugged her tighter.

Quinn pulled away. "I need to run inside a minute and freshen up."

She stood and made her way to the powder room.

On her way back outside a few moments later, she stopped to admire the gallery wall in her parents' great room. They'd always loved impressionist and postimpressionist paintings—had dealt in them for years—but could never in their wildest dreams afford the real thing. Three reproductions lined the gallery wall. Quinn had never studied art. It wasn't her passion the way it was her parents', and she didn't know much about it. But the vibrant colors always lifted her spirts.

Maybe Norah's being here had nothing to do with Quinn and her family. But she needed some reassurance that their lives weren't about to be upended. Hopefully her dad would come through on that score. But Quinn knew either way she was going to have to talk to Redmond, and she dreaded it. She couldn't live with the secret anymore. Maybe finally telling Hadley and Libba had emboldened Quinn. She did feel better, a bit. But she needed to share this particular burden with the man she shared her life with. Someone who, unlike her parents, always demonstrated he had her best interests at heart, always. She should never have listened to her parents to begin with. She had to make this right and pray Redmond could get past it for all their sakes.

Three Months before the Fall Meet and Greet

Chapter Twenty-Seven

Saturday, July 30, 2022, 5:00 p.m.
Monthly Meeting of the Sullivan's Island Supper Club—
Happy Hour
Home of Fish Aiken
Sarabeth Mercer Jackson Boone

July was so hot no one felt like cooking. Tallulah surprised us all and held supper club at Fish's house again and told everyone to remember to bring a swimsuit. The theme was Summer Salads, and everyone brought their favorite. To be honest, I wasn't sure it was a good thing how much control Tallulah was relinquishing two months in a row. I worried she was losing interest in supper club altogether, and it had been her raison d'être for as long as I'd known her. On the other hand, the heat was making everyone sluggish. Perhaps that's all it was.

Fish's house being oceanfront meant that the breeze off the water kept us cooler there than anywhere else outdoors. We were all on the pool deck again for drinks and apps, but at Fish's insistence, Tallulah had relented and let him serve gin and tonics and ranch water, two of our warm-weather favorites, from the pool house bar. Camille did the appetizers that night, three different kinds of skewers: watermelon feta, melon prosciutto, and caprese bites. I had found myself a spot in one of the hammocks and was relaxing, sipping on a gin and tonic and not really pining for company, when Birdie walked my way.

"I hope things have settled down for you," she said. "I heard things escalated online and got out of hand. I declare, I don't know what's wrong with people."

"I've left the Facebook group. I don't know what they're saying about me anymore. Frankly, I have bigger things to worry about. Although I would very much like to catch whoever is piling their doggie waste into my yard."

"You don't mean it." Birdie gasped.

"I'm afraid I do. Some the 'gifts' are in the little doggie waste disposal bags with messages written on them like GBWYFCF and MYOFB. We've worked it out. We think they mean 'Go back where you flippin' came from,' and 'Mind your own flippin' business.' Oh, and then there are the big piles of mess *not* in bags that we have to scoop up and dispose of."

"Oh, Sarabeth. How awful."

I nodded and felt myself tearing up. "It is truly one of the worst things that's happened. We wanted so much to be a part of things here, make this authentically our home. And to have some of our neighbors do such a disgusting thing..." I shook my head. "I just can't hardly bear it."

"Have you reported it to the police?"

"Tucker did. He's mad as fire, naturally. He's installed a few outdoor cameras to try to catch whoever is doing it."

"Well, I hope he gets pictures of the culprits soon," said Birdie. "Probably teenagers."

"You think?" I squinted at her. "My guess is it's whoever was in that hazmat suit and all their friends. We've gotten quite a few of those little messages every day for the past month. Most teenagers I know aren't that committed to anything aside from their Snapchat or what have you."

"You have a point," said Birdie. "Did the police ever identify the person wearing the hazmat suit?"

"Not that they've shared with me," I said. "Apparently the people who live in the house right in front of where the spraying was going on were out of the country, on a river cruise in Europe."

"I guess their alibis are solid then. Of course, they could've hired someone to do it."

"Or simply arranged for a friend or like-minded neighbor to take care of it," I said. What I left unsaid was that if I were the police, I'd be asking Vernon Markley what he knew about this. It was just crazy enough to be something Vernon would do. And he had well-documented issues with the flora growing between the first-row houses and the beach.

Birdie seemed to think that over for a minute, then she said, "Bless your heart, you don't need this to worry about on top of everything else. Did you find someone to fix your foundation?"

My stomach roiled. Tucker had to take money out of his 401(k) to fund the foundation repairs. "We did, thank you. Luke—the same guy who did our bathroom remodel—he's going to take care of it for us. His was the best quote, and his plan to fix it was exactly what the engineer recommended, only Luke never saw the engineer's report. We feel pretty good about him."

"Well," said Birdie, "I just hope this is the last of your troubles with the house."

"Me too, Birdie." I worried most about Tucker's stress level. Maybe when these repairs were finished, we should just sell the blooming house. Not doing the repairs wasn't an option, though everyone agreed the house had likely been off its foundation for years. But now that we knew about it, we couldn't sell it without disclosing the problem, and of course most buyers would insist something like that were fixed, but they'd still pay less for the house. As much as I loved Sullivan's Island and my friends here, I spent a lot of time wishing we'd stayed in Summerville. Our magical seaside empty nest had morphed into a full house of horrors.

Birdie scanned the pool deck, her gaze landing on Vernon, who was having an animated conversation with Knox. "I'd better go see what's going on over there."

I watched her walk away, thinking if it had been Vernon in that hazmat suit, I believed I was happier not knowing it. But surely he wouldn't have anything to do with putting dog mess in our yard. Vernon was our friend.

But some of his friends were definitely not our friends. But they were our neighbors.

Chapter Twenty-Eight

Saturday, July 30, 2022, 6:00 p.m.
Monthly Meeting of the Sullivan's Island Supper Club—Dinner
Home of Fish Aiken
Libba Graham

Libba wondered why Tallulah had gone to the trouble of having the long table she'd only bought last month removed from Fish's back porch. She'd replaced it with four tables of four, which was a departure from her typical setup. It likely had something to do with the Fitzgeralds.

After perusing all the salads on the buffet, Libba put a large serving of the Carolina shrimp salad she'd brought on her plate with just a touch of dressing, then added a small serving of a black-bean-mango salad Hadley had made. Anything Hadley brought would be healthy, they could all depend on that. Libba's mouth watered at the macaroni salad and the potato salad—she loved them both. They looked like the traditional, mayonnaise-dressed versions her mamma had always made—but Libba held on to her willpower and passed them both by. She added a scant spoonful of the pasta pesto salad to her plate, then found her place at table three with Jake, Norah, and Knox, which was perfectly fine with her.

Jake stood and held her chair for her, then lightly brushed her arm as he moved back to his seat.

A familiar but long-absent thrill shot through Libba like she'd grabbed ahold of a live wire.

For the first time in... she couldn't recall how long, she looked at her husband with lust in her heart.

Oh. My.

The new hormones. They must be starting to work. She'd seen a new doctor on Tuesday, with little enthusiasm but as sort of a Hail Mary. Dr. Giovanni had prescribed a blend of hormones with some testosterone in them. Who knew your ovaries produced a small amount of testosterone?

PRAISE THE LORD. Libba was horny.

Jake gave her a quizzical look. She flashed him a sly little smile. He smiled back but wore a confused look. Libba could well understand why. Oh please let this last. Let this be the beginning of things returning to normal in their bedroom. That would be a solid start.

Yes, she still had suspicions about Jake's relationship with Roxie. But the first thing she needed to do was get to feeling like her old self, then get her marriage back on track. She loved her husband, and she would fight for him if she had to. But first things first.

"So." Jake looked from Knox to Norah. "I'd ask if the two of you had big plans for retirement, but since Norah hasn't retired... how does that work exactly? Aren't you bored at home alone all day, man? At least tell me you have some interesting hobbies."

Knox laughed. "I've tried my best to get her to join me, but for some reason, the prospect of my company all day terrifies my wife."

"I wouldn't say it terrifies me exactly." Norah smiled. "Maybe I'm afraid you'll get bored with me."

"Oh, if Jake ever retires, I'll have to get a job," Libba said.

"Is that a fact?" Jake smiled at her. He seemed to be picking up on her playful mood.

"You know it." Please God, let this feeling last. Let her return to her normal self.

"I've tried playing a bit of golf," said Knox. "But most of the people I've met here are either not golfers or not retired or they don't live here full time. It's been a challenge."

"I like golf," said Jake. "I just don't have enough time for it to get very good at it. I'll play with you if you have absolutely no talent for it whatsoever."

"None, I'm afraid," said Knox. "Where do you normally play?"

"Wild Dunes is the most convenient, so usually there."

"Let me know what works for you. My schedule is fairly open."

"How about Saturday?" Jake said.

"Fantastic." Knox looked happier than Libba could recall seeing him.

"I'll set up a tee time," said Jake.

Norah was all smiles too. Libba met her glance across the table and read relief in her eyes.

"What else do you guys like to do?" Libba stabbed a shrimp and popped it in her mouth.

"We were getting out on our bikes a lot," said Norah, "before it got so freakin' hot. And we've spent some time exploring Charleston and the surrounding area."

"We've been exploring some of the local art galleries," said Knox. "And of course, Gibbes Museum."

"You looking for pieces for your new house?" asked Libba.

"We're always looking," said Norah.

"So you're collectors then?" asked Jake.

Knox tilted his head and made a face. "You might say that, I suppose. We have one or two pieces we acquired in the city that turned out to be good investments."

"We just like having pretty things on the walls," said Norah.

"Did you ever find the guy you were looking for," asked Jake. "The one with the stolen painting? A Van Gogh, wasn't it?"

Norah froze, then seemed to relax. "Not yet."

"Someone around here stole a Van Gogh?" asked Libba.

"No, no." Norah shook her head. "But a fugitive in a mess of a case involving bank fraud and art theft, who we suspect is in the area, is believed to have a Van Gogh that was stolen from a museum in Egypt in 2010. I asked Jake if he saw the painting when he was in a client's home. But it turns out that particular gentleman isn't our fugitive after all."

"What an interesting job you have." Libba missed her own job, and it did require an artistic eye. Maybe the kids were old enough now. Was it time to reclaim her career even if she had to start over—surely she wouldn't have to start all the way over. She needed to talk to Jake about this.

"Some days it is," said Norah. "And some days it's tedious, just like everyone else's job."

Jake's leg brushed Libba's under the table.

She caught her breath.

How early could they leave and not cause comment?

Chapter Twenty-Nine

Saturday, July 30, 2022, 7:00 p.m.
Monthly Meeting of the Sullivan's Island Supper Club—Dessert
Home of Fish Aiken
Quinn Poinsett

Quinn bit into her peaches-and-cream Popsicle. What a fantastic idea. Birdie had made homemade ice cream again, but to make it different—and allow them all to take their dessert back to the pool deck—she'd created a variety of gourmet Popsicles: coconut-chocolate-caramel cashew, tahini honey-roasted fig, banana-strawberry cheesecake, and peaches and cream, which was the vegan flavor. Quinn had tried one of each, and the peaches and cream were her favorite. She and Hadley shared a hammock and polished off their treats while Redmond and Cash perched on the shelf inside the pool with the rest of the guys drinking after-dinner bourbon.

"I cannot believe I ate four Popsicles," said Quinn. "I have never had seconds on dessert—let alone fourths—in my life."

"These things are addictive," said Hadley. "Besides, we had salad for dinner, so you're allowed."

Norah and Libba meandered over to join them. "Are you guys going swimming?" asked Norah.

"Swimming, no," said Quinn. "I think I'll change and go sit in the water like the guys are doing. I have to admit, that looks inviting." Quinn had heard nothing from her dad. It had been radio silence since he agreed to check in with the marshal's service and see what he could find out about the mobster her parents had testified against. She wanted to wait to talk to Redmond, hoping she'd have more information to share, an update. Or was she procrastinating yet again? She was petrified of his reaction. Was it better to live with the secret and the fear he might leave her, or tell him the truth and live with the consequences? And what would be the cost to him of knowing the truth? Even if he stayed, would he have as many sleepless nights after learning what threatened them as she did?

"Yeah, me too," said Hadley. "In a minute. Right now I'm loving this hammock."

"Let me pitch you an idea while you swing," said Norah.

Quinn and Hadley looked at her expectantly.

"I know Tallulah organizes supper club, but I was hoping to get your buy-in on coming to our house next month," said Norah.

"Ah—" Quinn felt like a possum in the headlights. There was no precedent whatsoever for anyone else making any arrangements at all for supper club. And Norah was still very new, and frankly, only here because Sarabeth kept inviting her and Tallulah couldn't figure a graceful way out of it. Quinn turned to Hadley.

"That sounds fun," said Hadley. "I bet Tallulah would appreciate someone else doing it once a while. It's got to be a lot of work."

Quinn squinted at Hadley. "You know as well as I do that Tallulah relishes being in charge of supper club. It's her baby."

"That's true," said Hadley, "but I also know it must be stressful doing all that every month. She should spread some of that around. Put the rest of us to work."

"We haven't had anyone over since we moved in," said Norah. "I'd love for you guys to be the first."

"It's fine by me," said Libba. "If you can talk Tallulah into it, that is. But Quinn's right. It's always been her pet project."

"Leave Tallulah to me," said Hadley. "I bet I can gentle her into it."

"I will take that bet," said Quinn. "I think you've lost your mind."

"We shall see." Hadley exchanged a glance with Norah.

What was going on between the two of them? Quinn wondered.

"Knox and I have a small art collection," said Norah. "It's a shame for no one else to enjoy these pieces. Having supper club will allow us to show them off. And... it will help me to integrate my skittish husband into polite society. Really, guys. I could use your help."

"What sort of art do you collect?" asked Quinn. "My parents were dealers when I was a child. That was their occupation before they retired anyway. They specialized in impressionist and postimpressionist painters." The second the words were out of her mouth, Quinn panicked. What on earth compelled her to mention her parents to Norah of all people? But if Norah were there to investigate them, she well knew who they were, so did it really make any difference? Was she subconsciously trying to bring things to a head? Maybe. Or maybe all this had been eating at her so much it just popped out.

"Really?" Norah smiled. "I'd love to get their opinion on a piece we have. It's a bit controversial."

"You have controversial art?" asked Libba. "I definitely want to see that."

"Me too," said Hadley. "It's not obscene, is it?"

"Obscenely expensive," said Norah. "We like postimpressionist painters. This piece is a vase of five sunflowers, and the dealer we bought it from insisted it was a Van Gogh, though it's never been authenticated. Supposedly it was a near duplicate of

Six Sunflowers, which was destroyed during World War II in Ashiya, Japan, in a bombing raid."

"Why wouldn't the previous owner have tried to get someone to determine if it was real or not?" asked Libba. "Surely he could've gotten way more money that way."

"Exactly," said Norah. "We've always assumed it was *not* a Van Gogh for that reason. I mean, come on. But... it really does look like his work. I'd love to see what Quinn's parents think—get their expert opinions."

Quinn tried to focus on her breathing so as not to hyperventilate. Why oh why had she opened her mouth? Her heart raced. Her blood pressure must've skyrocketed. She felt sick to her stomach. Was she having some sort of seizure?

"Seems like a lot of painters would've tried to paint like Van Gogh over the years," said Hadley. "I bet there are a lot of Van Gogh lookalikes."

"Exactly," said Norah. "But it makes for great dinner party conversation."

"Quinn, you okay?" Hadley scrutinized Quinn. "You went white all of a sudden."

"I just had too many Popsicles." Quinn climbed out of the hammock. "Excuse me." She scooted towards the pool house and the closest bathroom.

Chapter Thirty

Saturday, July 30, 2022, 9:15 p.m.
Monthly Meeting of the Sullivan's Island Supper Club—Dinner
Home of Fish Aiken
Tallulah Wentworth

Tallulah and Fish said goodbye to the last of their friends just before nine o'clock. She hadn't felt like getting into the pool earlier, but now she fancied a swim. She changed into her teal one-piece suit in the pool house and walked towards the zero-entry saltwater pool. It was so near the ocean it almost seemed like a part of it. With soft moonlight glinting on the surface of the Atlantic spotlighting the foam atop the waves, it was as if the ocean beckoned her. Tallulah would never get in the ocean, not in the daytime, and certainly never at night. But this bit of salt water hosted no creatures with sharp teeth.

Fish was already relaxing on one of the foam floating mats. "Want me to grab another raft?"

My goodness, Fish was a fine figure of a man stretched out on that lounger in his swim trunks. His body, toned and tanned, testified to the hours he spent in the gym. He'd aged quite well. "No, thank you. I feel like bobbing a bit."

"I thought tonight went well," he said.

"Better than expected," said Tallulah. "After last month, I was worried when Sarabeth told me she'd invited the Fitzgeralds back. But it worked out all right. He's not so bad really."

Fish gave a little side nod indicating he conceded the point. "Maybe he's not the insufferable lout I originally thought."

"I'd like to think we helped steer him in a better direction," said Tallulah. "Our Camille seems to have given up wrestling me for a spot on your dance card." There'd been a moment when Tallulah felt like there might be a rift in her relationship with Camille. She'd brazenly challenged her about dating Fish but then backed off. Tallulah assumed Tennyson was the reason. He must've been pursing Camille, which suited Tallulah just fine.

"I'd say Tennyson has her full attention these days," said Fish.

Tallulah splashed him. "Does that tweak your ego?"

"Hey," Fish protested. "Hardly. I like Camille. She's a friend. I've never minded being her escort. But there's no question whose company I prefer."

Tallulah smiled, feeling suddenly shy. What was wrong with her? "I think I will get that float."

"I'll get it for you."

She waved him off. "You're comfortable. I'll grab it."

She waded out of the pool and grabbed a raft from the wooden float corral near the potting shed. She tossed it into the pool, made her way back around, sloshed back into the water, and climbed onto the lounger. A billion diamonds were scattered across the night sky. The warm breeze off the ocean caressed her skin, the salty air stirring the jasmine, their fragrances mingling. They floated in companionable silence for a while.

"This is heavenly," said Tallulah.

"Indeed. Tallulah?"

"Mmm-hmmm?"

"I've enjoyed our dinners alone of late," said Fish.

"Me too. I love supper club, but I do enjoy the opportunity to have a deeper conversation. It's difficult to do that in a large group, especially when one has hostess obligations."

"So you're okay with it then?" asked Fish.

"Whatever do you mean? Okay with what?" Tallulah arched her neck to look at him upside down.

"Our dating."

Tallulah bolted upright on the float, then fell off into the pool, going all the way under. Seconds later, she popped back up, splashing wildly, her hair, previously untouched by water, now all in her eyes and dripping water. "We're not *dating*. Whatever gave you that idea?" She swiped the hair from her eyes.

"Well..." Fish gestured as if handing her the answer. "I picked you up and took you out to restaurants, just the two of us. We had lovely dinners, lots of interesting conversation, some reminiscing. We're seeing each other a couple of times a week, just the two of us, aside from time with the group. What would you call it?"

"I'd call it friends having dinner. Why does it have to be anything more than that?"

Fish winced. "It doesn't have to be, Tallulah. I just thought that it was."

She could tell she'd hurt him, and that hurt her. But it seemed important to clear things up. She was loyal to Henry's memory... She could hear Birdie in her head, reminding her of what she already knew... that there was no marriage in the next life. She shooed that thought away. "Why would you think that?"

"Perhaps because I wanted it to be."

Tallulah was having a hard time catching her breath. "Fish, I —" What was wrong with her? Was she making a huge mistake? Was it silly to continue holding a candle for one's late husband?

"It's all right, Tallulah." His eyes were soft and kind. He spoke gently to her, as if he were soothing a skittish horse.

"I don't think it is. I just... You know Henry was... you know what he was to me." But Henry was gone. He wouldn't be coming back. And when she saw him again—and she knew she would—he would no longer be her husband.

"Of course, Tallulah. I'm not trying to take Henry's place. No one could ever do that, and I probably know that better than most."

"Well, what then?" Tallulah realized she sounded hopeful. Did she want him to convince her?

"Well, I think Henry would be the first one to tell you that you shouldn't be alone. He's been gone now for more than six years. I don't think we're meant to live alone, any of us, and I've spent most of my life that way. I feel like I'm finally getting it right, after all these years. I missed my chance when we were young. I thought we had all the time in the world. But no one ever really does. That's an illusion of youth."

Everything was roiling inside Tallulah. She needed a towel and a glass of water. She headed out of the pool. Henry wouldn't want her to be alone. She had imposed that on herself.

"Tallulah, wait." He slid off the float and followed her.

She kept moving. The sound of waves breaking gently on the sand and the moonlight on the water made her dizzy, or maybe lightheaded. She was having some sort of transcendent episode, like she was watching them on a movie screen. Something inside her was unfolding, blooming.

She'd made it to dry ground and taken two steps towards the pool house when Fish caught up to her. He laid a hand gently on her arm and she stopped walking. Something fluttered in her chest.

He rubbed her arm, and she gasped as warm honey washed through her, unleashing passion that had long been dormant. How? Why? She hadn't expected to ever feel this again.

She turned and looked up at him and was lost in his kind blue eyes.

He held her by the shoulders, at arm's length. "I will never push you somewhere you don't want to go. You understand that, right?"

She nodded. She'd lost the capacity to think about anything but him and his strong arms.

He cupped her face in his hands. "But I will do everything in my power to make you want me. To make you choose us." And before she found her wits, he kissed her and she was lost.

When he pulled back, there was a question in his eyes.

She nodded.

And then he picked her up and carried her towards the pool house.

"Fish! You're courting a heart attack before we've even gotten to the bedroom. Put me down. Men your age shouldn't—"

"Hush woman." He chuckled. "I've been training for this moment for years now."

Chapter Thirty-One

Wednesday, August 10, 2022, 10:00 a.m.
O'Leary Home
Quinn Poinsett

"So, to be clear, we're not being invited to *join* your supper club?" asked her father.

It was too hot that morning, even in the shade of the backyard, to be outside. The three of them sat in the bright, airy great room, with the air-conditioning turned to frigid, or maybe it was just that Quinn was shivering from nerves. Her emotions were all over the place. On the one hand, this idea of inviting her parents into her friend set—especially at Norah's house—was the worst possible idea that could easily blow up her entire world. The entire affair was against her better judgment. Quinn should never have mentioned it. She should've lied and told everyone her parents declined the invitation.

On the other hand, after living in a state of constant anxiety for so long, unable to put things right because she was literally immobilized by her various fears, she had a bizarre compulsion to see where this all led. It felt inevitable. Or maybe she was a coward and this was her easy way out. The way to make something happen without confronting her problem head-on. Was she a coward? All Quinn knew for sure was that she was near her breaking point.

"No," said Quinn. "It's a onetime invitation. The Fitzgeralds are hosting supper club, and you're invited to join us for purposes of looking at their art collection. I told them I didn't think you'd want to come—"

"Why on earth would you say that?" demanded her mamma.

"Because my whole life, I have never known the two of you to attend a dinner party. Because you don't generally enjoy the company of strangers, or acquaintances for that matter. I've never actually known either of you to have friends."

"That's harsh," said her father.

Quinn closed her eyes, blew out a breath, then gathered herself. "I apologize. I didn't mean to sound harsh. But you have to admit, you guys don't socialize—ever."

"Fair enough," said her father. "Tell me more about the painting."

"They have several," said Quinn. "A small collection, Norah called it. Most of the pieces are impressionist or postimpressionist—"

"Get to the Van Gogh." Her dad made a rolling motion with his hand.

"It's highly unlikely, of course, that it is actually a Van Gogh," said her mamma.

"Exactly," said Quinn. "*Very* unlikely. I had the impression they know it's not. It just makes for interesting dinner conversation."

"But is it a portrait? A landscape? A still life?" asked her dad.

"It's a vase of five sunflowers," said Quinn. "Supposedly painted around the same time as the other sunflower paintings."

"Five sunflowers?" Her dad's voice crackled with excitement. "There are seven known versions of sunflowers in a vase. None of them have five flowers." He locked eyes with Quinn's mother.

"We have a reproduction of *Three Sunflowers in a Vase*," said her mamma. "The original was purchased by a private collector in 1996. *Six Sunflowers* was destroyed in World War II, in a bombing raid in Japan. Then there were five versions of *Sunflowers* with twelve to fifteen flowers. I've never heard anyone mention a vase with five sunflowers."

"It was very likely painted by some wannabe," said Quinn. "I'm sure it's nothing to get excited over."

"You don't want us to come then?" said her mamma, her voice laced with hurt and accusation.

"It's not that, Mamma," said Quinn. "But think about it. Norah is a US marshal. I should think you'd want to steer as clear of her as possible." Quinn had lost her mind. That was the only possible explanation for her mentioning this to her parents.

"Now why on earth would you say that?" her father asked. "She clearly has no professional interest in us. If she did, we surely would've heard from her by now. She's our neighbor, who happens to have a job with the marshal's service. Nothing more."

Was it Quinn's imagination, or did her mamma look queasy? "Mamma?"

"What?" Myrna's tone was cranky. "It feels like you're ashamed of us."

"Don't be ridiculous," said Quinn. "I'm trying to protect you. Protect all of us."

"Quinn, I think your obsession with this woman is unhealthy," said her mamma.

"I'm not *obsessed* with her," said Quinn. "Did you call your contact? Find out anything about the guy you sent to prison?"

"Hmm?" Her father seemed lost in thought. "Oh... No. It slipped my mind. But honestly, Quinn, there's nothing you need to be worried about. And I think it would be good for your mother and me to get out a bit, meet some of the neighbors. You're right, of course. We've never done much of that sort of thing, but perhaps it's time we shook things up a bit, hmm?"

"If you're positive there's no chance this can backfire," said

Quinn, who was reasonably certain it would. Their opinion on the subject was meaningless.

"I'm positive," said her father.

"And… if you'll promise to be on good behavior. No spectacles."

"Oh for goodness' sake," said her mamma. "We're not children."

No, but they sure did act like it sometimes. There were so many ways this could go badly. Quinn parked her elbows on her knees and rested her head in her hands.

Her mother moved closer to her on the sofa and put an arm around her. "I promise we won't embarrass you."

"I'm not worried about you embarrassing me," Quinn lied. "This is just all… this is just icing on the cake. My nerves are just shot."

"For the life of me, I don't understand why," said her mamma.

"Seriously?" Quinn's voice climbed the scale as she lifted her head.

"Yes, seriously." Her mother wore an innocent look.

"Oh, I don't know, Mamma, maybe I'm nervous about the fact that I haven't been honest with my husband of thirteen years. I love this island so much. It's the only home I've ever known. But every day we've lived here, I've lived with the knowledge that one little thing could happen, the wrong person could decide to come here on vacation, or somehow the mobster you sent to prison might discover where we are, or who knows what tiny little thing might give us away, and we'd have to pack up and leave in the middle of the night, like all the times we did after we left Alabama, before we came here.

"And now I have a family of my own. And I live with the knowledge every day that your past might come in the middle of the night and hurt my children. Or that I might have to decide one day between leaving my family or staying behind while the two of you are relocated, knowing that whoever comes looking for you will find me instead—and my children. What might they do to us to get us to give up where you are?"

Quinn's parents exchanged a long look.

"I can't bear this burden anymore," said Quinn.

"What do you mean?" asked her mamma.

"I mean... I can't go on living with Redmond and not telling him the truth."

"Quinn... you're not going to leave Redmond, are you?" Her mamma gave her an incredulous look. "He adores you. I can't—"

Ooooh! Of course it would never occur to her mamma that Redmond—Quinn's *husband*—was Quinn's first priority. "No, Mamma," she said. "I would never willingly leave Redmond. I am going to do what I should have done before we were married. I'm going to tell him the truth. The whole truth."

"You can't do that," her mamma said flatly.

"Absolutely not," said her father.

"I have to," said Quinn.

"No," said her dad. "That would be a betrayal of your mother and me. I forbid it."

Quinn stood. "The two of you are unbelievable. I have to go."

"Quinn..." Her mamma grabbed her by the shoulders and looked into her eyes. "Don't do anything foolish."

"I've already done the foolish thing," said Quinn. "I've been lying by omission to my husband for thirteen years. It's time I fixed this." She pulled away from her mother.

"Katie Quinn," her father coaxed. "I tell you what... let me make that phone call. Let me see what I can find out. Give me a few more days—a week, okay? It might take some time for them to get back to me. Just... wait a while longer. Will you do that for me, Katie Quinn?"

Quinn tried to read what was in her father's eyes, then her mamma's. They seemed sincere, but they always did when they wanted something. Why were neither of them not more concerned about her? About how all of this impacted her children?

"I will think about it," Quinn said.

Her dad nodded. "Good. I'll let you know when I hear something. Just... don't do anything until we've spoken, okay?"

Reluctantly Quinn nodded. After all this time, another week wouldn't change things, would it? That was part of the problem. Every day felt like the next round of Russian roulette.

"Good girl," said her dad. "And Quinn?"

She lifted her chin and met his gaze.

"Let us know the particulars on that dinner party. I really would love to see that painting."

Chapter Thirty-Two

Norah was waiting for me near the lighthouse again that morning. We'd walked together most days for a few weeks now. I liked Norah—she was good company. And I wanted to be there for her. It seemed certainly within the realm of possibility that she was the victim of some form of abuse. What kind of person would I be to turn my back on her? But honestly, I could've used the time alone in the mornings to gather my thoughts and work out what I was writing that day. I was still behind, even further behind than I had been. The words were dripping slowly onto the page.

We turned left at the end of the walkway and headed up the beach. It was cloudy that morning with the smell of impending rain mingled in with the salt.

"You didn't have another mess in your yard this morning, did you?" asked Norah.

"Sadly, yes. It's pretty much a daily thing."

"People are disgusting."

"Some of them can be." I offered her a little smile. "How's Knox? Has he played golf with Jake yet?"

"Yes, actually. A couple of times. I think they hit it off. Well, Knox enjoys spending time with Jake. I hope it's mutual. He's probably just being nice."

"Oh, I'm sure Jake enjoys it. You know how guys are... give them something sporty to do and a few beers and they're happy as clams," I said. "Does it seem to be helping? Is Knox... feeling more at ease?"

"He seems to be," said Norah.

"How's he handling the upcoming supper club at your house? That's not a stress point, is it?"

"Well... I won't say it hasn't been stressful, but I think it'll be a good thing actually. One step at a time. Hopefully he'll settle in. How are things at your house?"

I sighed deeply. "Tucker's in Indiana this week. The bathroom is still a work in progress. There's a delay with the tile guy. But at least all the subfloors are back in. This whole project has taken far longer than we thought it would."

"That's got to be awfully stressful, especially with the kids in the house."

"It does make things more challenging, for sure," I said.

"Any idea how long they'll be staying?" Norah asked.

I gave a little half chuckle and shook my head. "That's anybody's guess. It depends on Deacon getting a more stable job. But even then, it's hard for him to manage the girls by himself."

"But he's their dad, right?"

"Of course."

"I mean... look, it's none of my business, but have you considered maybe giving him a deadline?"

"No, I think Deacon knows me well enough to know I'd never kick them out, so what's the point?"

"Is this a pattern? Have they moved in with you and Tucker before?"

"Oh yes. Several times. Twice when there were more of them

—when he was married to the girls' mother. She has a son from a previous relationship."

"So, a family of five moved into your home and stayed for...?"

"Two years the second time. The first time... honestly, I don't remember."

"What does Tucker say about all this?" Norah asked.

I shrugged, watched a flock of seagulls float by. "What can he say? Neither of us are happy about the situation. But what can we do?"

Norah shook her head and sighed, looked out to where the cloudy sky met the sea.

"What?" I asked.

"Nothing."

"No, tell me what you're thinking," I said.

"I'm thinking maybe you're a bit of a people-pleaser, and you need to stand up for yourself."

This may surprise you, but that was not the first time a friend had suggested such a thing to me. But it always confused me.

"If by people-pleaser, you mean I'm there for my family when they need me, I guess I'm guilty as charged. The thing is, this is the way I was raised. This is what I've been taught my whole life, at home and at church. You make sacrifices for others, especially family. And if you want to claim the name Christian, and I do, you put other people first."

"But Tucker is your family too," Norah said.

"Well, of course, but in the hierarchy of whose needs come first, children come before adults."

"I'm just suggesting you might need to establish healthier boundaries."

"I wish I knew how to do that and not have homeless grand-children," I said.

"Do you really think they'd be homeless?" asked Norah.

I thought about that for a minute. "I think my granddaugh-ters would be living in an environment I couldn't tolerate... maybe with a roommate they shouldn't be exposed to in a broken-down apartment on the not-real-safe side of town. I couldn't live with that. But I'm curious... and I know your background is different from mine... but don't you think family should take care of family?"

"To a point," said Norah. "But I think you passed that point a long time ago, and forgive me, but I think your son is taking advantage of you. I don't have kids, so I may be way off base here, but I'm wondering if pushing him to stand on his own two feet might not be the best thing at *this* point. You and Tucker are entitled to enjoy the home you've worked for and dreamed of on your own terms, don't you think?"

"I think I couldn't be happy if I knew my granddaughters were simultaneously living in squalor."

"Squalor, really?" Norah gave me a look that might've meant she thought I was being melodramatic. "Do you think it would be that bad?"

"I do. Everything is so expensive, especially rent. Deacon didn't finish college. Heck, he barely started it. The jobs he can get, they don't pay enough for someplace nice, in a good school district. And, well, I've seen the way my son keeps house."

Norah sighed. "Most men, in my experience, are not particularly fastidious housekeepers. I shouldn't have said anything. It's your family and your business."

"You're my friend," I said. "I get it. My life is a hot mess, of course you want to help me fix it. But trust me, you're not suggesting things I haven't thought of myself. It's just that I have to be able to live with the consequences of my actions. And I know what I can and can't live with."

"What about Tucker?" Norah asked. "This has got to be putting a strain on your relationship."

"Tucker could no more live with the girls in a bad situation than I could. There are many things putting a strain on both of us," I said. "So many things, happening all at once. It's like we're under siege. But... so far at least, we're under siege together. I pray it stays that way."

And I prayed every night that Deacon would find a good job that paid enough to support him and the girls. I further asked God every night to send him a good strong woman, one he loved enough to want to build a different kind of life with—one that would be good for his daughters.

So far, God has had a different plan.

And I am just trying to hold on.

Two Months before the Fall Meet and Greet

Chapter Thirty-Three

Saturday, August 27, 2022, 4:30 p.m.
Monthly Meeting of the Sullivan's Island Supper Club—Before
Fitzgerald Home
Sarabeth Mercer Jackson Boone

Norah's house reminded me of Eugenia's—Fish's house. They were both that old-fashioned beach house style with high ceilings, lots of white paint, and lots of porches. But Norah's had even more of that coastal retreat vibe going on with heart pine floors throughout, that bead-board ceiling, and painted tongue-and-groove paneling. It was simply gorgeous. I had just a teentsy bit of house envy, I confess. I would've just loved for our house, although it was much more modest, of course, to have that same feel when we finally finished it. If we ever did.

Now I just want to get this out right up front. I was not myself that evening. I love my granddaughters—and my son, though to be perfectly honest, and I just hate admitting this, but it's occurred to me recently that he and I are not meant to live under the same roof. The boy—I'm sorry, the full-grown man—is a slob, and I did not raise him that way. And those sweet, beautiful, innocent granddaughters... no grandmother wants to be in the position of explaining that Gigi and Granddad are going to take a l'il nap so please don't come knocking at the door, okay?

Tucker and I were in desperate need of alone time. It was extremely hard to come by in a house with a grown son, two teenaged granddaughters, two dogs, and an iguana Tucker is convinced is a rare species found only in the Cayman Islands that is illegal for us to even have in the house. One of his stress points is that the department of natural resources is going to raid our house, or possibly PETA, and we're going to be a headline in the *Post and Courier*. It's a thing with him, not being a headline in the *Post and Courier*.

When you layer all that on top of our recent troubles with the house and resulting financial ruin and sprinkle in the melodrama about the trees I've gotten myself mixed up in, maybe you can understand how I was on edge. It does not excuse my behavior, I'm not suggesting that.

Anyway, Tucker and I had come early, at Norah's request, and I was surprised to find Cash and Hadley already there too. Norah said she wasn't much of a cook. Poor thing didn't have the time. So I suggested she call Hamby's to cater, and they had set things up on the long butcher-block island in a kitchen that looked like something the realtor probably described as a "chef's fantasy kitchen." It had commercial-grade stainless steel appliances, white-and-grey quartz countertops, glass-front upper cabinets, and a breakfast bar with stools that stood separate from the island.

The three of us—Norah, Hadley, and me—were in the kitchen, putting the finishing touches on things, and the guys had gotten drinks and wandered out to the screened porch over-looking the cove on the back side of Sullivan's Island.

"I think we're all set," said Norah.

"Everything looks fantastic," I said, and it really did. You'd never go wrong with Hamby's. Eugenia had taught me that.

"How's Knox holding up?" asked Hadley.

Norah made a gun with her finger and thumb and pantomimed shooting herself in the head. "I'm going to kill one of us before this is over. At first he was dead set against hosting. Then, once he got onboard with it, he wanted to micromanage everything. It's good he started drinking. Maybe that will settle him down."

"Aww—but at least he's enthusiastic about it," I said. "That's progress, right?"

"Let's get drinks before everyone else gets here." Norah led us over to a wet bar in what turned out to be one of three living rooms, which was open to the kitchen. A lot of the first floor of the house was an open concept with just the bare minimum in the way of walls to hold up the second floor.

"There's whatever you want," said Norah. "I'm going to have a gin and tonic. I hope this is okay. It's well stocked, but it's self-serve. I know Tallulah likes to have a bartender, but I'd rather not have strangers in my house all evening."

"You've gotta be kidding me," said Hadley. "You've got a liquor store here." Tall cabinets to the left held all kinds of top-shelf liquors with an equal number of liqueurs to the right. A selection of stemware hung from the center shelf, with stemless glasses above, and the whole thing was mirrored. A hammered copper bar sink occupied the center of the bar, with a wine chiller and another small refrigerator to the left, and an ice maker to the right. A tray of lemon, lime, and orange wedges sat to one side. Norah might not cook, but she clearly knew how to entertain.

"I set the things I thought most everyone would want on the counter. There are mixers in the refrigerator. Knox picked the wine." Norah gestured to the ice bucket and row of chillers. "They're all French. There's a champagne, a couple of whites, and a couple of reds. Knox is into wine. He has a walk-in cooler next the pantry with a bigger selection. If you encourage him in the slightest, he'll talk to you about the soil the grapes grew in for every bottle in there until your ears bleed."

"Gin and tonic sounds good to me," I said. "That's my hot weather go-to." When did I become a woman who nearly always drinks liquor? Up until a year ago, I was a wine drinker. With all the stress, apparently, I'd upped my medication.

"Yeah, me too," said Hadley.

Norah mixed three gin and tonics because that was just as easy as making one, she said, and we all toasted the evening.

"What I want to know," I said, looking at Hadley, "is how on earth did you get Tallulah to agree to relinquish control of supper club for the evening?"

Hadley waved a hand dismissively. "That was easy. I hypnotized her."

"No, seriously," I said.

"Seriously, I think she's distracted right now," said Hadley.

I squinted up my face at her. "Distracted? By what?"

"It's not what," said Hadley. "It's who."

"Oh yeah," said Norah. "Tallulah's in love."

"What?" I might've gaped at her a few seconds, then remembered myself and closed my mouth. "With who? Y'all, I have missed happy hour most of this month. I'm clearly behind. What is going on with Tallulah?" And how did Norah know this and I did not?

"Fish." Hadley smiled. "And can I just say, they are so stinking cute together."

"Oh-ooh! Well, I'm so happy for them," I said. "When did all this come about?"

"It's been about a month," said Hadley.

"I have got to stop missing happy hour," I said. "Tallulah must really be head over heels for sure. She agreed to having supper club here *and* having Quinn's parents join us. My goodness."

"What's going on with you?" Hadley asked. "Why've you been missing happy hour? Something else break? You got more contractors coming around?"

"They've finished the foundation work," I said. "But I've been taking the girls back-to-school shopping and running back and forth to Florence. My mamma's not doing well. She... aah... she has cancer."

Okay, I had not intended to talk about that. I can't. If I let myself even think about it, I fall apart. And I have no time to fall apart. None. I felt my eyes tearing up.

"Sweetie, I'm so sorry." Hadley put her hand on my arm, and they both said all the sympathetic things, and for the next few minutes, I explained all about how they'd thought they'd caught it early—at least that's what Mamma told me. But she'd had surgery and chemotherapy, and now she was going to need radiation. And then there was my daddy, whose cognitive decline was declining and exacerbated by Mamma's cancer. He simply could not deal with her being sick at all.

"She's going to be fine," I said, though I wasn't convinced at all. "The doctor said they caught it early." I'd never actually heard the doctor say that, but Mamma kept repeating it, and my sister was the designated medical overseer for the family because—well, mostly because she's the bossiest one and it's just easier to go along.

"You've had a rough year," said Hadley.

"I have." I took a big sip of my gin and tonic.

"I mean, my gosh," said Hadley, "the kids moving in with their pets, the house falling apart, your parents, the trees... and all that ugliness. You've just had a parade of one thing right after the other."

"Yes." I nodded. "And I march in the front of this parade of insanity and twirl the fire baton."

We all started giggling, then we laughed and laughed. It was such a blessing to have friends you could laugh with, maybe especially when so many things weren't one bit funny. "But I have so much to be grateful for." I was healthy. I had the best husband in the world, and I adored him and he truly must adore me back, because what man would live with an illegal blue iguana if he was not truly in love?

The doorbell rang, and the three of us looked up to see the

rest of our group on the street-side screened porch looking in. Norah crossed the room to open the door.

"I just hope there's no ice cream for dessert this month." Hadley grinned. "I've heard Quinn's parents are prone to slinging it."

I sorely wish I could tell you that Quinn's parents were the source of the evening's drama.

Chapter Thirty-Four

Saturday, August 27, 2022, 5:30 p.m.
Monthly Meeting of the Sullivan's Island Supper Club—
Happy Hour
Fitzgerald Home
Libba Graham

Libba was no expert. She'd had a few art classes in school, sure, but she had no idea if the painting of an apple-green vase with five yellow sunflowers on a teal background was a Van Gogh or not. "It looks very similar to his other paintings of sunflowers," she offered. It was important to contribute to the conversation, especially when it had to do with art. Libba should've studied up on postimpressionist art. Her husband was an artist, for heaven's sake. She should be conversant on all the artsy topics.

Most of the group gathered in the wide hallway that ran behind one section of the larger living room. The Fitzgeralds' art collection was scattered between the living rooms, dining room, and this gallery and consisted of several impressionist landscapes, a few seascapes, and the painting of a vase of sunflowers, which hung alone on the short wall near the pass-through to the dining room. They all studied it as they sipped their cocktails.

"Well, clearly there would be no interest in the painting at all otherwise," said Finn O'Leary. He and his wife, Myrna, stood closest to the painting. He studied the painting with a loupe for five minutes or so, then stood back and regarded it skeptically. "Someone has gone to a great deal of effort to make it look realistic, but this is no Van Gogh."

"Eh, that's what we thought as well," said Knox. "But it's a pretty piece, isn't it?"

"True enough," said Finn. "We have several reproductions of his still-life paintings, all of flowers—irises, sunflowers, and poppies. They're good reproductions, and they're quite lovely. They bring us joy, just as any beautiful thing does. No one with a trained eye would mistake them for originals." He shrugged. "But you never know, do you? A museum in Connecticut was bequeathed a version of poppies in a vase in 1957. Van Gogh painted seven different versions of paintings with poppies. He didn't have money to pay models, you see, so he focused on still lifes. Anyway, they didn't believe the painting was an authentic Van Gogh, the museum. They put it away in a closet. Then, thirty years later, the Dutch authenticated it. It's worth... best guess? Fifty million."

"Well, I'm glad to know our insurance doesn't need an additional rider," said Knox, who seemed to be in an almost jovial mood.

"You've got some really nice pieces here," said Myrna. "I mean, none of them are Van Goghs, but I'd say you need a stiff rider on your insurance and a top-of-the-line alarm system."

"Seriously?" asked Norah. "I mean, well... we have CPI. It's a decent alarm system, but there are no sensors in the walls here. This isn't the Louvre. We didn't pay *that* much for any of these. We just like pretty things on the walls."

"Hmm..." Myrna raised her chin and her eyebrows and looked down her nose at Norah, all superior. "Perhaps you should educate yourselves on the current value of your collection."

"I'm sure your system is sufficient," Finn said, his voice soothing. He flashed Myrna an annoyed look, and then there was this awkward, long few minutes when everyone went back to looking at the sunflower still life. Finally Finn turned to Knox and said, "So tell me about where you acquired your other pieces."

Knox said, "So there's this gallery in New York..." He drifted into the living room, and Finn and Myrna followed.

That Myrna was starting to work Libba's nerves. Where did Norah get to? Libba wandered into the kitchen.

Norah and Hadley had their heads together over by the sink.

"Hey, what are y'all up to in here?" asked Libba. She didn't mean anything by it or expect that they were actually up to anything other than maybe setting out serving spoons, but the looks on both their faces when they stepped back and turned to her seemed to indicate otherwise.

What was going on? Libba smiled at them and waited to be let in on whatever it was.

"We were just admiring all this food," said Hadley.

"Sarabeth nailed it when she told me to call Hamby's," said Norah.

It stung being left out. And Norah was so new to the group. Why did she have secrets with Hadley? Come to think of it, Libba'd noticed them talking privately after happy hour Friday before last. They sure were fast friends.

"Is it time to eat?" Libba asked weakly.

"I think so," said Norah. "It's six o'clock. I guess I should round everyone up." She stepped towards the living room. "Knox? It's time for dinner. Everyone?"

Norah stepped back into the kitchen and moved towards the far end of the butcher-block island. Most everyone else gathered towards the kitchen end of the great room. Norah found Knox in the crowd and gave a little gesture with her head for him to come over there with her. He seemed nervous, Libba thought, but he moved to Norah's side.

Where was Jake?

"Knox and I are so glad everyone could come this evening,"

said Norah. "I know we got off to a bit of a rocky start here, but we want to make Sullivan's Island our home, and we're grateful to have wormed our way into your group."

Laughter rolled through the room. Everyone seemed in good spirits. Tallulah and Fish sure looked happy, Libba thought. The two of them seemed to only have eyes for each other.

"Because I can't cook, and the rest of you have done the heavy lifting the past two months, I called in the cavalry," said Norah. "Hamby's has put together a buffet for us, and there are several selections for the plant-lovers among us. There's a table in the breakfast room to the left that seats eight, and of course the dining room is at the end of this hall to the right, and there are ten places in there. Everyone, please sit wherever you like."

Libba searched the crowd for Jake. Where had he gotten to? She sauntered into the living room, her eyes sliding past the French doors to the screened porch. Movement to her left caught her eye. Someone was on the side porch. She crossed the room, pulled open the door, and stepped outside. The heat and humidity blasted her in the face. Thank goodness they were eating indoors.

The porch seemed empty. Libba wandered to the far end, looking left and right. Someone had been out here. Where'd they go? When she reached the corner of the house, she heard a man talking.

"I'm sure it's nothing to be concerned about." Not Jake. Whose voice was that?

Libba scanned the back porch, which was also empty. There, at the bottom of the steps leading to the back lawn, was Tennyson. He had his back to her and a phone to his ear.

Libba turned to head back inside.

"Call the doctor if you like." Tennyson's voice was harsh. She'd never heard him use that tone before. "But don't call me again."

"There you are." Jake rounded the corner and nearly collided with her.

She smiled up at him. "What do you mean 'There you are?' I came out here looking for you."

He wrapped his arms around her and pulled her in for a kiss. "Well, now that you've found me, what are you going to do with me?"

"I guess for now I'll feed you." Libba grinned and pulled him back towards the door. "You'll need your strength later on."

Jake grinned. "Remind me to send this new doctor a case of whatever she likes to drink."

Libba was very grateful for Dr. Giovanni. Phase one of Libba's plan to get her life back was on track. She was reasonably certain Jake had no time *recently* to spend with Roxie outside office hours. And things were good between her and Jake, if not all the way back to the way they used to be. But... Libba harbored suspicions about Roxie that she was going to have to find a way to resolve one way or another.

A board creaked, and they heard footsteps on the wooden stairs behind them. They both looked over their shoulders as Tennyson stepped onto the porch. "Awfully warm this evening," he said, his voice now the familiar honeyed drawl.

"Hotter than Georgia asphalt," said Jake.

"I'm burning slap up." Libba searched Tennyson's eyes.

Nothing to see here, his expression seemed to say.

"Allow me." He opened the door and held it for them, ever the Southern gentleman.

Who had he been talking to on the phone? It sounded quite personal.

Chapter Thirty-Five

Saturday, August 27, 2022, 6:00 p.m.
Monthly Meeting of the Sullivan's Island Supper Club—Dinner
Fitzgerald Home
Tallulah Wentworth

Tallulah picked up one of the cobalt-blue dinner plates and passed it to Fish, who was behind her in line, then got one for herself. "My, this looks delicious."

She served herself a large portion of the salad—it was Hamby's signature salad with the blue cheese crumbles and candied pecans—and then added just a taste of the red wine braised short ribs and a crab cake to her plate. A smidge of the garlic mashed potatoes, a few of the brussels sprouts—they had bacon, after all—and a scoop of the succotash and a bite of the vegetable pirlou rounded out her plate. Love had enhanced all her appetites. She and Fish had been gorging themselves on all manner of delicacies. She'd need to moderate herself a bit or else she'd pack on the pounds and lose her girlish appeal.

Fish piled his plate high and added one of the rolls and some salted butter. He picked up a second roll with the tongs and started to put it on her plate. "No, thank you, darlin', I'm watching my youthful figure."

"My dear, you would make Aphrodite herself feel dowdy." Fish spoke softly into her ear, making shivers run down her spine.

"Oh for the love of Pete," Camille muttered. She was right in front of Tallulah and apparently had excellent hearing. "Maybe you two should skip dinner and retire early."

"Careful dear, your green-eyed monster is showing," quipped Tallulah.

"Is that what you think?" Camille's voice rose, then she scanned the room and dipped her head to speak directly into Tallulah's other ear. "I'll have you know, I have no reason to be jealous of you. Tennyson and I are eloping."

Tallulah drew her head back and stared at Camille. "What? You can't be serious."

"Yes, ma'am. Shhh. Not a word. We're keeping it a secret."

"Why?"

"It's romantic."

"It's scandalous. You hardly know him."

"Ladies, our friends would like to have some supper as well." Fish patted Tallulah's arm.

"Yes, of course. My apologies," said Tallulah. "Sit by me." She gave Camille a meaningful look, thankful for the first time that Norah had chosen not to use place cards.

Camille sashayed down the hall towards the dining room.

Tallulah rolled her eyes and followed. Camille did have a flair for the dramatic.

In the dining room, Tennyson had taken the seat by Knox, who was at one end of the table, while Norah was at the far end. Camille sat by Tennyson, but Tucker had already taken the next chair, with Sarabeth across the table. Birdie and Vernon occupied the spots next to Norah, on opposite sides of the table. Birdie must love that. She would have to kick Vernon instead of patting him on the leg to keep him in line. Tallulah sighed. She'd have to finish her conversation with Camille later.

Tallulah took one of the two remaining seats, to Knox's left, across from Tennyson. He was a handsome devil, and Camille was positively radiant. Still, she hadn't known him nearly long enough to be thinking about marriage. Had she? Of course, none of them were getting any younger, and one did need to seize the day. Tallulah certainly had.

She felt flustered. Had Camille made that up about eloping just to get a rise out of her? Tallulah loved Camille, but she certainly wasn't above that sort of thing. That was probably it. She couldn't possibly be serious. Of all of them, Camille was the most cautious where men were concerned.

"Would you like some wine?" Fish set his plate on the table at the place next to hers.

"Yes, please," said Tallulah. "Something red. Thank you, darlin'."

Tallulah put her napkin on her lap and glanced around the dining room. "Norah, your home is lovely. It certainly looks like y'all are all settled in."

"Thank you," said Norah. "I think we're nearly there. Moving is the worst thing I've ever had to do. I told Knox this is it. They'll carry me out of here."

"I know exactly what you mean," said Sarabeth. "I *hope* to never have to move again."

Tallulah was on the same side of the table as Sarabeth and couldn't see her face. But there was something in the tone of her voice... maybe the emphasis on the word hope... that sounded uncertain.

"Well, you won't hear me suggesting the idea." Tucker smiled at his wife like he was trying to reassure her.

What was going on there? Surely there was nothing else wrong with their house. As it was, it would've no doubt been cheaper to tear the thing down and start over. Tallulah started to ask them if they were finally through with the unplanned projects when somebody's phone started ringing.

Tennyson was directly across the table from Tallulah, and he jerked like he'd been shocked. "Excuse me," he said, and he put his napkin on the table and strode out of the dining room. Why can't people learn to put their phones on silent at the dinner table?

"Did your video cameras catch your vandals?" Knox addressed Tucker.

"Sadly, no," said Tucker. "I'm going to add a few more, maybe some back in the trees. Our yard has several big planting beds and a potting shed. It's too easy for people to sneak around and get to the backyard. And cameras are so common now people know to look for them and avoid them on the house."

"This has just gotten completely out of hand." Fish set Tallulah's wine in front of her and took his seat. "Surely teenagers are responsible. I would hate to think our fully grown neighbors would stoop so low."

"All you have to do is read what they post online to know what their emotional IQ is," said Norah. "I wouldn't put anything past some of those people. Now, grant you, it's a minority. A very vocal and clearly uncivilized minority."

"I thought all that was settling down," said Tallulah.

"No," said Norah. "Sarabeth isn't in the group anymore. But they're still at it. In fact, if anything, it's gotten worse. But again, it's really just a handful of unhinged people."

Tennyson returned to the table. Camille said something to him, and he nodded and patted her on the arm. Everything appeared to be all right, Tallulah thought.

"You know, I have an idea I wanted to run past y'all," said Sarabeth. "All this Facebook stuff… I think people just get caught up in things online. Like a mob mentality or what have you. If we were dealing with each other face-to-face, things would surely be different. What if Tucker and I were to host a neighborhood meet and greet? Give everyone an opportunity to chat with each other in person. Just something casual, you know?"

"I think that's a very generous idea," said Norah. "I'm not sure you'll get the response you're hoping for. But I see the worst of people. It goes with the job. You shouldn't listen to me."

"I just think it's harder to demonize each other up close and personal. We've got to relearn how to disagree with each other and still be friends," said Sarabeth. "We've got to stop allowing that one thing that divides us from outweighing all the things that unite us."

"That's exactly what I was saying the other night," said Vernon.

"Vernon." Birdie looked at him sternly, but the dining table was wide, and Tallulah doubted Birdie could reach to kick him. Shame, that.

Camille said, "I doubt any of them will have an epiphany and realize we need to let Mother Nature have her way with the maritime forest instead of trying to manicure everything to suit us. But... it might make them less likely to throw dog poop in your yard."

"That's an interesting perspective." Knox twirled his wine-glass and studied the ruby elixir in the light. He had everyone's attention.

"What do you mean?" Camille squinted at Knox.

"That we should let Mother Nature rule the maritime forest," said Knox.

"I think that's precisely what we should do," said Camille. "Surely you don't support the cutters' position on this after all?"

"Not entirely." A slow smile tugged at the corners of Knox's mouth. "It's just that, if I understand everything I think I know about the situation, Mother Nature didn't install the jetties that set the whole thing in motion. Men built the jetties."

"Well, that had to be done," said Camille. "The harbor entrance just wasn't workable."

"Did it?" Knox raised an eyebrow. "If Mother Nature had been left in charge, as you suggest, we wouldn't have the accretion issue to begin with. We'd very likely be fighting erosion like Isle of Palms and Folly Beach, like up at Breach Inlet."

No one said a word for what felt like a very long time. Tallulah hadn't ever thought about it, but she supposed what Knox said was true, even if it did rankle to hear him say it. Vernon wore an expression like he was positively dying to say something but feared for his life. Birdie had him fixed with a death stare.

"Fair point." Fish gave Knox a sideways nod. "However, we can't rewrite history. It's unlikely they'll be taking the jetties down. We can only take the situation as it is now and do our best to protect the land we're stewards of."

Knox nodded. "Indeed. But I would submit there's a balance to be struck with those who have issues like our friend Vernon—with the critters and so forth. And I confess I do have sympathy for those who bought property with ocean views and are taxed for the value of the property that includes a view they no longer enjoy."

A loud clatter came from the far end of the table, followed by the sound of a chair being moved back.

Tallulah leaned in and looked to see what was going on.

Sarabeth stood, her face flushed.

Knox, Tennyson, Fish, and Tucker scrambled to rise, as gentlemen do.

"I have heard some of these very same points expressed in that vile Facebook group. *Those* are the talking points of the people who want to see our maritime forest scalped... who want every single thing that's grown since Hugo cut back to three feet, wiping out our protection from devastating storms."

"I beg your pardon—" Knox's tone was conciliatory.

"Well, you can't have it." Sarabeth tossed her napkin on her plate. "Excuse me." She bolted from the dining room.

Oh dear. Tallulah had been afraid nothing good would come from having supper club in this odious man's house. Why on earth did he feel driven to bring up divisive topics at the dinner table? Tallulah moved to stand but felt Fish's hand on her shoulder. She looked up, then followed his gaze.

Tucker's napkin was on his plate. "Perhaps I would find more sympathy in my heart for folks who've lost their multimillion-dollar views if our neighbors would stop demonizing my wife and trashing my yard. Excuse me."

"I am terribly sorry, truly," said Knox.

"Maybe a meet and greet is a good idea, Tucker," said Tallulah. "I'm happy to help."

"Let us get back to you on that," Tucker said as he strode out of the dining room.

"You would not catch me catering to that bunch," said Norah. "But if they decide to do this, I'll help any way I can."

"I wonder when they were thinking of..." mused Camille.

"When the weather cools off would be nice," said Birdie. "Maybe around Halloween?"

"I could help then," said Camille.

Later, Tallulah would wish she'd paid more attention to what Camille said that evening, and what she didn't say. But the truth was, Tallulah was too distracted by poor Sarabeth and too wrapped up in new love—a second chance at love—to pay much attention to anything or anyone other than Fish.

Chapter Thirty-Six

Saturday, August 27, 2022, 6:30 p.m.
Monthly Meeting of the Sullivan's Island Supper Club
Fitzgerald Home
Quinn Poinsett

Quinn was on eggshells the entire evening. How could she not be, with her parents there? Her mamma seemed miffed to be relegated to the breakfast room—like maybe she'd expected reserved seating by the hostess. But the apple-green painted table with ladder-back chairs in the window-lined breakfast room might've been Quinn's favorite spot in Norah's house. It was homey. Quinn was thinking she'd like to come back sometime when she wasn't wrangling her parents, maybe get to know Norah better. It seemed unlikely, as Quinn observed them all having a civilized dinner, that Norah would turn out to be the instrument of their downfall.

This night could not be over soon enough to suit Quinn. She'd hoped to catch her mother and have a private word, maybe hear what they'd learned from their contacts at the marshal's service, but so far her mamma had been persistently unavailable. When Myrna excused herself to go to the powder room, Quinn waited a couple of minutes, then excused herself and followed her mamma down the hall past the kitchen and through the alcove to the right that led to the powder room.

When Myrna opened the door, she couldn't avoid Quinn.

"Mamma?"

Myrna looked piqued. She held the door as if to usher Quinn into the bathroom.

"I don't need to go in there right now," said Quinn. "I've left you several messages. I need to know what you and Daddy found out."

"This is hardly the place or the time, Quinn."

Quinn stepped closer to her mamma. "Unfortunately, this is the only time you've been available."

"But I'm not, darling. This is a dinner party. We need to get back."

"He didn't even call did he?" Quinn hissed. "After he specifically asked me to wait another week—and it's been more than two —to give him time to reach out to someone."

Just then, Sarabeth darted down the hall, her head tucked towards her chest. She stopped short and looked from Quinn to Myrna. Sarabeth's face was flushed, her eyes bright with unshed tears.

"What on earth is the matter?" Quinn placed a hand on each of Sarabeth's arms.

Sarabeth shook her head. "Are y'all waiting for the powder room?"

Myrna stepped back and held the door. "I've just finished."

"Excuse me, please." Sarabeth went inside and closed the door.

Myrna turned to head back to the table.

Quinn started to follow her, but then Tucker came barreling down the hall and into the alcove.

"She's in here." Quinn looked at Tucker, her face creased in a question.

Tucker shook his head as if to say, *It's nothing.* He knocked gently on the bathroom door. "Sarabeth? Sweetheart?"

It was clearly something, but if Sarabeth wanted to talk to her about it, she would. Quinn had her hands full just then with potential parent drama. Quinn glanced into the dining room on her way back to the table. Everything seemed calm in there, but when she returned to her table, her parents seemed to be quietly bickering. This was usually a precursor to loud bickering, which always escalated. She fixed her mamma with a gaze that might've implored her to quiet down.

Quinn should've known better. Her mamma had never responded well to criticism, real or imagined.

Myrna raised her voice. "Finn, my migraine is back. I have the most awful migraines." She placed her hand in Finn's.

He kissed her hand and stood. "Let me get you home, my sweet."

What were they up to? This wasn't going according to script.

Myrna rose. "This has been lovely, but I'm afraid we're going to have to call it a night."

Everyone stood and said their goodbyes. Quinn's parents walked down the hall, said goodbye to the others, thanked the Fitzgeralds with something approaching normal etiquette, then quickly made their exit.

Something was definitely up with the two of them. Discreet exits weren't a part of their repertoire. Quinn picked up her wineglass and drained it. She was convinced her parents hadn't made the call they'd promised. In fact, now that she thought about it, Quinn was sure they'd only told her that to get her to agree not to spill everything to Redmond. Once again, they'd manipulated her. More and more, she realized this was a major theme in her life.

"Would you like another glass?" Redmond asked.

"Yes, please." Maybe she could relax a bit and enjoy the rest of the evening. What on earth was up with Sarabeth?

Libba and Jake and Hadley and Cash were in the midst of a lively discussion about the alligator found swimming in a tide pool earlier that week. Thank goodness the kids hadn't been on the beach at the time. Quinn knew she was overprotective of Oliver sometimes. But the things she had nightmares about actually did sometimes happen.

Quinn felt someone passing behind her chair. She glanced over her shoulder and saw Tennyson heading through the door leading to the porch, his phone to his ear. He wore an unpleasant expression. Quinn watched Libba tracking Tennyson. She tilted her head and sent Libba a look that meant *what's up?*

Libba rolled her eyes and shrugged, then moved one chair down to talk to Quinn. "He's been out the door once already on the phone, and he was out there before dinner. Apparently his niece is expecting and she's nervous. This is her first. That's what Camille said anyway. He's not very patient with her. I'll say that much."

"Dessert is on the bar whenever you're ready." Norah had slipped into the breakfast room. "There's a selection of min-tarts, lemon bars, and other goodies, plus some fresh fruit with lemon dip."

Sarabeth appeared at Norah's side and put a hand on her arm. "I just wanted to apologize to you for earlier. I'm just so sorry. I think we're going to head on home now." What had Quinn missed? It was hard to imagine Sarabeth had done anything that would require an apology.

"No problem," said Norah. "Knox should've kept his mouth shut. I'm the one who should apologize, or he is actually. In fact, I'm sure he'd like to." Norah made a move like she was going to get him.

"Please," said Sarabeth. "We'll talk later. I just need to go home."

"Okay, whatever you need," said Norah. "See you on the beach Monday morning?"

"Sounds good." Sarabeth nodded. "Thank you."

Tucker stepped up, placed a hand at the small of her back,

and they said their goodbyes to everyone and slipped out the side door.

Redmond set Quinn's glass of wine in front of her. It was such a lovely shade of red, so rich.

Everyone was chatting above her, or it seemed that way, she guessed, because Norah was standing there beside her and most everyone else had stood to say goodbye to Sarabeth and Tucker. So no one was sitting at the table with Quinn to watch her down that entire glass of wine.

She closed her eyes and took a deep breath and let it out.

It was time. Please God, let this be all right. Please don't let her husband leave her.

"Redmond?" She touched his hand, then slid hers inside it. His hands were so strong, so reassuring.

"Yeah, babe?" He squeezed her hand and bent down.

"I need to talk to you."

Chapter Thirty-Seven

Saturday, August 27, 2022, 7:45 p.m.
Near the Lighthouse
Quinn Poinsett

It didn't take them long to get home. Quinn and Redmond lived a block off the other end of the cove, near the kayak landing, between Station 18 1/2 and Station 19 on Central. Quinn loved their one-level raised beach house with its deep, wrap-around haint-blue-ceilinged porches. She prayed they'd all still be living there together tomorrow. They checked on the kids, fielded a few homework and scheduling questions, then took a quilt to sit on and headed towards the beach.

They were quiet as they walked down Station 18 1/2 Street, crossed Middle Street, then I'on. Redmond was giving her space. He was always good about that. They passed the lighthouse, then walked down the beach access path and went right on the beach. It was getting on towards sunset, and the prettiest view was across the harbor, behind the Ravenel Bridge.

"Would you like to walk or sit?" Redmond asked.

"Let's go on down a bit farther," Quinn said. "Then we can sit if you like." She needed another moment.

They walked on, past the spot where the Station 16 beach access trail ends, then Quinn picked a spot for the quilt. They spread it on the sand, then sat and stared across the harbor. The breeze off the water cooled the evening. Quinn inhaled a lungful of salt air and slowly let it out. It was time.

"There are things I've never told you," she said.

He nodded. "I know, Quinn."

"It's not that I don't trust you—I do. You are my rock... the center of my entire universe."

He pulled her close and waited.

"When we moved here, I was eleven. I told you that part, and I told you we'd moved around a lot after we left Alabama. But the part I left out was that my parents were in the witness-protection program." When the words were finally out, a massive weight rolled off her chest. She was nearly faint from the relief.

He pulled back and looked at her in disbelief.

She watched him carefully as she continued, attuned to every eye twitch. "They were art dealers, and we were living in New York at the time..." She told him everything, like they'd made her promise never to do—and she told him that part too.

He stared at the setting sun, quiet for the longest time, saying nothing.

"Please tell me you don't hate me," she whispered.

He hugged her close. "Quinn, you are everything to me. I could no more hate you than I could take an aerial tour of the island on my pretty pink flying pig."

She pulled back to look at him. "What are you thinking? Are you mad? You... you have to be mad..."

"I might be mad tomorrow, but I'm sure I'll get over it. Right now I'm thinking I'm just so freakin' relieved that it's *this* you've been hiding and not any one of ten things that would've been so much worse." He blinked, his soft grey eyes hard to read.

"What do you mean?" Quinn asked.

"I thought maybe you were in love with someone else."

She sat up straight. "How could you think that?"

"When you know something is wrong, but you don't know what, your imagination goes to the worst-case scenarios. If you were in love with someone else, I'd have to let you go. But that's the only way I ever would. If your happiness depended on it."

She put her hands on both sides of his face and pulled him close. And then he kissed her like he was starved for her. After a few minutes, he pulled back and looked at her.

"What else?" he asked.

"What do you mean?"

"What else is tormenting you?"

"That's all... It's enough, isn't it?" she said. "I mean, the rest is all connected. Like, what if they get relocated because they've managed to blow their cover after all these years?"

"Well, I'd hate it for them," he said, "but there's not much we could do about it. Why worry about things we can't control? I'm sure there's some way you could still see them occasionally."

"They've always assured me that's not the case. But my bigger fear is that the people who might hunt them down would find us and hurt you and Oliver and the twins to make some sort of point. I just... The guilt eats at me. Putting all of us in the worst kind of danger. I don't see how you can't hate me for that. I hate myself for it."

He swallowed hard and looked out over the water. "You're not responsible for this situation. You were a child when all this happened."

"But I should've told you before you married me."

"Yeah, I would've preferred that, I'm not going to lie. But Quinn, it wouldn't have made a damn bit of difference. We would still have gotten married. We'd still have Oliver and the twins. The only thing that would've been different is that you wouldn't have carried that burden by yourself all this time. And I guess maybe I wouldn't have dismissed some of your worries as being crazy over-protective."

"Seriously? You would've married me anyway?" Tears rolled down her cheeks.

He wrapped his arms around her. "Of course I would've."

"What are we going to do now?"

He thought that over for a few minutes. "Well, we'll just have to do whatever it takes to keep us all safe. Leave that with me okay?"

Quinn nodded. "Okay." She snuggled into him, weak with a mixture of relief and joy.

"What was your name?" asked Redmond. "I'm assuming they made you change your names."

"I was originally Delaney. Delaney Neve O'Sullivan. I think that's one of the reasons my dad was captivated by Sullivan's Island originally. It was named for an Irish sea captain named Florence O'Sullivan. My parents were Liam and Maeve."

"Did you ever think about talking to Norah about all this? Her being a US marshal and all?"

Quinn laughed. "No, but I was afraid for a while maybe she was here to check up on them. They've been acting so crazy lately, creating public spectacles. I don't know what's gotten into them."

"Did you ask her that? If she was supposed to check in on them?"

"No, they told me they have a specific contact, that her being here was a coincidence."

"That sounds right," he said. "But wait, have you not ever met anyone from the marshal's service?"

"What do you mean?" she asked.

"I mean like, when y'all were first getting into the program in New York, when they were getting ready to testify... you met the marshal assigned to their case then right?"

Quinn slowly shook her head. "No, I've never met anyone like that."

Redmond gave her a puzzled look.

"What's wrong?" she asked.

He shrugged. "Nothing. Everything is perfect. Far better than I deserve."

They held each other close and watched the sunset over the harbor.

One Month before the Fall Meet and Greet

Chapter Thirty-Eight

Saturday, September 24, 2022, 5:00 p.m.
Monthly Meeting of the Sullivan's Island Supper Club—
Happy Hour
Home of Tallulah Wentworth
Sarabeth Mercer Jackson Boone

I suppose it was to be expected after last month, which was mostly my fault, but we were back at Tallulah's house for supper club in September, although I will say she seemed to have relaxed a bit about certain things, which was a blessing. It wasn't as casual as being on Fish's pool deck, but things were a lot more laid-back than they had been in a while. Love was mellowing Tallulah.

The bartender handed Tucker and me our drinks—I had a spicy margarita and Tucker had a Corona—and we wandered over near the pool. It was a lovely evening, getting so close to October that I could smell it in the air.

"I just can't help feeling bad about Norah and Knox," I said to Tucker.

"Give it time. They'll be back."

"I'm not certain of that. You know I adore Tallulah, but I can't convince her that scene was all my fault. She holds Knox responsible, but really, he had a perfectly reasonable position, and honestly, he echoed some of the things I think myself when I'm feeling reasonable. I just wasn't in a reasonable place that night."

"Stop beating yourself up." Tucker rubbed my cheek. "Your posse is inbound. I'm going to go see what the guys are into." He kissed me on the cheek and headed over towards Redmond and Cash.

Hadley and Quinn meandered over and set their drinks on a nearby bar-top table.

"Have you tried these apps?" asked Quinn. "They're delicious. And everything is identifiable." She popped a cracker with pimento cheese into her mouth. Her plate held a deviled egg, two Angels on Horseback—fried oysters wrapped in bacon with a lemony aioli—and more of the pimento cheese.

"I haven't been over there." Honestly, I wasn't that hungry. The contractors had finally finished everything—at least everything related to the disaster with the primary bath and the foundation. But the financial fallout was ongoing.

I'd missed my deadline. Just yesterday, I was in tears on the phone with my editor—so unprofessional. She'd given me more time... would somehow adjust the schedule without moving my release date, which was an answered prayer, and I should've been feeling some relief from that, but I did still have to finish the book. I desperately needed to do something to get my creative juices flowing.

"Here, try this. I put way too much on my plate." Quinn handed me a toothpick with an Angel on Horseback.

"No, thank you," I said.

"Sarabeth," Hadley said in a firm tone. "Snap out of it. Norah and Knox will be back next month, you'll see. Stop beating yourself up. Tallulah invited them, you know."

"Tucker just said that same thing to me."

"Smart man," said Quinn.

"I know," I said. "But—"

"No buts," said Hadley. "Here, try this." She slid a bite of pimento cheese into my mouth.

"Mmm." I nodded. It really was good pimento cheese. "Y'all are sweet to worry about me. I'm sorry to be such a wet blanket."

"Do you have everything you need for the meet and greet?" asked Quinn.

"I think so," I said. "Y'all just don't know how much it means to me, everyone helping with this. I was just going to put out some iced tea and cider and pretzels or something. But my goodness, everyone is bringing so much... and Tallulah is sending over her favorite bartender. Sweet Norah has ordered several things from Hamby's, who I think actually might be cooking for them full time now. I just really appreciate everything so much."

Quinn waved a hand dismissively. "We all love a party."

"And we all want to get a look at the idiots," said Hadley. "Just so we know who to look out for."

"I'm starting to get nervous. It's unsettling, not knowing if we'll be entertaining the people who are harassing us with pet waste. Do you think people will really come?" I asked.

"Some will," said Hadley. "I'm not sure if the people who've been such jerks to you online will show or the idiots who keep trashing your yard. That would take more moxie than I'm guessing they have. But I think this will be good for all of us. The people who show up will build a few bridges."

"I'm proud of you for doing this," said Quinn. "I'm not sure I'd be so forgiving."

"I just keep thinking about my friend Frances. I told y'all about her, Frances Tennant? She's lived here since before Hugo, and her house was all but destroyed. It'll be worth it if we can help people understand how she feels. I'm certain she's not the only one."

"I've never met her," said Hadley. "Seems like she and Tallulah would be friends. They've both lived here a long time. This is a small town."

"We were at one time." Tallulah seemed to appear out of thin air. "Very good friends."

"Really?" I squinted at her. "What on earth happened?" I loved them both. It only made sense to me they should be friends.

"Remember what I said to Vernon," asked Tallulah, "when he had the bright idea to discuss politics?"

"Vaguely," I said, like the incident wasn't chiseled and bedazzled in my memory.

"Well, Frances was the old friend who worked beside me in the soup kitchen, whose children I watched play baseball and whose birthday parties I attended, who agreed with me on everything on God's green earth except the one. And when she found out who I voted for in the year 2000, she never spoke to me again. Said she couldn't be friends with someone whose priorities were so skewed."

"That's just awful." And horribly sad. Frances seemed so alone. Why would she deliberately cut herself off from friends like that?

"Yes," said Tallulah. "And that is why I never discuss anything to do with politics with anyone I care about. Now come to supper. Has anyone seen Libba?"

Chapter Thirty-Nine

Saturday, September 24, 2022, 5:30 p.m.
Monthly Meeting of the Sullivan's Island Supper Club—
Happy Hour
Home of Tallulah Wentworth
Libba Graham

"Come on, I want to show you something." Libba led Jake down the deck steps, past the table beneath the live oak tree Tallulah had set for dinner, and down another set of steps to the thick grass.

"Where are we going?" asked Jake.

"Shh." Libba placed a finger to her lips and grinned wickedly, then turned and ran across the lawn and through the door leading under the house. Like many raised beach houses, the garage was below the house, but a wide passageway adjacent to the garage led to a private courtyard on the far side of the house. Jake followed Libba into the enclosed patio.

"Wow," said Jake. "I never knew this was here." He turned around in a circle, taking in the wide bed of tropical plants that bordered the privacy fence.

"Me either." Libba laughed. "I was exploring earlier. It's a secret garden." She put her arms around his neck and pulled him down to her for a kiss.

"Ummm...," he murmured appreciatively.

Libba rubbed his leg with her foot.

"Sugar, what are you up to?" he asked.

"It's happy hour," she said huskily. "Imma make you happy."

He chuckled, but seconds later, when Libba pulled him over to the concrete wall at the side of the house and her full intentions became clear, he gasped. "Elizabeth Anne Frances. What would your mamma say?"

Libba kissed him deeper. Her mamma was the furthest thing from her mind.

"This is a side of you I've never seen before," whispered Jake. "This is scandalous behavior, woman. A stronger man would put a stop to it. But then I've never had a lick of sense where you're concerned."

She devoured her husband with wild abandon.

Chapter Forty

Saturday, September 24, 2022, 6:00 p.m.
Monthly Meeting of the Sullivan's Island Supper Club—Dinner
Fitzgerald Home
Tallulah Wentworth

"Here they come." Tallulah watched Libba and Jake climb the steps hand in hand. Libba was all innocent smiles, but Jake flushed and would not meet Tallulah's eyes. "Y'all enjoying a stroll?"

"Yes," said Libba. "Your yard is just stunning. I was just showing Jake your landscape lighting, which I've long admired. I want him to highlight our beds the same exact way."

"Well, it does deter prowlers in the bushes." Tallulah raised an eyebrow at Libba but had to chuckle to herself. At least they were both smiling.

"I'm so sorry if we kept y'all waiting," said Libba.

"Not at all," said Tallulah. "Everyone, tonight I've kept things very simple. I know you'll all be shocked. We're having Lowcountry boil and hushpuppies. Fish did everything himself, and it's all in serving bowls on the table. There's a blue bowl near

Hadley's place without the sausage. After Fish says grace, everyone find your places and dig in."

It was very liberating, keeping things simple. She made one last visual check of the table as Fish said amen. She'd brought out the Fiesta tableware this evening. A simple burlap table runner scattered with chunky candles in brightly painted wooden holders was all that adorned the farmhouse table aside from the dishes themselves, which were a random mix of sunflower, poppy, meadow, lapis, and turquoise. It was all quite colorful and happy, and the casual vibe suited the Lowcountry boil. Tallulah squelched the notion that she'd taken the easy way out this month.

She wasn't sure how much anyone cared about the food this month anyway. Most of them seemed to be in the throes of love. Fish gave her a sideways look as he moved behind her to pull out her chair. She'd put him at the head of the table, a place she usually occupied. She honestly couldn't say why she did that, only that it just seemed right. Fish had always been her partner in supper club in one way or another. That evening he'd prepared their food. He had settled quickly into the role of leading man in her life. It wasn't that she'd forgotten about Henry—not at all, never. She would always love Henry. But she loved Fish too. Those things weren't mutually exclusive. And Fish was here. Warm, strong, and tender. Tallulah felt the joy bubbling up inside her.

Hadley smiled at her from across the table. "Tallulah, you look radiant."

"Thank you, darlin'," said Tallulah.

"If I could have everyone's attention." Fish stood and everyone got quiet.

"Congratulations are in order. Tennyson, I don't imagine these ladies will ever forgive you for absconding with Camille and depriving them of a proper wedding. But we're happy you've both returned safely from your trip to Las Vegas, and we wish you many happy years together. To Camille and Tennyson." He lifted his glass and everyone echoed his toast.

Tallulah's eyes found Camille's as she lifted her glass. At the far end of the table, Camille certainly did look happy. And Tennyson played the part of attentive newlywed husband well. Was Tallulah wrong to worry? She did want Camille to be happy. But was it necessary to rush things so? Maybe at their age rushing things was the best policy. After all, there weren't that many shopping days left until Christmas.

Fish returned to his seat, and they all went about the business of scooping shrimp, corn, sausage, and potatoes onto their plates. Tallulah stole another look at Camille, who she'd swear she'd never seen this happy. What's done was done. Tallulah would be happy for her and trust the good Lord to take care of her and all the rest of them.

She glanced around the table. Camille and Tennyson were wrapped up in each other. Vernon and Birdie chatted across the table with Sarabeth and Tucker, something about the fall meet and greet, which they'd scheduled for the Friday before Halloween. To Tallulah's left, Jake and Libba were every bit as engrossed with one another as the newlyweds. Whatever had happened to turn things around for them, Tallulah was grateful for it. New hormones, she'd heard, and perhaps Libba needed to have them dialed back just a bit, or maybe not. As long it was her own husband she was dragging into the bushes, what did it hurt?

Quinn and Redmond seemed more relaxed and happy than Tallulah had seen them in a while. Quinn's parents surely were interesting people, though Tallulah didn't think having them at supper club on a regular basis was a good idea. They weren't easy to be around. Maybe that was her objection to Knox Fitzgerald as well if she thought about it. Sometimes he was comfortable in his own skin, and sometimes he wasn't. But Norah was a sweetheart. Tallulah genuinely enjoyed her company and was sorry they hadn't come this evening.

What was going on with Cash and Hadley? Tallulah

continued her sweep down the opposite side of the table. They'd been back together now for more than a year. Was Cash planning to pop the question? They seemed happy. What fun a wedding would be. Fish was right. Camille had robbed them of the perfect opportunity for a big celebration.

But why couldn't they plan a celebration after the fact? Tallulah could throw them a big reception. They could have it right here. Or maybe at Fish's house. Why was everyone so much more comfortable at Fish's house? Well, it was oceanfront.

Tallulah turned to Fish. "What would you think about throwing a wedding reception for Camille and Tennyson?"

"I think if it makes you smile, I'm all in."

Chapter Forty-One

Saturday, September 24, 2022, 7:00 p.m.
Monthly Meeting of the Sullivan's Island Supper Club
Home of Tallulah Wentworth
Quinn Poinsett

Dessert that evening was key lime pie, Quinn's favorite. Tallulah had set it up on a table near the bar and told them all to have some whenever they liked. Quinn had taken a piece over to a lounger by the pool. She delivered a bite of key lime pie to her mouth as she watched Redmond, deep in conversation with Cash on the other side of the deck.

What were they talking about? It looked serious, not like dinnertime conversation.

Or was she borrowing trouble?

For the first time in... since they'd been married, she should be able to relax. There were no more secrets between them. Redmond, true to his word, had upgraded their security system with a high-end company he'd found through Cash. Maybe that's what they were talking about. Redmond had also bought a gun, which she was ambivalent about. She hated having a gun in the house with the kids. You heard horror stories. But Redmond had put it in a gun safe by the bed that opened with his palm print or hers. And he was going to take her to the shooting range and teach her how to use the gun. Better safe than sorry. She'd sleep better knowing they could defend themselves if they had to.

And then there was the safe room Redmond had plans for. He was serious about easing her mind. The elaborate, steel-walled room would take the space currently occupied by a guest room they never used. His parents were nearby in Charleston. Hers were almost on top of them. Neither of them had siblings. They'd never miss the guest room, and again, the safe room would give them peace of mind.

So why had Redmond slow-walked the installation? He'd been gung-ho and had contractors ready to start the week before last, then he told her he wanted to wait and talk to someone else before they started. He'd been very vague...

She needed to get a grip.

She was married to the most wonderful, forgiving man, and he was the world's greatest dad. He was also very thorough in everything he did. If he wanted to talk to someone else about the safe room, it was no doubt for the best.

At least her parents were behaving better. They'd calmed down significantly over the past six weeks or so. There'd been no more public incidents, no more fighting. She had not told them that she told Redmond everything. They'd talked about it and decided against it, thinking it could only make a volatile situation worse.

"Is this seat taken?" Hadley slid into the lounger beside her.

"Yes, I'm sorry, my Latin lover went to get us a nightcap, but he'll be right back," said Quinn.

"Honestly, this vegan key lime pie has got to be as good as what you're eating." Hadley put a bite into her mouth.

"Let me taste it." Quinn took her fork and scooped a bite of Hadley's pie. She chewed thoughtfully. "It's really good. But I like mine better."

"You're a purist," said Hadley. "Hey, listen, what are you taking to Sarabeth's the night of the meet and greet?"

"Mini tomato tarts," said Quinn. "It's one of Redmond's mother's recipes, and they're delicious."

"I'm taking a cooler full of bottled water and a cooler of soft drinks, you know, for the imaginary teetotalers. But I guess you have to have that stuff just in case. Anyway, Cash has to work that night, so I'm going solo. Any chance I can bum a ride with you and Redmond? Think he'd help with the coolers?"

"Of course," said Quinn. "He'd be happy to."

"Excellent. Thank you," said Hadley.

"But it's a shame Cash has to work. I bet Sarabeth would've loved having him there, you know, as a deterrent. There's nothing like a police presence to keep people civil. Well, Norah will be there."

"I heard Norah has to work too," said Hadley. "But between you and me, I seriously doubt the troublemakers will bother showing up. They're not generally interested in efforts to make peace."

"I don't know which thing to hope for, that they come or that they don't." Quinn shrugged. "We'll pick you up at seven if that's okay. The invitations she sent said eight. That should give us plenty of time to set up."

Chapter Forty-Two

Saturday, October 8, 2022, 5:15 p.m.
Boone Home, I'On Avenue
Sarabeth Mercer Jackson Boone

When your house is generally full of teenage granddaughters and their friends—and your thirty-five-year-old son who is possibly becoming a hermit—you relish every opportunity for time alone. Tucker and I were enjoying the peace and quiet on the screened porch, gazing out over our backyard and sipping a drink called Holy City Smoke, which Hadley had introduced us to. It has mezcal in it, and I have to say, it's quite relaxing.

"The yard looks fabulous," I said. "I can't believe you got all all that scraggly brush out, got all those azaleas planted, and got everything mulched. Everything will look real nice for the meet and greet. But I worry you might've overdone yourself." Men Tucker's age should hire high school athletes to spread mulch. We didn't need to be courting trouble.

"Sarabeth, I need to stay active. The exercise is good for me. I don't want to get to the point where I can't do these things myself. You worry too much."

"Maybe so. But it would ease my mind if you'd just hire somebody to do the heavy stuff and then walk on the beach for exercise like I do."

"When will the kids be back?"

"Deacon took the girls to the outlet mall to do a little more school clothes shopping. He said they'd eat dinner out, so I'm guessing seven to seven thirty."

Tucker waggled his eyebrows at me. "Why don't I mix us another drink and meet you in the bedroom?"

I grinned at him. "Let me run through the shower right quick." A joyful little feeling bubbled up in me. It wasn't often we had privacy in our own home. I stood and gave him a kiss with a promise in it and hurried into the primary suite.

I have to tell you, after everything we've been through with our bathroom, I was so happy with the way it turned out. We designed it to have a spa-like feel to it, and it really did, all white subway tile and soothing tones of white, cream, beige, and grey. I turned the Sonos on and shuffled a playlist I'd named A Little Romance just in that part of the house. Kameron Marlowe was singing "Steady Heart" as I hopped into the shower.

After I dried off, I smoothed on a thick layer of my favorite orange-scented body butter and tied my blue sarong so that the knot below my right shoulder had a little flourish. Tucker and I had bought several brightly colored sarongs on a long-ago vacation in St. John. A shop in Mongoose Junction had them, and we thought they'd be fun around the pool. We ended up practically living in them, and well, now I guess they make us feel carefree, like we were in the islands. I wear mine like a dress, and he wears his around his waist. It's just a fun little thing we do.

I went into the bedroom and closed the plantation shutters and used the remote control to turn on the candles scattered around the room. I picked up my phone and skipped the Sonos to "Seven Days" by Kenny Chesney, which we were listening to on that trip to St. John. Then I fluffed all the pillows and arranged myself in what I hoped would be an attractive position and waited for my husband.

A few minutes later, he hadn't arrived from the kitchen. I was thinking he probably decided to bring a little snack with the drinks, which he often did, and I figured I'd help carry it. So I padded into the kitchen.

"Can I help with anything?" I asked.

Tucker whistled. "That outfit is quite helpful." He poured our drinks from the shaker into frosty glasses with a flourish. "If you'll get the drinks, I'll bring the nibbles."

I picked up a couple of cocktail napkins, then the glasses, and had taken one step towards our bedroom when the front door blew open and in came Lennox, Calliope, and Deacon.

There was no place to hide in our open floor plan house. They'd already seen us anyway. Tucker and I froze. I inhaled really sharply, making a noise that was somewhere between a scream and a gasp.

The girls stopped short in the entryway, mouths open.

Now, neither of us were indecent, exactly, in our sarongs. But it was quite clear to anyone familiar with adult pastimes what was going on.

After a few beats, Tucker said, "Sarabeth, I am not wearing this costume to the meet and greet. You wanted me to try it on, fine. I hope you're happy. I'm sorry, darlin'. I know it's Halloween, but I think we need to skip dressing up as Tarzan and Jane and just wear our regular clothes." It was a valiant effort to reframe the incident in the memories of our granddaughters. I had little faith in its success, but was willing to go along.

"But a costume party will be way more fun." I smiled and tried to sell it.

"I like the pirate outfit Granddad wore last year better," said Calliope, who was a little on the naive side.

Deacon, to his credit, said, "Girls, let's take your new clothes upstairs and put everything away."

Wordlessly, Lennox and Calliope scooted up the stairs.

Tucker closed his eyes. His shoulders rose and fell with a deep breath. I could just see the disappointment, and I was disappointed too. I think something might have snapped inside me. This was ridiculous. It shouldn't be this way. We should be able to have time to ourselves in our own home. At our age, we shouldn't be having to fit our lives around our children.

"Sorry about that," said Deacon. "We finished early and decided to come home for dinner." He averted his eyes and took a step to follow the girls up the stairs.

"Wait just a minute please," I said.

He looked at me like, *what's up*? "Ma'am?"

"Ninety days."

"I'm sorry?" Deacon wore a confused expression.

"You'll need to make other living arrangements for you and the girls. You're welcome to stay here with us for ninety more days. That should give you enough time to figure things out. It's already been five months."

"Mom—" There was an objection in his voice.

"I know there will be challenges, but you are a smart young man, and you will figure this out. I have faith in you."

"Well, Mother—" There was that patronizing tone again.

"No, now that's a mistake." I smiled sweetly at him.

He wrinkled his forehead. "I don't make enough—"

"First don't ever take that tone with me again. Do you understand me?"

"What tone?" He made air quotes.

"*That* tone." I hoped he could hear the warning in mine. "And second, if you have to work a second job to put a roof over your daughters' heads, well, that's what parents do. They make sacrifices for their children."

Deacon looked flabbergasted. "I don't know what you expect—"

"I expect you to grow up. It's time. As I said, you are a very smart young man. You will figure all this out. Now excuse us please."

I waggled my eyebrows at Tucker, and he followed me into the bedroom and closed the door.

"Who are you?" Tucker laughed as he set the plate on top of the picnic blanket on the bed. He walked over and stood next to me.

"I'm fixin' to show you." I smiled a wicked smile up at him and handed him his glass. "To an empty nest. Cheers."

I took a long drink from my cocktail glass. Something inside me had come unleashed. I felt positively giddy. Was this what standing up for yourself felt like? I could make a habit of it.

Well... I still believed in putting others first. But there had to be a balance in there somewhere, and I hadn't really learned that part yet.

Today the "others" I was putting first was my husband.

Chapter Forty-Three

Thursday, October 20, 2022, 7:00 p.m.
Graham Custom Woodwork
Hungryneck Boulevard, Mount Pleasant
Libba Graham

Libba checked her makeup in the rearview mirror. It was Jake's birthday, and he'd worked late finishing up a table for a client. She was going to surprise him with a gourmet picnic and a scandalous outfit. She climbed out of the car and gathered the picnic basket and her purse. Whoa. She'd have to move slowly across the parking lot in her black stilettos carrying the basket.

She glanced around the parking lot. Jake's car was still here, of course. But Libba was not expecting to see Roxie's Corvette—a college graduation gift from her overindulgent father. What was *she* doing here this late? She didn't work on Jake's custom orders. Roxie handled stock items.

Well.

Libba squared her shoulders. This was it. Tears welled up in her eyes. Things had been going so well between them. She'd almost convinced herself Jake's fling with Roxie—or whatever it was—was only in her head. It was time she found out exactly what was going on between her husband and his protégé.

She made her way gingerly across the parking lot.

The door to the showroom was open, but the lights were out. Libba let her eyes adjust to the dark, then crossed the showroom, passed the offices, and stood in the doorway to the workroom, which was bathed in candlelight.

Across the room, Jake stood behind a long, live-edge dining table. He had his hands on his hips. Libba watched as Roxie, who must've crossed the threshold of the room mere seconds before Libba arrived, sashayed across the room, clad only in a pushup bra, lacy panties, and heels the height of Libba's own. Roxie had a bow on her head and carried a cupcake with a candle in it. She sang "Happy Birthday" as she walked. Libba just stared in shock.

"What the hell are you doing?" Jake's voice boomed across the room.

Libba's lip quivered. He sounded so mad. He must've seen her though Roxie was now blocking her line of sight. Libba couldn't see Jake anymore. She could only hear him. What *was* she doing? She should've left when she saw Roxie's car.

"*Roxie,*" Jake yelled sharply. "Cut it out. Now. Put the lights back on. Where did all these damn candles come from?"

Roxie stopped walking. "What's wrong?"

"*What's wrong?* You can't be serious."

"I just thought—"

"Get some clothes on. And leave. Now."

Wait. What? Libba's heart lifted. Jake was rejecting Roxie. And he apparently didn't know Libba was there. Wait a minute. Did he? Could he see her?

"I don't understand...," Roxie said, her voice childish and pouty.

"It's crystal clear," said Jake. "You just crossed a line, a big one. Now get your clothes on and go home."

"But, Jake-ie...," she wheedled. "You haven't seen my birthday dance."

"That's it. You're fired. Get all your things. Get out. Now. I'll mail your final check."

She just stood there looking at him.

"*Go*," he barked.

Roxie turned around. When she saw Libba, she gasped, her eyes huge. "Oh."

"You're not moving. Why are you not moving?" Jake asked.

"I think she was surprised to see me," Libba said.

"*Libba?*" Jake leaned out to see around Roxie, then crossed the room in long strides. "Libba, this is not what it looks like."

Libba nodded, a little smile playing around her lips. "I'm pretty sure it is."

"You don't understand—"

Libba moved past Roxie and stood in front of Jake. She looked up at him. "I think I do." Then she turned to Roxie. "Roxie, why are you still standing there? *Move it right now,* or I'm calling your mamma."

Roxie dashed out of the room.

Libba was lost in Jake's eyes.

"Just tell me one thing," she said.

"I never—" he started.

She put a finger to his lips. "Did you really not see me there until I spoke?"

He shook his head. "No. I didn't. I swear." He raked a hand through his hair. "I'm so sorry, Libba. Baby, I would never—"

"I think I know that now." She smiled at him. "Better make sure she's gone."

Jake nodded. "Be right back."

"And Jake?"

"Yeah?"

"Better make sure the door is locked behind her. I don't have anything on underneath this trench coat."

Later, wrapped in the picnic blanket, she sat in his lap as they fed each other bites of the picnic she'd packed—a gourmet charcuterie board with cubes of filet mignon, grilled shrimp, cheeses, figs, pears, grapes, and nuts with toasted baguette, now atop the newly finished table.

Libba said, "Jake, I want to go back to work. The kids are old enough, don't you think?"

"Sure they are. And I can help with taking them where they need to go. I know you do a lot of running…"

"I know I'm not going to be able to step back into management. I'm going to have to, well, not start over entirely, but back up a bit. It'll take a while for me to make up the ground I've lost. But I'm okay with that."

He smoothed her hair and slid it behind her ear. "What if you didn't have to do that? Take a step backwards, I mean?"

"I just don't think that's realistic, but—"

"See, the thing is, I have a recent opening here at Graham Custom Woodwork. And I was thinking instead of hiring someone to help with the product end of the business, maybe I should hire an executive to manage the office and be in charge of marketing. What do you think?"

"You really think I could do that? I mean, could I actually be an asset? Because the last thing I want is for you to do this—and Jake, it's an amazing offer—but I don't want you to offer me this because you think it's what *I* need. I want it to be what *you* need."

"Baby, I have seen what you can do with marketing. You're amazing. And you have the business-management background to do everything I need and probably a lot of things I don't even know I need. I would be lucky to have you."

"Are you sure?" Libba gave him a look that was part tentative smile, part question.

"Heck, yeah. If you're willing to do it, you can start whenever you like. We probably will have to hire another product developer because I'm already busy and I have no doubt you'll drive more business."

"Well, let's open the champagne." She kissed him soundly to seal the deal.

Chapter Forty-Four

Monday, October 24, 2022, 5:45 a.m.
Beach near Station 26
Sarabeth Mercer Jackson Boone

Norah and I had been walking in companionable silence for a while when she asked, "How are things at home? I mean, since you gave Deacon his eviction notice?"

"Overall, pretty good. I still feel guilty sometimes. It just seems wrong on so many levels. I was raised a certain way. Family does for family. That's all there is to it. But... the difficult thing is when the right thing for some of the people you love is the wrong thing for someone else you love. I can't do for the kids anymore at Tucker's expense. And actually, that's something else my mamma has always said. In fact, she's drilled it into me: 'Sarabeth, you have got to put Tucker first.'"

"Maybe there's a reason she felt like that message needed extra emphasis." Norah smiled.

"Could be."

"Have you finished your book?"

My smile widened. "Almost. I have just a couple more chapters to go. Then of course there'll be edits and so forth. But it will be a huge relief to have the story down."

"I can imagine."

"I was really worried there for a while. I think dealing with the Deacon situation helped to..."

"It unbl—"

"No, no, no. Don't say that word. I don't believe in that word."

"Okay, okay." Norah laughed.

I made little circle motions with my hands. "Resolving that issue helped to loosen the flow of pent-up words."

"Okay then." Norah nodded. "I'm so happy things are flowing."

"Thank you. Actually, and I hesitate to say this because it might, I don't know, tempt fate or something, but... things are really good with Tucker. The house is... well, there's a lot we haven't gotten to that was on our list when we first bought the house. But all the pressing things had been taken care of. And I love our new bathroom. The foundation is rock solid. Everything else will come in its time, I guess."

"It sounds like things really are finally looking up," Norah said.

"They really are." We walked another minute in silence, and then I thought, well, there'll never be a right time to ask this question, so I may as well. "Hey, can I ask you a question?"

"Sure, of course."

I walked another few steps before I finally got it out. "Knox hasn't ever... gotten rough with you, has he?"

"Oh good grief, no. Absolutely not."

"Oh—whew! I mean, I just thought—"

"First of all, he wouldn't dare. I'm trained in multiple martial arts, and I'm always armed."

"I did recall that little tidbit. And I thought, yes, of course you can defend yourself. But—"

Norah nodded. "But I told you Knox tried to isolate me, and you know that's typical abuser behavior."

"That's right." I nodded. "I didn't mean to offend you. I was just worried about you."

"I'm not offended. I understand. And thank you for caring."

"Why, of course I care."

"Knox is gentle as a lamb. He would just never hurt anyone. I know he comes off as a jerk sometimes, but... he's doing better actually," said Norah. "He's really trying. I just keep reassuring him and telling him that we're building a life for the two of us here... He felt so badly about opening his mouth at supper club that night. I don't think you'll hear from him on the topic of the maritime forest ever again."

"I'm the one who's sorry about that night. Not my finest moment."

Norah waved the notion away. "Please don't give that another thought. Hey, are you getting nervous about Friday? The meet and greet?"

"I am. Really nervous. I'm wondering what the heck I was thinking. I mean, if the people brazen enough and... *despicable* enough to throw pet waste in our yard as a method of indicating their displeasure with me show up at all, it won't be because they want to shake hands and be friends."

"You never know," said Norah. "Sometimes people will surprise you. Worst-case scenario, you'll have a nice party. I hate that I have to miss it."

Chapter Forty-Five

Friday, October 28, 2022, 8:00–9:30 p.m.
Fall Meet and Greet
Home of Sarabeth and Tucker Boone
Sarabeth Mercer Jackson Boone

We had supper early the night of the meet and greet, Tucker, Deacon, me, and the girls. Deacon had plans and left right after, but the girls helped me get things set out. Hadley and Quinn and Redmond arrived about seven fifteen—they were such a big help. Norah and Cash both had to work, which I understood completely, but I was actually shocked that Knox came *by himself*.

Norah had arranged for Hamby's to drop off a bunch of food—she really went overboard. They came at seven thirty and brought platters of tea sandwiches, those little sweet potato biscuits with ham—regular ham biscuits too—and deviled eggs. And I want you to know, Knox was right there as they unloaded, carrying trays out and putting them on the buffet we had set up in the backyard. He was just as nice as he could be, and he didn't mention a single word to me about jetties or accreted land or anybody's views, which was a huge relief. Tucker and I hadn't seen him since the night I had that meltdown at their house.

Norah I had seen many times since, and I knew it was important to her to smooth things over.

The girls and I had put together a few simple things. A veggie tray, a fruit tray, and some sweets—you know, brownies, cookies, and lemon squares—and bowls of salty snacks, like pretzels, nuts, and popcorn. And we put big bowls of Halloween candy out—that was a big hit. Sweet Hadley brought a couple of coolers of water and soft drinks and extra ice. She is just so thoughtful.

Oh—I have to tell you, Quinn's tomato tarts were out of this world. All the food was so good I was wishing we hadn't had supper. Birdie and Vernon brought spinach and artichoke dip and pimento cheese and crackers. And Libba and Jake, bless their hearts, brought I don't know how many pounds of smoked chicken wings. Oh... Camille and Tennyson brought the little grape jelly meatballs and buffalo chicken dip. The bar outside, well, that was all Tallulah and Fish. They came a little after seven with the bartender and set all that up.

My friends arrived with a feast, is what I'm telling you. They came early, and they brought their best and favorite party foods, and they had my back. That just meant the world to me. And it's why what happened that night just broke me in ways I don't think I'll ever recover from.

So, let's see... Well, first of all, I was a little nervous but not too much really. I guess you might say I was riding high. Things were looking up for Tucker and me. I mean, we were still stretched thin financially. But we had a plan for rebounding from the past nineteen months or so, and aside from the sporadic "offerings" someone threw into our backyard, things were going pretty well.

Now, what we had in mind was *not* to have a group discussion about the issues and clear the air—not at all. There was no program. We simply wanted to spend time together, get to know more of our neighbors, and *humanize* each other.

At first you would never have guessed that the whole thing was planned to help mend a neighborhood rift. It was like any other party. I shuffled my beach music playlist on the Sonos.

Everyone likes beach music. Tucker and I stood near the front door and greeted people as they came in. Nearly everyone just went on through the house and into the backyard. That's where the bar and the food were after all.

I confess, I searched every face as people came in, trying to catch a clue from an expression—or something—as to whether I was welcoming someone who'd been hateful to me or Frances or someone else online or possibly harbored poop-tossing tendencies. Everyone was so gracious I just couldn't believe any one of them was one of the troublemakers. And it was sort of wonderful, actually, to have these strangers who were my neighbors, who I wanted to get to know better, along with my dear friends at our home. It really did feel like we were widening the circle of goodwill, like we were sinking deeper roots into this community that meant so much to us both.

A few people just went straight to the backyard, so there were people there we didn't meet, and honestly, most of the people whose hands I shook I can't recall their names—there were just too many new faces and names, all at once—and I couldn't tell you then or now if they were in favor of cutting trees or not. But there was an air of goodwill, I'll say that much. Everyone was on their very best behavior, and no one was discussing anything controversial. At least not at first.

It was a nice party. The weather certainly cooperated. It was one of those clear, crisp October evenings I wait for all year. The breeze smelled like salt and football and possibilities. We had everything decorated for Halloween, and yes... I know my granddaughters may be a little old for Halloween decorations, but they love them. And there have been years when they didn't have decorations and might've had to scrounge around for something to turn into a costume because maybe their father was distracted by a skirt or a job he was chasing or by his friends in low places. I tried to give the girls what I could as I could even if it was inadequate and often a little late. And I had promised myself that even after they lived under another roof, I would be watching closely to make sure they had what they needed. Any other grandmother would do the same thing, I'm certain of it.

About nine thirty, Tucker and I decided to make the rounds, and we let Lennox and Calliope man the door. Up until that point, I would guess maybe a hundred people had walked through our house, most continuing to the backyard. When we walked through the screened porch and down the deck steps to the patio, Libba and Jake and Quinn and Redmond were dancing, along with a few other couples I didn't know. Everyone else was standing around in little clusters chatting, with everyone in as close a proximity as they could manage to the bar.

"Feel like dancing?" Tucker asked.

"Why sure." I smiled up at him.

He took my hand, and we walked over to the corner of the patio that was serving as a dance floor. "Hold Back the Night" by the Trammps was playing, and everything was just perfect in that moment. We were at the home we'd bought together in the place we loved the most, surrounded by friends and some of our family anyway. I was as happy as I ever remember being.

Trouble had arrived. I was simply oblivious to it.

Chapter Forty-Six

Friday, October 28, 2022, 9:25–10:00 p.m.
Fall Meet and Greet
Home of Sarabeth and Tucker Boone
Libba Graham

Libba had forgotten all about the reason for the party. She was dancing with her husband, kicking up her heels, and being high on life again after feeling like she'd been dragged through the ditches of hell for the better part of a year. She might've been the slightest bit tipsy. The bartender was mixing prickly pear margaritas, and Libba was working on her second.

But about 9:25—it was right before Sarabeth and Tucker came outside—she noticed a group of thirtysomethings coming around the side of the house by the garage and felt a ripple in the force. There were maybe four or five couples and an unattached blond woman who was dressed to get the wrong kind of attention. If Libba had ever seen any of them before, she didn't recall it. They all went directly over to the bar, but Libba thought from the loose way they carried themselves that they weren't ordering their first drinks of the evening.

Libba might've alerted Sarabeth and Tucker to this clan, but just then her attention shifted.

"Oh good grief." She looked at her foot.

"What's wrong?" asked Jake.

"My sandal broke," said Libba. "Let me see if Sarabeth has a pair I can borrow."

"I'll be over by the bar." He nodded in the direction of Knox, Hadley, Quinn, and Redmond, chatting animatedly.

Libba found Sarabeth—she and Tucker had just joined them on the dance floor—and she said of course Libba could borrow a pair of shoes, just go find whatever she wanted in her closet. Fortunately they were both size eight. Libba moved cautiously up the steps, through the screened porch, across the lower floor of the house, and into the primary suite, which occupied the front corner of the house.

Sarabeth's closet was through the bathroom, which had just been completely redone and was stunning—all rippled white subway tile, with farmhouse sinks and an oversized glass shower. Libba took a moment to admire the big slipper tub with the oil rubbed bronze retro tub filler.

Sarabeth and Tucker had separate closets down a little alcove on the far side of the bathroom. Libba slid the pocket door to the right—obviously Tucker's—then closed it and opened the door to her left. Wow. They must've redone the closets while they were doing the bathroom. This looked like something from a closet design ad, with drawers and hanging sections of varying heights. Sarabeth's shoes occupied a wide floor-to-ceiling row of shelves at the back. Libba chose a cute pair of tan wedge sandals that would go with just about anything, including her transitional floral dress and jean jacket, and walked barefoot, carrying the sandals from the bathroom back into the bedroom.

She set the shoes on the floor and had one foot raised when she saw the small blue dinosaur about the size of a well-fed house cat.

Libba sucked in a long breath and held it. This was the iguana that moved in with Deacon and the girls. Sarabeth had not exaggerated. Libba had never seen anything like it. Did this thing bite? Was it poisonous?

The creature stared at her from the doorway of Sarabeth and Tucker's bedroom.

Libba had left her phone outside.

There was no way around it.

It hissed at her.

"Aah!" Libba jumped up on Sarabeth and Tucker's bed. A shiver ran down her spine.

"Help!" she called.

No one responded.

"*Help!*" she called louder.

The third time she raised her voice, it held a note of panic. "*Helllllp!* Somebody help me!"

She heard running footsteps, then watched through the doorway as Sarabeth's teenaged granddaughters, Lennox and Calliope, come to a screeching halt at the far end of the little hallway that separated the primary suite from the living area. Their eyes and mouths were wide with alarm.

"Oh no." Lennox, the older of the two, had dark honey-colored hair.

"How did Elvis get out?" asked Calliope.

"I don't know," said Lennox. "I'll call Dad." She backed away, presumably to find her phone.

"Does Elvis bite?" Libba asked.

"We don't know," said Calliope. "He's never bitten one of us, but we don't mess with him. We just look at him. He's beautiful, isn't he?"

"Stunning," said Libba in a flat tone indicating how unimpressed she was with Elvis at that moment.

Lennox came back, a phone to her ear, breathless. "He's not answering."

"What are we going to do?" asked Calliope.

The three of them stared at Elvis, who continued to occupy

the doorway, swiveling his reptilian head from Libba to Lennox and Calliope. He was trapped between them, at least for the moment. But Libba had no intentions of apprehending him, and she was effectively trapped in the bedroom.

She climbed off the far side of the bed, opened the plantation shutters, and looked outside to see if anyone was in earshot. But the window overlooked the side yard, not the back. Libba was about to step to the front window when movement caught her eye. Someone was standing in the yard beneath the window, between the house and the potting shed. Who was that? She was looking at the top of his head. It was Knox. And here came one of the group of thirtysomethings who'd just arrived. It was the tube top and miniskirt-wearing blonde. Why was she over there talking privately with Norah's husband?

Libba couldn't hear what they were saying, but Knox appeared to be doing most of the talking. The blonde crossed her arms. Finally she suggested something vulgar with her middle finger, turned around, and stalked off. What in the world?

Lennox and Calliope squealed.

Libba pivoted to the sound of running on hardwood floors.

Elvis and the girls had disappeared.

"Where'd he go?" Libba dashed out of the bedroom, looking both ways as she entered the family room.

Lennox and Calliope stood on the stone fireplace hearth.

"Into the kitchen." Lennox pointed. "We'd better get Gigi."

"No!" Libba reached out a hand. "Wait." Sarabeth had way more than she could handle hostessing such a large crowd. She did not need to know this creature was loose in her house. The dogs must've sensed something was wrong. They were barking their heads off. "Are the dogs penned up?"

Lennox nodded. "Upstairs in Gigi's office. Should we let them loose? Elvis doesn't like the dogs."

Libba thought for a minute. "No. That could end badly. We need brooms and mops. Anything with a long handle."

"Be right back," said Lennox. She circled behind the sofa, cut through the dining room, and darted down the back hall to the laundry room, then returned with two brooms and a Swiffer pole. She handed Libba a broom and kept one for herself. Calliope got the Swiffer pole.

"We need to shoo this thing outside, all right?" said Libba. "None of us want to touch it. There's no way to get it back in its cage. And it will be far happier outside. He can go live in the forest. This is the best thing for everyone. Right?"

"Right." Lennox and Calliope nodded enthusiastically.

"All right then," said Libba. "There's company in the back-yard. Elvis is leaving through the front."

Libba opened the front door wide, then circled back to one side of the kitchen island.

Lennox went around the other side. "Here he is. Shoo." She swept the broom gently into the iguana's tail.

Elvis obliged by darting towards Libba, who scooted out of the way and shooed the iguana in the direction of the foyer.

Calliope gave him a little push with the Swiffer pole and he must've seen freedom because he darted across the family room, through the foyer, and out the front door.

Libba closed it behind him. "Well done, ladies."

Upstairs, the dogs went to howling.

Chapter Forty-Seven

Friday, October 28, 2022, 10:00–11:00 p.m.
Fall Meet and Greet
Home of Sarabeth and Tucker Boone
Tallulah Wentworth

Everything was fine at first, though Tallulah was skeptical anything was being accomplished other than a good time. Having a good time with folks built bridges though, she supposed. It certainly wouldn't hurt anything. But then the trouble started around ten thirty.

Tallulah had pegged those four couples as trouble when they first arrived about an hour ago. No one knew who they were. They didn't introduce themselves or make any effort to engage anyone beyond their group. It didn't make sense at first. Tallulah thought they'd all come in together, but apparently they'd simply arrived at the same time, because two of the couples were conservationists, and two were cutters. That became crystal clear when they started raising their voices.

They stood in a circle in the middle of the deck, going back and forth, getting progressively louder. Tallulah could only make out a word here and there: accreted land, dunes, hurricanes, legacy, coyotes, views, fires, mosquitos.

"Did you see where Tucker went?" Fish glanced around the backyard.

"I think they both went inside a few minutes ago," said Tallulah. "The dogs were barking like crazy."

"This isn't headed anywhere good," said Fish.

Redmond, Libba, and Jake came over to where Tallulah and Fish stood on the opposite end of the patio from the bar.

"You think we should intervene?" asked Redmond.

"I'd like to see what Tucker thinks about that," said Jake.

Birdie, Vernon, and Camille joined their huddle.

"I could get the water hose," said Vernon.

"Vernon, behave yourself," admonished Birdie.

The volume on the argument went up another notch, and then a few more people jumped into the fray to defend their point of view. Before you knew it, the whole thing escalated.

"A coyote killed my wife's Yorkshire terrier. Do you know what I paid for that dog?"

"Are you flipping stupid? Keep your flipping pets on a flipping leash." The crude man used another word that started with *F*. He seemed fond of the word and used it several times in every sentence.

"What do you not understand about the effects of rising sea levels on a barrier island?"

"Talk to me when rats are running through your living room while your kids are watching television," a stocky, muscled man snarled at the red-haired woman.

"Watch your tone with my wife," said the six-foot-plus man in the golf shirt and pressed khakis.

"Here come Tucker and Sarabeth," said Camille.

"She needs to keep her flipping nose out of other people's business." The stocky man put his pointer finger on the tall man's chest.

That turned out to be a mistake.

Someone shoved someone.

They shoved back.

The first punch knocked the stocky man to the ground.

And then someone got a running start and plowed into a man standing too close to Tallulah.

Fish pulled her out of harm's way just in the nick of time.

"Hey! Knock it off!" Tucker yelled from the deck. He motioned at their group of friends. "Y'all come on inside." Then he pulled Sarabeth through the door.

Tallulah, Fish, Redmond, Libba, Jake, Birdie, Vernon, Camille, and Tennyson hustled up the steps.

"This is a disaster." Sarabeth was beside herself. "And everything was going so well. I don't understand."

"It's just a few people," said Tallulah. "A handful of uncivilized cretins ruined your lovely party."

Sarabeth sat heavily at the kitchen table. She seemed to be in shock, which Tallulah could certainly understand.

Tallulah watched from the window as Tucker walked back out onto the deck with an air horn, turned off the music, and hollered at them all to leave. And some of the crowd did go home. But that group—those four couples—they just turned on poor Tucker, shouting and carrying on.

Tucker came inside the house and said to Sarabeth, "Where are Lennox and Calliope?"

"They're upstairs," she said in a hollow voice.

He looked around the room, doing a head count. "What about Quinn and Hadley?"

"They were out on the front porch a few minutes ago," said Tallulah.

Redmond crossed towards the front door.

Tucker locked the back door as he dialed the police with his cell phone.

Things were happening in a blur; everyone was finding the best window to peer out of—it was chaotic inside Sarabeth and Tucker's house. Everyone was excited, all talking at once. Tallulah couldn't say how long it was before Redmond came back inside looking worried.

"Tucker, everything under control here?" asked Redmond.

"Yeah. Police are on their way."

"I'm going to head out. I need to catch up with Quinn."

"Oh, did she leave?" Sarabeth lifted her head.

"Quinn had to run by her parents' house," said Redmond. "I'll just take her home from there."

Within three minutes, the chief of police was there with two other officers, and they arrested the troublemakers. Tucker, Fish, Vernon, and Tennyson went outside to speak with the police. Birdie and Camille busied themselves straightening up in the kitchen. Libba and Jake sat with Calliope and Lennox in the den —the girls seemed excited, chattering and having a hard time sitting still.

Tallulah sat at the table with poor Sarabeth, who put her head in her hands. Tallulah just felt so bad for her. No one could ever say she didn't do her best to make peace. But there was no denying it had backfired badly.

Chapter Forty-Eight

Friday, October 28, 2022, 10:15 p.m.
Fall Meet and Greet
Home of Sarabeth and Tucker Boone
Quinn Poinsett

Quinn's mamma texted at ten fifteen:

> I locked myself out of the house. Please bring
> your spare key and let me in.

Quinn texted back:

> Be right there.

She looked for Redmond but didn't see him in the crowd. She climbed the steps to the house and made her way through to the front porch. Where was he?

"Hey, everything all right?" Hadley stood at the corner of the front porch. She pressed a button on her phone and slid it into a pocket.

"Yeah, I was just looking for Redmond," said Quinn. "Mamma's locked herself out again, and I need to take her a key."

An odd expression crossed Hadley's face. "Oh. Gosh. The car's blocked in."

Quinn's eyes followed Hadley's. Yep. They'd driven Quinn's SUV because of the coolers. They'd parked in front of the garage. Now there were cars parked on either side and three deep behind them in the driveway below.

She sighed. "It's not that far. I'll just walk over there right quick."

"Do you want to find Redmond first?" Hadley asked.

"No, I'll be back in just a minute. Tell him for me, would you?" Quinn started down the steps.

"Quinn, wait," Hadley said.

Quinn turned and looked at her expectantly.

"Do you have a copy of their key in your purse?" Hadley gestured towards Quinn's small crossbody bag.

"I keep one on my key chain. She's always locking herself out. One time Daddy was over in West Ashley and got held up in traffic. It was really hot, and she had to sit on the porch for two hours. She brought me a key the next day."

Hadley started to say something, then hesitated.

"What's wrong?" asked Quinn.

"Nothing, nothing." Hadley smiled. "I just hate for you to have to walk over there. Why don't I come along with you? For company?"

Quinn waved her off. "That's not necessary. You stay here. The natives out back are getting restless. I could use a few moments to myself. What on earth are those fool dogs barking at? I'll be right back."

As she reached the bottom of the steps, Quinn wished she had her bike. Should she pop home and get hers? It was only a couple of blocks home, but it was a little more than a mile each way to her parents' house. It would take her nearly half an hour each way to walk it but only a little more than five minutes on a bike.

Where did Sarabeth and Tucker keep their bikes? Probably in the garage.

Quinn made her way through Sarabeth's Halloween grave-yard, sweeping the fake cobwebs from in front of her face. It was creepy, too realistic in the dark. She walked over to the detached garage to the left of the house. She'd just try the door. If it wasn't open, she'd pop home. But the pass-thru door to the garage opened easily. She flipped on the light switch, grabbed the bright orange beach cruiser on the end of the bike rack, and pressed the button to open the garage door.

As she pushed the bike out the door, a woman in a tight miniskirt and tube top walked around the edge of the house. Quinn pressed the button on the keypad to close the garage door. The woman glanced her way, a wild, fearful expression on her face.

"Are you all right?" Quinn asked.

The woman nodded but didn't speak. She walked quickly across the front yard and headed left on I'on Ave.

Quinn mounted the bike. It was a straight shot to the right down I'on to her parents' house. Where was her father after ten o'clock on a Friday night? Why couldn't he have let her mother in the house? Were they both locked out? That never happened. Her dad always had his keys in his pocket.

Six minutes later, she turned left on Station 27 Street, then right on Middle Street and pulled into her parents' driveway.

Neither of their cars were there.

What the heck?

All the lights were on inside, the house lit up like Christmas. It was very unlike her father to leave lights on if they weren't home. He was frugal in some ways, not in others. Had her mamma found a way in after she'd called Quinn? But where was her car? She could've called Quinn back if she didn't need her help after all. Quinn sighed. It wasn't the first time her mamma had demonstrated a complete lack of consideration.

She parked the bike in the driveway near the base of the steps and jogged up to the porch.

"Mamma?" she called. "Daddy?"

She knocked on the door, rang the doorbell, and pulled out her key.

"Mamma? Daddy?" She opened the door and stepped inside.

Something felt wrong, off. Dread clawed at her chest.

"Mamma? Daddy?" She walked through the breakfast room and into the great room.

And she stopped short and stared at the wall.

All three of the Van Gogh reproductions were gone.

Taped to the wall in their place was an envelope with her name on it.

Quinn grabbed it and tore it open. She unfolded the single sheet of paper. A card fell out. She bent to pick it up as she read.

Darling Quinn,

Please forgive us.

This goodbye is not forever.

We'll be in touch when we can, but it will be a while.

This is for the best. You need a stable home, and we need to do the things that make us feel alive so we don't get bored and drive you crazy. The house and everything in it is in trust for you and always has been. Your attorney's card is enclosed. Burn this as soon as you get home.

All our love,

Mom & Dad

Quinn felt lightheaded, dizzy. She tried to make sense of what she was seeing. She stuffed the letter and card in her purse and zipped it closed.

Quinn ran down the hall to their bedroom and threw open

the closet. Their suitcases were gone along with some of their clothes.

She turned and started towards the door and stopped cold. Hadley walked down the hall in her direction, an expression filled with pain and sympathy on her face.

"Hadley?" Quinn whispered. "They've gone."

Hadley reached her and pulled her into her arms. "Sweetie, I'm so sorry."

"What... Why are you here?"

"I was afraid of what you might find. That's why I wanted to come with you. I took one of the other bikes and followed you."

"What is going on? I don't understand." Quinn pulled away and searched her friend's eyes.

Hadley sighed. "I need to call Norah. We'll explain everything." She tapped the screen on her phone.

"So they've been relocated then?" Quinn asked.

"No..." Hadley winced. She rubbed Quinn's arm. "Your parents aren't in witness protection. They never have been... Norah, hey. ... No... I'm with Quinn at her parents' house. ... No, they're not here. The paintings are gone. ... Right. Okay. We'll clear out of here then."

"What do you mean, they're not in witness protection?" Quinn took a step back. Confusion and angst swirled and simmered inside her. "Of course they were in witness protection. That's been the defining fact of my life."

"I'm afraid not," said Hadley. "It turns out Norah really was looking for them though she didn't know your parents were the couple she was after. And Quinn, it breaks my heart to have to tell you this, but I think this is probably partly my fault. When you wouldn't ask Norah why she was here, I was so sure she had nothing to do with them, and I just wanted you to feel better. So I started asking her the questions you wouldn't. I don't know... maybe she would've figured it out anyway. It's hard to say."

"Why was she looking for them if they're not in witness

protection? Please... Hadley... please tell me what's happening here."

Hadley sighed. "Part of what they told you was true. They used to be art dealers... well, and also art thieves."

Quinn gasped. Shock, horror, and disbelief wrestled for the upper hand.

Hadley continued, "And they did go to a mobster's house to appraise a painting. But while they were there, someone killed him, and instead of sticking around and becoming witnesses—in which case, they would've undoubtedly been in witness protection—they stole three paintings and a whole lot of money and ran. They've been running ever since. At least one of the Van Goghs that used to hang in their living room is real—*Poppy Flowers*. It's possible the others were real as well. Something about an appraisal scam to replace real paintings with high-end fakes... Norah can explain all of that.

"Norah didn't have enough to make her case. She suspected your parents were the couple she'd been looking for, but they'd been very clever. The paintings at Norah and Knox's house were bait. One of them was really valuable—I don't even know which one. Not the fake Van Gogh sunflowers. One of the landscapes was worth a couple million dollars—not Van Gogh level, but your parents would've known it was worth a lot of money.

"Norah invited them to come to supper club to see if they'd nibble. And with everyone at Sarabeth's tonight, Norah was staking out her own house, thinking it would be an opportunity they couldn't pass up. Apparently your parents are good at what they do, because somehow they got in and out of there and took the painting and the fake Van Gogh. Who knows why they took that. But they slipped right by Norah, who is heading to the airport right now to speak with someone at the private terminal. She thinks your parents flew out a little bit ago."

Quinn sat hard on the bed. She'd been frightened her whole life, out of her mind scared at times. She'd isolated herself as a child, never getting close to anyone from fear of somehow giving away their location to the monsters who pursued them. When all along, she'd been living with the monsters.

They'd lied to her.

Her entire life had been a lie.

But the worst thing of all was that they'd turned her into a liar too.

Quinn's phone rang. She and Hadley both stared at it for a second, then Quinn slid it out of the sleeve on her purse. "It's Redmond."

"Hey." She answered the phone and told him where she was and just that she had brought her mamma a key.

When she hung up, she looked at Hadley. "He knows, doesn't he? I could hear it in his voice. He was petrified when I told him I was here. He's on his way, by the way."

Hadley closed her eyes. "No, he doesn't know, but he suspects a lot. He's been asking Cash a lot of questions he couldn't answer. Redmond was suspicious of the whole witness-protection story because you told him you'd never met one of the agents."

Quinn nodded. "So... now they're fugitives." She was numb with shock.

"They've been fugitives for twenty-six years."

Chapter Forty-Nine

Saturday, October 29, 2022, 7:20 a.m.
Morning after the Fall Meet and Greet
Sullivan's Island, South Carolina
Boone Home, I'On Avenue
Sarabeth Mercer Jackson Boone

I went running down the front porch steps just as, for the second time in a twenty-four-hour period, the police pulled up to our house. Tucker backed away from our cemetery display beneath the live oak. He saw me and came walking towards me, arms outstretched like he was trying to keep me away from the body.

"Who is it?" I looked up at him.

"It's Knox Fitzgerald."

The wind just went right out of me. I gasped, and I knew my mouth was moving but I wasn't making any sounds. Through my peripheral vision, it registered then that Knox's silver Tesla was still parked on the far side of the driveway.

The chief of police got out of the car along with another officer.

Tucker shook his hand and said, "I'm Tucker Boone, and this is my wife, Sarabeth. This is our home."

"If y'all could just wait on the porch, please, or inside the house, even better." The chief nodded at us, but he was focused on Knox.

"This is a friend of ours, Knox Fitzgerald," said Tucker. "He lives over on Conquest. I should call his wife."

"We'll send someone to speak with her," said the chief.

Norah. Oh my goodness, poor Norah. "Would it be all right if I came along?" I asked. "She doesn't have any local family."

"All right." The chief spoke quietly to his officer and then said, "This is Officer Koontz."

Officer Koontz walked towards the car. "This way, ma'am."

I climbed into the front seat of the police car, and we drove the mile and a half over to Norah and Knox's house. I felt like I was having a horrible nightmare and couldn't wake up.

What in this world had happened? Had Knox had a heart attack? When was the last time I saw him the night before? Oh my Lord, had he been in our front yard all night? I sucked in air, and I guess I must've made some kind of noise, because Officer Koontz looked at me and said, "Ma'am, are you all right?"

I nodded. I needed to pull myself together, for Norah.

I guess Norah, when she saw me there at her door at whatever time it was in the early morning with a police officer... she must've known right off. She opened the door, and she didn't say one word. She just took one look at the two of us and went real still.

Tears just rolled down my face. I couldn't help it.

The police officer said, "Ma'am, could we come inside please?"

Norah just stood back and we walked in and she led us over and sat down on one of the sofas in the family room. She just kind of collapsed. I sat beside her and put my arms around her.

Officer Koontz sat in the chair to our left and said, "Ma'am, I'm terribly sorry to inform you, but your husband's body was found this morning in Mrs. Boone's front yard."

Norah doubled over with her arms around her waist, and she just rocked back and forth. "What happened?" she moaned.

I looked at Officer Koontz because I didn't have the first idea.

"We're trying to figure that out, ma'am. When was the last time you saw your husband?"

"Yesterday evening, a little after seven."

"He didn't come home last night?" he asked.

"No. I wasn't expecting him."

Officer Koontz's eyes narrowed, and he said, "Did he live somewhere else?"

"No," said Norah. "I am a US marshal. Our house was burglarized last night. Knox planned to stay in a hotel."

What? They were burglarized?

"I see," said Officer Koontz. "Okay, well... my condolences, ma'am. I don't have any further information right now. We'll be in touch as soon as we do."

"I need to see him," she said.

"Ah... those arrangements will be made, yes ma'am. I'm going to leave Mrs. Boone with you, and we'll be back in touch soon." He nodded, stood, and left.

"You don't have any idea what happened?" Norah was very pale but stoic. I knew she must be in shock.

"None." I shook my head in disbelief. "I was just trying to work out when the last time I saw him was."

"But he's still there? At your house?"

"That's right," I said.

"I'm going to get dressed," said Norah. "And then I'm going to take you home."

She seemed to be gathering strength from somewhere, Heaven only knew where. He wasn't even my husband, and I was distraught. But I needed to be there for her, to do whatever she needed. There would be time to process all of this later.

I nodded. "All right then."

It didn't take her five minutes to change.

We walked down a back hall off the kitchen, through a drop zone, and out the back door. The garage was connected to the house by a breezeway. Norah led me into the garage and handed me the keys to her Lincoln Nautilus.

"I know it's not far," she said. "But I'm in no state to drive."

I noticed then she was shaking.

"Of course not," I said, but I wasn't sure I was either. I drew a deep breath and climbed into the car.

By the time we made it back to our house—well, we couldn't —that was the point. The street was completely blocked. There were two more police cars, a sheriff's office car, and several other vehicles I couldn't even make out. There was crime scene tape across our front yard. I was thinking we should've stayed at Norah's house, but I also knew if it were me, wild horses would not keep me away from my husband. I turned down Flag Street and parked at the Hugers' house. I felt certain Josephine would understand. She knew our circumstances.

Norah and I parked to the side of the driveway so as not to block the Hugers in or out and walked across their backyard into ours.

"We should go through the house," I said. "They're out front, but they asked us to stay inside or on the porch. I figure we can step out onto the porch and speak to the chief of police."

Norah nodded and followed me as we climbed the deck steps and in through our screened porch.

Tucker was in the living room with Cash. They looked up, stopped talking, and stood.

"I sent Deacon and the girls to your parents in Florence," said Tucker.

"Thank you." I looked at Cash. "I'm so glad you're here."

"The Sullivan's Island police chief requested SLED assistance," he said. "The sheriff's department is also helping with forensics."

"Forensics?" Norah's voice was incredulous. "What happened to Knox?"

"Please," said Tucker. "Let's sit."

He and Cash waited until Norah and I were seated on the love seat, then sat back down, Tucker on the sofa and Cash on one of the chairs. I put my arm around Norah.

"Tell me what happened," she said. "Please."

"Blunt force trauma to the head," Cash said quietly. "It looks like a shovel from the potting shed was the weapon."

"Oh my Lord." I felt like I'd been punched in the gut. Someone at our party—a party I planned to spread goodwill—at our house, killed our friend with our shovel? "This happened last night? No, it couldn't have. Everyone left about eleven thirty. We walked out with Libba and Jake. We would've seen if—"

"Are you certain of that?" asked Cash. "It was dark. Those headstones are under the tree..."

"They have spotlights that come on at night," said Tucker. "The whole idea was to be able to see the spooky headstones. Yeah, it's dark everywhere else. But there's no way we could've missed him if he were out there when we locked up."

"Tucker, where all do you currently have the cameras?" asked Cash. "Are they motion activated?"

"They are. They're mostly in the backyard where someone was throwing their doggy bags and whatnot over the fence. The CPI system has one at each corner of the house, so all the windows and doors are covered. But... I turned those off last night before the party. I figured they'd run nonstop with that many people coming and going."

"Let's take a look at whatever footage you have from the backyard," said Cash.

"I'll get my laptop." Tucker stood and walked towards the bedroom.

"I'm going to need to talk to everyone who was here all evening and see what they remember," said Cash. "See if we can figure out who saw Knox last, if anyone noticed him arguing with anyone."

"You don't think he got into it with some of the conservationists do you?" I asked. "Because he wasn't involved in any of that drama last night."

"Well, he had an altercation with someone about something," said Cash. "Norah, do you know of anyone he had trouble with?

Before last night? Could someone have shown up here he'd had words with?"

Norah shook her head. Her eyes were bright with tears. "No. You guys are our social circle. There's no one else he talks to. I doubt he even knows anyone else in this town."

"It would be better if everyone cleared out of here for the time being," said Cash. "This is a crime scene. And from what I understand, more than a hundred people tromped through here last night. There's a lot to sort out."

I turned to Norah. "I don't think you should be alone right now. Why don't you and I go back to your house?"

"As soon as I see my husband," she said.

Cash nodded. "I'll arrange that."

Chapter Fifty

Saturday, October 29 Around Noon
Home of Fish Aiken
Sarabeth Mercer Jackson Boone

Tallulah suggested I bring Norah over to Fish's house. There's just something so soothing about the ocean, and we all needed soothing that day. I knew Norah would grieve in her own way, in her own time, probably for a long time. But that day, like the rest of us, she was still in shock. And she wanted to question everyone about the night before, so she really wanted to go over to Fish's house. In fact, she asked Tallulah to round up everyone else and get them over there. I guess I'd say Norah was wrapping herself up in the role of detective to avoid playing the part of widow.

That's how we came to be sitting in the cushioned lounge chairs on the far side of Fish's pool deck looking at the ocean— Tallulah, Libba, Quinn, Hadley, Norah, and me. Fish, Jake, and Redmond had made a provisions run. Tucker and Cash were still at our house, and Heaven only knew how long they'd be there. Birdie and Vernon said they'd be over later. We hadn't been able to reach Camille but figured she was wiped out from the night before.

"I'm just trying to get this straight in my mind." Norah's voice had a gravelly, cried-out quality to it. She was more composed than I would have been in her situation, but I had the impression she'd decided she would grieve once someone was in jail for killing her husband. "Libba, when your sandal broke at around 9:25, you saw Knox over by the bar?"

"Yes," said Libba.

"He was talking with Quinn and Redmond and me," said Hadley. "Then Jake came over."

"And how long after that would you say you saw him outside the window talking with the questionably dressed woman, Libba?"

Libba considered that for a few minutes. "Well, I did lollygag. I was admiring Sarabeth's new bathroom, then her closets. I took my time. Then there was the whole drama with Elvis."

"Thank you so much for ridding my household of that creature," I said. And then I felt stupid for not setting the thing free long before that. He was probably much happier than he had been in that terrarium that was too small in my opinion. How was I even thinking about that stupid iguana? Knox, our friend, our neighbor, who had just really started settling in to things, who Norah loved so much... was dead. The truth is, that first day, everything just felt surreal. Like I said before... we were all in shock.

"Happy to oblige," said Libba. "Norah, I'd say it was maybe fifteen minutes later. So let's say around 9:40, maybe 9:45."

Norah looked at Hadley. "Do you remember him leaving the group around then?"

Hadley got a faraway look in her eyes. "He was still standing there when I went to get a drink less than five minutes after Jake joined us. Quinn and Redmond went to dance when I went to the bar. So that left Jake and Knox."

"We need to talk to Jake," said Norah. "And we need to find out who the woman in the miniskirt was. I wonder if there's a picture of her on one of the cameras. Sarabeth, would you ask Tucker?"

"Of course," I told her. Now, I knew Tucker had his hands full at the house, but I texted him right then.

Libba said, "I'll text Jake."

We all watched the waves for a few minutes and sipped our iced tea. Tallulah had tried to get Norah to put a little bourbon in hers, but she insisted she needed a clear head. Norah was on a mission.

A few minutes later, Libba said, "Jake says he went to get some wings right after Quinn, Redmond, and Hadley left. Knox told him he was going to the bar."

"And when's the next time anyone saw him?" asked Norah.

Everyone thought for a few minutes, but no one came up with anything. It's like we just lost track of Knox. And that just hurt my heart. Because he came to be supportive even though Norah wasn't there, and he tried so hard to participate, be helpful, be a part of things... and instead of making sure he was comfortable and a part of things, I completely forgot about him.

"I don't remember seeing him after that," I said. "It didn't dawn on me until this morning, but I know he wasn't with us when everyone came inside right before Tucker called the police. Everything was so chaotic. I should've made sure we were all safely inside, but I just lost track."

"This is not your fault, Sarabeth," said Norah. "You had your hands full. Knox was a grown man. He didn't require babysitting."

No one said the obvious thing, that if we'd been taking better care of him, maybe he'd still be alive, so maybe we should all babysit each other a little more.

"Do y'all think this could possibly have to do with the trees?" I asked. "I mean... surely not. Is there a psychopath of some sort on the loose? Are the rest of us safe?"

"There's safety in numbers," Libba said. "I'm glad we're all here together."

Quinn said, "I saw that woman coming from the backyard as I was getting a bike from the garage at about ten fifteen. She walked between the house and the garage. She looked upset. I remember asking her if she was all right. She nodded and took off down l'on, to the left."

My phone dinged with a text. "Norah, Tucker sent this picture of her from one of the cameras. It's really grainy." I showed it to her.

"Do you know who she is?" I asked.

"Never seen her before in my life," said Norah.

Birdie and Vernon came walking across the pool deck, calling their hellos.

Birdie walked over and gave Norah a hug and told her how sorry they were.

"Thank you," said Norah. "I know I'm still in shock. It's just not sinking in. I don't have any idea what I'm going to do. Knox has been my best friend for... thirty years."

"It's something you'll never get over," said Tallulah. "But you'll learn to live with it."

"Why do y'all have a picture of Tennyson's niece?" asked Birdie, who'd been looking at my phone still in Norah's hand.

"Tennyson's niece?" I squinted at Birdie.

"Camille introduced her to us last night," said Vernon. "Have to say, she doesn't look very pregnant to me. Cute girl."

"Vernon." Birdie gave him a look that suggested he hush up.

"Why was Tennyson's niece at a neighborhood meet and greet?" I asked. "I mean, not that she wasn't welcome and all. I just don't understand why she'd want to be there."

"Who knows?" Birdie shrugged. "Nobody explained that to us. Tennyson didn't seem thrilled she was there at all."

"I have a very bad feeling about this," said Hadley.

We all looked at her. "Why?" I asked.

"Because Tennyson doesn't have a niece," she said.

"How do you know?" I asked.

"Because Tallulah asked me to do a background check on him

months ago. His wife, Zelda, passed away in 2018. They didn't have children, and neither of them have siblings. He has no family I've been able to find."

"What was that about her being pregnant?" asked Hadley.

"The night we were at Norah's for supper club, someone kept calling him," said Libba. "I overheard him talking on the phone—and he wasn't very nice to whoever he was talking to. But he told someone... who was it? That his niece was pregnant and nervous she was having a miscarriage."

"Has anyone spoken to Camille today?" asked Hadley.

No one spoke up.

Oh my stars. Was Camille okay? This "niece" of Tennyson's was surely trouble. But what about Tennyson? I was suddenly very scared for Camille.

"I'll try calling her again," said Tallulah.

A few minutes later she put the phone down. "She's still not answering. Why don't we ride over and check on her?"

"I think that's a great idea," said Norah.

We all hopped up and headed for the driveway, but when we got there, the guys had taken Jake's car, and Redmond's car was behind Norah's.

"I don't have his keys," said Quinn.

"My car's at my house," said Tallulah.

"I can drive," said Hadley, "but we won't all fit in my car."

"Let's take Morrison." We all turned to look at Tallulah. She walked over and punched in a code to open the garage. Fish's orange VW microbus was inside. It looked like a Creamsicle on wheels. "The keys are right here. He won't mind."

"Why'd you call it Morrison?" I asked.

"That's his name," said Tallulah. "Fish went through a Van Morrison phase about the time he bought it. He named him Morrison."

We all climbed into Morrison, and Tallulah drove us across the island to Camille's house. I was impressed as all get out that Tallulah could drive a stick.

I hadn't eaten anything at all that day, which was a good thing, because my stomach was doing flip-flops. I just could not wrap my brain around the fact that I had planned a party where some series of events which could not possibly have happened had it *not* been for the party I planned, had led to one friend's death, and now another friend was almost certainly in grave danger—though how those two things were connected were a complete mystery—and I thought up mysteries for a living.

Who could possibly have done this?

How had this happened?

What should I have done differently?

It was all my fault.

In the very back seat of Morrison, tears were rolling down my cheeks.

Chapter Fifty-One

Saturday, October 29, 2022, 1:00 p.m.
Home of Camille Houston
Sarabeth Mercer Jackson Boone

Camille lived on the end of Middle Street on the other side of Fort Moultrie, around the elbow, so to speak, of Sullivan's Island. She had her house built new when she first moved there. Built to look like an old white beach cottage with a metal roof, it was perfectly charming and with all the modern conveniences—including an elevator from the garage beneath the house to the living level. It wasn't huge like some of the houses on the island. But as Camille liked to say, it was plenty big enough for her. Tallulah pulled through the gate in the white picket fence and parked in front of the house. We all climbed out of Morrison.

Something gnawed at my stomach. I just knew Camille was in trouble. I think we all did. But we were hamstrung by our manners to a certain degree. It's like there was just enough doubt in our minds—because the whole thing was preposterous, like something from one of my books—that we couldn't bring ourselves to knock the door down with a battering ram and take them by surprise.

Tallulah, our unofficial leader, marched up the steps and rang the doorbell. We all gathered around her on the small front landing. No one came to the door. Tallulah kept ringing and knocking, and we all peered through windows. There was no sign of Camille.

"Does anyone have a key?" I asked. I was starting to feel panicky, though I wasn't exactly sure why.

"Not that I know of," said Tallulah.

"I'm going to check around back," said Hadley. She and Norah exchanged a look, and the two of them headed down the steps and around to the ocean side. Well, I guess technically, Camille's house was harbor front, sitting as it did on the end of the island.

A few minutes later, Hadley opened the front door and let us all in.

She held a finger to her lips.

Somewhere in the house, water was running. Where had Norah gotten to? It came back to me then, something I'd heard her say: that she always had her gun with her. Just then I was thinking that was a very good thing. Hadley rather famously refused to have anything to do with guns.

A soft ding called our attention to the elevator door.

We all held our breath. Who was on the elevator?

Seconds later, it slid open.

Tennyson drew back and looked at us with this sour expression.

I'll be honest, something about him wasn't right even before he opened his mouth. It's like he'd dropped all pretense of being a Southern gentleman—like he knew if we were there, the gig was up. Had he simply been after Camille's money the whole time? He and his "niece?" What did any of this have to do with Knox?

I looked at Hadley. She was on high alert with a spring-loaded look, as if she was ready to pounce.

Tennyson said, "At the risk of sounding inhospitable, what are you all doing standing in my home?"

"We came to our friend Camille's home to check on her," said Tallulah. "She wasn't answering the telephone. That's what we do. We check in on one another."

"Camille is resting," said Tennyson. "Last night took a lot out of her. She's nearly seventy, after all."

Birdie raised her chin at him. "She's sixty-eight, and the way I hear it, that's six years younger than you."

"Whatever is your point, Birdie?" asked Tennyson.

Norah came from down the hall. "I have a better question," she said. "What did you give Camille, and why won't she wake up?"

"I haven't given her anything," said Tennyson. "She said she was going to take a nap."

Well, I guess I panicked when I heard Camille wouldn't wake up. I'd lost one friend the night before, and I wasn't aiming to lose another. I pulled my phone out of my purse and dialed 911.

When they asked what my emergency was, I said, "Yes, this is Sarabeth Boone?"

Tennyson leaned in and took a step towards me like he was going to tackle me, but Vernon moved between the two of us.

"What's your emergency?" the operator asked.

"Y'all have already been to my house twice, but right now I'm over at Camille Houston's house on Middle Street?"

Tennyson tried to dart around Vernon.

That's when Norah pulled her gun. "Stop right there."

Everyone else gathered round, making a wall between me and Tennyson.

"Yes," I stammered, "that's house number 1017. I have reason to believe my friend has been overdosed with something. She won't wake up. Please hurry. Send an ambulance. Send the police. Send everybody."

I hung up the phone and said, "With my recent track record, I'm sure they'll be right over." Somewhere along the line, I'd started shivering and my voice was shaky.

The sound of running water stopped.

Tennyson glanced down the hall towards the guest room and office, then he stepped backwards into the elevator, the only place he had to go. He pressed the button.

Vernon reached out and put a hand on the door. "Don't be rushing off now. You have guests."

Tennyson pried Vernon's arm, trying to dislodge it.

Norah said, "Step off the elevator." She motioned with her gun.

This was all just surreal to me—like we were watching it happen in a movie. It was crazy. And we were all in shock before we even got there. Now this man who had sat at the dinner table with every one of us was trying to make a run for it after surely poisoning Camille.

And then Tennyson pulled out his own gun and pointed it at Vernon.

I leaned back in horror. Oh. My. Lord. Sweet Jesus, save us.

"Vernon, get away from there," said Birdie.

I jumped over towards the wall of windows overlooking the ocean, out of shooting range of anyone on that elevator. Everyone but Norah and Hadley scattered.

The door to the elevator closed.

Norah ran towards the front door, Hadley the back. The elevator only had two stops. Tennyson could only go down to the garage. They were off to intercept him.

Birdie said, "I'm going to see if there's anything I can do for Camille."

"I'll come with you," said Tallulah.

They headed down the hall past the kitchen towards the primary suite, and I started to follow them. How long would EMS take? What should we do in the meantime?

That's when Tennyson's niece—I recognized her from the picture Tucker had sent—came strolling down the hall from the other end of the house, wrapped in a towel. She stopped short when she saw she had company: Libba, Quinn, and I were the only ones left in the living room.

I stopped in my tracks, turned towards her, and said, "Hey, we're Camille's friends. I think you met a couple of us last night. I'm Sarabeth Boone. The party was at my house?" I held out a hand.

Libba and Quinn moved in on either side of me.

Now here's what I was thinking... *this woman is associated with a man who very likely attempted at least one murder, possibly two. At the very least, she's an accomplice.* But I didn't necessarily want to call her on that just then, given that Norah had left with the gun, Hadley had gone too, with whatever gadgets she might have for self-defense, and I had no training whatsoever in dealing with this situation.

The girl held on to her towel with one hand and reached out to shake my hand with the other. "I'm Arabella Fleming."

"And you're Tennyson's niece?" Libba asked in a way that suggested this was utter rubbish.

"Why are you here? Why are you showering at Camille's house?" Quinn asked. And I have to say here, that at that moment, none of us had any idea yet what had happened with Quinn's parents the night before, well, except Hadley and Norah. But the rest of us didn't know a thing. And Quinn was amazing —she stood there with Libba and me and stared that woman down.

Arabella's bit her lip and nervously scanned the room.

"He just left," I said. "EMS is on the way to check on Camille."

Arabella's eyes grew large. "If you don't mind, I'm going to get dressed."

"I think that's a *very* good idea." I tilted my head and nodded, like, *do you think?* She couldn't escape through the bedroom windows without risking a nasty fall.

EMS arrived moments later and two technicians dashed through the front door.

"She's that way." I pointed them down the hall, then followed.

"We'll stay here," said Libba. "In case the 'niece' decides to leave."

The EMTs went to work shining a light in Camille's eyes and checking her over.

I was just praying, *Lord please let Camille be all right. And please keep Hadley and Norah safe as they chase after that horrible man.* How had we all missed that he was some sort of psycho?

"I found these in the trash," said Tallulah. She handed one of the techs two empty medicine bottles, which had contained Ativan and Percocet.

"Good to know what she's taken," he said. "We're going to transport her."

"Is she going to be all right do you think?" I looked hopefully from one EMS tech to the other.

"You'll need to speak to the doctor," the taller one said. But then the stocky guy looked at me and nodded reassuringly.

I stepped back into the living room to get out of their way and took a seat. Hadley and Norah came in through the front door. "He left in his car," said Hadley. "I called Cash. He won't get far."

Arabella came down the hall, wearing one of those little knit athletic dresses. She looked warily around the room. "I guess I'll be going."

Hadley said, "If you don't mind, someone from the South Carolina Law Enforcement Division is on their way. He asked that you wait and speak to him before you go."

"Oh... well..." Arabella looked from me to Hadley. "Is that required?"

"Yes," said Norah. "Please have a seat."

Arabella looked at the floor, then nodded. She wore a defeated expression. "Is Camille okay?"

"We don't know yet," I said. "Would you happen to know anything about what she's been given?" Norah and Hadley both looked at me with quizzical expressions, and then it hit me I had no business asking this woman questions. There was one law enforcement officer in the room plus a private detective and a

SLED agent on the way. This was not one of my novels. I had no authority here.

"I'll just have a seat over here." I took a chair near the sliding doors that led out onto the deck.

"I didn't know she'd taken anything," said Arabella. "She was awake when I got into the shower about thirty minutes ago."

"Why wasn't she answering the phone?" asked Hadley.

"I think Tennyson turned her ringer off," said Arabella. "She was tired—she didn't sleep well last night."

The EMS technicians wheeled Camille out. She looked pale and frail. I went back to silently praying.

"Birdie and Vernon and I are going with her," said Tallulah, her voice a bit unsteady.

"Good," said Hadley. "Cash is on the way. He can drop the rest of us off."

"Actually," said Quinn, "it's not far for me. I'll just walk home. It's probably better for me to get out of the way."

"I'll go with you," said Libba, and they scurried out the door.

So that left me with Hadley, Norah, and Arabella, with Cash on the way. If it had not been for the fact that my house was still a crime scene, I might've walked home myself. But I confess to being plenty curious about Miss Arabella Fleming. And it might be that part of that was the author in me. For whatever reason, I stayed put.

It wasn't long before Cash showed up. He took a spot on the sofa by Hadley. Norah was in a chair to their right and Arabella directly across from them. Over by the sliding door, I was really more in a spectator's seat, which was fine by me.

"I'm Agent Reynolds," said Cash, "with the South Carolina Law Enforcement Division. Miss Fleming, is it?"

"Yes. Arabella Fleming."

"Miss Fleming, I need to let you know that you have the right to remain silent—"

She held up her hand. "I don't want to remain silent. I had

nothing to do with... whatever he has done. And I will not go down for this. I will gladly tell you everything I know."

Cash nodded. "All right. But just for the record, I do need to read you your rights." He proceeded to do that.

She nodded. "I understand."

"What is your relationship to Tennyson Sumter?" Cash asked.

"We've had a romantic relationship for about a year now," she said.

A year? A *year*? So the entire time Tennyson was courting Camille, he'd simultaneously been carrying on with this woman?

"So you're not his niece?" asked Cash.

"No," said Arabella. "That's the lie he told Camille."

No surprise there. I guess we all knew at that point that Camille—all of us—had been taken in. Poor Camille. Even if she fully recovered physically, would she ever recover emotionally from all of this?

"So you knew he'd recently married Camille Houston?" asked Cash.

"Yes." She nodded and looked at her lap.

"Are you expecting, Miss Fleming?"

"No," she said. "That's another lie he told. Look, he married Camille for her money, obviously. He was trying to keep me strung along. I admit to stupidity—nothing more. I honestly don't know how this would've worked out in his plan. I think he was making it up as he went along. But I've had enough."

Oh dear Heavens. Camille had always been so afraid, so cautious about who she dated. And now this. Would she ever trust another man?

"What were you arguing with Knox Fitzgerald about last night?" asked Cash.

"That's the man's name?" she asked. "The one I was talking to with the dark hair?"

"That's right," said Cash.

Fear flashed across her face. "He... overheard me arguing with Tennyson. He figured out we had a non-uncle/niece relationship.

He was asking me questions, like did I know Tennyson was a married man. He was giving me unsolicited advice."

"And you told Tennyson about that?" asked Cash.

"Yes," said Arabella. "I wish now that I hadn't."

"Why is that?" asked Cash.

"He said he was going to take care of it," said Arabella. "I didn't know what he meant by that. I guess I assumed he was going to talk to the guy maybe. I kept waiting for Tennyson to be honest with Camille and just put an end to this scheme. But that was the last thing on his mind. I didn't see him do it, so I can't say for sure he did, but later in the evening, I stumbled across that man... I didn't know his name... but he was lying behind the potting shed."

I sucked in air. I'd pretty much come to the conclusion that Tennyson had killed Knox, though I'd had no idea why. It seemed unlikely there were two people with murderous intent in our midst. Surely not. But it was still shocking, having it confirmed.

"And you believe that Tennyson killed him?" asked Cash.

"I'm afraid of that," said Arabella.

"How do you suppose Mr. Fitzgerald ended up on the Boone's front lawn by the Halloween display?" asked Cash.

She rolled her lips in and out and seemed to think long and hard. "Well, I don't know how that happened, but if I were to guess, my theory would be that Tennyson went back later, sometime around three a.m., and moved the body."

"Why would he have done that, do you suppose?" asked Cash.

"I think he recalled Sarabeth Boone having words with Knox during one of those dinner parties." She didn't look my way, just kept her eyes on Cash.

I did not care for my name in that woman's mouth.

She continued. "He maybe thought if he left... Mr. Fitzgerald... where he was, that he might not be found immediately. My theory is that he wanted there to be a lot of uproar and confusion today, and if possible, he wanted everyone to think Mr. Fitzgerald's death had to do with the trouble at that party last night, possibly throw suspicion on Sarabeth Boone."

Oooh! Of all the—

"Why did you go to the Boones' house last night?" asked Cash.

"I wanted to make something happen," she said. "Tennyson was telling Camille I was his niece and needed a place to stay. He talked her into letting me stay here. It was just too freakin' strange. I didn't want any part of that. But he wouldn't walk away from all that money. I was trying to force him into a decision one way or another."

"And I guess you did," said Norah, a tremor in her voice.

Oh my stars, poor Norah. It was such a random thing, Knox getting mixed up in Tennyson's scheme. He'd been in the wrong place at the wrong time and overheard something that put all of this into motion. I could see Norah was on the verge of falling to pieces.

Was Cash going to arrest Arabella? Was she possibly an accessory or something?

I stood and walked over to Norah, quietly moved behind her chair, and put a hand on her shoulder. "Maybe we should let Cash finish up here. He doesn't need us. And I think you have all the answers. Let's get you home, sweetie."

Norah looked up at me and nodded. "I could use some air."

We walked back to her house. Norah was quiet, and I just let her have her space. When we got to the steps, I said, "Do you want me to come in and stay with you a while longer?"

"I'd like that," said Norah.

"Do you think you could eat anything? You haven't eaten all day..."

"No, thank you. I can't stomach food. But I think I might take a shower."

"That's a good idea," I said as we walked into the living room that adjoined the kitchen. "I'll be here. Holler if you need anything."

"Thank you for being here," Norah said. "It just... it just breaks my heart. He was standing up for Camille, you know?"

I nodded. "I do." We were both crying.

"I think he was finally starting to feel like part of the group, like maybe we could be happy here... He was trying... harder than he ever has, to fit in."

"I know."

She swiped at her tears, then doubled over sobbing. I've never heard such a heartrending moan. I pulled her to the sofa and held her close as the sobs shook her whole body.

And I cried for the damaged child who'd become a damaged man who had tried so hard to fit in and went outside his comfort zone because he loved his wife... and after coming so far, he'd overheard a conversation and been dead within the hour.

And I cried for his wife, my sweet friend, who would never be the same.

Chapter Fifty-Two

Saturday, November 26, 2022, 5:00 p.m.
November Supper Club—Thanksgiving
Fish Aiken's Home
Tallulah Wentworth

"Everyone gather round." Tallulah stood with Fish at the edge of the pool deck with the ocean behind them. It was a glorious evening, warm for November. Thankfully, it was warm enough for them to be outside, which was where they'd both wanted to be. The Atlantic frolicked and splashed, providing the perfect soundtrack.

"Does everyone have their champagne?" Fish asked. "I've got toasts to make here in a moment."

"I may need a top-off." Camille looked around for the bartender, who doubled as a server for the evening, making sure the bubbles flowed.

Tallulah sent up a prayer of thanks that Camille seemed no worse for wear. She'd given them all a scare. Tallulah worried her friend may never go out with another man after the affair with Tennyson, who came with what had appeared to be a suitable background, if not a pedigree. The lesson they'd all learned was a hard one. Monsters sometimes came in pretty packages. Apparently now there were questions about Zelda Boykin Sumter—Tennyson's wife's death too.

Camille may never have anything to do with men again, but she wouldn't want for company. They'd all rallied around her, taking turns sitting with her as she recovered and dealt with Tennyson's betrayal. Tallulah knew a thing or two about loneliness and the dark places it could lead. She and Fish kept Camille close, making sure she didn't have the opportunity to be lonely. Tallulah chuckled when she thought about the parallel to how Eugenia had once kept her close, going so far as to install herself in Tallulah's house.

"Hank?" Fish motioned and here came Hank with a bottle of Veuve Clicquot.

"We have a surprise," said Tallulah. She couldn't stop smiling, but tears threatened as well. "Y'all know I had planned a wedding reception for this evening for dear Camille in celebration and in thanksgiving. And I guess we all know why that didn't work out, and hopefully we'll all toast Tennyson's very long prison sentence in a few months." Personally, Tallulah hoped he didn't strike a plea deal. She'd love to see him at the defendant's table while they all testified against him. She gave her head a little shake. Tennyson had no place here today.

Tallulah smiled wider. "But in the spirit of not being wasteful—"

"You're doing it wrong." Fish interrupted her with a grin.

"Am I now?" She grinned back at him.

"Why don't y'all let me handle this." Vernon made his way to the front.

"Well, that was the general idea," said Tallulah.

Vernon stepped between them and held out his hands, palms up. "It seems our friends have finally come to their senses and realized what any one of us could've told them years ago. They belong together. So by the power vested in me by the American Wedding Ministries dot com, I'm about to do the honors."

A ripple of awwws, aahs, and joyous laughter moved through their friends. Then they clapped and hooted.

"Let's save some of that for just a minute," said Vernon. "Dearest friends, we are gathered this evening to witness the union..." He'd memorized his part and didn't miss a line.

Tallulah and Fish had decided on the classic vows, which they said to each other in the falling light. It was magic hour when Vernon pronounced them husband and wife. Tallulah was happier than she'd been in quite some time. This felt so right. And she knew in her heart that somewhere, Henry was just fine with it.

"To my bride." Fish lifted his glass and they all followed suit.

"Y'all, everyone help yourselves to dinner now," said Tallulah. "The buffet is in the usual spot."

Laughing and happy, they meandered towards the porch.

"Where are y'all going to live?" asked Birdie. "Here or at your house?"

"Here," said Tallulah. "We both love the ocean. We're going to sell my place. We don't need both these big houses. And this just feels right."

"Eugenia would be so happy," said Birdie.

"I wouldn't be a bit surprised if she planned the whole thing," said Tallulah.

As they reached the steps to the porch, they all hung back to let Tallulah and Fish go first. They piled their plates with the usual Thanksgiving fare: two kinds of turkey, roasted and smoked, dressing, gravy, braised short ribs, garlic red-skinned potatoes, sweet potato casserole, macaroni and cheese, vegetable pirlou, green beans almondine, cranberry-orange relish, buttermilk biscuits, and sweet jalapeño cornbread. Tallulah flashed Fish an impish grin and chose a chair in the middle of the table on the back side.

"Y'all sit wherever you like." She chuckled when that caused a stir. She was letting go of some of her traditions but happily planning new ones.

Norah took the seat to her left. "This food looks amazing."

"Hamby's did every bit of it," said Tallulah. "How are you doing, darlin'?"

"As well as can be expected, I guess," said Norah. "It helps to have friends. I'm very grateful for all of you."

They'd bundled Norah up in the comfort of the group, making sure she had as much company as she needed—in truth, they'd likely given her far more in the way of company than she'd wanted—and kept her in casseroles and fried chicken and cakes. Sarabeth had continued taking long walks with her every morning and making sure she joined them for happy hour on the beach. Norah'd taken an extended leave from work, which Tallulah thought was a good idea, though knowing Norah, she'd soon need the distraction. Norah would probably never get over losing Knox the way she did. But they would walk with her through it and hold her hand. Truthfully, none of them would ever be the same.

Tallulah patted Norah's arm. "We're grateful to have you."

Sarabeth took the chair across the table from Tallulah, smiling at them both. The smile seemed genuine, not forced. Tallulah had been deeply worried about Sarabeth in the aftermath of the fall meet and greet. She seemed intent on taking blame for things that were not her fault.

"Did you get your book turned in, darlin'?" Tallulah asked.

"I did," said Sarabeth. "I finished the edits last night, as a matter of fact. Now I just need to figure out what the next book's about."

"Well, you have no shortage of material," Vernon chimed in from a few seats down.

Tucker slid into the chair next to Sarabeth. "Did you tell them?"

"Not yet." Sarabeth had a twinkle in her eye. She glanced around the table. "Tucker finally got some footage of the yard vandals on camera. They'd been sneaking in through the Hugers' yard."

"Who was it?" Tallulah asked. "I hope they've been arrested."

"It was a couple of teenagers," said Sarabeth. "Kids of a hedge fund manager who bought a house in the early 1990s, over near the lighthouse on Atlantic. They had an ocean view when they bought the house. The parents are definitely in favor of laying the forest low. But—and this is the part that restores my faith in the power of community—they were mad as fire at the kids, and they're making them take full responsibility. In fact, they're going to be doing some yard work for us for a while in addition to whatever penalty the court imposes. Yes, they have been arrested."

"Well, I know you're glad to have that solved," said Norah.

"I am," said Sarabeth. "And I'm just so, so relieved it was teenagers. I mean, everyone knows their brains aren't fully formed. It just hurt my heart to think our neighbors—our fully grown-up neighbors—would do such an awful thing. It made me question our decision to move here in the first place."

"I'm so glad things have finally settled down for you all," said Tallulah.

Tucker raised his eyebrows nearly to his hairline. "Me too. It's been a rough year—nearly two, I guess. But things are looking up. Deacon has a new job, everybody."

A celebratory wave of cheers went round the table.

"What's he going to be doing?" asked Vernon.

"He's tending bar and waiting tables over at Langdon's," said Sarabeth. "The hours aren't ideal for a single father, but well, we don't mind helping out with the girls, and they are getting older. Apparently he'll make good money there."

"He's a nice-looking young man," said Norah. "I bet he does well in tips."

Finally everyone found a place and settled in, then Fish said, "Shall we hold hands for grace this evening?"

Everyone joined hands, and Fish thanked God for all the blessings they enjoyed, chiefly among them the friends around the table.

Tallulah couldn't help but think of Knox. She had so many

regrets where he was concerned. If she'd listened to Fish to begin with and they'd never invited the Fitzgeralds to supper club, would Knox Fitzgerald be alive today?

Would Camille? Or would Tennyson have succeeded in his scheme to kill her and take all her money?

Even after they'd invited them to supper club and then Sarabeth kept inviting them back, Tallulah hadn't made Knox as welcome as she could have. He'd tried, in his way, to fit in. And he'd tried to help that young woman—and Camille too, no doubt. Camille had likely been his primary concern. The chance encounter between Knox and Tennyson and his paramour had cost Knox his life, but it may well have saved Camille's. Yes, Knox was flawed. But he was also noble. And the good Lord knew, they were all flawed.

Tallulah smiled as she watched Libba feed Jake a bite she'd put together for him. They seemed positively giddy these days. Tallulah was relieved to see it. She'd been worried about them there for a while. It was a fine idea for Libba to take over managing the office for Jake. Some couples weren't cut out to work together, but something told Tallulah they'd be just fine.

Quinn and Redmond had their heads together at the end of the table. She smiled at Redmond, love clearly shining in her eyes. Poor Quinn had weathered a rough patch too, but she seemed to be all right. She'd pitched right in helping to care for Camille and Norah. It was a massive blow, no doubt, to learn that your parents had lied to you your whole life. Quinn was so sweet-natured—had such a lovely smile. How could her parents have mistreated her that way? Narcissistic criminals... that was Tallulah's assessment. But Redmond was Quinn's rock. They'd built a happy life together and clearly loved each other very much. Love covered a multitude of problems.

What would Eugenia think of all this? Of what supper club had become? Tallulah looked around the table at all the precious happy faces.

She had found her other purpose. She had knit this group

together, with Eugenia's help, of course—and Fish's. Somewhere in their tiny town by the sea, did someone else need a group to belong to? She prayed God would help her be alert to the needs of others and find, as Eugenia had, the one in the crowd who needed a friend and to be that friend. May she continue Eugenia's mission.

"A penny for your thoughts?" Fish leaned in close.

"It's been an eventful year, traumatic even," said Tallulah. "But it's taught me a few things."

"Indeed?"

"Things may have changed here since Hugo, but the most important things are the same. It's still a community where people care about one another even if they disagree. You take that small group of troublemakers out of the picture—and of course, Tennyson Sumter—and I think what happened at Sarabeth and Tucker's house was quite wonderful. People came together in the spirit of community. Maybe we should have something like that every year... try to grow the event."

Fish swallowed hard. "You're looking to take that over aren't you?"

"Naturally." Tallulah smiled. "Consider it an extension of my hospitality operation."

Fish shook his head and smiled. "Whatever makes you happy."

"You make me happy." Tallulah's heart was near to bursting with joy. A little of it leaked down her cheeks.

"And you make me the happiest of men, Mrs. Aiken."

Later, after they'd all had dinner and dessert, Fish led her out to the dance floor he'd had set up on the far side of the pool deck, near the ocean, with white lights strung across it. Everyone followed and gathered around.

"May I have this dance?" He kissed her hand.

"There's no music." Tallulah smiled up at him.

But just then, the opening strains of "The Way You Look Tonight" wafted across the pool deck.

"You've thought of everything." She took his hand, and they danced under the stars while their friends looked on. "You're still the best dancer in the group."

"You flatter me, wife."

When the music changed, they all shagged to "With This Ring" by the Platters, with everyone taking turns dancing with Norah. They danced and danced to beach music and classic rock and standards until they were all danced out.

It was the most magical evening Tallulah could imagine. And the perfect start to the next chapter of her life.

Author's Note

I'm often compelled to explain a few things after putting a book out into the world. With this book, the urge is especially strong, and I've decided to indulge my urges.

First, should anyone who actually lives on Sullivan's Island—which is a very real place that I have visited quite a lot but have never lived myself—pick up this book, I want to say to you first how blessed I think you are to live in such a magical place. I'm so happy to have the chance to visit from time to time and to explore your island as my literary landscape. I do not take the privilege lightly. And secondly, I didn't mean to make light of your very real struggles with the issues surrounding the accreted land. It is, I know, a complex issue, one which I do not pretend to have answers for. I'd also like to stress what is on the copyright page of this and every other novel I've ever written—this book is fiction. While the place is real and the accretion issue is real, *everything* else is made up. I have no idea if the actual residents of Sullivan's Island argue online about this or any other issue. It's none of my business. I write fiction.

That bit—the neighbors arguing online—was actually *inspired by* a situation that shocked me to my core several years ago when the lovely neighborhood we lived in at the time was torn apart by a dispute over a playground. None of those neighbors are depicted in this book. I was deeply troubled by how things can escalate between neighbors online and wanted to explore that in fiction. That said, and I can't emphasize this enough, this book is entirely fiction.

And should any of my friends or family read this book, I know you will pick up on certain similarities between my life and that of Sarabeth Boone. Actually, all of these characters have some of me in them, naturally. But there are events in Sarabeth's life that I have unmistakably lived through. Again, I can't stress this enough—she is not me. Her children are not my children, nor her grandchildren mine. But I know where all those folks live. Her adventures are different from mine in very important ways, but they are of course, like everything I write, inspired by my own.

I so hope you've enjoyed the book.

Warmly,

Susan

Acknowledgments

Of all the things I write, the acknowledgments page stresses me the most, because I'm always terrified of leaving someone out. And it seems there is a longer list of people I am deeply grateful to with each book. *The Sullivan's Island Supper Club* is a story that's been brewing in the back of my mind for years, and so many people have contributed to it in ways large and small, some of whom will remain forever anonymous.

For continuing my education on all things Sullivan's Island, special thanks to Judy Linder. Judy had the great good fortune of growing up on Sullivan's Island, and the further blessing of being able to return. Thank you, Judy, for your time and insights, The things I got right are because of you and others who've contributed to my understanding of this unique barrier island. Any mistakes are purely my own.

Hugs, love, and thanks to the Fancy Girls: Karen Brown, Machelle Frick, Connie Harrison, Beth Huss, Jancy Ketchie, Diane Osborne, and Becky Rowe—who I literally, yes, twirled fire with. Some of these ladies are are my lifelong friends, and others I've known at least since I was a teenager. These special women inform my fictional group of women friends, The Sullivan's Island Supper Club, in countless ways.

It takes a team to publish a book. I am ridiculously blessed with the following people, who I have assembled into what I like to think of as "my team." I am over-the-moon excited to work with my team, and deeply grateful to each member. Thank you, thank you, thank you...

...Tiffany Yates Martin, my friend, who is also an author's dream editor. I'm so fortunate to have worked with you on this book.

...Annie S. at Victory Editing for your sharp eyes and careful proofreading.

...The enormously talented Courtney Patterson and all the folks at Curated Audio for everything they do to create the audiobooks.

...The fabulous team at Dreamscape Media who makes the audiobooks widely available.

...Marina Kaye at Qamber designs for the gorgeous original artwork used in my cover.

...Elizabeth Mackey for turning the artwork into a cover I adore.

...Kathie Bennett, at Magic Time Literary Publicity, for fabulous events.

...Susan Beckham Zurenda, the other half of the "Two Southern Susans."

...Veronica Adams, my able Marketing Manager, who has made herself indispensable.

...MaryAnn Schaefer, my long-suffering assistant, who I would be hard-pressed to function without.

...Ciera Washington, my retail assistant, the newest member of the team. Ciera handles a long list of things, including packing and shipping signed personalized books from the Worldwide Headquarters of Stella Maris Books, LLC. (Ciera is also one of the grand darlings.)

...Marc Duroe at New Wave Media Design, for excellent website design and maintenance.

...Ginger Jacks at Gingersnaps Catering for your creativity in bringing the flavors of the book to the launch party.

Readers...as always, my heartfelt thanks goes out to every reader who has connected with my novels. Because of you I get to spend my days doing the job I love. I am endlessly grateful.

Booksellers...as ever, I deeply appreciate every bookseller who has recommended my books to a customer or hosted me for an event. Special thanks to Jill & Lee Hendrix at Fiction Addiction bookstore, Amy Williams at As the Page Turns, Bess Long at My Sister's Books, and Hollie Woods and her team at Barnes & Noble at The Market Common in Myrtle Beach.

I also need to thank all the members of The Lowcountry Society, for your ongoing enthusiasm and support. And thank you to all the members of The Lowcountry Book Club for hanging out with me online and chatting about one of our favorite topics—books.

I am forever grateful to my Creator for giving me an overactive imagination and a love of words. I sincerely believe I'm doing what I was designed to do, and it is a joyful thing. If there is anything good in anything I have ever written, the credit is entirely God's.

Last, but certainly not least, my heartfelt thanks to my sprawling, boisterous family. I adore you all. Very special thanks to my sister, Sabrina Niggel, brother, Darryl Jones, and bonus brother, Joe Niggel, for their understanding and grace when I am elsewhere.

And thank you beyond measure to my husband, Jim Boyer, for your ongoing love and support. I could have looked the world over and not found a better man.

If I have forgotten someone, please know it was unintentional and I am deeply grateful to everyone who has helped me along this journey.

About the Author

Susan M. Boyer is the *USA Today* bestselling author of thirteen novels. Her debut novel, *Lowcountry Boil*, won the 2012 Agatha Award for Best First Novel, the Daphne du Maurier Award for Excellence in Mystery/Suspense, and garnered several other award nominations. Subsequent books in the Liz Talbot Mystery Series have been nominated for various honors, including Southern Independent Booksellers Alliance Okra Picks, the 2016 Pat Conroy Beach Music Mystery Prize, and the 2017 Southern Book Prize in Mystery & Detective Fiction.

Big Trouble on Sullivan's Island, the first novel in her Carolina Tales series, won the 2024 Independent Publisher Book Award silver medal in Southeast Regional Fiction and was a 2024 National Indie Excellence Award finalist.

Susan is a lifelong Carolinian. She grew up in a small North Carolina town and has lived most of her life in South Carolina. She loves beaches, Southern food, and small towns where everyone knows everyone, and everyone has crazy relatives. You'll find all of the above in her novels. She and her husband call Greenville, South Carolina, home and spend as much time as possible on the Carolina coast.

If you'd like to be among the first to hear about new releases, events, and sales, sign up for Susan's newsletter on any page of her website by scrolling to the bottom or waiting for the pop-up.

susanmboyer.com

Sunsplashed Southern Stories

BY SUSAN M. BOYER

Carolina Tales Series

Big Trouble on Sullivan's Island

Beginnings - The Sullivan's Island Supper Club (Prequel)

The Sullivan's Island Supper Club

Trouble's Turn to Lose (April 8, 2025)

Hard Candy Christmas (October 28, 2025)

The Liz Talbot Series

Lowcountry Boil (A Liz Talbot Mystery # 1)

Lowcountry Bombshell (A Liz Talbot Mystery # 2)

Lowcountry Boneyard (A Liz Talbot Mystery # 3)

Postcards From Stella Maris (Five Liz Talbot Short Stories)

Lowcountry Bordello (A Liz Talbot Mystery # 4)

Lowcountry Book Club (A Liz Talbot Mystery # 5)

Lowcountry Bonfire (A Liz Talbot Mystery # 6)

Lowcountry Bookshop (A Liz Talbot Mystery # 7)

Lowcountry Boomerang (A Liz Talbot Mystery # 8)

Lowcountry Boondoggle (A Liz Talbot Mystery # 9)

Lowcountry Boughs of Holly (A Liz Talbot Mystery # 10)

Lowcountry Getaway (A Liz Talbot Mystery # 11)

Printed in the USA
CPSIA information can be obtained
at www.ICGtesting.com
CBHW020237240824
13638CB00001B/1